"[*Darkwalk... ...*tically far-fetched, and a riveting read."

—Kings River Life Magazine

"Take Sherlock Holmes's London, change the name, and place it somewhere else with another cultural group nearby that transects it, and take the dark, dreary factor way up. This is where our story takes place . . . and it is mesmerizing . . . an outstanding debut novel."

—That's What I'm Talking About

"What a fantastic start . . . a dark fantasy detective story that takes readers on a dark, sometimes disturbing journey. E. L. Tettensor crafts a tale that makes you think even while you shudder—a delightful combination. *Darkwalker* is brilliant!"

—Fresh Fiction

"History and mystery spark in this effervescent series debut."

—My Bookish Ways

"A new paranormal mystery series featuring an intriguing main character and rich, thorough world building; once the story takes off, it does not stop . . . surprising and fantastic."

—The Bibliosanctum

"A fantastic debut novel set in a wonderfully realized world."

—Nothing but the Rain

Books by E. L. Tettensor

Darkwalker
Master of Plagues

MASTER OF PLAGUES

A NICOLAS LENOIR NOVEL

E. L. Tettensor

A ROC BOOK

ROC
Published by the Penguin Group
Penguin Group (USA) LLC, 375 Hudson Street,
New York, New York 10014

USA | Canada | UK | Ireland |Australia | New Zealand | India | South Africa | China
penguin.com
A Penguin Random House Company

First published by Roc, an imprint of New American Library,
a division of Penguin Group (USA) LLC

First Printing, February 2015

 REGISTERED TRADEMARK — MARCA REGISTRADA

ISBN 978-0-451-41999-6

Printed in the United States of America
10   9   8   7   6   5   4   3   2   1

For Danielle, with thanks for taking a chance

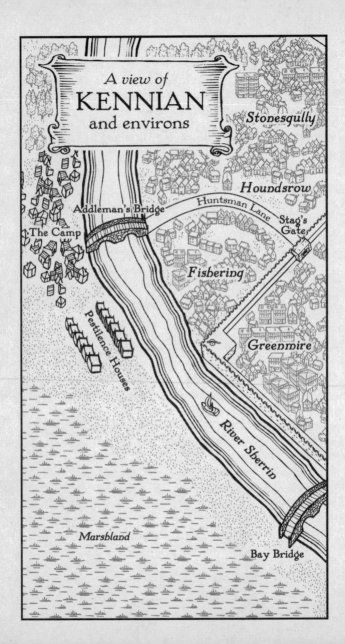

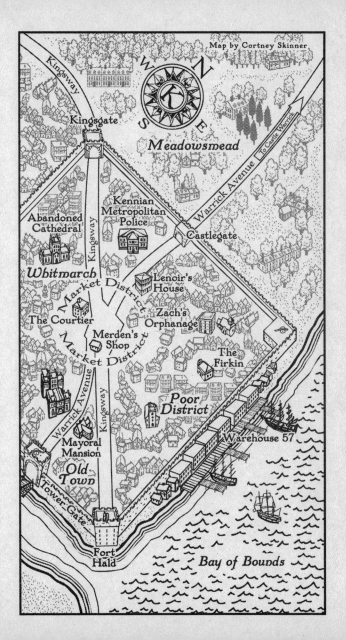

PROLOGUE

Drem lurched through the mist, putting one foot resolutely in front of the other, his boots slurping in time with the throbbing of his head. Cold, wet droplets soaked his brow. How much of it was weather, and how much sweat, he couldn't tell. He raised a hand to his forehead and found what he expected: warm, even through the damp. *It's fever, all right,* he thought. *Isn't that just perfect?* All he wanted was to lie down, to curl up in a corner of his shack and sleep, but if he didn't put in his time at the clinic, he wouldn't eat today. *Just a little farther,* he told himself. *Maybe Sister Rhea will let you rest a bit before she puts you to work.* The nun was a kindly sort— you'd have to be, running a clinic in a slum—and she wasn't likely to be too demanding once she saw the state Drem was in.

The mist turned to drizzle as he slogged on. Drem started to shiver. The fog swept in, a foul gauze clinging to the cankers that passed for dwellings, the seeping gouges that served as roads. The main avenue, already quiet, began to clear as the slum's residents fled the weather. A trio of ragged Adali children gathered their pebbles up out of the mud and scattered, bounding away like startled deer. On the other side of the road, a woman selling bread cursed a salty streak as she tried to hustle her wares inside before they were ruined. *Summer in the Camp,* Drem thought wryly. God, he hated this place.

He could hear coughing from several of the shacks he passed. Women and children, old men and young, they all sounded the same—gusty, crackling *whoops* that made Drem's chest tighten in sympathy. Half the Camp seemed to have it. *It's that damn cough that's doing it,* he thought. *Has to be.* Nothing but plague could account for so many deaths in such a short span of time. It didn't explain why no one had come to claim the bodies, but maybe that wasn't so strange. This was the Camp, after all; a bigger collection of indigent, anonymous wretches had never been. *Wretches like you, Drem Eldren.* If the cough got him too, would anyone care? Sister Rhea, maybe. Then again, maybe not. The nun had seen so much of death, especially these past few days. Most likely, the sight of Drem's corpse wouldn't inspire much more than the usual sigh and shake of her head. *Another of God's children called home,* she'd say, as though life were nothing more than the brief distractions of a child, a game of pebbles in the street.

Up ahead, a shape appeared in the fog: a blood-colored hand reaching, disembodied, through the veil. *At last.* With the clinic in sight, Drem managed to liven his gait a little. The healer's flag rolled gently as the rain picked up, the crimson hand seeming to wave him inside.

The stench hit him as soon as he pushed through the tent flap: sweat and bedpans, herbs and potions, pestilence and decay. Drem should have been used to it by now, but in his fevered state, it was almost too much for him; he had to fight down a wave of nausea.

"Ah, good." Sister Rhea glanced up from whatever medicine she was preparing, her warm eyes crinkling at the fringes. "I was beginning to think I wouldn't see you this morning."

Drem scanned the small vestibule, but saw only bloody rags and brown medicine bottles. "Just me today, Sister?"

"Not quite, but we're definitely shorthanded. It's the weather, I think." The nun meted out a few drops of dark liquid into a glass of water. Her shadow, grotesquely elongated in the lamplight, mimicked the gesture against the stained sheet separating the vestibule from the patient beds.

"Didn't see the wheelbarrow outside," Drem said. He hoped that meant one of the other volunteers had taken it. Let someone else collect the corpses for once.

"No, thank the Lord, it's still out back. We've not had any reports this morning. It's a blessed relief, after the last few days. I was beginning to think we had an epidemic on our hands. So many dead . . ." As she spoke, a tattered cough sounded from the other side of the partition, as if warning the nun not to count her blessings just yet.

"It's that cough, I reckon," Drem said. "Killing 'em left and right."

The nun hummed thoughtfully. "I don't think so. More like the flux, from the condition of the bodies, though that's not quite right either. The flux doesn't cause that kind of bruising, and it certainly doesn't do that to the eyes."

Drem shuddered. He'd almost managed to forget the eyes. He had no fear of dead bodies—could hardly work in a clinic if he did—but the ones he'd been collecting lately were different. *Those* corpses haunted his nightmares. The purple welts, the distended bellies—those were bad enough. But the eyes . . . He couldn't begin to guess what caused a man's eyes to bleed like that. He supposed he didn't want to know.

Someone moaned from the patient beds, calling for water. Sister Rhea scarcely seemed to notice; she was too busy looking at Drem. Her expression was pinched, unsettling. "Are you all right? You're white as a sheet."

Instinctively, Drem touched his forehead again. *Even*

warmer. "I'm fine, Sister. Thank you." He needed to put in at least a little work today, or he wouldn't feel right taking the food. If he'd wanted outright charity, he wouldn't have volunteered at the clinic in the first place.

"You don't look fine." The nun set the glass of water down on her medicine table. "You're sweating, and ... Is your nose bleeding?"

Drem's fingers brushed his nostrils and came away smeared with blood. He grunted in surprise. "Looks like. I didn't know." He accepted a handkerchief. "Thank you, Sister."

"Sit down, please." The nun gestured at her own chair. "Have you been coughing?"

"No, Sister."

"Pain in your chest? Shortness of breath?"

"No, Sister. Just woke up with a headache, is all, and now this fever. The nosebleed ... that's new."

"Take a deep breath, please." The nun pressed an empty glass between Drem's shoulder blades and bent her ear to it. Embarrassed, Drem did as he was told, breathing in and out, in and out, until Sister Rhea was satisfied. "Your lungs sound fine."

I could've told you that. "I do feel a bit light-headed, though." Even as he said the words, tiny specks of light swarmed in his vision. He felt something warm and sticky on his upper lip.

"Tip your head back!" Sister Rhea grabbed the handkerchief and clamped his nose with it. Moments later, Drem tasted blood at the back of his throat. Now he did cough, and once he started, he couldn't seem to stop. He hacked until his eyes watered, until he could hardly breathe. Droplets of red spattered the sheet wall in front of him, spreading like tiny ink stains. When at last the spasm subsided, he found himself doubled over and gasping for breath, clutching his nose and wondering how in the below a grown man came down with a gushing nosebleed.

He was going to ask Sister Rhea, but when he raised his head, the look on the nun's face made his heart stutter. "What is it, Sister?"

"Your eyes." The nun hesitated. "They're . . . well, I'm afraid they're bleeding."

CHAPTER 1

The shot almost took him.

If Lenoir had been wearing a hat, it would have been blown clean off. As it was, he felt his hair move as the bricks above his head exploded into dust, sending a shower of debris down the inside of his collar. Cursing, Lenoir ducked back around the corner of the building, fumbling for his own gun. *Fool. You should have guessed he would be armed.* Civilians rarely carried pistols, but this was no small-time thief. He had killed before, and left the auctioneer unconscious. *Slow down, Lenoir. Think before you act.* He would be damned if he got himself killed over a painting—and a crude, tacky, *Braelish* painting at that.

Cocking the hammer of his flintlock, Lenoir peered cautiously around the corner, but his quarry was nowhere to be seen. He stepped out from the cover of the wall, his gaze raking every trash heap, every doorway, every shadowed corner. The alley stretched on, empty, for another fifty feet before hitting Warrick Avenue. Lenoir hesitated, puzzled. *He cannot have run that fast. Where could he . . . ?*

A sound drew his eyes upward, and he caught a glimpse of movement. The thief was scrambling hand over hand up a drainpipe. Lenoir aimed his gun and fired, but he missed by a wide margin, earning himself a second dust shower. The thief did not so much as flinch, and within moments he was over the parapet and out of sight. Lenoir swore. He could not possibly follow; his body was thoroughly unequal to the task. His mind, though, might do better. He imagined himself standing on the roof, scanning his surroundings.

Warrick Avenue was too wide to cross from the rooftops. The thief would have to climb down first, and that would take too much time. He had not leapt across the alley, or Lenoir would have seen him. That left south toward Ayslington Street, or west toward Bridgeway. An athletic man might make the jump across Bridgeway—and the thief was obviously athletic, having made short work of the drainpipe. But it would be risky, and Lenoir doubted his man was any more eager than he to get himself killed over a painting, no matter how inexplicably valuable it might be. Ayslington would be the easier jump, for the streets were narrower than the avenues. *South, then,* he concluded, and sprinted back up the alley.

He banked onto Bridgeway and nearly collided with a fruit stand. Avoiding it landed him right in the thick of the foot traffic, and he had to put his shoulder into it, bowling a path for himself and ignoring the outraged cries that followed in his wake. He glanced up at the eaves as he ran, but there was no sign of the thief. *No matter. His course is clear.*

Just as he reached Ayslington Street, someone blasted into him from the side, throwing him into the path of an oncoming carriage. Lenoir might have met his end right there had he not been wrestled aside by a pair of meaty arms. The carriage rumbled past, so close that the hoofbeats seemed to ricochet inside Lenoir's skull, drowning out even the cursing of the startled driver.

"Sorry, Inspector." Sergeant Kody brushed at Lenoir's coat in a feeble attempt to right it. "Didn't see you coming."

"Clearly." Lenoir twisted out of the sergeant's grasp.

He was not sure what irritated him more: that Kody had stumbled onto the thief's trail through sheer luck, or that he was not even winded from the chase. Lenoir, for his part, had to brace his hands against his thighs to catch his breath. His eyes scoured the rooftops. Nothing. "Damn! We missed him!"

"I heard a shot, but I wasn't sure . . ." Kody trailed off as he followed Lenoir's gaze. "He's up there?"

Lenoir ignored the question. He squeezed his eyes shut, concentrating. Once again, he mapped out the block in his mind. *Bridgeway to his right, Warrick to his left . . .* They had reached the boundaries of Old Town, and Bridgeway would soon curve off to the west, leaving a narrow alley to continue on straight, like a tributary of a much larger river. *He could make that jump and head west, but . . .* Lenoir shook his head. "There is nowhere for him to go."

"How do you figure that?" Kody gestured at the rooftops across Ayslington Street. "The end of that block hits the water. He could jump in the river and just swim away."

"With a four thousand–crown painting in his pack? I think not."

"West, then. He could jump the alley where Bridgeway curves off."

"Old Town," Lenoir snapped. "Peaked roofs." Then it dawned on him. He turned and bolted back the way he had come, leaving Kody to follow. He could only hope the thief had lost time to indecision, or they might be too late. "Get your crossbow ready, Sergeant!"

By the time they got back to the alley, Lenoir was fit to collapse, but somehow he managed to calm his breathing as he trained his pistol on the narrow track of sky above his head, cocking the hammer of the second barrel. "Be ready."

The sergeant frowned down the sight of his crossbow. "How will we know where—"

"*Quiet.*"

They had only a fraction of a moment to react. The crescendo of footfalls, the scrape of roof tiles, the faintest grunt of exertion—then the fluttering black cloak appeared overhead. Lenoir fired. He knew he had missed the moment he squeezed the trigger, but as always, Bran Kody found his mark. The thief did not scream, but Lenoir knew the bolt had taken him, for the man missed his jump and slammed onto the edge of the roof. He scrabbled at the tiles, but it was a lost cause; he plucked them loose like so many feathers, sending them spinning to the cobbles below, and soon after he followed them. Now he *did* scream.

He was still screaming when Kody flipped him over and wrenched his arms behind his back. The feathered end of a bolt protruded from his thigh. Lenoir procured the iron cuffs, but he could not get the man to stop writhing for long enough to get them on; after a cursory attempt, he left the business to Kody.

"No offense, Inspector," Kody said, "but I'm not sure why you find these so difficult. They're simple enough. See?" He demonstrated, as if he were teaching a child how to tie his shoes.

"No, Sergeant, I'm afraid I do not see. These Braelish devices are needlessly complicated. Give me a T-chain, and I am content. One does not need to weigh two hundred pounds to subdue the perpetrator while one fumbles with one's keys. A simple twist will do the job."

Kody looked at him askance. "Sure will, and crush his wrists in the bargain. Kind of barbaric, don't you think?" With a final crank, he locked the second cuff and shoved the thief onto his belly.

"I was not aware the objective was to make the criminal comfortable."

"What if the guy's innocent?"

Lenoir stooped to retrieve the thief's fallen pack. "If he is innocent, you should not have him in restraints." He jammed his hand inside the pack, only to hiss and withdraw it again. A bead of blood appeared on his thumb.

"What is it?" Kody asked.

Lenoir drew out a ragged shiver of wood with a bit of canvas drooping from it. Slowly, forlornly, the rest of the painting followed, clinging to its shattered frame like a furled sail. "*Garden By Evening,* it would appear. What is left of it."

Kody winced. "Lord Einhorn won't be happy about that. Neither will the chief."

"Lord Einhorn's love affair with this monstrosity is obviously over, or he would not have put it up for auction. As for the chief . . . It is not our job to protect works of so-called art. We are policemen, not museum curators."

Kody did not look convinced, and he gave the thief a shove with his boot. The man moaned something about his legs. "Broken, most likely," Kody said. "Want me to carry him, Inspector?"

Lenoir did not doubt for a moment that the burly sergeant was strong enough, but the question still struck him as bizarre. "You are a sergeant, Kody, not some newly whelped street hound. Leave the heavy lifting to the watchmen."

"I'll go find one," Kody said, and he loped off toward Warrick Avenue.

Absently, Lenoir flattened the bedraggled painting against the wall. He scrutinized its bold colors, its harsh, clipped strokes, its muddy texture. *A garden only a Braelishman could love.* "I shall ask the magistrate to be lenient, my friend," he muttered to the thief, "for you have surely done a public service."

"Destroyed," said Chief Lendon Reck. "As in, *destroyed.*"

Lenoir shrugged. "Perhaps that is too strong. I'm sure it can be restored, though why anyone would wish to, I cannot imagine."

The chief gave him a wry look. "You're an art critic now?"

"I am Arrènais, Chief. We are all art critics."

Reck snorted. "Not to mention food critics, fashion critics, theater critics . . ."

"Criticism builds character."

"I guess that explains why you lot are such a *humble* people."

Lenoir's lip quirked just short of a smile. "Undoubtedly."

The repartee was short-lived. The chief's countenance clouded over again, his thick gray eyebrows gathering beneath the deep lines of his forehead. "You want to tell me what in the below my best inspector is doing running down a thief? That's *his* job." He jabbed a finger at Kody.

The irony of this lecture was not lost on Lenoir. *Small wonder Kody acts like a watchman, when you act like a sergeant.* "I was not precisely running the man down," he said, a little defensively. "I did not expect to meet the thief, merely to discover his hideout."

Reck spread his hands, inviting Lenoir to continue.

"The painting was stolen yesterday, from the auction house. His Lordship wished to recover it, and he asked for me personally. I intended to discover the thief's hideout and assemble some watchmen to bring him in."

"Didn't quite go to plan, though," Kody put in, helpfully.

"So you end up chasing him all over Evenside." Reck shook his head. "I don't know what's got into you, Lenoir. A few months ago, I could hardly get you to take an interest in a murder investigation. Now you're putting your life on the line for a stolen painting. You have a recent brush with death or something?"

This time, Lenoir chose to ignore the irony. "I thought you would want me to take the case, Chief. Lord Einhorn is a particular benefactor of the Metropolitan Police."

"Don't I know it! And now I have to explain to His Lordship how a valuable piece of art came to be destroyed!"

"I can explain it to him, if you wish."

The wry look returned. "No, thank you. I'd like to make it sound like we *regret* ruining his painting."

Lenoir shrugged. "As you like. And now if you will excuse me, I have a report to file. . . ." More accurately, Kody had a report to file, but Lenoir saw no point in bothering the chief with extraneous details.

"Later," Reck said, rising and grabbing his coat from the rack. "You're coming with me, Lenoir. We have business with the lord mayor."

Lenoir made only the barest effort to conceal his dismay. "*We*, Chief? I cannot imagine what His Honor could possibly—"

"Save it. I know how you feel about the man, but fortunately for you, it's not mutual. His Honor has a crisis on his hands, and he wants our best. That means you. Now let's go." Turning to Kody, he added, "I'll want that report when I get back."

Lenoir trailed the chief down the stairs and into the kennel, bracing himself for the throng. The shift was just changing over, and watchmen teemed in every direction, choking the narrow avenues between work spaces. Sergeants tucked themselves more tightly behind their desks, and scribes pressed up against walls and collected in corners, clutching their ledgers and ink bottles and waiting out the tide. The chief made no such accommodation, nor did he need to; as soon as his boots hit the floor, the pack of hounds parted as if by some collective instinct, standing aside to let their alpha through. Lenoir followed closely in Reck's wake, feeling the pack close up behind him.

The chief's carriage waited for them in the street, a pair of watchmen serving as driver and footman. Reck waved the latter off as he climbed in, and he was still scowling when Lenoir took the seat across from him. "If you hate the carriage so much, why do you take it?" Lenoir asked, amused.

"For the dignity of the Kennian Metropolitan Police," Reck said dryly. "If I showed up at the lord mayor's mansion on horseback, I'd never hear the end of it." He rapped his knuckles on the wall behind him, and the carriage started up.

The chief said nothing for the first several blocks, preferring to stare out the window, lost in the cares of his office. Ordinarily, silence suited Lenoir perfectly well, but he did not wish to arrive at the lord mayor's without any notion of why he had been summoned. "There is a body, I presume?" he prompted.

"If only it were just the one." Reck's reflection in the carriage window was weary. Lines crisscrossed his pale face, each one a journey, tread and retread, like game trails in the snow. He had been strong once, Lenoir judged, a heavy like Kody, but in the ten years Lenoir had known him, he had always seemed . . . *used*. Not for the first time, Lenoir wondered why the man did not simply retire. He had earned his rest many times over. And if there was no one around capable of taking his place . . . well, that was not going to change anytime soon. The Kennian Metropolitan Police had a few stray threads of competence, but they were tightly woven into a fabric of mediocrity. Unless the chief planned to cling to his post until he died, he was going to have to accept the fact that his successor, whoever he was, was most likely not going to measure up.

In the meantime, Reck had more than one body on his hands. A serial killer, or a massacre? Sadly, the City of Kennian was no stranger to either. "How many dead?" Lenoir asked.

"Over a thousand, at last count."

Just like that. A hard blow to the stomach.

Lenoir stared. "I don't understand. There cannot have been a thousand murders in the entire history of the Metropolitan Police."

"Who said anything about murders?"

Lenoir frowned. "It's not like you to be coy, Chief."

Reck scowled back at him. "I'm not the one being coy. All I know is what His Honor's letter said, and that wasn't much. There's some kind of epidemic at the Camp, and he's afraid it's getting out of hand."

"I have heard the rumors, of course, but . . . what has it to do with us? It is unfortunate, but hardly unusual. Disease is the wildfire of the slums. You can count upon it razing the ground every now and then. It is not a matter for the police."

"Tell me something I don't know." Lendon Reck, like Nicolas Lenoir, was not a man inclined to sentimentality. "Look, there's no point grousing about it. The lord mayor calls; we come running." The chief's tone left little doubt about his own lack of enthusiasm for this endeavor, and Lenoir decided it was pointless to press the matter further. He would have his answers soon enough.

The walls outside the carriage window soon gave way to sloping lawns and manicured hedges, signaling their arrival at the mayoral mansion. Lenoir could not suppress a sour turn of his mouth. Emmory Lyle Hearstings had been lord mayor of Kennian for three years, and in that time, he had thoroughly distinguished himself as one of the most fatuous creatures on hind legs. Lenoir had never been endowed with a great store of patience, but few taxed his meager reserves more thoroughly than His Honor. The sole stroke of good fortune was that Hearstings was generally too thick to notice. Still, Reck was taking no chances: as the carriage shuddered to a halt, he leveled a finger at Lenoir and said, "On your best behavior, Inspector, or I'll have you patrolling with the pups."

Lenoir might have declared such an activity to be preferable to the current enterprise, but he had no wish to antagonize the chief further, so he merely nodded.

They were shown to a frilly parlor and offered tea. They both declined. The chamberlain invited them to sit, indicating a delicate-looking sofa upholstered with elaborately embroidered silk. Reck frowned at it dubiously, as though he had been invited to sit on a poodle. He opted for a more functional-looking chair instead. Lenoir perched on the proffered sofa, if a little gingerly.

"A fine piece, newly commissioned," the chamberlain said, his pride evidently piqued by the chief's rebuff.

"It's . . . nice," Reck said, a peace offering. "Goes with the style of the room."

"Arrènais," the chamberlain said, and Lenoir succumbed to a fit of coughing.

His Honor kept them waiting, as was his wont. It would not do for him to seem too available. Reck folded his arms and scowled at the carpet. Lenoir drummed his fingers on his trousers (the only genuinely Arrènais fabric in the room, or he was a fishwife). The clock on the mantel measured out the passage of time with prim precision. The chamberlain reappeared now and then to update them on His Honor's unavailability, and to offer tea. Eventually, he was obliged to draw the curtains against the increasingly intrusive slant of the afternoon sun.

By the time Hearstings graced them with his presence, even Reck had had enough; he sprang to his feet like a scalded cat. "Your Honor."

"Chief Reck." The lord mayor's improbable mustaches perked up as he smiled. "I hope I haven't kept you waiting too long. And Inspector! I trust you are *par rinn* . . . er, *par renne—* "

"Very well. Thank you," Lenoir said before further violence could be done to his mother tongue.

"Yes, well. Very good. Please, gentlemen, take a seat." Hearstings lowered his own ponderous girth into an armchair. Even as he sat, he reached inside his jacket and consulted his pocket watch in a gesture contrived enough to grace a portrait, or perhaps even hard currency. "How are things at the station?"

"Fine, thank you, Your Honor," Reck said.

"A lovely graduation ceremony last week. You must so enjoy welcoming the new lads."

"One of the privileges of the job."

"Excellent food too. We must be allocating too much coin to the Metropolitan Police!" His Honor barked out a laugh.

A vein swelled in the chief's forehead, a sign every hound knew and dreaded.

Hearstings was oblivious. "By the way, Reck, are you looking into that business of Einhorn's?"

"Yes, sir."

"Oh, good. I heard there was quite an incident at the auctioneer's. Why, did you know—"

"Excuse me, Your Honor, I thought you wanted to discuss the Camp?"

"Ah, indeed." The lord mayor assumed a solemn look, running his thumb and forefinger along his mustaches. "I'll come straight to the point."

Somehow, the chief managed to nod without a hint of irony.

"We have an epidemic in the Camp," Hearstings said. "Horrid disease, from what I hear. Men bleeding to death from the inside out."

Reck grimaced. "Sounds ugly."

"That's an understatement. Have you ever heard of anything like it?"

The chief shook his head. "You, Lenoir?"

"No, Chief, I have not."

"Neither has my physician," said Hearstings. "So far, it's confined to the Camp, thank God, but it's making a damn mess of the place. If it gets out of hand, I'll have panic on my hands."

Lenoir did not doubt that was true, but he still failed to see where the police came into it. So did Reck, apparently, for he asked, "What exactly do you need from us?"

Hearstings fluttered his hand, as though shooing a fly. "I'm sure it's nothing, but I promised Lideman I'd send for you. Head out there first thing in the morning. Talk to him. Hear him out, let me know if you think there's anything in it, that's all."

Lenoir and Reck exchanged a blank look. "Lideman? And he is . . . ?"

"From the College of Physicians. Head of Medical Sciences. He's been out at the Camp the past few days looking into this. He has . . . theories."

"About what, exactly?"

"Why, about the disease, of course. About where it came from."

"No doubt that is a fascinating puzzle for a physician," Lenoir said, "but it is not the concern of the Metropolitan Police."

Reck shot him a warning look. "What Lenoir means, Your Honor, is that my hounds are hardly qualified—"

"You misunderstand," the lord mayor said. "I'm not asking you to solve a medical mystery. I'm asking you to look into a potential crime. You see, Lideman doesn't think the disease reached the Camp on its own. He believes it was planted."

For a moment, Lenoir was not sure he had heard right. "Planted. Meaning, deliberately."

"Yes."

Reck leaned forward, his chair creaking beneath him. "You think someone started a plague *on purpose*?"

"It sounds outlandish, I know, but Lideman is absolutely convinced. If he's right, it means someone is trying to commit mass murder."

More than a thousand bodies, the chief had said. And that was just the beginning. "If he is right," Lenoir said, "someone is succeeding."

CHAPTER 2

"I don't get it," said Kody.

If he had all day, Lenoir could not possibly enumerate all the ways in which that was true. "Could you be more specific, Sergeant?"

"It just seems kind of far-fetched. I mean, why would anybody want to start an epidemic?"

Lenoir guided his horse toward the stone archway that marked the Stag's Gate, nodding at the guard as he neared. It had always struck him as a quaint anachronism—putting guards on a gate that no longer held any significance, the old walls having long since been outstripped by the growth of the city—but he played along. It was still theoretically possible for the guards to refuse someone passage, and in Lenoir's experience, minor authorities enjoyed nothing better than flexing their muscle. It was best not to tempt them. Instead, he held his horse patiently while the guard made a great show of inspecting a handcart before waving it through, as though the old woman wheeling it were passing from the countryside into the city, instead of from Houndsrow to Whitmarch.

"And if you *did* want to start an epidemic," Kody went on, "why do it in the Camp? Why not somewhere more central, like Greenmire or Stonesgully?"

The sergeant had a point. If the goal was to spread the disease as rapidly as possible, it would make more sense to plant it somewhere within the city walls, where conditions were ripest. The population density, the location—the inner city slums made ideal breeding grounds for disease. The Camp outdid them all for sheer squalor, but it was far enough on the outskirts of the city that some did not even consider it part of Kennian proper.

"Those are the right questions," Lenoir said, "but this is not the right time to ask them. It is far too early to guess at motives. We do not even know if this Lideman's theory is correct, and the disease was planted deliberately."

"I wonder if he's the real thing. Most of these so-called physicians are charlatans, if you ask me. Although, I suppose if he's Head of Medical Sciences at the college, he must have some credentials. . . ."

The sergeant continued to prattle on, but Lenoir had stopped listening. In moments like these, he pined for the good old days, when Bran Kody had despised him too much to indulge in idle chatter. Like a plant that wants nothing but air to survive, Lenoir had been content for his relationship with Kody to subsist entirely on cold silences. Alas, those days were gone.

"Speculation is fruitless, Sergeant," he interrupted. "We have not a shred of evidence to go on. For the moment, we must content ourselves with observation." *Silent observation, God willing.*

Kody took the hint and subsided.

As they drew farther away from the old walls, the scene around them grew ever more disorganized. Where the inner city was a complex warren of narrow, twisting alleys, and the more distinguished suburbs of Morningside an ordered procession of genteel houses, the streets of Houndsrow seemed almost to exist by accident. Eight-story tenements vied for space with ancient stone farmhouses capped with thatch, the latter looking for all the world as if they had sprouted up between the gaps like furry little mushrooms after a rain. The tenements were topped with timber jetties that slanted out over the streets, giving the buildings a precarious lean, as if they had suffered a paralytic stroke. Every inch of space was accounted for, yet few of them well. Every now and then, Lenoir and Kody would pass a cobbled square with a fountain, or an ancient church, or some other remnant of a village that had long since been swallowed by Kennian's voracious appetite for expansion. Mostly, though, the Evenside suburbs were a place of semipermanence, a haphazard landscape sketched in rough, hasty lines. Lenoir and Kody wended their way through the jumble until they reached Addleman's Bridge, a narrow path of stone arching over the slow, moody waters of the River Sherrin. The river marked the edge of the city proper. On the near bank stood the modest suburb of Fishering; on the far bank, the Camp. In between, Addleman's Bridge marked the last bastion of civilization.

Kody sighed. "Here we are."

Lenoir shared the sergeant's lack of enthusiasm. The last time he had been here, it was in the company of a supernatural creature who wanted him dead. Somehow, he had survived that night, and even found an ally in the vengeful spirit who had once hunted him. But that did not mean he was eager for a reminder of the experience. It made the scar on his right forearm squirm a little, as though maggots wriggled just under the skin.

"Let us be as quick as we can about it," Lenoir said, and he spurred his horse.

He could see the pestilence houses from the bridge, their pale peaks looming over the hovels like a range of snowcapped mountains. They could not have been there long, judging from the crisp white color of the canvas, but there were already at least two rows of them. *There will be more,* Lenoir thought, *before this thing is done.*

As they neared the foot of the bridge, he felt increasingly uneasy. The cold clatter of their hooves intruded upon an eerie hush, as though they were barging uninvited into a funeral. Mercifully, the sound died away as the horses passed from stone onto earth, their hooves beating out a dull, irregular rhythm, like the stutter of a terrified heart. The street was nearly deserted. A few people stirred here and there—carrying water, or firewood, or sacks of flour—but they went about their business in hurried silence. No children played in the street. No idle youths loitered about. Even the stray dogs sat subdued as the horses plodded past.

Kody threw Lenoir a grim look, but he did not speak. Disturbing the silence seemed disrespectful somehow.

The pestilence houses had been erected a short distance from the river, for ease of access to the water. The ranks of white tents looked like the camp of some invading army. Both sights were familiar to Lenoir, and they often coincided, as they had during the revolution in his home country. Lenoir's beloved city of Serles had suffered greatly under the twin scourges of violence and disease; his adolescence had been a study of death in every possible shade.

More delightful memories. The Camp seemed to be full of them.

They found Lideman in the largest of the tents, where the procedures were performed. A row of cots lined the space on either side, each one occupied by a patient. Lenoir spotted the physician immediately: he strolled between the rows, hands folded behind his back, as though he were taking a leisurely walk in the public gardens. Behind him trailed a younger man, furiously scribbling notes in a ledger. They had not yet noticed the visitors, and Lenoir could not prevent his gaze from roaming over the patient beds in morbid curiosity.

He immediately wished he had not.

Men, women, and children of every shape and size occupied the cots, about fifty in all. Their pale flesh gleamed with sweat, and their hair clung to their scalps in matted

MASTER OF PLAGUES **23**

clumps. Some seemed to suffer only from fever, but others presented ghastlier symptoms, looking almost as if they had been beaten half to death. Their arms and chests were covered with massive purple welts, and their limbs appeared swollen. Dark blood trickled out of nostrils, from the corners of mouths. Bloody tears streaked faces white as death. The smell of rotting flesh hung in the air, like a butcher's on a hot day. Lenoir threw his arm up over his nose and mouth to prevent himself from retching. Kody did the same, backing away instinctively until he bumped against a table and was forced to grab it to steady himself. Instruments rattled, and Kody cursed quietly.

Lideman and his young assistant turned at the sound. Both men wore scarves tied around their faces. "Gentlemen, you should not be here!" the physician called. "It is not safe!"

"We are with the Metropolitan Police," said Lenoir through his sleeve. "We have been sent by the lord mayor."

Lideman grunted. "Good. But it is still not safe. Wait outside, and I will be with you directly." Turning to his assistant, he said, "Ten more minutes of draining, and not a moment more. These people have little enough blood to spare."

Draining? Lenoir looked again at the nearest cot, and he realized that some of what he had taken for bruises were actually leeches. *Of course.* Braelish physicians and their leeches.

Kody's nose wrinkled behind his sleeve, and he glanced at Lenoir. *See?* the look seemed to say. *Charlatans.*

They quit the tent without any further encouragement, waiting for Lideman to join them. In spite of what they had just seen, neither man spoke; the strange hush had descended over them again. They watched mutely as a steady procession of nuns moved between the tents, carrying bloody rags, pails of dark liquid, and assorted other items Lenoir did not care to scrutinize. A pair of young men, presumably medical students, appeared at the mouth of one of the tents, bearing a litter with a sheet draped over it. A child, judging by the length of the body.

"Where do you bury them?" Lenoir asked, breaking the silence as Lideman joined them.

The physician tugged the scarf down, revealing a kind face lined with care. "A trench near the edge of the woods. We don't have time for individual graves anymore." He held out a hand. When Lenoir hesitated, he smiled. "You are wise to be cautious, but you needn't worry. I touch nothing with my bare hands."

Even as he spoke, Lenoir noticed the leather gloves stuffed into the physician's coat pocket. The coat itself appeared to have been treated with some kind of wax, and the hem was unusually long, reaching almost to the ground. The physician was taking no chances. "Inspector Nicolas Lenoir," he said as he shook, "and this is Sergeant Kody."

"Horst Lideman, from the College of Physicians. But I suppose you already knew that." He gestured at a small green tent set apart from the others. "This way, please, Inspector. It's not much safer out here than it is in the treatment tent."

They followed Lideman into the green tent, which appeared to be a makeshift office. A desk laden with books and ledgers crowded the space, leaving only enough room for a few extra chairs. A soft globe of light from a pair of lanterns was all that illuminated the space. *A gloomy place for gloomy work,* Lenoir thought, taking one of the proffered chairs.

"I'm glad His Honor sent you," Lideman said as he sat behind the desk. "I wasn't sure he would. He didn't seem to put much stock in our theory." There was no bitterness in the words; it was simply a statement of fact.

"*Our* theory?" Lenoir arched an eyebrow.

"The college is of one mind on this. The disease was definitely planted."

"And what leads you to this conclusion?"

"It is quite straightforward, once you know the characteristics of the disease."

Lenoir was not eager to know the details, but he was obliged to ask. "How so?"

"There are three factors," Lideman said, holding up as many fingers. He assumed a professorial tone. "First, we have never seen this disease in Braeland before, though we have heard rumors of it appearing much farther north, beyond Adaliland. I have written to my colleagues all over Humenor, but I am virtually certain they will confirm that the disease is unknown to their shores as well."

"Kennian is a port city," Lenoir pointed out. "Exotic diseases are often brought in by ship. That is how the pox reached Arrènes thirty years ago."

"That brings me to the second factor, Inspector. This disease is exceptionally virulent. It kills more than three quarters of those it infects, and it does so with remarkable speed. For the first day or two, the symptoms appear remarkably like influenza. But after that, the patients deteriorate rapidly. Vomiting. Diarrhea. Bleeding from various orifices. After the lesions appear, it is more or less a lost cause. Death typically follows in less than twenty-four hours."

"Those people in the tent . . ." Kody said.

Lideman shook his head. "We're doing what we can, but I'm not hopeful. Some of them will survive, but those with the bruising . . . I haven't seen a single patient come back from that."

"How long does it take for the patient to fall ill?" Lenoir asked.

"It's difficult to be sure, but what we've seen so far suggests that symptoms begin appearing three to four days after infection. Perhaps five, if the patient is especially hale."

"Approximately a week between infection and death," Lenoir summarized.

"In most cases, less."

"Which means that whoever carried it into Kennian cannot have come from a very great distance, even by ship. He would not have survived the journey."

"He might, if he was very lucky, but not without infecting others, two thirds of whom would have perished."

"But he *must* have come from a long way," Kody said, "and fast, or we would have heard about this disease before now."

"Precisely." The physician bestowed an approving nod, as though on a particularly bright pupil. "The only thing that spreads faster than an epidemic is word of it. Kennian is a port city, as you have pointed out, full of the comings and goings of foreigners. If a disease this devastating was headed our way, we would have heard about it."

"Could a person be infected without showing signs?" Lenoir asked.

"Unlikely, and even if it were possible, I do not believe such a person would be contagious. The college has been here for over a week, and what we have seen in that time suggests that patients are not contagious until *after* they have presented with symptoms."

"And for how long do they remain contagious?"

Lideman smiled. "Excellent question, Inspector, and that is the third factor. Patients are contagious for as long as they display symptoms, and they grow steadily more contagious as the disease progresses. So a patient in the early stages with flu-like symptoms is not terribly infectious, whereas someone with the lesions is dangerously so. As soon as they recover, however, they cease to be a danger. The battle is won, whether by the grace of God or modern medicine, and they have driven the enemy off the field. When they perish, however, they remain quite infectious, for the disease invades completely. It continues to feed on their dead flesh."

Lenoir was beginning to understand. "It came to us through a corpse."

"Or corpses," Lideman said, with an arch of his eyebrow.

"In that case, Doctor, I am inclined to agree with your assessment. It seems very likely that this epidemic was started deliberately."

"Sorry, Inspector, but ..." Kody had the awkward, self-conscious look of a man who suspects he is about to ask a stupid question. "Are we sure about that? Maybe someone died on a sea voyage, and whoever unloaded the body didn't realize it was infectious."

"You have obviously never been on a ship, Sergeant," Lenoir said with a thin smile. "Sailors are not known for their sentimentality. If a shipmate dies, he is tossed overboard, not transported lovingly into port. Especially if the crew fears that whatever killed him is contagious."

"Besides," Lideman said, "the disease seems to have cropped up in several places more or less simultaneously, suggesting multiple sources of infection."

A rustle at the tent flap distracted them. The young assistant Lenoir had seen earlier poked his head through. "Excuse me, Doctor, but I've brought the nun you wanted to see."

"Ah." Lideman rose, smiling. "Excellent timing. Show her in." A small, birdlike woman in white robes slipped into the tent, nodding gravely at each of them. "Sister Rhea," Lideman said, indicating the last remaining chair, "thank you for coming back so soon. These men are from the Metropolitan Police." Lenoir introduced himself and Kody. "I wonder if you could repeat for them what you told me yesterday, regarding the bodies you found."

"I'm happy to tell what little I know," the nun said. She was probably in her early thirties, but just now, she looked much older. Dark circles sagged under her eyes, and when she went to rub them, her hand revealed a slight tremor. *She has not slept in days,* Lenoir judged. "I didn't find the bodies, exactly. They were reported to the clinic by local residents. I sent my volunteers out to collect them and bury them, after I had blessed them."

"Volunteers?" Lenoir echoed, curious in spite of himself.

"Those who are willing to volunteer at the clinic receive a hot meal for every day they work," the nun explained. "It gives them a sense of dignity to earn their keep."

"Collecting corpses is a tough way to earn a meal," Kody said.

The nun sighed. "And dangerous, apparently. It wasn't a common activity until about a month ago. Usually, when someone dies in the Camp, his friends and relations bury him, or at least bring him to the clinic for us to take care of. When a body turns up in the street, it's usually because the victim had no connections to speak of."

"Plenty of people like that in the slums, I reckon," Kody said.

"You would be surprised, Sergeant." The nun's tone was gently admonishing. "Life is hard here, it's true, but these people look out for each other. Even if a man has no family or friends, his neighbors generally wouldn't leave him lying in the street."

"These bodies your volunteers collected," Lenoir said, "did anyone recognize them?"

"Not that I know of, and no one came looking for them, the way relations do when their loved ones have gone missing."

"Did you notice anything else unusual about the bodies?"

"You mean besides their condition?" The nun paused, considering. "Well, I suppose it's a little strange that none of them was Adali."

Lideman gave a thoughtful grunt. "The Camp must be twenty percent Adali, at least. Considering how many bodies you picked up, one would expect to find at least one Adal among the dead. Yet more evidence that these corpses came from elsewhere."

"How many were there?" Kody asked, stealing the question from his superior's lips. Lenoir shot him an irritated look, and was rewarded with a slight flush. The sergeant's discipline had taken an unfortunate turn since the incident with the necromancers. Quite on his own, Kody had come close to cracking the case, and the success seemed to have gone to his head. Lenoir hoped he would not have to remind the sergeant of his place.

"There were eleven in all," the nun said, "if I only count that first wave, the ones who were never identified."

Lenoir drummed his fingers on his arm, thinking. "This first wave, as you call it—you found them over what period of time?"

"Four days. Perhaps five."

"No two in the same place," Lideman said. "All over the Camp, in fact."

"Like sowing seeds in a field," Lenoir murmured.

"Precisely," said Lideman. "So you see, Inspector, it is quite obvious. Even if we presume the highly unlikely scenario of infected corpses somehow arriving in Kennian by accident, the odds of all of them turning up in the Camp, yet no two in the same place, are so minuscule as to defy belief. This epidemic *was* started deliberately, and whoever is behind it, he was thorough."

Kody's mouth tightened into a thin, angry line. Even he could not doubt it now.

"Exactly how infectious is this disease?"

Later, it would seem to Lenoir that his question had somehow tempted fate.

Before the physician could answer, a crack of sunlight appeared, signaling the return of the young assistant. He hesitated at the tent flap, looking afraid. "Doctor, you had better come. There are some men outside. They brought a warrant."

"A warrant?" Lideman rose, looking bewildered. "A warrant for what?"

"You'd better come."

Lenoir had to shield his eyes against the glare as he trailed Lideman out of the tent, Kody and the nun following. Two men stood arguing with one of the nuns. Lenoir studied them closely. *Pressed slacks, laced shoes, buttoned coats.* The raiment of the urban professional, but of modest make—too modest for bankers or lawyers. Officials of some kind, then. They could have been hounds, but Lenoir would have recognized them. *From the City,* he concluded, but before he had time to reflect on that, he realized they were not alone: Sergeants Innes and Izar stood at a discreet remove, their expressions grim.

The chief expects trouble. It was obvious from his choice of sergeants. Izar was a towering Adal with a permanently serious expression, and Innes looked like he had been hewn from the side of a mountain. Each of them was intimidating in his own right. Most people would think twice about crossing one of them, let alone both. In pairing them, Lendon Reck was sending a signal to anyone with eyes.

"Sergeants!" Lenoir called, startling them. They had not seen him emerge from the tent.

Izar and Innes came over, while Lideman hurried to join the nun arguing with the officials. "What are you two doing here?" Kody asked as his colleagues drew near.

"Chief sent us," Innes rumbled. "Said we might find you here."

Lenoir swallowed his irritation at this nonanswer. Innes was a capable enough sergeant, but that was mostly owing to his immense strength and ability to follow orders. His mental faculties were decidedly less remarkable. Lenoir addressed Izar instead. "These men—they are city officials?"

The Adal nodded. "They are here with a writ," he said in a low voice, "from the lord mayor. The chief already got word, and he sent us to keep an eye on things, to see that they don't get out of hand. There are watchmen on the way too, and lots of them."

Lenoir had a sinking feeling. "The lord mayor is afraid the disease will spread." Izar nodded again, gazing down at Lenoir with solemn golden eyes.

"Chief's snarling mad," Innes added. "Says he should have been told this was in the works when you all went to see His Honor yesterday. Says he doesn't have the manpower to do it."

"To do what?" Kody asked, looking between Izar and Innes in confusion.

Lenoir swore quietly in Arrènais. The sinking feeling had become a great hollow pit. "How much of it is he sealing off?"

"All of it, Inspector," Izar said. "As of now, the Camp is under quarantine."

CHAPTER 3

"Hearstings is a fool," Lenoir growled, watching as the city officials conferred with Lideman over the arrangements. The physician looked grave, but determined. Most likely he approved of the decision.

He was not the only one. "Maybe it's for the best," Kody said, "if this thing is really as bad as they say."

Lenoir clucked his tongue impatiently. "Closing off the Camp may be prudent, but he could have waited a few hours at least, until we finished a first round of interviews. Instead he has torched our investigation."

Kody gave him a skeptical look, as if he thought his superior was being dramatic.

Nettled, Lenoir said, "What do you suppose the residents of the Camp will make of the quarantine, Sergeant?"

"I don't suppose they'll like it."

"And whom do you think they will blame?" To aid Kody's thinking, he gestured at the watchmen swarming the foot of the bridge into town.

Kody's brow smoothed as the situation dawned on him.

"That's right, Sergeant. They will blame the hounds preventing them from fleeing this death trap. They will blame *us*."

Kody sighed. "They won't tell us a bloody thing."

"Except, perhaps, to join the ranks of the damned. So we had better hurry and get what we can, because in a few hours, we will be about as welcome as this plague."

"Where do we start?"

"I have no idea." Lenoir scratched his jaw. Two days' worth of stubble answered irritably, but gave him no inspiration. Then he spotted the nun lingering near the green tent. "Sister Rhea," he called, heading over.

The nun seemed not to hear. Her eyes followed the officials as they pointed at the riverbank, gesturing along its length.

"Sister," Lenoir said again.

Rhea did not turn. "They're condemning these people to death," she said, as if to herself. "We might have got it under control, but now . . . if people can't leave, they *will* get sick. And they will die."

Better the slums than the whole city. The thought hovered, unspoken, in the air.

"The volunteers who collected the bodies," Lenoir said. "I presume they fell sick also?"

Rhea turned at last. Her eyes were dull and gray, like clouds burdened with unshed rain. "There was just the one, actually. An exceptionally hard worker. Drem." She shook her head. "He started showing symptoms a few days after the first body turned up. That would be about four weeks ago now."

"I'm sorry," Kody said. He knew better than to wait for Lenoir to say it.

"Did he mention anything before he died that might be helpful?" Lenoir asked, sticking to the practical. "Something he saw, perhaps, or something he heard?"

To his surprise, the nun smiled, albeit wanly. "Oh, he didn't die. Drem is exceptional in that way too. He's one of the few survivors. He's still very ill, but he will recover."

Every man appreciates random strokes of luck, but to an inspector, they are diamonds in the dirt. Lenoir permitted himself a rare smile. "In that case, Sister, I should very much like to speak with him."

"If he's strong enough," Kody added, but that was pure theater. He knew perfectly well that Lenoir would conduct the interview regardless.

"That should be possible," Sister Rhea said. "Follow me."

The red hand of healing was visible from a long way off, waving gently in the breeze. Lenoir could not suppress a shudder at the sight. Aside from the general queasiness he experienced in any encounter with Braelish "medicine," he found the crimson hand to be a singularly macabre image. Was it meant to represent the stained hand of the barber? The lifeblood of the dying man? The frantic wave of someone signaling for help? The universal symbol of healing should be a source of comfort and solace. Instead, it was a vivid reminder of blood, of death and violence—or so it seemed to Lenoir.

The inside of the clinic was scarcely more reassuring. Flickering candlelight picked out the angles of a cramped space littered with the trappings of human suffering. Scalpels, scissors, and stained bandages lay scattered across one table; brown medicine bottles crowded another. Bedpans leaned in a precarious stack next to a washbasin. A familiar, funereal silence stifled the place.

"Most of the patients have gone," Sister Rhea said, speaking softly. "Those afflicted with the plague were sent to the pestilence houses, and those with the cough have mostly fled. They would rather die of consumption than catch the plague, and I can't say I blame them."

"So there's no plague in here?" Kody asked, visibly relieved.

"No longer. We have converted the clinic into a convalescent house." Rhea sighed. "Which is why it's nearly empty."

"But you did treat plague patients initially?" Lenoir asked.

"I tried to. About two dozen patients came through here before the pestilence houses went up. I lost all but Drem."

"That is to be expected, from what Lideman told us. In fact, it is fortunate that you yourself did not fall ill. How do you account for it?"

Her answer was predictable. "By God's grace. He obviously has plans for me yet. This way, please, Officers." She brushed aside the thin sheet separating the vestibule from the patient beds.

The clinic had a similar layout to the treatment tent presided over by Lideman, albeit on a much smaller scale. Two rows of cots lined either side of the tent, the passage between them barely wide enough to permit a man to pass. Most of the cots appeared to be empty, though it was difficult to be sure in the dim light. A single figure moved at the back of the tent; a nun, judging by the silhouette.

"Sister Ann," Rhea called quietly, "would you excuse us a moment?"

"Of course." They stood aside to let her pass, and she vanished without another word.

Rhea led them to a bed near the back of the tent, where they found a thin figure huddled under a blanket. Pale, translucent skin stretched tightly over cheekbones, hung loosely beneath sunken eyes. Ashen lips moved wordlessly, as though in prayer. *This man is near death,* Lenoir thought. And he was one of the lucky ones.

"Drem." The nun rested a hand against his shoulder. At first, the only reaction was the scuttling of eyeballs beneath bluish lids. After a moment, the waif called Drem opened his eyes, his pupils coming slowly into focus.

"Sister." The voice scraped out, barely audible. "I'm so cold."

"I'll bring you some tea. In the meantime, do you think you can manage a brief chat? This is Inspector Lenoir of the Metropolitan Police, and he wants to ask you a few questions."

"It will not take long," Lenoir added, feeling a stab of pity for the man, despite himself.

Drem's watery gaze darted to Lenoir. "Police?"

"We are trying to learn about the disease," Lenoir said. He did not elaborate, having already decided not to discuss the criminal aspect of the case openly. Rumors would spread quickly, and that could result in conspiracy theories, accusations, and worse. People instinctively wanted someone to blame for tragedy, and when they found that someone, real or imagined, retribution was usually swift. Word would get out eventually, but Lenoir had no desire to add fuel to the fire. He made a mental note to speak to Lideman and Rhea about the need for discretion.

Fortunately, Kody did not need to be told. "We think if we can trace it, maybe we can learn something that might help us treat it." The sergeant had good instincts, Lenoir had to admit. He was already competent; if he learned to challenge his mind a little more, he might even be more than that one day.

Drem struggled to sit. Rhea helped prop him up with a pillow before heading off to procure the promised tea. "Don't know what I can tell you," Drem said.

Neither do I, Lenoir thought, but he had to try. "The first body you found—do you remember exactly where it was?"

"Sure. You don't forget something like that." He shivered, as if to emphasize the point. "It was in the river."

Interesting. "Who discovered it?"

Drem shook his head. "You'll have to ask Sister Rhea. I wasn't there when she heard about it. She just asked me to get the wheelbarrow, because someone had drowned in the river. Only when I got there . . . I'm no healer, but even I could tell he hadn't drowned."

"What exactly did you find?"

"He was mostly underwater, but his leg was up on the bank, tangled in some logs. That's what was holding him there. I fished him out—wasn't easy—and soon as I saw him, I knew something was wrong. Figured he'd been beaten to death, covered in bruises like that. Sister Rhea thought so too, until the others started turning up, all looking the same."

"While you were collecting the body, did you see anything else that struck you as strange?"

"Like what?"

"Anyone watching, for example?"

"Don't think so." Drem furrowed his brow. "No, I reckon not, or I'd have asked 'em for help. Had a demon of a time getting him out of the river."

"What about the next body?" Lenoir continued, though his hopes were dimming. "Where was that?"

"Just off the market road, in a heap of rubbish. He was . . ." Drem paused, a hand swiping at his eyes. "Sorry. I'm just . . . dizzy. . . ."

Lenoir waited until Drem had recovered. "After the rubbish heap?"

"After that . . ." He stared into space for a moment before shaking his head. "After that it all starts to . . ." He trailed off.

Lenoir finished the thought for him. "It all starts to bleed together."

Drem swallowed, nodding. He drew his blanket more tightly around his shoulders.

This is not getting us anywhere. Lenoir was running out of questions, and judging by the frustrated look on Kody's face, the sergeant could not think of any either. "Forget the bodies," Lenoir said, grasping. "Over the course of those few days, did you see anything out of the ordinary? Anything at all that struck you as strange, no matter how seemingly insignificant?"

"When I was picking up the bodies, you mean?"

"At any time."

Drem closed his eyes, remembering. "I don't think . . . Wait." He paused. "Guess there was *that* . . ."

"What?"

"It's probably nothing, but ... I do remember seeing an Inataari. Just walking, mind—nothing suspicious about him. But you did say *anything.*"

"An Inataari?" Kody frowned. "Are you sure?"

"Positive. Seen their kind before, when the circus came through a few years back."

"I remember that," Kody said. "Never got a chance to see it myself."

"Me neither, but I saw 'em in the street, juggling and such."

"Thank you for your time," Lenoir interrupted, before the sergeant could lead them farther down Irrelevant Lane. "I wish you a speedy recovery." On cue, Sister Rhea appeared with the tea.

As soon as they were outside, Kody let loose. "That's something, isn't it, Inspector? The Inataari?"

"Why so?"

Kody looked surprised. "Well, have you ever seen one?"

"Once or twice."

"Once or twice, and look how old you are. That means it's rare."

Lenoir scowled. "Rare, yes, but that is hardly definitive. The Inataari trade more and more with Braeland, and aside from the docks, the Camp is the first place one would expect to find them."

"So ... we just dismiss it?" Something like the old disdain colored Kody's voice.

"Of course not. We make a note of it and move on, and do not allow ourselves to be distracted by what is most likely a meaningless detail."

"I guess that makes sense."

"I am delighted you think so, Sergeant," Lenoir said coldly. He quickened his step, heading for the pestilence houses. He would say a few words to Lideman and the sergeants, collect his horse, and depart. There was nothing more to be gained in the Camp, at least not today.

By the time they reached Addleman's Bridge, a crowd

had already gathered, drawn by the spectacle of dozens of watchmen erecting a barricade. For now, the Camp's residents were too stunned to be angry, but that would not last. The watchmen knew it too; a cache of rifles could be glimpsed between the timber planks of the barricade. On the opposite bank, an identical barricade was going up. Barely noon, and already the work was almost complete; Lenoir and Kody had to dismount and lead their horses through the small gap remaining between the barricade and the edge of the bridge. The next time they came through, it would have to be on foot.

"Look at that," Kody said as they made their way across the no-man's-land between barricades.

Lenoir followed his gaze to the far side of the river. The barricade was not the only hive of activity. Watchmen lined the riverbank in both directions, stacking sandbags as though preparing for a flood. *They are building a wall,* Lenoir realized. Glancing downstream, he could see watchmen patrolling at intervals, conspicuously armed with rifles. He wondered how much of the river the hounds could possibly cover.

"The chief must have every watchman we've got out here," Kody said into his thoughts.

"So it would seem."

There was a stretch of silence, broken only by the hollow clacking of the horses' hooves. Slowly, almost reluctantly, Kody said, "Even if we find whoever started this thing . . ."

"It will do nothing to stop the plague," Lenoir finished. "That is true, Sergeant, just as finding a murderer will do nothing to bring his victim back to life. Sometimes, the best justice has to offer is vengeance."

Vengeance was something Nicolas Lenoir knew all about.

As they passed through the barricade on the Fishering side, Lenoir scanned the crowd of watchmen in search of whoever was in charge. He did not have to look far: Lendon Reck himself prowled the scene, pointing fingers and barking out orders. Lenoir handed the reins of his horse to Kody and made his way over.

"Chief."

Reck made a dismissive gesture. "Not now, I'm— Oh, it's you." The chief glanced him over, as though looking for signs of success. "Find anything?"

"Very little, but I am"—*Confident? Optimistic?*—"still investigating."

Reck understood the subtext well enough. He grunted and made another impatient gesture. "Look at this damned mess, will you? I could throttle Hearstings with my bare hands. A few days of this, and the city will tear itself apart."

Lenoir frowned. "What do you mean?"

"I'm under *direct orders*"—he spat the words out— "to do everything in my power to make sure the Camp is sealed off."

"So?"

"So, this festive little crowd you see is not temporary. When they're done here, these hounds will be deployed along the banks of the Sherrin, as far as we can stretch them."

"What, all of them?"

"That's right. Virtually every watchman and sergeant on the force, right here."

"But the rest of the city . . ."

"Will tear itself apart," Reck repeated.

Good God. As foolish as he knew Hearstings to be, Lenoir would never have thought the man capable of something this catastrophically stupid. "Did you not explain to him—"

"Of course. Told me I was overreacting. *Don't worry,* he says. *In times of crisis, people come together.*" He glanced at Lenoir, and they shared a brief, bitter laugh. Politicians might traffic in such comforting platitudes, but experienced hounds knew the truth: in times of crisis, people ate each other alive.

"Where to now?" the chief asked, sounding only half interested. He had bigger worries now.

"The docks."

"Got a lead?"

"No. Merely a deduction."

"Let's hope it's a good one."

Lenoir was not sure it even mattered. Kody was right—catching whoever did this would do nothing to stop the plague. It would do nothing to contain the panic. And it would do nothing to protect Kennian from herself.

Even a small city needs a police force to prevent it from sinking into anarchy. Kennian was home to hundreds of thousands, including some of the most ruthless criminal networks in the world. With the quarantine in effect, word of the plague would spread in hours, and nothing provoked chaos more quickly than panic. What would happen when people realized that only a skeleton crew of hounds patrolled the streets?

They were about to find out.

Twenty feet away from the Fishering barricade, in a secluded spot on the far side of the street, a curious bystander observed the activity. He watched as the chief of the Metropolitan Police gestured angrily at the river, explaining the situation to one of his men—an officer of some rank, judging by the civilian clothes. The officer had just come from the Camp, accompanied by a younger partner who hovered nearby deferentially. The younger man wasn't in uniform either. That meant he was at least a sergeant, which in turn meant that his superior must be at least a senior sergeant, if not an inspector. That wasn't good news. It could be a coincidence; maybe they were investigating a murder or some such, and just happened to be in the Camp when the quarantine was declared. More likely, though, it had something to do with the plague.

The curious bystander cursed quietly. Had they figured it out already? It hadn't really occurred to him that anyone would bother to ask where the plague had come from, at least not right away. He'd assumed that everyone would be too busy panicking. The disease was highly contagious, after all, and it killed with ruthless efficiency. *Maybe that's the problem,* he mused. *Maybe that's how they worked it out.* Regardless, the Camp was now swarming with hounds, and it was about to get a whole lot harder to keep an eye on his little project. He needed a plan.

He'd foreseen the quarantine, of course. The Camp was tantalizingly easy to cut off, what with the river doing most of the job on its own. And the lord mayor and his council had little to fear in the way of political consequences. The slum rats had no voice of their own, and even the most dewy-eyed humanitarian would find his principles sorely tested by the prospect of plague. The city would quietly turn its back on the Camp. It had already begun. He'd predicted this, and it didn't get in the way of his plans. In fact, he'd counted on it.

What he hadn't counted on was how quickly it would happen. It wouldn't be too difficult to sneak past the hounds—there just weren't enough of them to watch the entire length of the river, especially after nightfall—but that was assuming you were healthy. An infected person would never make the swim, and a boat would easily be spotted. *But that quarantine can't be allowed to hold. It'll ruin everything.*

An idea was already forming in his mind. It wouldn't be easy, and it might get a little messy, but luckily, he wasn't squeamish. Still, he couldn't do it alone. He needed eyes and ears in the Camp—that, and maybe a little muscle. Fortunately, he knew just where to look.

He hadn't anticipated having to kill hounds, but that was the thing about plans: the best ones always took a little improvising.

CHAPTER 4

Bran Kody didn't like the docks.

There was no escaping them, not if you were a hound. Like the slums, they were familiar hunting grounds, especially for the lower ranks. As a watchman, Kody had spent at least half his time prowling these stinking piers, arresting smugglers and breaking up tavern brawls. He'd been stabbed—twice—and had his nose broken by the biggest man he'd ever seen, a slave trader from some country Kody couldn't pronounce, let alone locate on a map. He'd seen all sorts of awful things—a beggar kid who'd been beaten to death, a pretty whore called Clari carved up until she was unrecognizable. Once, he'd fished the bloated corpse of one of his fellow watchmen out of the bay. Avoiding the docks, and places like it, was one of many reasons Kody had been so eager to be promoted from watchman to sergeant. The higher ranking you were, the less time you spent in the filth. That was the theory, anyway. Yet here he was, alongside Lenoir, an inspector.

Some things were just part of the job. You couldn't escape them, at least not entirely. Not until you were chief of the Metropolitan Police.

He tried to console himself with that thought.

"We're starting with the dockmaster, I suppose?" he

grumbled as the familiar stench of fish guts drifted up the alley to meet them.

Lenoir did not respond. The inspector's hands were jammed in his pockets, and he had the collar of his coat turned up, in spite of the midday heat. Kody had come to recognize this posture as a sign of deep thought. It was as though Lenoir was trying to shut himself off from the world, to retreat into a place of darkness and silence, free of distractions. Maybe it helped him to concentrate. Or maybe he was just cranky.

Kody spotted the dockmaster from a long way off, even though he'd never seen the man before. It wasn't so much the uniform—though the bright red jacket did draw the eye—but the way the man carried himself, crusty and confident, like a sea captain. The wharf was his deck, the dockhands his crew, and he presided over them with an air of absolute authority.

Apparently, that authority extended over Lenoir and Kody too—in the dockmaster's mind at least. "Got some business down here, Officers?" the man asked as they approached. He'd pegged them for hounds as easily as they'd pegged him for dockmaster. "I'm real busy here," he added, gesturing at the massive ship moored beside him. She was an impressive vessel, with towering masts and an elaborately carved prow. Foreign, Kody reckoned, but he wasn't an expert. A steady procession of dockhands marched down the gangway from her decks, unloading her cargo; they reminded Kody of ants ferrying eggs.

Lenoir dismissed the dockmaster's self-importance with three simple words: "Come with me."

Captain Crusty didn't like that one bit. He squared off to face Lenoir, giving the inspector a full view of his broad chest and meaty arms, like a bird puffing up its feathers to intimidate a rival. *Ex-sailor,* Kody thought. They usually were. "Maybe you didn't hear me," the dockmaster said. "I'm real busy."

Lenoir greeted this display with a look of perfect

boredom. "The City of Kennian thanks you for your industriousness. Now come with me."

The dockmaster turned an ugly shade of pink, and Kody tensed, frisking the man with his gaze. No sword, but Kody would bet a day's wages there was a knife hidden on him somewhere. Sailors were seldom without them. Kody's hands curled into fists, ready. He'd leave his own sword in its scabbard unless he really needed it.

The dockmaster wasn't that stupid; he wilted a little in submission. Lenoir's bland confidence had carried the day again. "Better be quick," the man said sullenly.

Lenoir ignored the remark. He turned and walked back up the pier, leaving the dockmaster and Kody to follow. They found a quiet spot near some fishing boats, most of which had already been scrubbed down for the day. One or two pairs of ears still loitered about, but it was as much seclusion as they were likely to find at this time of day. Lenoir paused, looking the dockmaster up and down. Kody would have given another day's wages to listen in on the inspector's thoughts, but all he heard was the creak of rope and the gentle slapping of water against the hulls of the boats.

"How long have you been dockmaster here?" Lenoir asked.

The man regarded him warily. "Seven months. Why?"

"And you have been on duty every day for the past few weeks?"

"Except on prayer day," the dockmaster said. "And I got witnesses to that."

He thinks he's being accused of something. Kody wasn't surprised. If the man had been a sailor, chances were he'd been a smuggler too. The words were practically identical in Kody's lexicon.

"Have you seen any unusual activity over the past six weeks or so?"

The dockmaster blinked. He hadn't expected that question. "What do you mean, *unusual*?"

"Braelish is not my mother tongue, but I believe I am employing the customary definition of the word. As in, *out of the ordinary*."

The man's jaw tightened, but he swallowed his anger. "Hard to say what's ordinary around here, Officer."

"Inspector."

"Oh." The dockmaster shifted uncomfortably. "Well, anyway . . . I can't say anything unusual has caught my attention, unless you count a couple of escaped monkeys."

"Monkeys?" Kody echoed, incredulous. "Yeah, I'd say that counts."

"Filthy little buggers." The dockmaster spat into the water for emphasis. "Got out of their cages down in the hold, only the crew was too stupid to notice. Little vermin came boiling out of there the minute we opened the hatch. One of my men got bit rounding 'em up."

Kody felt a little pang of excitement. *That could do it, couldn't it?*

"When did this incident occur?" Lenoir asked.

The dockmaster hitched a shoulder indifferently. "Five days ago. Maybe six."

Damn. So much for that idea.

"Lucky my man was wearing heavy gloves," the dockmaster said, "or he might've got rabies or some such."

"You managed to catch them?" Lenoir asked.

"Took us over an hour, but yeah, we managed."

"No one else was bitten?"

"Not that I know of."

"Five or six days ago, you said. You are absolutely certain?"

"You can check the records if you doubt me."

"I shall. Thank you. I'll need to see everything from the past six weeks, starting with the oldest."

The dockmaster's mouth dropped open. "Six weeks? You got any idea how many ships come in here every day?"

"Quite a few, I should imagine, and I will need the cargo and crew manifest for each and every one."

Kody stifled a groan. *We'll be here for hours.* He could only hope that Lenoir would deign to help sift through the ledgers. Usually, he left such menial tasks to Kody.

"Before we get to that, however," Lenoir said, "I have one more question. Have you had any recent reports of disease among the arriving passengers or crew? Deaths, perhaps?"

The dockmaster smirked. "Don't know much about sea voyages, do you, Inspector?"

"Answer the question," Kody said, crowding the man a little.

The dockmaster gave him a sulky glare. "Sure, I've had reports. Every day, practically. Just part of being at sea, isn't it? They're out there a couple of weeks, they get sick. They die. Sometimes lots of 'em die." He shrugged. "Just how it is."

"But the dead are not typically brought into port," Lenoir said.

"Pretty rare. A loved one, maybe, but most folks would rather bury 'em at sea than leave 'em to rot in the hold. You can imagine the smell."

Kody could imagine it all too well. He grimaced.

"Have any been brought in recently?" Lenoir asked.

"Dead bodies? Not so as I've heard."

Kody sighed. *Dead end.*

Lenoir thought so too; Kody could tell from the sour look on his face. Even so, he said, "We will see those records now." Apparently, he was determined to be thorough.

He really has changed, Kody mused. A year ago, Lenoir could barely be convinced to take up a case, and when he did, he haunted the streets aimlessly, like the ghost of a hound long dead. He'd been irritable, arrogant, and apathetic, to the point where he and Kody were barely on speaking terms. Things were different now. *He* was different. Still irritable and arrogant, maybe, but Kody found those foibles easier to put up with now that Lenoir had rediscovered his edge. Something had happened to him during the case of the corpse thieves, something that had reminded him of who he was: the finest detective in Braeland.

But even the finest detective needs leads, and right now, they had none. Lenoir was convinced that the disease had come to Kennian by ship, and he was probably right, but without evidence, the knowledge did them no good.

Sometimes vengeance is all justice has to offer, Lenoir had said. For now, it seemed that justice could not even offer that much.

Kody winced, massaging the kink in his neck. He had a corker of a headache, and the insides of his eyelids felt like rasps. Sorting through the ledgers had taken way too long, and turned up way too little. "Who knew Kennians were so fond of spices?"

"Of course," said Lenoir, buttoning his coat. "How else could one tolerate Braelish cuisine?"

Kody rolled his eyes, but otherwise let the remark pass. He'd learned long ago that it was pointless to dispute the cultural superiority of the Arrènais. "I guess we're calling it a day?"

"Not quite."

Kody checked a sigh. "Where to?"

"You look like you need a drink, Sergeant," Lenoir said archly, and he headed for the street.

Kody stared after him, stunned. Inspector Lenoir had never invited him anywhere, not socially. As far as he knew, Lenoir didn't have a social life. And if he did, he wouldn't spend it with a junior officer whose company he obviously found irritating.

Must have something to do with the case, he decided. Regardless, when your inspector invited you for a drink, you didn't refuse. Kody caught up in a few short strides.

Evening had fallen, and the harsh glare of the dock-master's lantern still stained his vision, giving depth to the shadows and sketching the street in charcoal and ash. Up ahead, soft globes of light blossomed one by one as the streetlamps were lit. Kody trailed Lenoir in silence, his confusion only growing as they made their way toward the poor district. He would have thought Lenoir had had enough of the slums for one day.

It had been a while since Kody had been in this part of town after sunset, and he was surprised at how lively they found it. The more respectable neighborhoods had already shuttered their shops and retreated indoors, but the poor district buzzed with activity. Revelers poured in and out of taverns, and hawkers still lined the streets, flogging humble wares like cooking oil and tallow candles and old boots. A man selling a miracle tonic grabbed at Kody's sleeve as he passed. "Cures what ails you! Only a quarter!"

"A quarter crown for a pint of liquid?" Kody laughed. "You've got a sense of humor, mate."

"Small price for your health," the man retorted, but he knew a lost cause when he saw it; he turned his attention elsewhere.

Two blocks later, they reached their destination: a slightly rough-looking alehouse called the Firkin. Kody shook his head, bewildered. *Wouldn't have thought Lenoir would set foot in a place like this, not unless he was on the job.* But then, how much did he really know about his superior, anyway? Lenoir didn't confide in him. Could barely stand to talk to him. Could barely stand to talk to *anyone*, as far as Kody could tell. To describe the man as "private" would be like calling water wet.

Lenoir paused just inside the door, scanning the crowd with narrowed eyes. He must have spotted what he was looking for straightaway, for he plunged into the melee, leaving Kody to follow. When they had shoved their way into the heart of a group of friends toasting flagons, Lenoir stopped. Kody was just about to ask what was going on when the inspector's arm jerked, as though he had caught a fish somewhere between the bodies.

"Hey, hands off! I wasn't doing nothing!"

Lenoir ignored this indignant protest, dragging his catch through the crowd to an open space in the corner. Only then did Kody get his first glimpse of the owner of the voice: a ragged, squirming boy with sandy hair poking out from under his hat like straw from the stuffing of a scarecrow. He looked to be about seven, judging from his height, but Kody knew better. The boy was ten, and he was called Zach.

"Don't have to be so rough about it," the boy grumbled, straightening his shirt and tucking the ends back into an ill-fitting pair of half breeches. "You could've just shouted, you know."

Lenoir regarded his favorite informant with a wry expression. "I could have, at peril of my dignity, but you would have finished with that baker's purse first."

Zach glanced back to the crowd with a shrewd eye. "Baker, huh? How can you tell?"

"Flour on his trousers, oven burn on his right wrist."

The boy sighed. "Not much coin to be had there. Wouldn't have bothered if I knew."

He doesn't even try to deny it, the little delinquent. What in God's name did Lenoir see in this boy? Something, obviously; Kody suspected it was Zach's kidnapping that had shaken Lenoir out of his torpor last winter. The inspector hadn't been the least bit interested in the corpse thieves until Zach went missing. *But why should he trouble with a pint-size cutpurse?* "Like calling water wet," Kody said under his breath.

"What's that, Sergeant?"

"Nothing." *Just pondering the mystery that is Nicolas Lenoir.*

"Was he your first victim this evening?" Lenoir asked

the boy. "Or do I have to turn in a few purses to the barman?"

Zach twisted away protectively. "I earned this money fair! Beat those drunkards at bones, twice!"

Kody and Lenoir turned to look at the drunkards in question, a trio of hard-luck types who could barely keep themselves upright. "I'm not sure I would call that fair, Zach," Lenoir said, but he sounded more amused than admonishing. He turned away to get the attention of the barmaid.

The boy, meanwhile, eyed Kody curiously. They had met twice before: once at the kennel, when Zach had given a statement following his abduction, and another time in a place much like this. Then, as now, Zach had stared openly at Kody, fascinated by something only he could see. It made Kody uncomfortable. "All right, kid?" he asked awkwardly.

Zach shrugged. "Still alive."

The barmaid came over with a flagon of ale and two cups of wine. The beer went to Kody, and Lenoir handed one of the cups to Zach. The boy sighed as he took it, casting a longing glance at Kody's flagon.

"Do you really think he should have that?" Kody asked the inspector in an undertone. "At his age?"

"It's only wine, Sergeant."

"But he's a child."

Lenoir gave him a blank look. "Do children not consume wine in Braeland?"

"Er, no. Not generally."

Lenoir frowned into his cup. He took a sip, swirled it in his mouth, and shook his head, mystified. Kody decided to let it go.

Zach took a swallow too, and his face puckered. "Tastes like vinegar."

"Agreed," said Lenoir, "but it is still better than beer. One day, I will buy you a glass of proper Arrènais wine."

Zach looked skeptical, but a free drink was a free drink—he took another big draft from his cup, wincing as he swallowed. "I have a task for you," Lenoir said.

The boy brightened. "What's that?"

"I need you to spend some time at the docks for the next few days. As much as you can manage."

Kody tried not to look surprised. He knew Lenoir sometimes gave the boy odd jobs, but he'd assumed nothing important. Plus, the wharf was no place for a kid.

Zach, for his part, looked pleased at the prospect. "The docks, huh? Sounds good."

"You like the docks?" Kody asked, a little incredulously.

"Sure. Most interesting place in town. All sorts to see and do down there. And the money's not bad, either."

Kody shook his head in disbelief. Drunken sailors might be easy marks for a thief, but they were dangerous ones too. Make a mistake, and you were liable to get your throat cut, child or not. "Keep that up and you won't live long."

"Live better while I do, though."

"That's some philosophy for a ten-year-old," Kody said.

Zach shrugged. To Lenoir, he said, "What am I looking for?"

"I'm not sure. Keep an eye on the cargos. I want to know what is coming in and going out. And see if you can wheedle some tales out of the crews. Anything strange or interesting they may have come across, here or abroad. Do not trouble too much if the stories are true—at least not for now."

"Really?" Zach's eyes widened with his grin. "Wow, this is the best job ever!"

A ghost of a smile flitted across Lenoir's face. "I thought you would like it."

"Listening to tall tales from all over the world? What's not to like?"

It was a rhetorical question, but the answer came to Kody anyway, in a vision of the beggar boy he'd found beaten to death all those years ago. *I hope this one's as clever as you think, Inspector.*

"I'm especially interested in reports of disease," Lenoir said.

"Like the one in the Camp?"

Kody and Lenoir exchanged a look. *Word is spreading already.* Panic would not be far behind.

"Where did you hear about that?" Lenoir asked.

"Everybody's talking about it." Zach lowered his voice conspiratorially. "They say you bleed your guts out through your nose."

"Who says that?"

"Everyone."

"What else do they say?"

Zach did not miss the edge in Lenoir's tone. "What's the matter?"

"Just answer the question."

"I don't know," the boy said, looking a little wounded. "The usual stuff. How the Adali are the only ones who know how to cure it. How they brought it here in the first place."

Kody sighed and muttered an oath. "Can't say I didn't see that coming." The Adali were already despised as heathens and sorcerers, and frequently blamed for everything from crime to bad harvests. The fact that the plague had started in the Camp, where a disproportionate number of Adali lived, all but guaranteed they'd take the blame. "It's going to get ugly, Inspector," Kody said, "and soon."

"Most likely."

"You think people will make trouble for them?" Zach asked. "The Adali, I mean?"

He is a clever one at that, Kody thought.

"Hopefully it will not come to that," Lenoir said, but Kody could tell he didn't believe it.

So could Zach. "But it's just a stupid rumor. They don't *know*."

"Sometimes a rumor is enough," said Lenoir.

"But it's not fair." The boy scowled. "It's like the nuns at the orphanage. They always think I'm in trouble, even when I'm not. They don't *know*, but they think they know. They hear a rumor and *wham*—I'm scrubbing pots!"

Lenoir's mouth twitched, as if he were wrestling a smile. "It is true that people are often treated as if they are guilty, simply because they cannot prove they are innocent."

"You can prove it," Zach said, with absolute conviction.

Aha. Kody was beginning to understand what Lenoir saw in the boy.

"I'm surprised you care what happens to the Adali," he said, "after what they did to you."

Zach cocked his head. "What do you mean?"

"Well, you were kidnapped by Adali."

"The ones who took me are dead."

"Well, sure," Kody said, "but some people would hold that against the whole lot."

Zach just looked at him as though he were babbling nonsense.

"Consider his life, Sergeant," Lenoir said in an undertone. "He has been on the streets since the age of six. He has seen evil in every race, in every age and sex. He cannot hate them all." Turning to the boy, he said, "Let the sergeant and me worry about the plague. You have business at the docks." Zach presented an open hand, into which Lenoir dropped a few coins. "No beer," he said, one eyebrow arched to show he was serious. "I will know."

Zach rolled his eyes. "You don't have to say that every time."

"If you hear anything interesting, find me straightaway. Otherwise, we will meet in two days. But not here—we will do it at the Courtier. My stomach cannot handle any more of *this*." He frowned down at his wine cup.

"Fine by me, as long as I can have some steak." The boy headed for the door, his small frame weaving easily through the crowd. It took Kody and Lenoir longer to negotiate their way; Zach was already outside when they caught up with him. "So you're gonna find a way to stop the plague?" he asked as they parted.

"I am an inspector, Zach, not a physician."

"But you find things. You could find a cure."

"A cure is not something you track down as you would a murderer. It must be discovered through science, and I have no gift for science. We must rely on others to find a way to stop this plague, and I am afraid that will not happen quickly."

"Oh." Zach's brow furrowed as something new occurred to him. "What if I get sick? What if you do?" The boy seemed equally worried by either prospect. *He really looks up to Lenoir,* Kody thought. So the inspector wasn't entirely friendless after all.

"Go home, Zach," Lenoir said. "You are safe, for now. We both are."

Kody could tell he didn't believe that, either.

CHAPTER 5

"Three thousand and some," Kody said, sliding the report across Lenoir's desk. "That's more than fifteen hundred deaths in the past three days."

"I can count, Sergeant." Lenoir reached for the report, then changed his mind and left it alone. What could it tell him that he did not already know?

"You talked to the boy last night, didn't you? He find anything?" The barest hint of hope colored Kody's voice.

"Nothing yet."

Nothing. It had become their watchword, their constant companion. *Nothing* was what came of the day spent at the College of Physicians. The stagecoach, the post, and the river ferry had turned up still more of it. "So much nothing," Lenoir said, sounding every bit as resentful as he felt.

Kody nodded, and for a moment, the two of them just stared at the report, a malignant thing lying there between them, mocking their impotence. Lenoir's thumb tapped out an erratic rhythm against the surface of the desk, and his knee bounced against his chair. He had rarely felt so helpless. The plague was like a boulder tumbling down a hillside, picking up speed as it fell. Meanwhile, Lenoir was no closer to finding out who was responsible, and the odds of that happening dwindled with each passing day.

Inevitable, the rational part of him argued. *This was always a fool's errand.* They had no evidence. No hint of motive. The crime was unlikely to be repeated. In short, they had none of the elements required to solve a case. Not so long ago, Lenoir would simply have given up. Oh, he would have gone through the motions—a man must earn a living, after all—but his lack of progress would not have vexed him overmuch. As Kody had already pointed out, catching whoever was responsible would do nothing to slow the plague. From that point of view, little enough hung in the balance beyond some vague notion of justice, and it had been a long time since Lenoir had been taken in by her deceptions. Justice was a mirage, a shimmering ideal on the horizon that kept men plodding onward, hoping in vain to reach her. Lenoir had seen through that illusion long ago.

No, it was not justice that spurred him. It was something much more primal, much more urgent. It was *necessity.* For if he did not have the case, what did he have?

Nothing.

The Darkwalker had spared him. Given him back his life. A precious gift, yet Lenoir found he did not entirely know what to do with it. After so many years of being marked for death—of not caring, not allowing himself to be cared for—Lenoir scarcely knew how to *live.* He had no family. No real friends. No dreams or aspirations, at least not for himself. He had divested himself of those things long ago. Once, he had filled the void with liquor and indolence. These days, he filled it with the Case. It was not enough, but it was all he had.

And it was going nowhere.

For once, Kody's voice was a welcome intrusion. "Did you hear they reassigned Izar?"

Lenoir looked up. "No."

"Chief said it was too dangerous to keep him on the barricade. People had started throwing rocks at him." Kody shook his head. "How do you like that? Throwing rocks at a hound!"

"He is not a hound in their eyes," Lenoir said. "Right now, he is only an Adal."

"Ingrates. Anyway, they moved him to the other side of the bridge. I guess they figured there were enough Adali in the Camp that no one would give him trouble."

Lenoir winced. That meant Izar was the one enforcing the quarantine, keeping the Camp's residents from entering Kennian proper. "The gatekeeper against his own people."

"Rough," Kody agreed. "Chief didn't have much choice, though. At least it means we've got one of our best on it."

Somehow, Lenoir doubted that would be much comfort to Sergeant Izar.

He reached for the report, scanning it listlessly. The scribe, whoever he was, had started to write down the names of the dead, only to give up when it became clear there were too many. *Death rate has quadrupled in the past week,* it read. *If current trend continues, Camp population will be halved by the end of the month.* Lenoir swore in Arrènais and pushed the report away, sorry he had given in to his curiosity.

He paused. He grabbed it back.

He felt his lips moving as he read, but he did not care. He leaned in close enough to smell the ink on the paper. *Milswaith, Brandton, Filimore.* With each successive name, he became more convinced. But how could he test his theory?

The idea came to him almost instantly, yet he hesitated. *This is not your task,* he thought. *But still . . . so many are dying. . . .* "Get your coat, Sergeant," he said, rising.

"What is it?"

"Something the boy said. Now go." Kody needed no further encouragement; he bounded out of the office like a foxhound let off his lead. By the time Lenoir joined him at the bottom of the stairs, Kody had his coat buttoned, his sword belt on, and his crossbow slung over his shoulder. If he had had a tail, it would have been wagging.

Lenoir shared the sergeant's enthusiasm, even if he did not show it. After three days without a lead, even a long shot felt like a breakthrough. And though this would bring him no closer to the perpetrator, it was *something*. A purpose.

A purpose was all he needed.

He kept a brisk pace all the way to the market district, Kody following resolutely, and best of all, silently. It was so blissful that Lenoir was almost in a good mood when they arrived at their destination: an anonymous building in the market district, wedged between a butcher and a tailor. Then he remembered what lurked behind that shroud of curtains, and his momentary cheer vanished.

"What is this place?" Kody asked.

"It is . . ." Lenoir paused, unsure how to describe it. "There is someone I need to speak with," he finished awkwardly, reaching for the door.

Dozens of candle flames shuddered against the breath of wind that followed them inside, their glow flickering against mysterious shapes. Horns dangled in spirals and spikes from the rafters, as though a herd of exotic antelope grazed upon the ceiling. Smooth orbs of glass glinted in the dark like the eyes of a nighttime predator. Shelves lined the walls, as high and crowded as any library, their shadowed recesses only hinting at their contents. Woven twigs and dried bushels of herbs swallowed the light; the sharp facets of crystals threw it back. Lenoir had to duck beneath a brace of pheasants suspended just inside the door, their blood dripping noisily into a tin pail below.

From behind the counter, a pair of golden eyes watched his progress curiously.

"What in the below?" Kody hesitated in the doorway. Lenoir had done the same the first time he visited this place.

"Greetings, Inspector," said a deep, resonant voice. "I hope you will not think me rude if I say that I am surprised to see you again."

Surprised to see me alive, you mean. "I am still a little surprised myself," Lenoir said.

Merden tilted his head thoughtfully. Candlelight burnished the prominent peak of his left cheekbone, melted away into the hollows of his angular face. "How did you survive?"

Lenoir shot a look at Kody, who still lingered warily near the door. He had never told the sergeant the whole story; he could hardly believe it himself. "That is a tale for another time," he said, hoping Merden would take the hint.

"A shame. I should very much like to hear it."

You have no idea. Aloud, Lenoir said, "This is Sergeant Kody."

Merden turned his golden-eyed gaze upon Kody, allowing the sergeant to experience that profoundly wise, profoundly unnerving stare. The Adal said nothing, but inclined his head in greeting. Kody ducked awkwardly in return.

"Merden is a soothsayer," Lenoir said.

"Okay." Kody stayed where he was.

Turning back to Merden, Lenoir said, "I need your help."

"Plainly."

Lenoir had forgotten how sharp—and how sharp-tongued—the Adal could be. "Are you aware of the disease that has been ravaging the Camp?"

"I do leave this shop occasionally, Inspector." The dryness of his tone cut cleanly through the lilting accent.

I will take that as a yes. "And its symptoms—you have heard them described?"

"I have."

"Is the disease familiar to you?"

There was a long pause. Merden considered him carefully. "I would be very disappointed, Inspector, if this was a roundabout way of asking me whether the Adali are responsible for bringing this plague to Braelish shores."

"Not at all." Lenoir raised a hand in a mollifying gesture. "I am merely asking whether, in your experience as a practitioner of"—he hesitated, darting another look at Kody—"of traditional medicine, you have come across this disease before."

"If you mean *khekra*, you can say it," Kody said from the doorway. "I'm not stupid."

Merden glanced at him. "You would not be stupid to fear dark magic, Sergeant. On the contrary, you would be a fool not to."

Silence descended on the room like a fine layer of dust. *Khekra* was rarely spoken of openly, not even among the Adali. Few southerners had even heard the word, and those who had invariably wished they had not. Fewer still were those, like Lenoir, who had witnessed its power. He cleared his throat. "You did not answer my question."

"The disease is known to my people," Merden said warily.

Lenoir could not help smiling. "As are its secrets. Is it not so?"

The soothsayer made no reply.

Lenoir shook his head. "I should have seen it sooner. All the signs were there."

"What signs?" Kody directed a mistrustful stare at the tall man behind the counter. "Sorry, Inspector, but I don't follow."

"It was the report that finally made me see it, though it has been in front of us all along."

"What has?"

"No Adali among the corpses brought into the clinic.

None in the treatment tent, or the convalescents' tent. Not a single Adali name listed among the dead. And then there was the rumor Zach mentioned, about the Adali having the only cure. Is that true, Merden, or are your people simply immune?"

The soothsayer's eyes narrowed.

"That is not an accusation," Lenoir was quick to add.

"Isn't it?" Merden's rich voice sounded a dangerous note, and for the first time, Lenoir found himself wondering what this man might be capable of. He had seen enough of the occult to know he had reason to fear.

"No, it is not. As I told you, I need your help. If you have a cure, you must share it."

Merden eyed him for a long moment, as though weighing Lenoir's intentions. The Adali rarely discussed their traditions with outsiders, still less with the police. *I should have been more diplomatic,* Lenoir thought. Tact had never been his strong suit, but he should have made more of an effort. If Merden turned them away, there would be no second chance.

"*I* do not have a cure," the soothsayer said at length. "If I had, I would have told someone by now. Or do you think me a barbarian?"

"Of course not," Lenoir said, but it sounded defensive, even to him.

Merden went on as though he had not heard. "It is quite possible, however, that a cure is known among the northern clans, for this plague has struck them before."

"When?"

"Not in our lifetime, but the Adali pass such knowledge from father to son, from mother to daughter, for every season comes again."

"Death isn't a season," Kody said, annoyed.

Merden raised an eyebrow. "What an odd thing to say, Sergeant. Death is the most reliable season of them all."

Lenoir clucked his tongue impatiently. "Someone in Kennian knows this cure. Otherwise, there would be

Adali victims, and many of them." The Camp was nearly a quarter Adali, after all.

"Perhaps there are," Merden said. "It may simply be that the Adali who fall ill do not present themselves at your Braelish clinics. My people have little faith in your medicine. We prefer to seek treatment among our own kind."

"That is possible, but it bears investigating. Will you help?"

"How can I help? I have already told you that I do not know the cure, if indeed such a thing exists."

"The Camp is under quarantine, a blockade enforced by the Metropolitan Police, and I am about to go canvassing the locals about Adali magic. I would think the matter is plain."

The soothsayer grunted. "I suppose it is at that."

"So you will come?"

Merden sighed, his eyes roaming regretfully over the shop. "The summer months are best for business," he said, "for spirits grow restless when the sun is near."

Lenoir had no idea what to say to that.

"I will come, Inspector, but give me a moment to prepare."

"Certainly. We will wait for you outside."

"You sure this is a good idea?" Kody asked as they stepped out onto the street. "With tempers the way they are, it might not be safe for him to walk around town right now."

"No more than it is safe for us to walk around the Camp. Hopefully, we can avoid drawing attention to ourselves. In any case, Merden can take care of himself, just as we can." He patted the sword at his hip for emphasis.

Kody eyed it dubiously. "You carrying a gun too?" The sergeant did not have much faith in Lenoir's ability to wield a blade, a misgiving that was not entirely unwarranted.

Lenoir pulled his coat back, exposing the butt of a

flintlock. Kody looked reassured. *As though I am any better with the damn pistol,* Lenoir thought.

A moment later, Merden came out of the shop. At the sight of him, Kody groaned softly, and even Lenoir struggled to hide his dismay. The soothsayer had donned a traditional Adali cloak, a spectacular garment of dyed purple wool and bloodred embroidery. Horn beads fringed a wide, drooping cowl, and a rune of some kind was picked out in tiles of bleached bone down the back. It was the most elaborate specimen of its kind Lenoir had ever seen, and though undeniably handsome, it would not exactly blend in with everyday Kennian attire. In the unlikely event that the casual observer should fail to notice the cloak, Merden had helpfully chosen a seven-foot tall walking stick of ebony and bone. They wanted only a herd of cattle to complete the picture.

The soothsayer hoisted a sling of leather pouches over each shoulder and locked the door to his shop. "I am ready, Inspector."

"We'd better get horses," Kody said. "Can you ride, Merden?"

The Adal stared at him.

"Right," Kody said, coloring. He might as well have asked a fish if it could swim.

Lenoir started off toward the station. Already, he could feel the eyes of the entire market square upon them, though whether hostile or merely curious, he could not tell.

This day was about to get very interesting.

CHAPTER 6

They left the horses at the Fishering barricade and crossed Addleman's Bridge on foot. Already, Lenoir could see that the pestilence houses had swelled in number, overtaking the view from the river. Ahead, the barricade loomed forbiddingly, its timber frame packed in with sandbags and capped with spear points. Watchmen armed with crossbows manned makeshift towers at both flanks, and a dozen more sat slumped against the bridge side, resting, cooking, cleaning rifles. The main force stood guard on the other side, facing the Camp; it was there they found Sergeant Izar.

"Inspector," the sergeant said, "I didn't expect to see you here again." He started to say something else, but then he spotted Merden, and his golden eyes widened. He dropped his head low and murmured something in Adali. Merden inclined his head in return.

Izar's gaze shifted between Lenoir and Merden. Lenoir could almost hear the questions, but he did not have time to explain. "How are things here, Sergeant?" he asked, scanning the barricade. The men looked edgy, and most of them wore scarves tied around their faces.

"Quiet, for the moment," Izar said. "We had an incident this morning. A mother tried to get one of the watchmen

to take her children through. She was very determined.
We had to subdue her, and that made some people angry."

"Where is she now?" Kody asked, glancing around.

"Unconscious. She was taken to the clinic."

Lenoir winced. "Anyone else hurt?"

"A few, but nothing serious. Good practice for the
men, I suppose, for when it gets bad."

When, not *if.* It hardly took a soothsayer to make that
prediction; one look at the faces of the crowd milling
around the barricade—angry, fearful, desperate—was
evidence enough. *It is only a matter of time.*

"I hear you had some trouble on the Fishering side,"
Kody said.

Izar smiled wryly. "Good thing the chief moved me
here, where I can stay out of trouble."

Kody said something in reply, but Lenoir had stopped
listening. Instead, he watched as Merden made his way
over to the crowd. Many of the watchers were Adali, and
they all bowed their heads the way Izar had done, some
putting their hands to their chests. A gesture of respect,
it seemed. They recognized him as a soothsayer, or perhaps as a witchdoctor. The cloak, Lenoir presumed.

"Izar," he said, interrupting the sergeants. "That rune
on the back of Merden's cloak—what does it mean?"

"*Mekhleth.* The Wise. Few men have the right to wear
a cloak like that."

"Do you know him?" Kody asked.

"Only by reputation."

"And he's some sort of . . . what? A holy man?"

"Not exactly. More like a shepherd. It's . . ." Izar shook
his head. "The word doesn't translate. *One who knows
the way,* I suppose."

"If he's so special, what's he doing living in Kennian?"

"That is a very good question, Kody." Izar's gaze followed Merden as he spoke with the crowd. Several of
them were pointing and talking animatedly.

"Time to go," Lenoir said. "Carry on, Sergeant."

As they approached Merden, the voices around him died, replaced by silent, distrustful stares. A woman said something sharp in Adali, but Merden raised a hand and spoke a few quiet words, and she subsided. "I have asked these people where they go for healing," the soothsayer said. "If you will follow me, Inspector, I think I know the way."

Lenoir nodded, only too happy to move away from the tense scene at the barricade. They made their way down to the main road, a wide track of earth flanked with market stalls. Pickings were meager today, Lenoir saw; the vegetables looked tired, the fruits dull and withered. They passed only a single butcher, and he had no beef to sell, only a bloody slab of mutton and a crate full of tatty, resigned-looking chickens.

"Look at the price of cooking oil," Kody said in an undertone, inclining his head at a nearby table. "Three times the price they were charging in the poor district the other night."

Three days in, and already the quarantine was biting. "It will get worse," Lenoir said, "and quickly."

"The women I spoke to at the barricade mentioned this," Merden said. "They want to keep their children inside where they will be safe, but they dare not leave their livestock unattended."

Lenoir sighed. "Livestock is the least of their worries. Cooking oil and sugar will be the first to go. Then the flour, and that is where the real trouble begins."

Merden glanced sidelong at him. "It sounds as though you speak from experience."

"I lived in Serles during the revolution. I was barely an adolescent, but I remember it as if it were yesterday. The city was not under siege, but it may as well have been. It was too violent, and people too afraid of the pox, for any trade to come. In the worst neighborhoods, people began eating dogs. By the end, the dogs were eating them." Lenoir shuddered at the memory.

They continued on in grim silence, following Merden's lead as he turned off the main road and struck out between the hovels. Their path was little more than a gutter, and they picked their way between puddles and glistening sinkholes of mud, clinging to the narrow strips of high ground like a small herd of ungainly goats. It smelled like a privy and looked like a swamp, but Lenoir barely noticed, too absorbed in the sight of a family of six loading their meager belongings into a wheelbarrow. Leaving, it seemed, but where would they go? They would not be allowed into Kennian. Out into the countryside, then? Or would the lord mayor have the highway blocked too? They were not the first to leave, either; Lenoir noticed several boarded up shacks along the way.

Nearly everyone they passed had a scarf tied around his face, and nearly every face was Adali. In quitting the main road, they had passed the informal boundary separating the Adali quarter from the rest of the Camp. The square shacks of tin and timber favored by Braelish and other southerners gave way to the distinctively dome-shaped tents of the Adali. Less distinctive were their colors, for while the traditional dwellings of the nomadic Adali were invariably brightly hued, these were drab and dingy, stitched together with whatever their owners could find. Here and there, an old tent could be spotted that had once known the touch of the famously vivid Adali dyes. These might have been red or gold in days gone by, but years of steeping in the grimy haze of the city had rendered them all the same forlorn shade of dun, making them scarcely distinguishable from the others.

"Mekhleth," a voice called. *"Mekhleth anir!"*

They turned to find a man hurrying out of his tent after them. He approached Merden respectfully, bowing his head as the others had done. After a wary glance at Lenoir and Kody, he said something to Merden in a hushed, urgent tone. They conversed for a few moments, and Lenoir could tell from the man's expression that he was disappointed. Merden put a hand on his shoulder and said something that was surely meant to be reassuring; the man nodded resignedly.

"His neighbor's son is sick," Merden explained.

"He asked you to help?"

"If only I were able."

"I thought there was a witchdoctor somewhere nearby who knows the cure," Kody said. "Isn't that why we're here?"

"I believe you mean a healer, Sergeant," Merden said coolly, "and, yes, there is one nearby. With so many ill, however, he is having difficulty keeping up."

Lenoir grunted thoughtfully. "So the Adali are not immune after all." He could not help feeling relieved. If it had simply been a question of physiology, there would be nothing to learn from the witchdoctor. *Healer,* Lenoir corrected himself. Like Kody, he had not realized the term *witchdoctor* was offensive, though he supposed it was not surprising. *Khekra* was a forbidden subject; it stood to reason that any term evoking dark magic would be similarly frowned upon. "Does this man know where we can find the healer?"

Merden repeated the question in Adali, and the man nodded, pointing. "We were headed in the right direction," Merden said. "It is not far now."

Sure enough, they came across the healer's tent a few minutes later. Lenoir did not have to be told which one it was. Aside from its impressive size and the traditionally bright shade of gold, a great throng of people teemed outside its entrance. At first, Lenoir thought they were clamoring to get inside, but as he drew nearer, he saw that the crowd was surprisingly subdued. Small groups clustered together, conversing quietly. Some sat slumped in the mud, though whether from illness, exhaustion, or just boredom, Lenoir could not tell. Many were certainly sick. Signs of fever were everywhere, and some already had nosebleeds. Husbands propped up wives, and mothers rocked crying children in their arms.

A ring of stakes had been driven into the ground around the perimeter of the tent. *Some sort of fence?* If so, it was not working. Decorative, perhaps—that would explain the horn beads and bits of bone dangling from leather thongs at the top of each stake. Merden seemed to take an interest in them; he nodded, as though a suspicion had been confirmed.

Kody held up, looking uncertain. His hand disappeared into his coat pocket, but he hesitated.

"Put it on, Sergeant," Lenoir said, reaching for his own scarf. "It does not make you cruel, or a coward. It only means you are not a fool."

Merden, for his part, drew his thumb across the underside of his nose, leaving a smear of what looked like fresh mud. "I should warn you, Inspector, what you see inside may be alarming, but you must remain calm. Above all, you must not distract the healer. To do so could be the death of us all." He gestured at the ring of stakes, as though that explained everything.

Kody looked startled. "What do you mean, *the death of us all*? What in the below is going on in there?"

"Khekra," the soothsayer replied, and he led the way into the tent.

CHAPTER 7

Passing through the tent flap was like being swallowed by some great beast. Darkness engulfed them, and for a moment, Lenoir stood rooted to the spot, blinking away the sunlight. His eyes adjusted quickly, but it did him little good; the cavernous space was lit only by a few tapers, and these stood in a tight semicircle in the center, a flaming sickle that devoured the eye and blotted out everything else.

A shadow shifted at the fringes of the light. Lenoir squinted, trying to make it out, but it had no distinguishable shape. He could not tell where the shadow ended and the darkness began, and yet it moved, twisting and sinuous, like a column of smoke. A dry, rattling sound accompanied the motion, peppering the air in short bursts—soft, then manic, then soft again—before falling abruptly silent. The darkness ceased its dance.

The flames ducked, as though disturbed by a sudden movement, but they bent *toward* the shifting shadow, rather than away. Something tugged subtly at the center of Lenoir's belly.

He could hear Kody's breathing behind him, too rapid by half. To his right, Merden watched calmly. A pungent scent pricked at Lenoir's nose, even through the handkerchief. Something familiar, something his subconscious branded as deeply unsettling, but he could not place it. He took an involuntary step back, but Merden's hand closed firmly around his wrist, exerting a gentle but meaningful pressure. *Do not move.*

Something *hissed* in the darkness.

Lenoir went rigid. Merden's fingers tightened around his wrist in warning, but the soothsayer need not have worried. Lenoir would not have been able to move if his life depended on it. He stood, transfixed, as the shadow resumed its sinuous dance. Lenoir felt another tug at his middle, sharp this time, too sharp to be merely a product of his own nervousness. For a moment, he feared he would be sick. Beside him, Merden let out a long, steady breath, as though blowing on something to help it dry.

A gust of wind rolled out from the center of the tent. The candles snuffed out. Everything went dark.

Silence.

"Mekhleth," a voice said, and a flame flared to life. The gaunt face of an elderly Adal appeared, etched in amber and shadow. He turned away to light a candle—not one of the tapers that had formed the sickle, but a short pillar with several wicks, as big around as a supper plate. He lit several more until a soft glow suffused the center of the tent, revealing the outlines of a cot with a figure lying on it. The patient, presumably.

But what in the depths of the below did they just see?

"Welcome," the man said in Braelish, having noticed his pale-skinned guests.

"I am Merden. These men are Inspector Lenoir and Sergeant Kody, from the Metropolitan Police."

The man arched an eyebrow, but did not otherwise reply.

"How did you know?" Merden asked him.

"That you were *mekhleth*?" The man smiled, a thin, weary thing. "Your breath. Who else could have lent such strength?"

Merden nodded, apparently satisfied with this unfathomable answer.

"I am Oded," the man said. "Please, come inside. It is safe now."

Lenoir gave the healer a thorough once-over with his eyes. He looked to be at least seventy, and judging by his drawn-out vowels and richly rolled *R*s, he had not lived many of those years in Braeland. Like Merden's, his skin was a rich copper hue, but the tips of his fingers were blackened. Evidence of his art, perhaps. Lenoir made a mental note to ask Merden about it later. More evidence of the healer's art, or at least his recent practice of it, could be discerned in the sagging lines of his thin frame. The Adali were a fine-boned race, and tended to be long and lean. Oded might once have been lean, but he had lost weight since, and the stoop of his shoulders took several inches off his height. *The man is exhausted,* Lenoir thought. Like Sister Rhea, Oded was sacrificing his own health for that of his patients.

Speaking of which . . . "This woman," Lenoir said, gesturing at the figure in the cot. She slept, or so it seemed, a thin sheen of sweat glistening on her brow. "You were treating her?"

Oded nodded.

"Will she live?" Kody asked.

"Time will show," the healer said. "Most get better, but a few—it is too late for them." He glanced at the tent flap, and Lenoir could read his thoughts. *He is having difficulty keeping up,* Merden had said. The more people gathered outside, the further behind he fell. It was a race, and the healer was losing.

"What happens to the ones who die?" Kody asked.

"They are burned."

"It is our way," Merden added.

"It will be our way soon, I suspect," Lenoir said, "in the Camp at least. According to the College of Physicians, the bodies are highly contagious. Burning seems like the safest option."

Oded made a face. "Physicians. *Pala.*"

Lenoir did not know the word, but he doubted it was complimentary.

Merden sounded a few low notes of laughter. "No doubt they are persuaded that leeches will improve the matter."

"They are quite attached to their leeches," Lenoir agreed, "if you will forgive the pun. I can only assure you that not all Humenori medicine is quite so backward. Science on the continent proper is rather more advanced." He glanced at Kody just in time to see the sergeant roll his eyes. As for the Adali, they traded a doubtful look.

"How do you treat the disease?" Kody asked.

"There are two parts." Oded gestured at the cot. "This was the second part, where the strength is restored."

"And the first part?" Kody's tone was wary, as though he was not sure he really wanted to know.

"It depends. If it is caught early, a potion is usually enough, but not always. Sometimes, it is harder."

"Harder how?"

"First, I must draw out the . . ." Oded paused, frowning. He looked at Merden. *"Hatekh."*

"Demon," Merden translated matter-of-factly.

Kody raised his eyebrows. "Demon, huh?" He flashed Lenoir a significant look.

No doubt he expected to find an ally in his skepticism, but Lenoir knew for a fact that such creatures existed. After all, he had nearly been killed by one. If the Darkwalker was not precisely a demon (Lenoir had never been sure what to call him) the distinction was subtle enough to be unimportant. "What makes you think a demon is involved?" he asked, ignoring Kody's snort.

"This has been known to my clan for generations," said the healer.

"That's not really an answer, is it?" Kody said.

The healer cocked his head. "Is it not?"

"Okay, fine, how did your ancestors know it was a demon?"

"By the marks." Reaching for the woman in the cot, the healer drew down her blanket to reveal a dark purple welt on her forearm. *The lesions,* Lenoir thought, *the ones Lideman says no one comes back from.* "These are the marks of the demon," the healer said.

"They're bruises," Kody said.

"Bruises, yes. From the demon."

"Oh, for the love of—"

"Enough," Lenoir said. "It does not strictly matter, does it?"

"My thoughts exactly, Inspector," said Merden. "What is important is that Oded is said to be treating the disease effectively, and for that, he deserves our respect."

"Indeed." Lenoir congratulated himself for bringing the soothsayer along. It helped to have another dispassionate, analytical mind involved, someone he could bounce ideas off, and that was certainly not a role Kody was going to fill. "Oded, can you show us how it is done? Can you teach others?"

It was Merden who answered. "That depends. Can others be taught?"

Good question. Somehow, Lenoir had a difficult time imagining Horst Lideman accepting medical advice from an Adali witchdoctor. But what choice did they have? "We have to try."

The healer looked uncertain. "There is not much time. You see how many wait for me outside."

"There will be more," Lenoir said. "More than you can ever hope to heal yourself. This is an epidemic, and it is running out of control."

"The inspector is right, my friend." Merden gestured at Oded's thin frame. "You give a little of your own strength each time you heal a patient. How much do you have left? You cannot do this alone. You need help." He added something in Adali, touching his chest.

The healer looked down at his patient, lips pursed. He sighed and shook his head. "Very well. I will try to show your . . . *physicians* . . . how to heal this sickness. But they will not listen. They will do as this one does." He gestured dismissively at Kody. "They will not believe."

Kody sighed. "Look, I believe you're doing *something* to help these people. I don't know what it is, and maybe you don't really know either. But if you told me right now that standing on one leg and barking like a dog would help this woman get better, I'd do it. I might not believe it, but I'd do it, because at this point, I'll try anything. I'd be willing to bet those physicians feel the same."

Lenoir gave him a wry look. "Eloquently put, Sergeant."

"Actually," Merden said, "it was."

If the healer was appeased, it was buried beneath layers of exhaustion. "I must rest. Come back tomorrow."

Kody scowled, and Lenoir opened his mouth to argue, but a sharp look from Merden stole the words. "As you say." Lenoir reached up to tighten the scarf around his face. "Until then." He gave a curt nod and withdrew.

"It would have been pointless to press the matter, Inspector," Merden said as they wove their way through the crowd of patients waiting outside. "His strength is gone. He would not have been able to show your physicians anything."

Lenoir did not answer. He turned his collar up against the evening and jammed his hands in his pockets. His mind whirred. Had they made progress today, or was it merely the illusion of progress? What evidence did they really have that Oded's treatment worked? For the moment, Lenoir did not give a flying fruitcake whether or not the disease had anything to do with demons. All he wanted was to find a way to stem the tide. With Merden's help, he had found a witchdoctor who claimed he could cure the disease, but even if that was true, Oded was just one man. Could he really teach Adali magic to a bunch of Braelish physicians, presuming they were even willing to learn? And if he did, would it be enough? *Death rate has tripled in the past week,* the report had said. Lenoir could still see the words, stained in black ink. *Camp population will be halved by the end of the month.* What could even a handful of healers do against such a deluge of death?

Lenoir gave his head a sharp shake. *Stop this. It achieves nothing.* He had learned long ago that it was useless to let the enormity of a task overwhelm him. A good inspector did not permit himself to become obsessed with minute details at the expense of the whole, but neither did he become paralyzed by the complexity of the challenge before him. *One piece at a time, Lenoir. Do not lose perspective, but do not lose hope, either. You are one step closer today. That is a victory, however small.*

He swam in his own thoughts for a long while. By the time he came up for air, they were nearing Addleman's Bridge. He could tell right away that something was wrong. So could Kody; the Sergeant quickened his gait, throwing a worried look over his shoulder at Lenoir.

"The crowd is bigger," Merden said. "A great deal bigger, in fact."

"Bigger," said Lenoir, "and a great deal more dangerous."

"How can you tell?"

"All men," said Kody. "All *young* men, or near enough. That's never good."

Lenoir unbuttoned his coat, for ease of access to his gun. "Be ready, Sergeant, but do not show your weapon unless you have to." He broke into a jog.

The crowd rippled like a small sea, currents and eddies stretching from the barricade back up the main road, overflowing between the hovels. Kody dove in first, taking full advantage of his size to elbow a path for himself and Lenoir. Merden followed somewhere behind, but already, he had been swallowed by the throng; the only sign of him was the tip of his ebony staff bobbing above angry faces. The closer they got to the barricade, the tighter the press became, until Kody was grabbing shoulders with both hands and wrenching people apart. "Stand aside! Police coming through!" Over the shouting, Lenoir could hear dogs barking.

They burst through the head of the crowd into a sort of no-man's-land, a tiny, tense pocket of air between two storm fronts—one turbulent and thunderous, the other icy and grim. The hounds at the barricade stood shoulder to shoulder, rifles in hand, a pair of dogs baying viciously as they strained at their leads. Lenoir had seen dogs used this way on the continent, but never in Braeland, and he doubted the beasts had been trained for the purpose. *Bad idea,* he thought, but it was too late to do anything about it now.

"Izar," Kody demanded of no one in particular, and one of the watchmen pointed. The Adal stood, stoic and determined, at the far end of the barricade, eyeing a civilian as big around as an oak. The civilian eyed him back, and Lenoir could tell the man was weighing his chances. They were poor indeed, but it was impossible to tell if the man realized that.

Kody called out. Izar flicked him a glance, but did not dare move; he waited where he was while Lenoir and Kody made their way over.

"What's going on?" Kody asked when they were near enough. "How did this start?"

"How do they ever start? With rumors. The woman who was injured this morning—apparently the story going around is that we killed her. And her children. Beat them to death with cudgels."

"That's ridiculous!" Kody protested.

Izar shrugged at the irrelevance of this appraisal.

"Those dogs . . ." Lenoir said.

"Not my idea, Inspector."

Lenoir had assumed as much. No Adal would be naive enough to release untrained dogs into a herd, whether of cattle or men. "We need to calm this situation, Sergeant," he said, though he knew he was stating the obvious. "Perhaps—"

"You there!" Izar stepped away and jabbed a finger at one of the watchmen. "Put that rifle up, fool!"

But the watchman could not hear over the crowd. He brandished his weapon in the face of a young Adali man, threatening, until one of his more sensible fellows grabbed the muzzle and jerked it upright, saying something heated. *These men are no more trained for this than the dogs,* Lenoir realized with a sinking feeling. As a young watchman in Serles, Lenoir had been instructed in crowd control, using tactics developed by the Prefecture of Police during the revolution. But Kennian had never known revolution, and Lenoir had not thought to recommend such training to the Metropolitan Police.

"Where's Merden?" Kody cried, whirling around.

"Here." The soothsayer appeared at Kody's elbow.

Lenoir did not have time for relief. The shouting around them kept growing in volume, the space between storm fronts shrinking inch by inch. Demands and accusations drifted like sparks over tinder, just waiting to catch light.

"—cannot keep us trapped in here like animals!"

"—just supposed to wait here to die?"

"Stand back! I'm warning you—"

"—not sick! Open your eyes! Can't you see that I'm not—"

A stone sailed through the air. It struck a watchman in the head, near his temple. He staggered.

The shouting swelled into a feverish crescendo. Izar surged, long arm reaching, crying out something even Lenoir could not hear.

A gunshot rang out.

Lenoir closed his eyes in the sudden silence.

When he opened them, the weapons were everywhere—rifles and blades, sticks and rocks, a length of what looked like lead pipe. The dogs tore into the crowd, set loose or simply broken free, and now there was screaming on top of the shouting, and the two fronts met in a brutal crash of bodies. Lenoir tried to reach for his pistol, but someone barreled into him, smashing him up against the barricade and pinning him there. He could hardly even see for the flurry of limbs. The edge of a log pressed painfully into his ribs. The pressure grew and grew as the crowd heaved against the barricade, trying to overwhelm it. If Lenoir did not break free, he would be crushed.

Another gunshot sounded, and another. It seemed only to whip the stampede into more of a frenzy. Lenoir thought he heard Kody shouting nearby, but he could not pinpoint exactly where. He heard a *crack* and a grunt, and the pressure against his chest loosened a little. Another *crack*, and the body against Lenoir's went slack. Merden appeared, his herder's stick clutched in both hands. "This way!"

The hounds had clustered together in a chaotic semicircle, creating a small, protected space between themselves and the right side of the barricade. Lenoir and Merden slipped behind them. It bought them some time, but little else; there was no way out except back through the rioting crowd or up over the barricade, and Lenoir did not want to risk being gunned down. The watchmen in the towers were firing warning shots at anyone foolhardy enough to attempt the climb. So far, the threats were doing the job, but Lenoir doubted it would last. "We have to get to one of those towers!"

"How?"

Lenoir had no idea. Izar was nowhere to be seen. They had lost Kody too. Lenoir drew his pistol, for all the good it would do him. He had two shots, and then it would be the sword. Even a skilled fighter would have trouble wielding a long blade in such a melee; in Lenoir's hands, it was as likely to end up in his own belly as someone else's.

The watchmen were not having much more luck with their rifles. The weapons were effective deterrents, but virtually useless at close quarters. Most of the men were using them like staves, cracking them across the faces of anyone who got too close. Somewhere within the horde, the dogs could be heard snarling and snapping. Still the rioters pushed in, pelting the police with stones and landing as many blows as they could with fists and sticks and whatever else they had managed to get hold of.

"Look!" Merden pointed. The hounds had dragged some of the sandbags out from the base of the nearest tower, and were smuggling their injured through the opening. Lenoir bolted toward it, pistol raised, hoping the sight of it would be enough to dissuade anyone from attacking him. The hounds held the line, keeping the tide at bay. The gap at the base of the tower was tantalizingly close, a light at the end of the tunnel of bodies.

He never made it.

The line broke just before Lenoir reached the gap. The tunnel of bodies collapsed in on itself, rioters flooding in through the breach. Izar appeared, grappling with someone. He had a pistol in his hand, hammers cocked and ready, but instead of firing, he was trying to subdue the civilian by hand. The sergeant paid for his mercy. Someone cracked the side of his face with a shovel, and he spun with a spray of blood before sinking down beneath the waves of humanity.

Lenoir dove at the spot where Izar had disappeared, but something struck the back of his head. White light flared in his vision, and then everything tilted, the bodies whirling away sickeningly as the ground rushed up to meet him. He went down hard, crashing against the barricade as he fell.

The last thing he remembered was the taste of blood.

CHAPTER 8

When Lenoir opened his eyes, he found himself staring at his own bedside table. For a moment, he wondered if he had dreamed it all—the witchdoctor, the hissing shadow, the riot. Then a bright flash of agony arced through his skull, and he knew better. He groaned and started to roll onto his back, but a rich voice said, "No."

Lenoir froze. "Merden?"

"Obviously."

He waited for more, but the soothsayer had apparently said all he wished to. Lenoir scowled. "Why am I not allowed to move?"

"You may move, Inspector, but you may not lie on your back. That would have unfortunate consequences for your split skull."

"Split?" If Lenoir had considered moving before, the notion left him quite completely.

"You need not be too concerned. It is not that bad."

The pain in Lenoir's head begged to differ. "Are you sure?"

Merden's only answer was an impatient expulsion of breath.

"What is that smell?" Lenoir asked.

"A poultice."

Instinctively, Lenoir reached for the sore spot at the back of his head. His fingers touched something cold and wet.

Merden *tsked*. "Really, Inspector, are you such a child? Must I tell you not to touch it?"

Lenoir struggled to a sitting position. The curtains were drawn, but a single oil lamp was enough to illuminate all four walls of his tiny flat. By its light, he took in the usual disarray: cupboards ajar, hearth unswept, threadbare blanket pooled carelessly at the foot of a single upholstered chair. He found Merden seated at the table with a cup of tea.

Another man might have felt uncomfortable at having a near stranger left unattended for hours in his home, but not Lenoir. There was nothing private for the soothsayer to find. Papers were scattered across Lenoir's writing desk, but none of them were personal correspondence. Portraits hung on the walls, but they were not friends or relatives. The only truly personal touch in the room was his books, one of which lay open in front of Merden.

When Lenoir recognized the title, his surprise momentarily overtook his pain. "You read Arrènais?"

"Not yet." The soothsayer sipped his tea.

Lenoir let that go. "How did I get here?" Even as he asked the question, an image passed through his mind, brief and hazy, like a half-remembered dream: someone grabbing his arm and hoisting him over a shoulder. "Did you carry me?"

Merden's eyebrows flew up. "I am flattered you think me capable of such a feat of strength, but no—it was not I who carried you. It was Sergeant Kody."

Lenoir grunted. It was as close as he could bring himself to verbalizing his satisfaction at the news that Kody had escaped the riot unscathed. "Where is he now?"

"At the station, I presume."

"And Izar?"

"The Adali sergeant? I do not know."

"What happened back at the barricade?"

Merden shook his head and took another draw of tea. "I do not think the wall was breached, but I cannot be certain. The riot was still in progress when we got you out."

"And how long ago was that, exactly?"

A look of irritation crossed Merden's face. "Perhaps it would be best if you asked all your questions in one go, Inspector, and spared me this tedious interrogation. Or shall I guess them?" He started to tick them off on his long fingers. "You have been out for approximately ten hours, mostly due to the healing tea I gave you. You were struck in the back of the head by a rock. I do not know who threw the rock. I do not know who survived and who did not. I do not know if the quarantine still holds, or if infected Camp residents are swarming all over the Five Villages in the first wave of the world's ending. Anything else?"

Lenoir gave him a flat look. "I think that covers it, thank you. But let us not pretend it is my questions you find tedious. You are annoyed because you are full of questions yourself, but have been obliged to sit here watching over me, and so have been unable to learn the answers."

Merden drank his tea.

Lenoir stood, gingerly at first, and was surprised to find that aside from the headache, he felt more or less intact. He washed his face, did his best to arrange his hair over the blot of healing mud at the back of his head, and checked his cupboards for something to eat. (The latter was wishful thinking; he never had anything to eat.)

"We had best head to the station," he said. "We can find out what happened, and see whether it will be possible to go back to the Camp today. Hopefully, Oded is still expecting us."

"As you wish."

"And Merden . . . thank you."

The soothsayer's golden eyes looked up from the

page. "I have remarked on it before, Inspector, but you are vested with an uncanny store of luck."

"So it would seem. Now, shall we go press it some more?"

Merden smiled and grabbed his cloak.

"Izar's alive," Kody said, "but he won't be on his feet anytime soon."

Lenoir nodded, looking relieved. The inspector had never said so, but Kody figured he liked Izar pretty well. The Adal was quiet, reliable, and clever, all traits Lenoir admired—in that order.

"Who else was hurt?" the inspector asked.

Kody ran through the list—those he could remember, anyway. More than a dozen watchmen and two sergeants had been seriously injured in the riot, and many more had bumps, bruises, and broken bones. As for the civilians . . . "Eight dead and countless injured," he said, concluding the briefing, "but at least they didn't get through the barricade."

Lenoir sighed and leaned back in his chair. "It will take years for the reputation of the Metropolitan Police to recover from this, especially in the Camp."

"Not like we were exactly popular before," Kody said with a rueful grin.

Lenoir didn't see the humor. "Do not be naive, Sergeant. Effective police work depends in no small measure upon the trust and goodwill of the population. If that trust is broken . . ."

"Very true," Merden put in from over Kody's shoulder. The soothsayer was drifting around Lenoir's office, inspecting its meager contents with detached curiosity. Kody had almost forgotten he was there. "My people are an eloquent example. How often do you find the Adali helpful in your investigations?"

"Seldom," said Lenoir. "At best they are uncooperative; at worst, actively obstructionist."

"Because they do not trust the police," Merden said.

With good reason, maybe, but as for what happened yesterday . . . "The hounds didn't start that riot," Kody said.

"Debatable," Merden said, "and irrelevant."

Kody opened his mouth to protest, but thought better of it. There was no point in arguing with the soothsayer. Like Lenoir, Merden seemed to think he was the smartest person in the room most of the time. And like Lenoir, he was probably right most of the time. *Good thing the two of them agree on just about everything. I'd hate to see those egos clash.*

"We had best hope things have calmed a little overnight," Lenoir said, rising and reaching for his coat. "If we cannot pass through the barricade, all our progress will be undone. I doubt very much Oded will present himself to Horst Lideman of his own accord."

"And if he did, no one would listen," Merden said.

"They still may not, but perhaps we will get lucky." Lenoir flashed Merden an enigmatic smile and shouldered his way out the door.

They grabbed the last three horses in the livery and headed out at a brisk trot, taking advantage of the light traffic at this early hour. The ride was uneventful until they reached the old Stag's Gate. Then things started to feel a little . . . *off.*

Small things, at first—the streets a bit quieter than they should be, the people a bit more careworn. Gradually, though, the signs became more obvious. Morning was well under way, but a lot of shops were still closed. Others had signs on their doors warning the sick not to enter, or advertising miraculous healing products. They passed a kid hawking newspapers with cries of, "Riots in the Camp! Can the hounds hold the line?" A few people even had scarves tied around their faces. *The only thing that spreads faster than an epidemic is word of it,* Lideman had said. The disease might still be confined to the Camp, but fear of it had infected half the city.

And there was something else.

"Not a hound in sight," Lenoir said, slowing his horse to a walk as he scanned the empty street corners. He shook his head and swore quietly.

Kody shared the sentiment. "I wonder if it's started yet."

Merden glanced back and forth between them, his brow stitched. He wasn't a hound; the progression of their thoughts wasn't obvious to him. "If what has started?" he asked.

Lenoir put it into terms any Adal would understand. "We hounds sometimes refer to ordinary citizens as *chickens*. Did you know that? Scattered about, scratching a living. Vulnerable. With no hounds to keep watch . . ."

"They are easy prey for the foxes." Merden nodded. "I see."

"This neighborhood has more than its share of foxes," Kody said, "and chances are, they're on the prowl already. We're not going to be very popular here, either, Inspector."

"No." Lenoir kicked his horse back into a trot. "Come. We are nearly there."

A few minutes later, Addleman's Bridge came into view—or it would have, had it not been completely obscured by the crowd of hounds manning the barricade. Two dozen at least, Kody reckoned, looking grim and ready for action. He wondered how many more they would find on the far side of the bridge.

"You sure you want to go in there, Inspector?" Sergeant Kelliman, the ranking officer, asked as he took Lenoir's bridle.

"What I want is immaterial, Sergeant. If I have ridden all the way out here, you can be certain it is important."

"Wouldn't be doing my job if I didn't ask," Kelliman

said, unfazed by Lenoir's brusqueness. The sergeant was older than God, and had been a hound since before Kody was born. He'd seen dozens of inspectors come and go, some of them even ruder than Lenoir. Presumably.

They left their horses in the care of some watchmen, and Kelliman led them to the makeshift gate at the foot of one of the towers, letting them through with a look that said, *On your heads be it.*

A surprise greeted them on the other side. A second barrier had been erected at midspan, a bristling palisade of man-size thorns that stretched from one guardrail to the other. It must have gone up overnight.

Kody whistled. "They really are worried, aren't they?"

"With good cause," Lenoir said. "The barricade was nearly breached last night."

"If the crowd does break through, a bunch of sharpened logs won't stop them."

"No, but it will slow them down long enough to make easier targets for the rifles."

Kody grimaced. "Do you really think they'd do it? Open fire on a bunch of unarmed civilians?"

"I'm not sure."

Kody was silent for a moment. Then, tentatively, he asked, "Would you give the order?"

Lenoir flicked him a glance. "I'm not sure."

Another surprise awaited them at the foot of Addleman's Bridge. Just inside the makeshift gate, a small man with flaming red hair stood at the center of a cluster of sergeants, giving orders. Kody's mouth dropped open. "Crears! What's he doing here?"

Following his gaze, Merden said, "By the looks of it, he is in charge of this operation. Is that unusual?"

"Crears is constable of Berryvine," Kody said. "He left Kennian years ago."

"The chief must have called him in," Lenoir said, sounding more than a little pleased. He headed over.

"Morning, Inspector. Kody." Crears shook hands. "Figured you'd be back. How's the head?"

"Painful, but not serious, apparently. When did you get here?"

"Couple of hours ago. Chief called up reinforcements from the outer villages last night. Me, plus two-thirds of my volunteers." Crears made a face. "Left my town pretty wide open, to tell the truth. Hope it doesn't come back to bite us."

"I daresay they will do more good here, Constable," Lenoir said. "It was a wise decision. Particularly putting you in charge."

If Kody had been on the receiving end of a compliment like that from Nicolas Lenoir, he'd probably have blushed. Crears, though, just nodded, like he'd heard it before. Which he probably had. Before he was Constable Crears of Berryvine, he'd been Sergeant Crears of the Kennian Metropolitan Police. He'd also been Lenoir's deputy, and the inspector made no secret of the fact that he considered Crears to be the best officer he'd ever worked with. In fact, he'd rubbed Kody's nose in it more than once. Kody might have resented Crears for it, were it not for the fact that the constable deserved every bit of that praise, and was a stand-up bloke besides.

"Got a line on who's behind this, Inspector?" Crears asked.

"Unfortunately not, but we may have found someone who can help treat it."

Crears glanced at Merden. "Even better."

If it works, Kody thought, but there was no point in saying it aloud.

"The crowd is smaller this morning," Lenoir said.

"It's early," said Crears.

Kody scanned the mob. Sullen faces stared back at him, but nobody looked openly challenging. "Maybe last night knocked some sense into them."

It sounded naive, even to him, and of course Lenoir

just snorted. Kody gritted his teeth. *Another tick in the minus column.* Lenoir was forever evaluating him, forever finding him wanting. *So quit making it so easy for him to judge you a fool.*

Crears was more charitable. He just shrugged and said, "Can't hurt to hope."

"We will leave you to it, Constable," said Lenoir, taking out his scarf and tying it around his face. "You have more than enough on your hands without us distracting you."

Crears didn't disagree. He left them with a brief nod and the typical farewell of a hound: "Good hunting, Inspector."

They headed up the main road, giving the mob as wide a berth as possible. Kody couldn't help brushing his hand over his coat, feeling the reassuring shape of the gun at his hip. He preferred his crossbow—more accurate, and less likely to blow up in his face—but it hadn't done him much good last night. It was too slow to reload, and anyway, even a flintlock was hard-pressed to miss at point-blank range. Still, he didn't much fancy putting a lead ball into a civilian's shoulder just because the guy was dead scared. He hoped he wouldn't find himself in that position again anytime soon.

Kody felt himself tense up as soon as the witchdoctor's tent came into view. It was just as well he hadn't gone to bed last night, or he'd have had nightmares about what they'd seen in that tent yesterday. He wasn't quite ready to admit it was magic, but he didn't have a competing theory. All he knew for sure was that *something* had happened in there, something that made every hair on his body stand on end. Some of it was probably in his head, but that tugging in his guts—that had been real. He'd nearly puked. And when the candles had been lit and he looked at Lenoir's face, he knew the inspector had felt it too. If there had been anything less than thousands of lives at stake, Kody wouldn't have gone back into that place for love or money.

They threaded their way through the crowd and slipped between the stakes marking the perimeter of the tent. Kody's shoulder brushed one of the dangling bits of leather as he passed, setting the beads clacking and the bones tinkling. He shivered.

Inside, a single figure stood silhouetted against the washed amber glow of the candles. "Good morning," the witchdoctor said in his lilting accent.

"Oded." Lenoir inclined his head in greeting. "I trust you are feeling stronger?"

"As strong as it is possible for me to feel."

"Are you ready to accompany us?"

A soft sigh preceded Oded's answer. "I am."

Something stirred in the darkness. Kody went rigid, his hand straying to his gun as a long, thin sinew of gloom moved near the table at the far end of the tent. A voice sounded from the depths of the shadows. "Interesting."

Kody cursed under his breath and let his hand drop. How in the Holy Host had Merden crossed the tent without him noticing? The Adal had been standing at Kody's elbow only moments before. *Witchdoctors,* he thought irritably.

Merden shifted, and now Kody could see him clearly, hunched over the table, scrutinizing it closely. He pointed at something and asked a question in Adali, and Oded responded. Merden held up a bottle and asked another question, and so on. Sharing trade secrets, Kody supposed. He was grateful not to be able to understand a word of it.

"And your patient?" Merden asked, switching back to Braelish.

"Resting with her family." Oded gave a tired smile. "She will recover."

"How can you be sure?" Kody asked.

"Experience." It wasn't much of an answer, but Kody let it go; the witchdoctor would have to endure more than enough skepticism today.

"If we are through here," Lenoir said, "let us be on our way. Time is not on our side."

"No, it is not," said Oded, "and we are about to waste more. Your physicians will not take my help."

"They will," Lenoir said, "if they know what is good for them."

Merden gave him a wry look. "And if they do not? What will you do, Inspector? Throw them in prison? Threaten to shoot them?"

"I might."

For the life of him, Kody couldn't tell if he was kidding.

CHAPTER 9

"**Y**ou cannot be serious."

Horst Lideman gaped at Lenoir as though the inspector had just ordered him to hop on one leg and bark like a dog. Which, Kody supposed, was about what it amounted to in the physician's eyes.

"I am perfectly serious," Lenoir said. "From what we have seen, the treatment appears to work."

Lideman knitted his fingers atop his desk and took a deep breath, as though to compose himself. "I am a physician and scholar, Inspector, and without wishing to give offense, these"—he glanced at the two Adali hovering behind Lenoir—"*traditional remedies* have no basis in science."

"That is true," Merden said. "They do, however, have a basis in fact, unlike most of your science."

Not helping, Kody thought.

Lenoir agreed; he fired an irritated look over his shoulder at Merden. "This is not a competition. Lives are at stake, and I would hope that healers such as yourselves could put aside your philosophical differences, for now at least."

Lideman shook his head gravely. "You don't understand, Inspector. If this were merely a question of philosophical differences, I might be persuaded to indulge in experimentation. But under the circumstances, it is quite impossible. These patients are under my care, and it is my duty to ensure that they receive the best medical treatment known to science. To do otherwise would be unethical."

"A curious argument," said Merden, "since the vast majority of the patients under your care are dying. A man of science such as yourself must surely recognize that repeating the same experiment over and over is unlikely to yield a different result. Your hypothesis is faulty, and it is past time for a new one."

Lideman turned an ugly shade of pink. "How dare you—"

"There is no point to continue," Oded put in. "It is always the same. These *physicians* care only for their pride."

"You know nothing about me, sir," Lideman said icily.

Lenoir growled and pinched the bridge of his nose, as though he were struggling not to explode. Meanwhile, the Adali and the physician continued to bicker. Kody could feel the conversation slipping away from them, and with it, their only shot. Before he could think better of it, he blurted, "What about the bruises, Doctor?"

"What about them, Sergeant?"

"The other day you said you'd never seen anyone come back from that."

"So?"

"So we have. Yesterday." Technically, that wasn't quite true; they'd *heard* the woman would recover, but they hadn't actually seen it for themselves. But Kody was pretty sure none of his companions was going to contradict him.

It didn't matter. Lideman wasn't buying it. "Is that so? Only yesterday, you say? And how do you know he has recovered, and is not merely experiencing a temporary improvement?"

Oded opened his mouth to reply, but Kody cut him off, determined to make his point before the argument deteriorated again. "How many times have you seen a temporary improvement in a patient who's that far gone?" Based on what Lideman had said the last time they'd met, Kody was pretty sure he knew the answer.

The physician shifted in his seat. "None."

"If those bruises are pretty much a death sentence, where's the harm in letting Oded try to heal one of the patients who has them? He can't make them any worse, right?"

Lideman sighed, regarding Kody with watery, blood-shot eyes. "Logic like that may sound compelling in the abstract, Sergeant, but these are human lives we're talking about. Each and every one is sacred. You and I do not have the right to decide who is beyond help, and who is fit to be experimented upon."

"But surely—"

"Are you married, Sergeant?"

Kody frowned. "Not that it's any of your business, but no."

"You have loved ones, I imagine. A mother, perhaps?"

"And?"

"Imagine your mother, God forbid, came down with this dreadful disease. How would you feel if I told you she was beyond help? That I would stop trying to save her, and instead planned to subject her to some heathen ritual that would almost certainly achieve nothing except to terrify her in the final hours of her life? What would you want me to do?"

It was a fair question. Kody didn't believe in demons, and he didn't want to believe in magic. He *did* believe in God, and he wasn't at all certain God would approve of experimenting with witchcraft, however desperate the circumstances. But if it were his mother, and this was her only chance . . . "I'm not sure, but I would at least want to be given the choice."

Lideman's eyes narrowed thoughtfully. Sensing an opening, Lenoir said, "You are right, Doctor—none of us here has the right to decide the fate of those who are ill. So let us ask the loved ones of a patient you deem to be terminal. Let them decide whether it is worth taking the chance."

Lideman looked at Oded, his teeth worrying the inside of his cheek. He was hooked, though they hadn't landed him yet. "How does it work?"

Kody winced inwardly, knowing the answer Oded would give. "It depends," the witchdoctor said. "For the very sick ones, I must first draw out the demon."

Lideman's eyes snapped back to Lenoir, his mouth twisting sardonically. Lenoir held up a hand. "The explanation may not convince you, Doctor, but the results are undeniable."

Merden *tsked*. "I do not understand you southerners. You believe in an all-powerful God, to whom you routinely pray, particularly when your loved ones are ill. How is this any different?"

"I rarely prescribe prayer, sir, and if I were to do so, it would be for the comfort of it, not the healing properties."

Merden was undaunted. "And do you ever administer yellowdrum mushrooms for infection?"

"Of course. It is a highly effective treatment."

"A highly effective treatment that has been used by my people for generations, yet has only recently been adopted on the Humenori continent, when the evidence before you finally became too compelling to ignore. Do you know how it works?"

Lideman didn't answer, but he didn't need to; his scowl said it all.

"My people believe the mushroom is a fragment of the ancient god Anadar, lord of the underworld. His tendrils lie just below the surface of the ground, spread across the land in a vast web, always searching for a means of escape. The mushrooms are his fingertips. Like an earthworm, the god can be severed and segmented and still survive, and when the mushroom is eaten, or its spores spread over a wound, Anadar is taken into the body. If you know a little of traditional Adali religion, you know that the god of the underworld feeds upon the flesh of the dead. That is one of the reasons we burn our departed ones. But Anadar cannot consume the living. Thus, when he is taken into an infected body, he consumes the dying flesh, and when it is gone, and all that remains is healthy, living tissue, the fragment of Anadar starves to death, and he is gone, leaving the patient recovered."

"Superstitious nonsense," Lideman declared.

"I am certain you think so, and I am equally certain that your rejection of that explanation will not deter you from administering yellowdrum in the future. Life is full of theories that cannot be proven, and results that cannot be explained. You believe in God, in spite of the lack of tangible proof, and you administer yellowdrum, in spite of the fact that you have no idea how it works. Theory without evidence, and evidence without theory. What does it matter?"

"There is a scientific explanation for yellowdrum," Lideman said. "We simply have not discovered it yet."

Merden shrugged. "Perhaps. And perhaps the same is true of Oded's treatment."

Lideman grunted, as if he'd just swallowed a hook.

"Let us find someone who is willing to try," Lenoir said.

The physician sighed and shook his head. "I will take no responsibility for this, Inspector, and if I am asked whether I think it will work, I will tell the truth."

"That is reasonable," said Lenoir. He looked relieved, and so did Merden.

As for Oded, he just scowled and said, "We must be quick, then. We have wasted too much time already."

"There we agree," Lideman said. "If my calculations are correct, in the time we have spent discussing this, three more people have fallen ill."

Kody swallowed hard. "How many have died?"

Lideman fixed him with a grim look and said, "You do not want to know."

It wasn't hard to find someone willing to try something desperate. The first family Lideman brought them to refused on the grounds that witchcraft was a sin against God, but the second family didn't share those misgivings. "If God had planned on answering my prayers, He'd have done it by now," the father said bitterly. "Maybe the Adali gods will do better. Besides, I hear you people can cure just about anything."

"Medicine is the gift of the Adali," Oded said. "Even so, I cannot promise for your son. For some, it is too late."

The man nodded resignedly. He'd already given up. *Poor bastard,* Kody thought. There were thousands of others just like him, and more by the minute. *God, I hope this works.*

They set Oded up in a private tent. It was smaller than the one he used in the Adali quarter, but he said it would serve, and anyway, they couldn't risk moving the boy that far away. Kody couldn't help grimacing when he saw the kid, covered in great purple welts, his fingers and toes grotesquely swollen.

The witchdoctor looked his patient over ruefully. "This may not work. The demon eggs already are hatching inside. The young are born strong. They will fight."

"You will conquer them," Merden said.

"Perhaps, but this will not be good for teaching. It is not . . ." Oded hesitated, searching for the word.

"It is not typical," Merden supplied.

"We can't back out now," Kody said. "We promised those people you'd try to heal their son."

"And so I will, but what I must do, I cannot teach. Not to Braelish."

Lideman drew himself up stiffly. "In that case, there is no need for me to be here."

Oded made a weary gesture. "You misunderstand. For most cases, I can teach. For this . . . it is different."

"Still," said Lenoir, "it will have to serve. At least we can see for ourselves whether the treatment works. Not that we doubt you," he added hastily, but Oded just snorted and set about his preparations.

"To my people, the disease is known as *Hatekh-sahr*," Merden explained as he watched Oded work. "It means *marks of the demon,* for the bruises covering the body." The soothsayer's amber eyes followed Oded's every move, tracking back and forth like the quill of a scribe, recording everything. Kody couldn't help wondering if Merden's fascination was purely intellectual, or if he planned to put what he learned to good use. "Tradition tells us that the sickness is caused by a demon entering the body through the nose and mouth. The bruises are left behind after it grapples with its victim in the dream-world. Once inside, it lays its eggs, crowding the victim's organs and causing them to bruise and bleed. The demon spawn feed upon the blood."

Kody grimaced. "Durian's arse, do we really need all the details?" He wasn't usually so crude, but really— bleeding organs?

Lideman, though, seemed intrigued; he gave a thoughtful grunt from behind his scarf. "Superstition aside, it is true that when we cut open the first few cadavers, we found massive internal hemorrhaging."

"What does that mean?" Kody asked, curious despite himself.

"It means bleeding," said Lenoir. "They are bleeding to death from the inside out."

"So we agree, roughly, on the cause of death," Merden said.

Lideman gave him an incredulous look. "Very roughly indeed, sir. The College of Physicians does not consider that the disease is a result of supernatural fiends turning the human body into a crucible of the damned."

"And what does your College of Physicians have to say about how the victim contracts the illness?" Merden seemed to be fully engaged in the conversation, yet his gaze continued to follow Oded's progress, narrowing every now and then as something particularly interesting caught his eye. Just now, Oded was positioning a cluster of crystals in a semicircle along the boy's left flank. The sickle shape seemed to be important somehow; it was echoed in the placement of the candles, and in a row of what looked suspiciously like human finger bones.

"It is obviously the air," Lideman said.

That tore Merden's gaze away from the preparations, if only for a moment. He regarded Lideman with an arched eyebrow. "Indeed?"

"Nearly a third of my medical staff has fallen ill, several of them without ever coming into physical contact with an infected person. Bad air is the only explanation. I have ordered miasma masks for all my staff as an extra precaution. They should be ready soon."

"Bad air." There was more than a hint of dryness in the soothsayer's tone. "And what causes this . . . *bad air*?"

"There are a number of theories," Lideman said, folding his hands behind his back and assuming a professorial manner. "Some think it a punishment from God. Others argue that the miasma is like a storm, simply passing through. Myself, I am inclined to believe that it results from the burning of corpses."

"Divine punishment, an itinerant weather system, or burning flesh." This time, Merden's tone was as dry as those finger bones.

If Lideman noticed, he chose to ignore it. "We have firmly established that the corpses are highly contagious, and it would explain why the plague began in the Camp.

The burning of corpses is common in the Adali quarter, is it not?"

Oded glanced up sharply, wrath brewing behind his eyes. But Merden spoke a few words in Adali, and the witchdoctor subsided, shaking his head and muttering, "*Pala.*" The word sounded like someone spitting on the floor, and Kody reckoned it meant roughly the same thing.

After a bit more fussing, Oded approached Merden, a wooden bowl in one hand, a dagger in the other. Without hesitation, Merden took the dagger and drew it sharply across his hand.

Lideman hissed. "What are you doing?"

"All magic requires blood, Doctor," the soothsayer said. He made a fist over the bowl; a steady *tap, tap* counted out the droplets as they fell. Lideman shook his head, disgusted.

Kody was disgusted too, but he couldn't help asking, "Why yours?"

"He is *mekhleth*," Oded said, as though it were obvious.

Kody let it go.

When he was satisfied the bowl contained enough blood, Oded handed Merden a cloth and said, "I am ready."

Merden turned to the others, his expression solemn. "If you would leave, do so now. Once the ceremony begins, it must not be interrupted, no matter what. To do so would certainly kill the boy, and very possibly the rest of us as well."

Lenoir and Kody had heard this warning before, but Lideman looked shocked. "What do you mean, *kill the boy*? What are you planning on doing to him?"

"I must cast out the demon young," Oded said. "They will not wish to be cast out. They will fight me, and when they fail, they will seek a new place. I must bind them so they cannot jump from the boy to us."

"If Oded's focus wavers at any stage, the demons will break free," Merden said.

Lideman wore that same wry look as he had before, when Oded had first mentioned demons. Lenoir saw it too. "Whether you believe in demons or not," the inspector said, "I can assure you that what is about to take place here will disturb you, and you will certainly have the instinct to recoil, if not to flee altogether."

"I did," Kody put in. *In fact, I'm having it right now.*

"As did I," said Lenoir, "even though Merden had already warned us not to. Be as skeptical as you like, Doctor, but at all costs, follow his guidance."

Lideman sighed and rolled his eyes. "Very well, Inspector, I shall not move."

"Nor make a sound," Merden said, looking at each of them in turn. Then he nodded once at Oded. The witchdoctor returned the gesture before turning his back on them.

Here we go.

CHAPTER 10

Lenoir took a deep, steadying breath. He would rather be just about anywhere else, but he had started them on this path, and he had to see it through. He jammed his hands in his pockets in case they should start to tremble. It would not do for him to look like a frightened child in front of Kody.

It began innocuously enough. Oded lit the sickle of tapers along the boy's right flank, speaking a word with each one, which Merden echoed in his cavernous baritone. (Apparently, the rule about keeping silent did not apply to him.) The light from the tapers glinted against the crystals on the opposite side of the table. The boy's prone silhouette appeared in the mirror of the facets, wreathed in flame, giving the eerie impression that he was trapped within. *Like the flaming prisons of the below,* Lenoir thought with a shiver.

Oded dipped his fingers in the bowl of blood, then flicked them, sending a spray into the darkness. He spoke a single word, sharp-edged and delicate. The candles flared, searing the darkness and forcing Lenoir to avert his eyes. When he looked back, the boy's figure seemed to be made entirely of shadow. A trick of the light, surely, but no matter how hard Lenoir squinted, only the boy's outline was visible. Yet somehow, his silhouette inside the crystals had become more detailed; Lenoir could even see the contours of his face. *What in the below?*

Oded let out a shriek and leapt upon the boy, hands wrapping around the child's throat.

Lenoir started. Beside him, Lideman moved as if to intervene, but Merden's hand shot out and seized the physician by the arm, his fingers digging into the man's clothing. The urgent look in Merden's eyes seemed to be enough; Lideman subsided, visibly distressed. A few feet away, the shadowy form of the boy writhed and kicked. Oded leaned into him, bringing all his weight to bear, his face twisted grotesquely as he throttled his patient. Kody swayed a little on his feet, fighting the urge to rush to the boy's aid. Lenoir had to look away lest he give in to the same impulse. His eyes strayed instinctively to the crystals, to the reflection of the boy trapped within.

The reflection was not moving.

Lenoir started. His gaze snapped back and forth between the crystals and the cot, unable to reconcile what he was seeing. Oded and the shadow continued to grapple, but the image of the boy in the crystals remained motionless—peaceful, even—a surreal counterpoint to the brutal struggle taking place only a few inches away. *Impossible,* Lenoir's mind told him, but the evidence of his eyes was undeniable. Whatever was happening on that cot, it did not seem to be affecting the boy. *But if that is not the boy, then what . . . ?*

The shadow on the cot bucked violently and froze, back arched, as though suspended from a cord tied to its navel. Still, the reflection in the crystals did not move. Oded straightened, his grip slackening, his expression wary.

The shadow exploded.

A rush of stinging wind blasted Lenoir full in the face, forcing his eyes closed. Then a buzzing unlike anything he had ever heard surrounded him. When he opened his eyes, he saw what looked like a massive swarm of black hornets gathered above Oded's head. Except they were not hornets, but fragments of shadow, somehow visible in spite of the gloom, each one an impenetrable blot of dark against dark. Lenoir glanced down at the cot. The boy was gone, yet his reflection remained in the crystal, still as a painting.

Lenoir could see the whites of Oded's eyes. The healer stood there, immobile, watching the swarm as it darted and roiled, stretched and twisted, moving like a flock of starlings. *He does not know what to do,* Lenoir realized in growing horror. Whatever had just happened, Oded had not been expecting it. Neither had Merden, judging from the look on his face.

Panic welled up in Lenoir's chest. Merden's warning still rang in his ears, but it was slowly being drowned out, subsumed beneath the numbing drone of the shadow swarm. The buzzing filled his ears until his skull seemed to vibrate. His heart pounded so badly that he could feel it in his throat. All he could think of was how much he wanted to *get away from here*. He looked at Kody and saw his own fear reflected in the sergeant's wild-eyed gaze. Lideman, meanwhile, looked ready to faint.

Just when Lenoir had made up his mind to move, Oded came alive. He grabbed a bundle of herbs from the table and plunged it into the flames. They took light, sending up a dense plume of smoke, and Oded dove at the swarm, brandishing the bundle like a torch. The shadows veered away from the smoke. Oded dove in again, tracing an arc with the flaming bundle, and once again, the shadows twisted over themselves to avoid the fumes. Oded circled the swarm, trailing smoke, letting a wall of it rise toward the ceiling. Everywhere the smoke touched, the swarm receded, and soon Oded had it surrounded. The smoke climbed higher, drifting above the swarm in a lazy canopy. The healer had succeeded in weaving a net of the smoke, but what he intended to do with it, Lenoir could not guess.

Beside him, Merden stirred, watching Oded's progress with frightening intensity. He seemed to understand what the healer was doing, but he made no move to help. Perhaps he did not dare.

Oded continued to tighten the noose. The fragments of shadow drew together, tighter and tighter, until they formed a dense cloud.

Merden twitched, his eyes blazing, as if to say, *Now!*

Oded produced a knife from somewhere inside his cloak, a wickedly curved sickle of what looked like bone. He reached inside the ring of smoke and slashed at the air. In an instant, the swarm began to stretch, pulled toward the spot where Oded had sliced the air, as though he had opened some invisible drain in the fabric of the world. The buzzing grew louder, angrier, as the swarm was drawn into a shrinking swirl. And then, as suddenly as it had begun, it was over. The last fleck of shadow vanished, leaving only . . . darkness.

Oded lunged at the spot where the swarm had disappeared, grabbing empty air and twisting his fist in a harsh movement. He shouted a string of words and drew the knife across the back of his arm, trailing a dark line of blood. Then he turned back to the cot. Swiping a hand across the cut he had just made, he waved a bloody palm over the sickle of small bones arranged near the head of the cot. The bones began to judder and shimmy. They moved, rearranging themselves into a shape Lenoir could not see. Then another gust of wind, a sudden darkness, and silence.

It was over.

A *thump* sounded in the gloom. Lenoir felt Merden move away from them. The soothsayer murmured a few words.

"Mekhleth," a familiar voice said weakly. Merden responded in hushed tones.

Lenoir's fingers closed convulsively around a small box in his pocket: his precious stash of matches. He rarely used them, for they were difficult to find and monstrously expensive. But he did not hesitate now. A flame hissed to life in his hands, and by its trembling light Lenoir saw that Oded had collapsed near the cot. Merden was helping him to stand. As for the cot itself, it held a small boy who appeared to be asleep. Lenoir approached on shaky legs, and saw that the boy's chest rose and fell in a regular, if shallow, rhythm. He lit the nearest candle just as the match started to sputter between his fingers.

"What in the name of the Holy Host did we just see?" Kody whispered.

"The demon young were strong," Oded said, as though that were any kind of answer. "I nearly failed."

"But you did not," Merden said. "A creative solution, my friend. Well done." He might have been congratulating the healer for solving a particularly tricky riddle, so matter-of-fact was his tone.

"You attacked the boy!" Lideman was shaking violently, whether from rage or fear, Lenoir could not tell.

Merden gave him an icy look. "You are mistaken."

"Leave it." Lenoir had no patience for squabbling, especially not now. "What matters is whether the boy will recover. Oded?"

"He should. But that is only the first part of the treatment. The second part you saw yesterday. Once I have rested, I will begin. After that, the boy must be given this." He held up a flask. Lenoir could not see what was inside, a fact for which he was profoundly grateful. "A few drops in water every hour for the first five days, and three times a day after that, until the potion is gone."

Lideman eyed the flask suspiciously, but he took it. "What's in it?"

"I will give you the list of ingredients," the healer said. "But now, I must rest."

Lenoir, Kody, and Lideman could not get out of the tent fast enough, and as soon as they were outside, Lideman unleashed his outrage. "*Madman! Charlatan!* I don't know how he achieved that awful spectacle—illusions and distractions and sleight of hand—but it is a scandal that he should be permitted to perform it on a sick child!"

"What if he healed the boy?" Kody said.

"Don't be ridiculous! If there is any actual healing being done, it will be due entirely to *this*." Lideman held up the flask.

"Perhaps," Lenoir said, "but as long as it works, I, for one, am grateful."

"You cannot possibly expect me to go through that"—Lideman waved vaguely in the direction of the tent—"that *ghastly* bit of theater. You should arrest that man, Inspector, not encourage him! He could have killed the child!"

Lenoir felt his own temper stir. "If it was merely theater, Doctor, then the child was not in any danger. You cannot have it both ways. If you are incapable of being open-minded, at least be logical."

Lideman colored, but he took a deep breath, and when he spoke again, his voice was calmer. "I sincerely hope this experiment does not backfire, Inspector. As for my adopting this ritual as a form of medicine . . ." He gave a mad little laugh and shook his head. "That is *quite* impossible. Good day." With that, he spun on his heel and stalked away.

A moment later, his assistant appeared, carrying his ever-present ledger. "Excuse me, Inspector, was that Dr. Lideman?"

"It was."

"Oh. I wanted to tell him that Sister Ora found some others who are willing to try."

"Perhaps you should tell him, then."

The assistant did not take the hint. "Four patients should be enough, don't you think?"

"I would not know."

Still the young man hovered, his eyes darting nervously to the tent. He lowered his voice. "How did it go?"

"I am not a physician, sir," Lenoir said, letting ice crystals form on the words. "As for Dr. Lideman, I am quite certain he will not hesitate to give you his opinion on the matter. If you hurry, you can catch him."

At last, the assistant fled.

There was a long stretch of silence. Lenoir and Kody watched the comings and goings about the pestilence tents, priests and nuns and medical students crisscrossing one another in a steady stream of industry. It was comforting somehow.

"What do you think we saw in there, Inspector?" Kody asked quietly.

"I don't know. Perhaps it is as Lideman says, and it was all an illusion."

"That would be some trick."

Lenoir shrugged. "A few judiciously placed mirrors, some smoke to divert the eye . . ."

"And that giant swarm?"

"Perhaps Oded is a talented beekeeper."

Kody gave a weak laugh. "Maybe."

"Perhaps it does not matter. If the boy's condition improves, Lideman may be persuaded to make more of the tonic, and perhaps that will be enough."

"A lot of *perhaps* in that formula."

Lenoir could not disagree.

"What happens now?" Kody asked.

Lenoir rubbed the back of his aching head and sighed. "We go home."

The hounds were walking straight toward him. Nash looked down, pretending to consult his notes. At the same time, he reached up and adjusted the scarf around his face so that it covered more of his features. He was being paranoid, he knew; there was no way the hounds could possibly recognize him from the riot. Yet it was impossible to suppress the instinct to hide, as if they somehow *knew* what he'd done. He stopped and turned away, writing furiously on his ledger to cover the furtive movement.

Footfalls sounded on the road. His pulse quickened. If the hounds looked closely, they'd see right away that he wasn't a medical student. He was too old, and his clothes were too modest. And if he wasn't a medical student, or a priest or a physician or a hound, then he had no reason to be here. He'd already invented a cover story that let him move freely among the men and women caring for the sick, but that story wouldn't appease the hounds. On the contrary, it would probably land him in jail. *Keep walking, chaps,* Nash bid them silently as they passed. *Nothing to see here.* He didn't even dare to glance at them, but kept scrawling crude oaths on the page in front of him, just to keep his pencil moving.

Gradually the footfalls receded, and when Nash looked up, the hounds were still headed toward Addleman's Bridge, pulling the scarves from their faces as though they were on their way out. He sighed, half in relief, half in disappointment. Part of him actually wanted to get into it with the hounds. He was tired of sneaking around. As smug as he felt about inciting a riot with nothing more than a few whispered words, he preferred a more direct approach. On the other hand, he'd be crazy to confront them out in the open, where they could easily call for backup. Better to deal with them quietly, if it came to that.

Bloody hounds. His employer had been right to worry. Day after day they'd come, sniffing around, asking questions. Nash was sniffing around too—after the hounds. His employer wanted to know what they were up to, how much they knew. That way, he could stay one step ahead of them. And if they got too close, it was Nash's job to take care of them. Nash didn't mind. It wouldn't be the first time he'd had to put down a troublesome dog.

And they *were* troublesome, though what exactly they were up to, Nash couldn't say. One minute, they seemed to be investigating the source of the plague, and the next, they were looking for a cure. Now they'd dragged a pair of Adali witchdoctors into it. Creepy folk, those two. Nash wasn't eager to cross them. He was pretty sure all that magic business was bollocks, but that didn't mean he fancied putting his theory to the test. And besides, tying off loose ends was supposed to be Sukhan's end of the deal. Still, Nash couldn't let the hounds and their Adali friends get in the way of his employer's plans.

No, there was nothing for it. Nash was going to have to get his hands dirty. And he was going to have to do it tonight.

CHAPTER 11

Zach lifted the corner of his card and peered underneath, the way Brick had taught him. He had to be careful—his hands were a lot smaller than Brick's, and he was pretty sure the bloke to his left was trying to cop a look—but Zach reckoned it was worth the risk. It showed that he knew what he was doing, and that was half the battle in this game. Brick's First Law of Crowns: *always look like you're winning, even when you're losing.* Zach adopted a confident expression.

The tip of a sword peeked out from under the card. He lifted a little higher, and saw another sword, and another after that—just as he'd seen thirty seconds ago, when last he looked. Zach had a good memory, but this hand was taking *forever*, and he was getting bored. Sailors, it turned out, could talk the ear off a donkey.

"She was *big*, mind you," the man across the table was saying, cupping his chest to demonstrate. "And a mouth to match!"

"So long as she puts it to good use," said the red-haired man, the one who was supposed to be Zach's partner. His name was Hairy—at least that's what it sounded like—and the name suited him. He had more fur on his arms than Zach had on his head, all of it rust colored. *"From spilling so much blood,"* he'd said. Zach knew bluster when he heard it (and he'd heard plenty of it today), but he reckoned there was some truth in it too. Hairy looked like the kind who'd spill blood just for the fun of it.

"Enough about whores," said Gerd. "Play the game!" The Sevarran rapped a knuckle against the table for emphasis.

"Patience, patience." Hairy played his card, a bushel of wheat with ten pips.

Durian's balls, Zach cursed inwardly. Ten was a high card, but wheat? That was a peasant card. Plus, he couldn't follow suit. *Just my luck. I finally get a mittful of swords, and my partner plays sodding wheat.*

"Better hope the boy has gold, Hairy, or you're buggered," the first man said, playing shields.

"He won't let me down, will you Short Shank?" Hairy winked, but there was just enough malice in his eyes to make Zach swallow hard. Would Hairy kill a kid over a game of cards? Zach couldn't be sure. That was the thing about the docks—you just never knew.

Gerd tapped his fingers against the table, eyeing each of the players in turn, as though he could read their minds if he stared hard enough. He was peasants this time around, and he didn't have much to go on. *He should hold out for another round,* Zach thought. Brick's Second Law of Crowns: *don't commit until you're sure, and that goes double if you're peasants*. Nobody had played a sword yet, so it was anybody's guess who would go on the attack first. Gold could mean anything. And as for sodding *wheat* . . . Zach puffed out a breath, but otherwise managed to keep his expression blank.

"Pass," Gerd said, though he didn't sound happy about it.

Zach didn't really have to think about his move. All he had was swords, and there was no point in wasting a high one, since he would be breaking suit. But he had to at least make it look like a tough decision, or he'd give away the rest of his hand. *Good time to get the conversation flowing,* he decided as he slid a thumb under his cards. "You all come in on the *Serendipity*?" he asked. "She's a handsome one."

"She's a bucket of piss," Hairy said, "but she's home. To Bevin and Gerd and me, at any rate. As for this one"—he inclined his chin at the man to Zach's left, a brooding Lerian named Augaud—"met him only this morning."

"Been anywhere good lately?" Zach asked, pretending to reorganize his cards.

"Play, kid," Gerd growled.

Zach shrugged, his eyes still on his cards. "I can talk and play at the same time. I'm clever like that."

Bevin snorted appreciatively. "Clever mouth, anyway."

"Come on," Zach said, putting just enough childish whine in his voice. "I'm stuck here all day, nothing to do. You must have *some* good stories."

"Tell you what," Hairy said, "you put down a nice tenner of gold, and I'll tell you all about my evening with Dockside Daisy."

Zach made a face. Suddenly, his lack of gold didn't seem like such a bad thing. He tossed a sword onto the pile, shooting a look at his partner that said, *Get it?*

Hairy shot him a look right back. He got it, sure enough, and he didn't like it. Zach squirmed in his chair.

Bevin barked out a laugh. "Bless my balls, kid, that's beautiful! Breaks suit and wastes a sword besides. Beautiful!" His partner, meanwhile, didn't even hesitate—he threw a big fat shield on the pile and grinned.

We're getting walloped, Zach thought ruefully, *and I'm getting nowhere.* He didn't fancy having to tell the inspector that he'd failed. Informants shouldn't fail, especially if they were hoping to become hounds one day.

Bevin was still sniggering about Zach's play. "All right, kid, just for that, I'll tell you a story. About Hairy here, and how he nearly got his manhood snipped by a pirate in Inataar." He elbowed his companion in the ribs. Hairy glared at Zach even harder, and a muscle in his jaw twitched.

Zach sighed. At least there were pirates.

They went round again, and it was even worse this time. Hairy threw a torch, which made no sense at all, and Bevin played a heap of gold. At this point, Gerd could safely declare a side, which he did, giving Bevin and Augaud a huge advantage. With the peasants as allies, they didn't even need any swords; they could just sit back and let Gerd do all the work. At least Zach could follow suit now. He used a fiver of swords to knock out some of the shields, but of course they still had their gold, and their peasants, and all Zach's side had was sodding *wheat.* And then Augaud broke out a real big torch, and they didn't even have that.

"So there he is, hopping from tavern to tavern, trying to win enough coin to hire some sellswords to protect him." Bevin was laughing so hard that he couldn't keep his ale in his flagon; it sloshed over the sides and spattered the table in little foaming puddles. "Except you can see what a cardplayer he is, so now he's broke *and* hiding, and not just from the brother and the rest of the pirates, but from the blokes he owes money! Now, Hairy owing money is nothing new—owes me about a year's wages—but these fellows are serious business, connected to half the criminal underworld in Darry, and they're out for blood. Suddenly, the brother and his pirate friends don't seem half bad."

Even Gerd was warming to the story now. He threw down a hammer, adding double to his allies' shields. "Then word comes in it's to be a duel at sundown."

"A duel?" Augaud frowned. "What does it mean, *duel*?" His accent was similar to Lenoir's, but harsher. *Peasant Arrènais,* Lenoir called it, though Zach doubted he would say so to a Lerian's face. Especially not this one. Augaud had a big knife at his hip, the kind fur traders carried, and fur traders were not known for their social graces. They *were* known for their skill with big knives, and that meant it was best to stay on their good sides.

"A duel is when two men fight for honor," Zach explained.

"Except in this case, the honor would be having your balls cut off if you lost," Bevin said.

Zach had to admit it was a good story, but it wasn't giving him any useful information. It wasn't helping his game, either; he still had two swords, both big ones. He really only had one choice if he wanted to earn his money back. But if he did it ... Brick's Third Law of Crowns: *never betray your partner.* Zach licked his lips nervously. "So what happened?" he asked, stalling for time.

"Nothing," Hairy said. "Not a damned thing. Now play your card, boy."

"Aw, don't be like that, Hairy," Bevin laughed. "Not the kid's fault. Can't you see he's got nothing but swords?" He took a long, loud swig of ale. "Anyway, Hairy's right, more or less, even though he's about as gifted a story-teller as he is a cardplayer. The brother never showed. Came down with the plague, if you can believe it. His mates too—most of 'em, anyway. I heard that whole ship got wiped out, and half the town besides."

Zach sat forward a little, his dilemma temporarily forgotten. "The plague, huh?" Hadn't the inspector said he was especially interested in reports of disease? *Keep your cool, Zach. This is your chance.* If he got what the inspector needed, he'd be sure of another job, another step on the path. He forced himself to slide down a little lower in his chair, trying to look casual. "What kind of plague?"

"Who knows?" Bevin upended his flagon, belched, and waved for the barmaid. "Some kind of bleeding disease, like the one they got in the Camp."

"Sort of like that, or exactly like that?"

"Can't say I've thought about it much. Guess it could be the same."

"How long ago was this?"

Bevin had swiveled in his chair to watch the barmaid, but he turned back around now, eyes narrowing.

Zach could have cuffed himself. He'd overplayed it. He could have found a subtler way of asking, shifted the conversation back to the pirates first.

"Four, five years ago," Bevin said warily. "What's it to you?"

Zach shrugged as indifferently as he could manage. "Just wondering if maybe one of these ships brought the plague here, that's all."

Hairy wasn't interested in plagues or pirates. He leaned forward and stabbed a finger at the table. "Boy, I'm not gonna tell you again. Play. Your. Card."

There was nothing for it. Zach snapped his card down, the biggest sword in his hand. Then, with a deep breath, he flipped his crown over, the blue one that matched Hairy's on the other side of the table.

Bevin, Augaud, and Gerd all whooped at this unexpected drama. "He's going it alone!" Gerd cried. "I don't believe it!"

"Abandoning your partner in the second-last round!" Bevin laughed, raising his empty flagon in salute. "You've got stones, boy!"

Hairy took it badly.

"You little—" Whatever came next was drowned out as Hairy upended the table, scattering cards and coins. The barmaid shrieked and leapt back, spilling ale down the front of her frock. Hairy shoved her out of his way. "I'll wring your neck for you!" He started around the table, his eyes fixed murderously on Zach.

Bevin grabbed his arm. "Take it easy, mate. It's just a game of cards. Not even much coin in it."

"And he is only a child," Augaud added. He gave Zach's shoulder a friendly thump, fueled with the strength of one too many ales. Zach tottered on his feet.

A soft *chink* drew everyone's eyes to the floor. Augaud had knocked a coin purse out of the inside pocket of Zach's waistcoat. A blue-and-white one, with the Lerian rose stitched damningly on the side. *Isn't that just like a Lerian,* Zach thought ruefully. *So proud.*

Augaud looked up, his eyes widening as they met Zach's. "You were leaned in so close," Zach said helplessly. "I thought you were looking at my cards . . ."

"Why you little—" The Lerian went for his knife.

Zach bolted, leaping over an upended chair and diving for the entrance in a perfect demonstration of Brick's Fourth Law of Crowns:

Always sit nearest to the door.

"Interesting," said Lenoir.

Zach eyed the inspector doubtfully. As much as he wanted to believe he'd turned up something important, he didn't see how he could have. He reckoned Lenoir was just trying to make him feel better, not letting on how disappointed he was. He did that sometimes—pretended not to be disappointed. Zach always saw through it, and it was always a blow. This time was especially bad, because it was so important. People were dying.

At least he could show the inspector that he was smart enough to see where he'd come up short. "It's not even a sure thing they were talking about the same disease," he said, sawing off another forkful of steak. He dragged it through the juices, the way Lenoir always did. "Plus, he said it was years ago."

"True."

Zach talked around his meat. "And even if it was the same disease, and it did come over on the *Serendipity*, I don't see why they would spread it around in the Camp. What would they get out of it?"

Lenoir gave him a funny little smile. "That's good, Zach. You are thinking like an inspector."

Zach squirmed in his chair, trying not to look pleased.

"Motive is the most important element to work out,"

Lenoir said. "Once you understand why a crime has been committed, who stands to gain, you are much closer to solving it." He sighed and took a sip of his wine. "Which is why you are right to be skeptical. It is indeed hard to imagine what a few ordinary sailors could possibly gain from murdering thousands in the Camp."

"Maybe they've got something against the slums?"

"They probably live in the slums themselves when they are not abroad. No, I think it very unlikely they are involved. Still, I will question them, just to be sure."

Zach winced. "Could you do it without mentioning me?"

Lenoir gave him a knowing look. "Pinch a few purses, did we?"

"He was looking at my cards!"

"Honestly, Zach, how do you expect to do your job if half the sailors in town are baying for your blood?"

"It's not *that* bad. Anyway, I don't have to do this for much longer, do I?"

"I thought you liked the docks."

"That was before I spent five days straight listening to sailors talk about whores."

Lenoir laughed into his wine cup. "Surely that is not the only thing they discuss."

Near enough, thought Zach, and in enough detail to leave little to the imagination. Not that Zach had any imagination. He didn't spend a lot of time around girls, and the ones he did encounter were pretty much the same as boys, as far as he could tell. Maybe they'd have been more . . . *girlish* . . . if they were born into different circumstances, but where Zach came from, there were no crisp frocks, no ribbons in your hair. Life on the streets wore you down. It was like those rocks in the river: whatever form God had originally given them, after a few years of being beaten down by the currents, they all became the same.

Which was why it was so important to get out of those fast-moving waters and onto solid ground.

"What about the cargos?" Lenoir asked. "Did you look into those?"

Zach pulled out a scrap of paper and pushed it across the table. "See for yourself."

Lenoir peered at it. "This is illegible, Zach."

"Huh?"

"Illegible." The inspector waved the page irritably. "It means *impossible to read.*"

Zach scowled. "There's appreciation for you. The only orphan in the Five Villages who can write, and you're complaining about my penmanship."

Lenoir was unmoved. "You can write because I paid for your lessons, but I find myself questioning whether I got my money's worth."

Zach stabbed sulkily at his steak. "It doesn't say anything anyway. Spices and cotton, cotton and spices. A little bit of wine and spirits." Zach shrugged and popped his fork into his mouth. "That's it."

"This is everything that has come in since you have been watching the docks?"

"Pretty much. I also put down stuff that came in earlier that was being unloaded. When I could find out, anyway." He pointed at the page.

"Anjet worm?" Lenoir read bemusedly. "Yellow mule?"

Zach snatched the page from Lenoir's hands. *"Angel wort and yarrow root,"* he said, handing it back.

Lenoir's eyebrows climbed his forehead. "We really must discuss your spelling, Zach."

"What is that stuff anyway?" Zach asked before Lenoir could make good on the threat.

The inspector scanned the page with a shake of his head. "I don't know. More spices, most likely, judging by the quantities. You might be eating it right now."

Zach considered his plate, but all he saw was steak and blood, butter with a bit of parsley in it. He didn't really like parsley, but at least he had something green on his plate. Sister Nellis was always telling him he had to have something green.

"Nothing else, then?" Lenoir said.

Zach shrugged. "I met a bloke who knew Sergeant Kody. Didn't seem to like him much. I think maybe the sergeant put him in jail once."

"Quite possible. Kody spent a great deal of time at the docks as a watchman."

"Oh yeah?" Zach lowered his fork and knife. Here at last was a subject that really interested him. "How long did he have to be a watchman before he became a sergeant?" Zach had been trying to do the maths, figure out how long it would take him to get from street hound to inspector, but he didn't know enough about it to make a reasonable guess.

"Less than five years, but that is exceptional. Sergeant Kody was promoted very young."

"How come? 'Cause he's so big?"

Lenoir sniffed into his wine cup. "Come now, Zach. If that was so important, would I be an inspector?"

"I suppose not." Lenoir wasn't small, but he wasn't big either.

"Kody was promoted to sergeant, on my recommendation, because he is a competent investigator. Much more so than most of his peers."

"What makes him so special?"

Lenoir cocked his head, peering at Zach as if he could look through his eye sockets straight to the back of his skull. "Tell me, what do you see when you look at Kody?"

My future, hopefully. Aloud, Zach said, "I'm not sure what you mean."

"If you were an investigator, what might you deduce about Bran Kody by examining the facts before you?"

This game again. Lenoir loved it. Zach liked it sometimes, but only when he did well. Otherwise, it just made him feel like a dumb kid. He frowned, thinking.

"How old do you think Sergeant Kody is?" Lenoir prompted.

Zach shrugged. "Twenty-something."

"Twenty-six."

That didn't sound very young to Zach, but he didn't say so. It would only make Lenoir feel older. "Okay, so he's twenty-six. So what?"

"A handsome fellow, wouldn't you say?"

"I guess. Can't say I've really thought about it." That wasn't strictly true. Even Zach had noticed the way the barmaid at the Firkin looked at Sergeant Kody the other night. She hadn't looked at Lenoir that way, or any of the other patrons.

"A handsome fellow," Lenoir said, "and twenty-six, with a respectable job. And yet he is unmarried." He leaned forward, one eyebrow raised. "What does that tell you?"

"Maybe he doesn't want to be married." Zach could certainly understand that. Marriage didn't make a whole lot of sense to him. Sharing what little you managed to scrape together with someone else? No, thanks.

"It is possible that marriage does not interest him," Lenoir allowed. "More likely, however, it is evidence of his dedication to his job. And of his ambition. Sergeant Kody wants to be an inspector one day, and perhaps even more. For now, all his energy is focused on that. And that, Zach, is what makes him so special."

Zach chewed on that as he chewed on his steak.

"So, is that why you're not married?"

Lenoir's snort was almost too soft to hear. "Eat your supper, boy."

"Hey, how come you're not eating?" Zach had been so busy inhaling his steak, he hadn't even noticed that Lenoir hadn't ordered anything.

"No appetite," Lenoir said with a grimace, "not after what I saw today. And before you ask—no, I do not wish to discuss it. Not right now."

Zach didn't try to hide his disappointment, but he didn't press the matter, either. That never got him anywhere with Lenoir. The inspector opened up when he good and felt like it, which wasn't often. There was no point in trying to convince him. Zach was pretty sure Lenoir was that way with everyone. In fact, he had a feeling the inspector talked to him more openly than he did to most adults. That felt good, even if Zach didn't really understand it.

"Going back out there tomorrow?" he asked.

Lenoir nodded. "Tomorrow, we find out whether Oded's treatments worked and the patients he saw will recover."

"You think they will?"

"I don't know." There was something in the way he said it—sad and weary, even more than usual—that made Zach's supper curdle in his belly.

"There was a plague in your town once, wasn't there?" It had been a while since Lenoir told him the story about the revolution, and Zach had been more interested in the exciting bits—the soldiers and rebels and great chanting mobs—but he remembered something else too, buried beneath all the adventure, something about everyone getting sick. When Lenoir told that part of the story, he'd worn the same sad, weary look he wore now.

"There was a plague, yes," Lenoir said, the words almost lost inside his wine cup.

"What stopped it?"

"Nothing. It stopped when it had killed everyone it wished to."

Zach swallowed. "How many people died?"

The inspector's dark eyes considered him for a moment. He drained his cup and reached for his coat. "Finish your supper, Zach," he said, and was gone.

CHAPTER 12

"Did you get any sleep last night?"

"If you need to ask, Sergeant, you are in the wrong line of work." It was needlessly irritable, even for Lenoir, but his nerves were stretched over a razor's edge. It did not help that he had a lump the size of an apricot at the back of his head, a lingering reminder of the riot. His neck was so stiff that he could hardly turn his head.

"Me neither," Kody said tartly, as though Lenoir did not already know. The sergeant was sporting a thin coat of stubble, which was a first, and his boots were so improbably shiny as to suggest a vigorous polish sometime in the past few hours, meaning it had been done well before dawn. Such fits of restless industry were intimately familiar to Lenoir, though it hardly took a chronic insomniac to recognize the signs.

"I suspect we will find more of the same in there," Lenoir said, inclining his head at the small green tent where Horst Lideman and the others awaited them. "Let us hope Oded, at least, is rested. He has a lot of work to do."

"Assuming he actually healed those people."

Lenoir growled under his breath. The one thing he had always been able to rely on from Kody, whether he wished it or not, was foolish optimism. Now, when it might actually come in handy, Kody was trying on a new face. "If I wanted extra negativity, Sergeant, I would carry a mirror."

Kody passed a hand over his eyes. He looked more than tired, Lenoir decided. He looked *worn*. "It's just . . . this doesn't feel like our lucky day," he said, pulling the tent flap aside.

By the light of a paraffin lamp, Lenoir took in the expressions arrayed around Lideman's desk, and he sighed. "It appears you are right, Sergeant. This is not our lucky day."

"It is not anyone's lucky day," Lideman said. He sat behind his desk, hands folded primly before him. Across from him, Oded sat rigidly upright, gazing into nothingness like a soldier under inspection. Merden hovered in a corner, his countenance inscrutable.

"What happened?" Lenoir asked, though he could already guess the answer.

"The treatment failed." There was no smugness in Lideman's tone, only regret. "The patients died."

"What, all of them?" Kody's tone was a mixture of despair and disbelief.

"It is not so surprising," Lideman said. "Their diagnoses were terminal, remember, and the disease kills quickly."

"It *is* surprising," Oded said, so quietly he might have been speaking to himself. "The woman . . . I knew she was lost. I said so last night. But the others . . . they were out of danger. For all four of them to die . . ." He shook his head, his gaze still abstracted. *He is in shock,* Lenoir thought.

"I do not deny your good intentions, sir," Lideman said in an apparent attack of amnesia, "but as I told you, your remedy has no basis in science."

Oded continued as if the physician had not spoken. "I cannot understand it. I did everything right. The demons were cast out, the strength of the patients restored. They were out of danger, all but one."

"Maybe it was our fault," Kody said. He rubbed his forehead, as though the idea pained him. "Maybe having other people in the room distracted you."

The healer shook his head. "That cannot be. You were only present for the first treatment, with the boy. After that, it was only Merden, and he is *mekhleth*. His power helped make the patients stronger, not weaker."

Lenoir swore under his breath. He had not come here expecting good news—it was still too early for that—but he had at least expected some ambiguity. Some *hope*. Some bit of improvement, however modest, in one or two of the patients. To face such unmitigated failure, and so soon . . . "It makes no sense."

"No," Merden said from his corner, "it does not."

But if Oded had no power over the disease, then why were the death rates so much lower among the Adali? "Perhaps your people are immune after all," Lenoir said.

"I'm afraid not, Inspector," Lideman said. "One of the four patients Oded saw yesterday was Adali. He was the first to perish."

Oded gave a dismissive wave. "Many of my people have died, just not so many as yours. We are not immune."

Lenoir shook his head, bewildered. "I cannot account for it."

"It makes no sense," Merden repeated, his golden eyes fixed on Lenoir.

"Nevertheless," said Lideman, "we cannot dispute the facts. I applaud your efforts, Inspector, and those of your companions, but I'm afraid I cannot devote any further time to this experiment. Good day, gentlemen."

Oded rose slowly, his posture stiff and straight, his head held high. Beneath the armor of his dignity, however, the healer was visibly wounded. Whether he understood it or not, his patients had died, and the skeptical Braelish physician had been proven right. For a brief moment, Lenoir wondered which of those unpleasant facts bothered Oded more. Then he saw the grief in the old man's eyes, and he had his answer.

"I will return to my tent," Oded said once they were outside. "I must continue my work."

"Do not allow this incident to shake your faith, my friend," Merden said. "Your gift is real, and it is sorely needed."

Oded nodded wearily. He said something in Adali, bowed, and took his leave. Lenoir watched him go, something suspiciously like guilt tugging at his gut. He had brought the healer into this—distracted him from his work, subjected him to ridicule and derision, deprived the Adali of his care. If, after all that, the only thing they had achieved was to damage the healer's confidence . . . *Not only have you failed to improve the situation, Lenoir, you may actually have made things worse.*

But there would be time enough for self-recrimination later. For now, something else demanded his attention. He turned to Merden. "You were trying to tell me something in there. What?"

Merden grunted. "I did not think you noticed."

"Of course I noticed, but why the guile? Why not just speak your mind?"

"Because I do not trust that physician."

"Lideman?" Kody cast a hasty look at the green tent and lowered his voice. "What are you talking about?"

Lenoir's eyes narrowed. "Do I take it to mean you think someone . . ."

The soothsayer arched an eyebrow.

"But why?"

"To discredit Oded."

"And you think Horst Lideman—?"

"I think nothing in particular about the man. But *someone* did, and if it was not Lideman, then it was one of his people."

"Did what?" Kody asked, his gaze cutting back and forth between them. "What are we talking about?"

Lenoir squeezed his eyes shut and took a deep breath. Sometimes, the sergeant could be impossibly dense. "Sabotage," he said.

"Murder," the soothsayer added.

For a moment, Kody just stared at them. When understanding finally dawned, his mouth dropped open a little. "You think the head of Medical Sciences murdered four of his own patients?"

"No," Lenoir said, "I do not, and I suggest we take this conversation elsewhere." He gestured meaningfully at the green tent a few paces away.

"This way," Merden said, and he headed toward the river.

When they were at a more discreet remove, Lenoir said, "Your theory is flawed, Merden. Lideman has no motive."

"Does he not? It would certainly be embarrassing for him if Oded's *heathen ritual*"—his voice dripped with sarcasm—"was able to achieve what his College of Physicians could not."

"That's not much of a motive for murder," Kody said.

"Agreed," said Lenoir. "The fact is, Lideman did not believe for a moment that Oded's treatment would work, and if he had been that concerned about being proven wrong, he would never have agreed to try in the first place."

"One of his people, then," Merden insisted doggedly.

"Look," said Kody, "I get that you want to protect your friend's reputation, but this is just silly."

Merden fixed him with a cool look. "I met Oded two days ago, Sergeant. It is not as if he is a brother to me. It is not loyalty that moves me to speak, but reason. Consider: the patients we saw yesterday were all terminal, according to Lideman, but they were not all suffering from precisely the same symptoms. Some could have been expected to die within hours, while others had longer. Yet they all died overnight, possibly within minutes of one another. We will never know, since no one was there to witness it."

"So?"

"*So*, does it not strike you as highly improbable that all four patients died at roughly the same time?"

"Not really. You just said it yourself—they were all terminal."

Merden sighed. "Very well. And what if I were to tell you that there was a fifth patient, one who did not yet display the bruising?"

"Lideman said there were four patients," Kody said.

"To the best of his knowledge, that was true."

Lenoir stared long and hard at the soothsayer. Merden returned his gaze evenly, without a hint of shame. "If you were to tell us that," Lenoir said, "it would mean that you and Oded treated someone in secret, without the permission of his family or physician."

Merden fluttered a hand, as though dismissing a meaningless detail. "If, hypothetically, we decided that the parameters of the experiment were flawed and undertook to treat a fifth patient, and if, hypothetically, that patient also died at the same time as the others, despite having been nowhere near as sick, would you then conclude that something highly improbable had occurred?"

Kody scowled. "You're a real piece of work—you know that? How do you know it wasn't the ritual that killed those people? Maybe all the stress of having that . . . *whatever* it was going on around them is what did it!"

"Do not be ridiculous. They were unconscious at the time."

"That doesn't excuse—"

"Enough, Sergeant," Lenoir said. He needed to think, and he could not do it with Kody throwing a fit of righteous outrage. "What's done is done. For now, we must focus on what it means. If what you are telling me is true,

Merden, then it does indeed appear as though someone
has interfered with the patients. The question is who, and
why?"

"I must see the bodies," Merden said.

"What for?"

"To determine what killed them. If I am successful, it
may shed some light on who did this."

"Very well. As an inspector of the Metropolitan Police, I can compel Lideman to release the bodies to us.
But you must be careful, Merden. The corpses are highly
contagious."

"I appreciate your concern, but I will take appropriate precautions."

"In that case, we must hurry," said Lenoir. "In view of
the risk, they will wish to dispose of the bodies as quickly
as possible."

Merden was already moving. "I will begin immediately."

"Here," the soothsayer said, gesturing along the dead
man's jaw, "and here." He wore leather gloves covered in
some kind of grease, but even so, he did not touch the
corpse any more than was necessary. He had cast off his
cloak in favor of a dun jerkin and trousers, and even his
boots appeared to be different. Lenoir had no idea where
Merden had obtained any of these items, or what he had
done with his own clothing, but the sight of it made Lenoir nervous, for he and Kody had no protection beyond
the scarves they wore. He had already made the mistake
of peering over the edge of the trench, and the sight of
the corpses—stacks upon stacks of them, lined up like
matches in a matchbox, covered in flies and reeking of
rot—was enough to make him light-headed. He wondered how the gravediggers managed it. They were
wrapped from head to toe, only their eyes visible, as
anonymous as executioners. Just now, they stood at the
edge of the trench, leaning on their spades, watching as

the hounds, the soothsayer, and the physician argued over the morning's crop of corpses.

Horst Lideman scowled behind his scarf. "So they have bruises. What does that prove?" He gestured irritably with a gloved hand. "They had bruising before they died. It was how we chose them, for Durian's sake! Please, Inspector, I do not have time for this nonsense!"

Merden tilted the corpse's face away from them. "Look harder," the soothsayer said. "These are finger marks. The killer was right-handed, and he stood here." On his knees, he positioned himself level with the dead man's shoulder and hovered his hand over the bruises.

Lenoir studied the corpse. The marks were there, to be sure, but they did not greatly resemble fingers to him. "When a victim is smothered, the bruises are typically well defined," he said.

"The internal bleeding would account for that," Lideman said grudgingly. "If you will forgive the analogy, these patients are like overripe fruit; the slightest pressure causes them to bruise badly. What would cause a clear outline in a healthy person would bleed much more profusely in someone suffering from the disease."

"So you agree those look like finger marks?" Kody asked. From his tone, it was obvious the sergeant did not see the resemblance either.

"It's impossible to be sure," Lideman said. "I must admit, however, that it's strange for all four patients to have so much bruising around the nose and mouth. Typically, the bruising is more pronounced in the trunk and extremities."

"Could it have happened postmortem?" Lenoir asked. "Were the bodies washed in any way, or otherwise handled in a manner that could account for a bruising pattern like that?"

"Not that I know of."

Merden *tsked*. "Why do you all strive to deny the obvious? These people were murdered."

Lideman shook his head, but it was more in amazement than denial. "I cannot fathom it. Who would do such a thing?"

The same sort of person who would deliberately start an epidemic. Lenoir kept the thought to himself. "Who had access to the treatment tent?"

"Myself, my students, and any number of nuns and priests," Lideman said. "Are you implying that one of us is a murderer?"

"I am not. Aside from the lack of obvious motive, the fact that the victims were smothered suggests that it was not one of your people."

Lideman blinked, half mollified, half curious. "Why is that?"

Lenoir was not inclined to explain himself. Unlike Lideman, he took no pleasure in edifying others; indeed, he found it reliably tedious. Kody, however, had a more generous nature. "Smothering isn't the easiest or most reliable way of killing someone," the sergeant explained. "It usually means the killer is hoping the crime will go unnoticed."

"But smothering typically leaves well-defined bruises. You said so yourself."

"But most murderers don't know that," Kody said. "They think what they're doing is invisible."

"Presumably, that rules out anyone with medical expertise," Merden said. "They would know that smothering leaves traces, so they would at least have used a pillow."

"Precisely," said Lenoir, doing his best impersonation of Horst Lideman.

If the physician realized he was being mocked, he did not let on. He rubbed his chin, seemingly fascinated by this new discipline. "Interesting. So what else can you deduce?"

Kody was only too happy to oblige. He dropped to his

haunches to inspect the body, his invisible tail wagging again. "Well, it suggests that the murders weren't planned, or at least not very well. Most likely a crime of opportunity."

"Perfectly sound, Sergeant," Lenoir said, "but not terribly useful, since we knew that already. The murders could not possibly have been planned in advance, since we selected the patients only hours before their deaths."

"Meaning our murderer knew what we were up to, or had access to someone who did," Kody said. "That ought to narrow the field."

"Indeed. Aside from ourselves, Doctor, who knew about Oded's treatments?"

"No one," the physician said, "apart from myself and Sister Ora. I could hardly let it get about that I was permitting something like *that*."

"Yourself and Sister Ora." Lenoir arched an eyebrow. "Is that all? Are you not forgetting someone?"

Lideman looked lost, so Kody supplied the answer. "Your assistant."

"Oh, yes! I'd quite forgotten . . ."

"Also the loved ones of the patients themselves," Merden added.

"Unlikely," said Lenoir. "The patients were already terminal. If a family member had wanted one of them dead, they need only have refused treatment."

"And anyway, there were four of them," Kody pointed out, "with no connection to each other except the disease and the treatment."

Lenoir started back toward the pestilence tents. He had seen all he needed to, and had no desire to prolong his exposure to the corpses. "I will need to speak with Sister Ora and your assistant immediately," he said.

Lideman frowned, but he nodded. "And the bodies?"

"You are free to dispose of them."

The physician signaled to the gravediggers, and they

resumed their grim task. Lenoir could not help wondering how many men it took to keep up with the deluge of death. The three he had observed were only part of the crew; others had been hard at work farther down the trench, expanding the pit. And Lideman had mentioned a second trench, identical to this one, on the far side of the encampment. *They will have to begin burning soon,* Lenoir thought, *pestilent air or not.*

Lideman conducted them back to his office, where he left them while he searched for his assistant. "He's dealing with this pretty well, considering," Kody said.

"Do not forget, Sergeant, it was Lideman who first theorized that the plague had been started deliberately. Murder is quite pedestrian in comparison."

"Maybe," Kody said, "but it's also pretty crafty, when you think about it. If Merden and Oded hadn't treated that fifth patient in secret, we might never have noticed anything was wrong."

Lenoir paused. *The fifth patient.* He had forgotten all about it. "Merden, should we not have checked whether the fifth patient showed the same bruising pattern?"

A clever smile tugged at the soothsayer's mouth. "There was no fifth patient, Inspector."

"Pardon?"

"It appeared you needed additional convincing, so I offered a scenario. I did say *hypothetically.*"

"Wait—are you saying you made it up?" Kody stared, incredulous. "But if there was no fifth patient, how did you know it was murder?"

"It was the only explanation."

"Hardly," Lenoir said. "There were, in fact, a number of explanations, of which murder was by no means the most plausible."

The soothsayer shrugged. "I had . . . What do you southerners call it? A *hunch.*"

Kody shook his head. "Unbelievable."

"I will not apologize for it, Sergeant. We are now virtually certain it was murder, which means that Oded's treatment may well have worked. That gives us hope."

"It gives us more than that," Lenoir said, his irritation easily eclipsed by something much more important. At last, they had the scent of their quarry.

At last, they had a lead.

CHAPTER 13

The kid looked like he was going to cry.

Kody wasn't sure what Lideman had told him, but the assistant obviously knew why he'd been summoned. His eyes were downcast as he entered the tent, and his thin shoulders trembled. When Lideman gestured for him to sit, he obeyed silently, without asking any questions. He definitely looked guilty. The question was, guilty of what? He weighed maybe ninety pounds with a full belly, and he had the pale, soft-looking hands of a scribe. Kody had a hard time believing the young man was capable of anything more sinister than squashing a spider.

Lenoir sat behind Lideman's desk, watching, his gaze taking silent inventory of everything. *What does he see?* Kody wondered. The guilty look, certainly. The soft hands and the trembling shoulders too. Was there anything else, something Kody might have missed? Kody caught himself squinting, and he felt foolish. The assistant was no more than three feet away; anything there was to see was right there in front of him. Besides, Lenoir's genius wasn't really in close observation (though he was no slouch). It was in making sense of what he *did* see, assembling it all into a meaningful whole. He didn't get attached to this theory or that, didn't obsess over every little detail. He gathered, he analyzed, he explained. *He's gathering now,* Kody thought, studying the way Lenoir sat in silence, staring at the assistant, letting the tension build. Lenoir was a master of silence. It was his shield and his weapon, and Kody had never seen anyone wield it more effectively.

When at last Lenoir spoke, he didn't go for the throat straightaway; he circled his prey instead. "What is your name?" he asked the young man.

"Brice," Lideman supplied. Since Lenoir had taken the liberty of installing himself behind the desk, the physician was reduced to hovering in the corner with Kody and Merden. "His name is Brice Wenderling." The introduction was delivered with an accusing scowl—directed not at Lenoir, but at Brice himself.

Interesting. Kody has assumed that Lideman would be protective of his assistant, and continue to play the role of the skeptic. Instead, it seemed that young Brice's flinching manner had dismissed any doubt in the physician's mind, as it had in Kody's, that his assistant had done something wrong.

Lenoir glanced up at Lideman, annoyed. "From this point on, I should be grateful if Brice answered the questions himself." He returned his gaze to the assistant. "You know why you are here, Brice, do you not?"

"Yes, sir." The young man spoke to his lap.

"You gave someone information about the treatments the Adali healer was administering."

"Yes, sir."

Lideman made a disgusted sound. "Brice, how *could* you? The confidence of a patient—"

"Doctor," said Lenoir, "if you interrupt again, I will have you ejected."

Lideman blinked. "This is *my* office!"

Lenoir ignored him. He let the silence settle again, then asked, "Whom did you speak to, Brice, and what did you tell him?"

For a long moment, the young man just sat there,

head bowed, shoulders shaking. A tear worked its way down his left cheek. Kody found himself feeling sorry for the kid. Sorry and angry and maybe even a little guilty for not picking up on the signs. The kid had been entirely too curious yesterday. He should have noticed that.

The whole thing gave him a headache.

Lenoir, though, was unmoved. "A name, Brice. Now."

"Burell. He didn't tell me his first name. He said he was ..." The young man paused, gazing ruefully into nothingness. "It sounds so stupid now ..."

"Go on."

"He said he was with one of the newspapers. The *Herald*, I think. He was doing a story on the plague, and he—he wanted to know why the Metropolitan Police were hanging around."

"What did you tell him?"

"I told him ..." Brice shot a guilty glance at Lideman. "I told him the College thought the plague had been started on purpose."

Lideman growled under his breath. "Of all the foolish ..."

"I thought it would help!" The young man swiveled in his chair to plead with his employer. "I thought maybe, if he printed that, maybe somebody saw something, and they could report it! The hounds are so busy at the barricades, and on the river ... I thought they wouldn't have time to ask around. I only wanted to help, Doctor!"

"If you truly wish to help," Lenoir said, "you will save your protestations for later, and focus on the matter at hand. This Burell—when did he first approach you?"

"Two days ago."

Lenoir sat back in his chair and closed his eyes. "Take me through it. Spare no detail. He approaches you, introduces himself. What does he look like?"

Brice considered. "About forty, I guess. Dark hair. Average height. He asked me—"

"No. We are not through with the physical description. What else can you recall?"

"Er . . ." Brice gazed at him helplessly.

Lenoir sighed. "Any distinctive markings? Scars? Tattoos?"

"Not that I saw."

"Was he fit?"

"He looked pretty strong, yeah."

"Pale skin, or tan?"

"Tan, I guess."

"Accent?"

"I . . . Pardon?"

Lenoir opened his eyes just enough to give the young man a flat look. "His accent, Brice. What did it sound like? Was he Braelish?"

"Yes."

"Kennian?"

"Definitely."

"Morningside or Evenside?"

"Dockside."

Lenoir grunted. "Not educated, then."

Brice blinked, as though someone had just snapped his fingers in front of his face. "I guess not, now that you mention it."

Couldn't have been a reporter then, could he? Kody rubbed his temples. People were so thick sometimes.

Lenoir must have been feeling generous, because he let it pass without comment. He just closed his eyes and said, "Continue."

"He asked me if I could comment on the treatment, how it was going. At first I gave him the usual answer—that we were making progress, doing what we could and all that. Then he asked why the hounds were coming around the pestilence houses day after day. I said they were—you were—trying to find out if maybe someone had started the plague deliberately."

Lenoir grunted. "How did he react to that news? Did he seem surprised?"

"Maybe not as surprised as you'd expect," Brice said in a tone that implied he'd thought as much at the time. *Probably disappointed that his gossip wasn't quite as explosive as he'd hoped,* Kody thought.

"What else did you tell him?"

"I said you were onto a new treatment, maybe even a cure. I thought that might give people hope, you know? So I told him about the Adali healer." The young man's gaze darted fearfully to Merden, as though he thought the soothsayer might turn him into a lizard. "He said his readers would be interested in that. He asked me to tell him how the treatment went." Brice's voice started to tremble. "So I did. Except I couldn't tell him much, because we didn't really know for sure. The witchdoctor said they would recover, and that's what I told Burell. I never thought . . . How could I know he was going to . . . ?" He trailed off, overcome.

"When and where did you last see him?" Lenoir asked. "I need you to be as specific as possible."

Brice swallowed hard. "Last night, just before dark. It was near the treatment tent. I watched him walk away, back toward the main road. I guess he must have come back . . ."

"Kody." Lenoir opened his eyes and straightened. "Find a watchman and have him ride back to Kennian. Tell him to fetch our best sketch artist."

"On it."

"I didn't know," Brice said, turning again to look at Lideman. The boy's eyes were red and pleading. "Until you told me a few minutes ago, Doctor, I swear to you, I didn't know."

Lideman just shook his head and said nothing.

Kody started for the tent flap, but he found his path blocked by Sister Ora. "Janice said you wanted to see me, Doctor?"

"I asked for you, Sister," Lenoir said. "Please, come in."

The nun approached with a bemused expression, taking in the strange sight of Lideman ejected from his own desk and young Brice weeping openly in a chair. "What's happened?"

Lenoir ignored the question. "Sister, did you at any time observe Brice here conversing with a man called Burell, who claimed to work for the *Herald*?"

"I'm not sure. What did he look like?"

"I introduced you," Brice said. "The dark-haired man with the ledger. I didn't say who he worked for."

Ora nodded. "I remember."

"Did he say anything to you?" Lenoir asked.

"Just hello. I was too busy to chat."

"And was that the only time you saw him?"

"Well, no. He was around for most of the day yesterday. He kept out of the way, and I suppose we all assumed he was with Brice, so no one asked him to leave. Why, has something happened? Has he stolen something?"

"He has murdered someone, in fact," Lenoir said, his eyes slightly narrowed as he watched her reaction.

Ora's hand flew to her mouth. "God have mercy! How awful! Who?"

She didn't know, Kody decided. Lenoir thought so too; Kody could tell by the way he nodded.

"And you're sure it was that man, the one Brice was talking to? Why, I only just saw him this morning!"

Lenoir leaned forward. "Wait. You saw him this morning? At what time?"

"A little over an hour ago."

Kody and Lenoir exchanged a look. An hour ago, they'd been on their way to examine the bodies. *Why would he be hanging around after committing murder? Why risk getting caught?* The answer came to Kody almost instantly. "He wanted to see if we would figure it out."

"And we did," said Merden. "He must have realized

that we suspected something when he saw us heading out to the graves."

Lenoir shot to his feet. "Oded is in danger."

"Oded?" Kody frowned, bemused.

"*Fool!* I should have seen this coming!" Lenoir was already halfway to the door.

Kody started to ask why, but thought better of it. Seeking an explanation would only earn him another dose of contempt, and the inspector probably wouldn't answer anyway. *Think it through,* he told himself as he followed Lenoir outside.

Those people were murdered so it would look like Oded's treatment didn't work. Whoever killed them didn't want Lideman and the other physicians to think there was a cure, because if there *was* a cure, then the plague could be stopped. *That means our killer is almost certainly the one who started the plague.* Fine—he'd figured that much out already.

Lenoir paused at the edge of the pestilence houses, seemingly undecided about whether to go back to the barricades for a horse or make the journey on foot. He chose the latter, breaking into a jog as he headed up the main road. Kody was grateful; he didn't fancy trying to navigate around these crowds with a horse. Besides, if they hurried, they should reach Oded's tent in about twenty minutes, and it would take half that time to reach the barricade.

Kody continued to mull it over as he ran. The exertion was making his head pound, but he had to stay focused.

So things are going fine for our killer until the hounds show up. They start asking questions. They obviously think something's up, but they can't prove it—so far, so good. But then Lenoir decided to involve an Adali witch-doctor, introducing a complication. The killer was forced to improvise. *So he decides to make it look like the treatment doesn't work. All he has to do is discredit the witch-doctor, and he's back on track.* Except things didn't go to plan. The killer *hadn't* managed to discredit Oded, because Merden had proved that the victims were murdered. If anything, the fact that the killer had gone to the trouble lent credence to the idea that Oded's treatment worked. Instead of undermining the witchdoctor, the killer had unwittingly boosted his reputation.

Which means Oded is still a threat.

The killer had gone the soft route the first time around. It didn't take much to murder people who were already dying, especially if you were the sort of madman who would start a plague on purpose. More importantly, if he succeeded, nobody would be the wiser. But now his cover was blown, and he had no choice but to go the more extreme route.

Lenoir was right: Oded was in trouble. Big trouble. And he was the only one who knew the cure. If they didn't get there in time . . .

Kody pushed himself into a flat-out sprint.

CHAPTER 14

Kody had left Lenoir and Merden well behind by the time he reached Oded's tent. He arrived, panting, temples throbbing, to find that the crowd waiting outside was bigger than ever, and they didn't look happy. Those that could stand were on their feet, milling about in restless, muttering clusters, and when Kody started to shoulder his way through, it earned him more than a few dark looks. It reminded him of the crowd at the barricade on the morning of the riot. *Tinder waiting for a spark. Isn't that all we need?*

He was hardly surprised when a tall man stepped in front of him, blocking his path. "Can't you see there are people waiting?"

"Police business," Kody said. "Stand aside."

"Police." The man sneered. "You think we're stupid? We know what this is. You Braelish need our medicine. You need our healer, so you take him away from us. All day I sat here yesterday. All day, waiting my turn for my daughters. The healer never came back!"

People were staring now, and the man's words drew noises of approval. *Careful, Kody.* "He's here now," Kody said between gritted teeth, "and I need to talk to him. Right away."

"Here, yes—seeing another Braelish man! You think because you have pale skin, you can just jump to the front of the line?"

Another Braelish man? Kody swore and tried to move past the Adal, but the man shoved him hard in the chest. Kody's fist curled, but he didn't dare take a swing. The crowd was too ugly; they'd tear him apart. He'd have to talk his way through this one. "The Braelish man—what does he look like? Does he have dark hair?"

"What do I care? You Braelish all look the same to me."

Kody got right up in the Adal's face, close enough for the man to see how deadly serious he was. "That Braelishman shouldn't be here. Let me through and I'll take him away. You can have your healer all to yourself." *For now, at least.*

The man glared at Kody for a long, torturous moment. Then, grudgingly, he stood aside. Kody barreled ahead before anyone else took a notion to get in his way, and when he reached the tent flap, he ducked through without hesitating.

He plunged into the darkness of the witchdoctor's tent, pausing at the threshold to let his eyes adjust.

"Oded?"

His voice sounded small and flat, swallowed by silence. Only now did it occur to him that the witchdoctor might be in the middle of a ritual. The thought sent a new stab of pain through his skull.

Something moved in the shadows. Kody tensed. "Oded?"

A low moan sounded at the back of the tent. Kody felt the hairs on his arms stand on end. He reached for his crossbow, then changed his mind and went for the flintlock instead. Just as his fingers brushed the gun, he sensed something move, and he jumped back. A shadow flitted in front of him, black on black, and he felt a breath of air. He pulled his gun and trained it on—what? Whatever it was fled deeper into the darkness, and Kody backed up against the side of the tent, keeping his gun leveled in front of him. His heart thudded in his throat.

This is ridiculous, he told himself. *It's not a demon, it's a man, and odds are he's a lot smaller than you. If he had a gun, he'd have fired it already. So quit cowering like a little girl.*

Kody stepped farther out into the tent. "Oded, are you here?" He started to move in the direction the sound had come from. He had almost reached the cot at the center of the tent when he sensed movement behind him. He pivoted in time to see something flash in the darkness. Pain blazed down his arm, and he dropped his gun. The thing flashed again, but Kody managed to twist out of the way. He threw a punch with his left, and it connected—with flesh and bone. Someone staggered in the darkness.

"Got you, you piece of—"

His attacker came at him again, and this time, Kody caught a glint of metal. A knife, and not a small one. He leapt back, narrowly avoiding a swipe to his midsection, and collided with the empty cot. Stepping around it, he put the cot between himself and his attacker. He reached over his shoulder and grabbed his crossbow. "You'd better hope your night vision is better than mine, mate, because I never miss."

For long moments, all was still. Kody held his breath, listening, sweating, but all he could hear was his own heartbeat. Somewhere in that silence, maybe only inches away, Oded waited. He was obviously hurt. Maybe worse. The temptation to look for him was almost overwhelming, but Kody knew better. He stayed where he was, waiting for his attacker to make the next move.

He didn't wait long. The dark shifted, and Kody fired. He hit his target dead on. When it shattered, Kody knew he'd been duped. A clay pot, by the sounds of it. He swore, tossing the useless crossbow aside. He drew his sword and braced for the counterattack, but it never came. Instead, something ripped near the back of the tent, and a blade of sunlight appeared. Kody tried to get there, but with the cot in his way, he knew he would never make it. Another slash of the knife was all it took to set his attacker free. The outline of a man slipped through the hole and vanished.

Kody started to follow, but froze halfway through the hole. His quarry had already vanished amid the tightly clustered tents. Kody might catch him, or he might not. Oded might need help, or he might be beyond it. It was a risk either way, and Kody lost precious seconds to indecision. But the cure was more important than catching a killer, so he grabbed the ragged flap of tent and pulled, tearing the opening wider to admit the sun. The light fell on a pair of boots lying where they didn't belong. Kody rushed over.

He found Oded facedown near the table at the back of the tent. Kody rolled him over, tucking his fingers under the witchdoctor's jaw in search of a pulse. Nothing. He leaned in close, listening for breath as he patted Oded down. Just below the rib cage, he found what he'd dreaded: a sodden patch of clothing, still warm. Kody slipped his fingers through the tear and searched for the wound. He found it. And then he found another, and another.

His mind catalogued the details as though he were writing a report: *multiple stab wounds to the midsection, large blade, upward thrust.* The assailant was right-handed, and what he lacked in precision, he made up for in brutality. The knife most likely punctured the heart. Kody swore and sat back on his heels. He was too late.

The tent flap opened, and Lenoir and Merden entered, both of them out of breath. Kody's posture and the gaping hole at the back of the tent told them everything they needed to know, so he didn't bother to say anything. He just stared into Oded's lifeless face and thought, *I'm sorry.*

Merden said something rueful in Adali, and then he was kneeling beside Kody, scanning the body as though hoping to find something Kody had missed, some sign that Oded could still be revived. Kody left him to it; for all he knew, the soothsayer had some mysterious Adali trick up his sleeve. But it would have to be some trick, because the witchdoctor was most definitely dead.

A moment's examination was all it took for Merden to reach the same conclusion; his posture sagged. Lenoir spat out an oath in Arrènais, then added one in Braelish for good measure. "The killer?"

"Gone. I might have been able to catch him, but I thought maybe I could still help Oded, so I let him get away." The words came out with remarkable calm, considering that he was moments away from being fired. He'd failed Oded. Worse, he'd failed Lenoir. The inspector didn't tolerate incompetence. He didn't even tolerate mistakes.

"How long ago?" Lenoir asked.

"Two minutes, maybe. I'll go after—"

"Don't bother. I'm sure he is long gone."

The shame brought heat to Kody's cheeks. "Sorry, Inspector."

Lenoir made an impatient gesture. "Flagellate yourself if it pleases you, Sergeant, but the matter was decided before you ever got here."

Kody blinked in surprise. Lenoir never missed an opportunity to criticize him.

Except, perhaps, when he was too busy criticizing himself. "If anyone is to blame, it is I. I should have seen this coming. Regardless, neither your regret nor mine will improve the situation, so it is pointless to indulge."

Merden began to murmur over Oded's body, one hand on the dead man's chest, the other on his forehead. Kody watched for a moment, curious despite himself. Lenoir, though, was not the least bit interested in Adali funeral rites. He paced the tent like a caged animal, scratching the stubble on his jaw and muttering the occasional curse.

What do we do now? The question was on Kody's lips,

but he didn't dare utter it. He'd narrowly escaped Lenoir's wrath moments before; it would be foolish to risk it again. Besides, the inspector obviously didn't have an answer. "We can still get the sketch artist," Kody offered, wiping his bloody hands against his trousers. "At least we'll have a likeness of the killer. And we can have posters put up all over the Five Villages . . ." It wasn't much, but it was all he could think of.

Lenoir wasn't even listening. He froze midstride. "Zach."

"What about him?"

"He found some sailors who encountered the disease overseas. Perhaps, if we show them a sketch of the killer . . ."

Kody grimaced. "Bit of a long shot."

"More than a bit. But they may also be able to tell us something about the disease, something that might help us to find a treatment."

"We have a treatment." Merden rose from his crouch, his long body unfolding like a pocketknife.

"We *had* a treatment," Kody said. He was being negative, he knew, but his head was killing him, and the taste of failure was still bitter on his tongue. "Now that Oded's gone, nobody knows how to do it."

"I do," said Merden.

Lenoir turned. "You can perform the ritual? Oded taught you?"

"I observed him closely while he worked on each of the patients. I understood most of what he was doing, and the rest, I asked him to explain."

"And you are certain it will work?"

The soothsayer smiled wryly. "I had better be, Inspector, since any mistake could well be fatal."

"Apparently, the ritual isn't the only thing that could be fatal." Kody's gaze dropped meaningfully to the body at their feet.

"We were caught unprepared," Merden said. "That will not happen again."

"No," Lenoir said, "it will not. We will place you under guard. I'm not certain how many watchmen I can persuade the chief to spare, but you shall have the maximum."

Merden made a face. "I hardly think that will be necessary—"

"It will be done," Lenoir said.

"What about them?" Kody hooked a thumb over his shoulder, at the doorway. "Those people want their healer back. They gave me a bit of a rough time coming in, and now this . . ."

"I must treat these people first," Merden said. "It is only right. After that, it will be first-come, first-served— Adali or Braelish, no discrimination."

"Will they go for that?" Kody asked doubtfully.

Merden's amber eyes were serene. "Leave that to me, Sergeant. My voice carries some weight among my people."

"That may be," Lenoir said, "but you are still only one man, and this is an epidemic. We are no better off than we were before."

Merden shrugged. "Perhaps a little, if you will forgive the lack of humility. Aside from the fact that I am younger and stronger than Oded, I am also *mekhleth*. My powers run deeper than most. Even so, you are right—I am but one man. I can save many lives, but this disease is like a stampede, and it will take more than a single shepherd to stop it."

"I think we can assume that Horst Lideman and his colleagues will be no help," Lenoir said.

"Even now?" Kody asked. "If Merden picks up where Oded left off, he can still prove that the treatment works."

"I do not think it is doubt that holds him back," said Lenoir. "It is fear."

"It was always an unlikely solution," Merden said. "From the beginning, I have assumed that I would need to take this on, though I hoped we would at least have

Oded." He gazed regretfully at the body of his slain countryman.

Kody shook his head. "Wherever he is now, he must be furious. He's lost to his people because of us." *Because of me.*

"He did not feel that way," Merden said. "He died angry and confused, but also proud of the work he had done in life."

"So you assume," Kody said.

"So I know." Merden closed his eyes and gestured vaguely around him. "It is written in the air."

Kody frowned. *I'm probably going to regret this, but . . .* "What does that mean?"

"When a man passes out of this world, something of him lingers for a time, like a perfume that clings to the air after the lady wearing it has gone. Feelings, mostly, but if the soul is strong enough, even thoughts can leave a trace. I can sense them."

"You can sense them," Kody echoed, stupidly. "And . . . how is that?"

"Because he is a necromancer," Lenoir said, looking uneasy.

"I thought he was a soothsayer."

"All soothsayers are necromancers," Merden said, "though not all necromancers are soothsayers."

"Okay," said Kody.

The soothsayer/necromancer looked back down at Oded's body. "He must transcend, ideally before nightfall."

Kody knew enough about Adali tradition to figure out what that meant. "You're going to burn him."

"It is our way. I would perform the rites myself, but I fear I do not have time. Hopefully, Oded had kin here in the Camp."

"Speaking of . . ." Kody glanced back at the tent flap. "Who's going to tell those people what happened?" He was pretty sure the news was not going to go over well.

"I will do it," Merden said.

Lenoir glanced at the hole in the back of the tent. "Would you think less of us, my friend, if we availed ourselves of the new exit?"

"I would think you fools not to."

"Do you have everything you need?"

Merden nodded. "And you?" He cocked his head meaningfully at the body.

"The matter is regrettably straightforward," Lenoir said. "The Metropolitan Police have viewed the crime scene and examined the body. I consider our duties discharged. All that remains is for me to round up a protective guard. They should be here by midmorning."

"In that case, Inspector, Sergeant—I have a great deal of work to do."

Kody gathered up his fallen weapons, pausing to load a quarrel into the crossbow before they hit the road. He didn't much fancy sneaking out the back like a murderer, but he saw the wisdom in it, so he followed Lenoir to the rear of the tent and held the ragged flap aside for the inspector to pass. He was halfway out himself when he paused and looked back. "Good luck, Merden."

The soothsayer had already been swallowed in darkness, but his deep voice reached out of the gloom. "And to you, Sergeant. I daresay you will need it."

Kody stepped out of the tent into a bright afternoon. The sudden change in light was enough to force a sneeze from him, and then another, and he had to blink furiously to banish the glare. As his vision came into focus, he saw that he still had blood on his hand. He thought he'd wiped it all off.

Better wash up properly before we go, he thought.

The last thing he needed was to catch plague.

CHAPTER 15

Kody scanned the docks with a weary expression. "Sorry for asking, Inspector, but what exactly are we hoping for, here?"

A miracle, Lenoir might have said, but he kept the thought to himself. The sergeant knew perfectly well how desperately unlikely this lead was, and as for Zach, Lenoir did not want to look like a fool in front of the boy. He told himself that this was not pride, but merely a desire to preserve the mystique of police work in Zach's eyes. The boy wanted to be a hound someday, and had little else to strive for in life. It would be a shame to disappoint him so soon. "We are following the only lead we have, Sergeant, which is a trio of sailors who may have encountered this disease before. It may come to nothing, but we will not have wasted our time. All the signs point here, to the docks."

"What sort of signs?" Zach asked, a little less brightly than usual. The boy was nervous about being reunited with his card-playing mates following the unfortunate incident of the day before. Ordinarily, Lenoir would not have brought him along, but Zach would save them valuable time. He knew what the men looked like, and would not have to ask around. Besides, the boy needed to learn that there were consequences to his actions, and this would be a safer way to learn the lesson than most.

"First," Lenoir said, ticking off on his fingers, "we know that the disease almost certainly came to Kennian by sea, probably carried by corpses. Second, we have your sailors, who spoke of a similar disease in a foreign land. Third, we have the account of Brice Wenderling, who described our killer as an athletic man with tanned skin and a crude accent."

Kody grunted thoughtfully. "You reckon he could be a sailor."

"The description fits."

"It also fits a bricklayer, or a carpenter, or just about anybody who works with his hands."

"It is tenuous," Lenoir admitted, "but it fits too well to ignore. Moreover, it is all we have at the moment." His gaze skimmed over the salt-scoured, windblown jungle before him, towering timber and dangling rope and a canopy of furled sails that blocked the sun. Somewhere in this strange wilderness was an answer, Lenoir felt sure. They just needed to find it.

"There it is." Zach pointed. "The Port. That's where I met Harry and the rest."

Lenoir squinted. The tavern was jammed in with the row of warehouses lining the boardwalk, with nothing to distinguish it from the adjoining buildings save a faded sign reading simply, ALE.

"I've been there," Kody said. "Full of brigands and cheap whores." He glanced at Zach, incredulous. "You were playing cards in there?"

The boy scowled. "Would've won, too, if my partner wasn't dumb as an ox."

"Whereupon you would have celebrated by buying a round from the Lerian's purse." Lenoir walked away before the boy could embark upon his customary protests, making for the tavern in purposeful strides. It was early yet, but *Serendipity* was still in port. Lenoir liked their chances of finding Zach's sailors more or less where the boy had left them.

His faith was rewarded. As soon as they entered the tavern, Zach pointed again, subtly this time, his sharp features tense with worry. "Can Sergeant Kody go first?" The boy gazed hopefully at Lenoir's burly deputy.

"No, but he will be right beside you." Lenoir gave the room a quick once-over. Aside from the front door, he located three exits: a door behind the bar, presumably leading to a storeroom, a passage to the kitchen, and a set of stairs heading up to the rooms where the whores plied their trade. Of the dozen or so patrons strewn about, only the cardplayers looked lively; the rest were wharf rats and bored-looking whores, many of them too far into their cups to know whether it was night or day. A group of Mirrhanese sat isolated from the others, drinking tea and playing tiles, but they barely glanced up when the hounds entered; they were unlikely to pose a threat. That left the barkeep. A hard-bitten fellow, he made no secret of the fact that he was watching Lenoir, and his expression said, *Stay out of trouble.* Lenoir had no doubt there were weapons stashed under the bar, and they had probably seen plenty of use. "Barkeep," he said in an undertone.

Kody nodded almost imperceptibly. "Got him."

His inventory complete, Lenoir started across the room. The cardplayers paid no attention, too busy heckling one another to notice the newcomers.

"A hammer!" one of them cried, driving a fist into the table and whooping with laughter. "He plays a hammer! Bless my balls, if he isn't the worst cardplayer in the Five Villages!"

Lenoir felt a tug at his sleeve. "That's Bevin," Zach whispered. "The one to his left is Gerd, and the red-haired one is Harry. I don't know the other two." He sounded relieved.

"Are ye offer yer nut, Harry?" said a small, weathered man, one Zach did not know. "We got no shields and no swords. What good is a sodding hammer?" He had the hard-edged accent of southern Braeland, almost strong enough to pass for Sevarran. "Small good yer peasants'll do us." He tossed a card onto the table in disgust.

The red-haired man opened his mouth to respond, but then his eye fell on Zach, and he scowled. "Well, well. You got some stones coming back here, kid."

"Stones," Kody said, "and friends." He leaned against the adjoining table in a posture that was casual, confident, and just happened to expose the butt of his flintlock.

"Hounds," the one called Gerd growled.

"Very perceptive, sir," Lenoir said. "Hopefully we can put those keen powers of observation to good use."

Gerd started to reply, but the man called Bevin put a hand on his arm, and Gerd subsided. Bevin, for his part, fixed Lenoir with a long, unflinching gaze. Abruptly, his face split into a broad grin, and he waved for the barmaid. "Ella, lass—bring us some drinks for these brave lads! Hounds on the hunt deserve a bit of the fine foam."

This one is dangerous, thought Lenoir. Aloud, he said, "Thank you, but no—we are on duty."

"It's a sorry sort of employment that won't let a man wet his gullet," Bevin said, still grinning, "but don't worry. I'll drink 'em in your honor."

The red-haired man was still glaring at Zach. "Might've known he was a *bitch*," he said.

Most street folk would take offense at being called a *bitch*, with all its graphic innuendo about "taking it" from the Metropolitan Police.

Not Zach. "That's right, I'm with the hounds." An impudent little smirk hitched one side of his mouth. "It was that or playing cards for a living, and I just didn't think I could compete with the likes of you."

Bevin laughed loudly at that. "He's a clever one, your little pup," he told Lenoir. "Worth twice what you pay him, I'm sure."

Just now, Zach could best demonstrate his cleverness by holding his tongue, but Lenoir spared the boy and did not say so aloud. Instead, he said, "I hope you will indulge me, sir, by answering a few questions."

Bevin smiled. "Whoever he was, it was self-defense."

"Very amusing," said Lenoir, without a flicker of amusement. "Let us begin with names. You are called Bevin?"

"That's right." Bevin pointed a thick finger at each of his fellow cardplayers. "This is Harund, this is Gerd, this is Marius, and this skinny scrap of leather is Stew. And you are?"

"Hounds," Kody said, "and that's all you need to know."

Bevin's smile turned brittle. "Not quite, Big Dog. I also need to know why you're here."

"We are interested in a voyage *Serendipity* made approximately four years ago," Lenoir said. The sailors exchanged glances, genuinely bemused. "On the voyage in question, you encountered some sort of plague."

Bevin grunted. "The plague, is it? I remember now— your little pup was asking about it. What do you want to know?"

"Where was it?"

"Inataar." It was the small man, Stew, who answered. "Darangosai. *That* was a trip, and no mistake."

Inataar. Lenoir and Kody glanced at each other. Could it be a coincidence? The sick man, Drem, claimed to have seen an Inataari while gathering corpses in the Camp. A rare sighting, but not significant in itself—not unless it came up again. And now it had. "Why was it such a significant trip?" Lenoir asked.

Stew hooked a thumb at the red-haired man, Harund. "Well for starters, Harry here got into it with some pirates, and almost got himself nutted—"

"We've all heard the story," Harry snapped.

Lenoir had not heard the story, for which he was profoundly grateful. "I asked about the plague."

"What about it?" Gerd frowned suspiciously over the rim of his flagon.

"What were the symptoms?"

Stew started to answer, but Harry cut him off. "How should we know? We didn't get it, did we?"

"You have eyes and ears. In my experience, when plague strikes a city, people tend to talk about it. In fact, they talk of little else."

Harry shrugged. "Maybe I wasn't paying attention." He gazed at Lenoir in open challenge.

Lenoir obliged him. "Sergeant."

In one smooth motion, Kody stepped behind Harry's chair, wrenched his arm behind his back, and slammed his face down onto the table. Gerd and Stew started to move, but Lenoir reached for his flintlock, and they thought better of it.

Kody produced the iron cuffs. "Paying attention now?" he growled into Harry's ear.

Lenoir leaned over the table, close enough to smell the ale on each sailor's breath. "Perhaps I have been unclear. I believe that you men have information that may be useful to my investigation. As an inspector of the Metropolitan Police, I have considerable authority under the law to compel your cooperation. You are welcome to explore the boundaries of that authority, but I doubt very much you will find it a pleasant experience."

Bevin smiled that slow, dangerous smile of his, spreading his hands in a mollifying gesture. "Inspector, please. There's no need for that. Our Harry is a bit of a hothead, that's all. You have our full cooperation."

"Excellent." Lenoir nodded at Kody, and the sergeant let his man sit up—though he did not remove the cuffs. "Now," said Lenoir, "am I obliged to repeat the question?"

"The plague," Bevin said. "We can tell you what we know, but it isn't much."

"Let me be the judge of that."

"All right, then. Let's see ..." Bevin scratched his beard. "We weren't in port long, I remember that. Just long enough for Harry here to dip his quill in the wrong inkpot. It was like you said, though—all of Darry was whispering about the plague. Even that first night, we heard about it. Folk reckoned it was being passed between the sheets. 'Stay away from the whores,' they told us. Funny enough, that turned out to be bad advice for Harry." Bevin turned and grinned at his red-faced shipmate. "Whores don't tend to have brothers protecting their honor."

Lenoir suppressed a growl. *Zach was right. These men cannot go five seconds without mentioning whores.* Aloud, he said, "Focus, please. Aside from advice about which inkpots to avoid, what else did people say about the plague?"

"There were lots of places you couldn't go," Bevin said. "They'd quarantined whole neighborhoods. The fun ones, mostly. Made for a dull shore leave."

"Captain didn't want to stay long anyway," put in the sandy-haired man, the one called Marius. "He'd been hearing things about ships losing half their crews within a matter of days. Said we'd unload and go, no dallying about."

Highly contagious, and deadly within a few days. It certainly sounded the same. "And the symptoms? What did you hear about that?"

The small one, Stew, made a disgusted face. "Didn't have to hear. Saw it with my own two eyes. Beggar woman calls out to me as I'm walking by. I look down, and she's got blood in her eyes, and the next time she opens her mouth, she's coughing it up!" He shuddered at the memory. "I hightailed it out of there, I can tell ye."

Lenoir and Kody exchanged another look. It was not ironclad proof, but it was as close as they were likely to get. "It sounds as though that disease has made its way here to Braeland," Lenoir said, watching the men carefully.

Bevin did not trouble to look surprised. "Figured as much, after your pup there brought it up yesterday."

"It was only a matter of time," Marius said. "Humenori been sailing across the Grey for near a century now. The Inataari got our rats, and we got their plague. All part of the trade between nations. God bless progress." He hefted his flagon in mock salute.

"Actually, Inspector, that's a good point," Kody said. "When we looked through the dockmaster's ledgers, how much of it was spices from Inataar and Mirrhan? Half? Maybe more? There must have been dozens of crossings between Kennian and Darangosai in the past four years. Seems strange we haven't heard of this plague until now."

"Lots of crossings," Marius said, "but not many ships. Not every captain willing to take on the Grey. She claims her share of tribute, and may God rest 'em well before he musters 'em up." He raised his flagon again, and this time his shipmates joined him.

"As for those of us who do make the crossing," said Bevin, "I promise you, we've *all* heard of the plague. If we don't talk about it, that's only because it's a fool of a seaman who tempts fate."

"You have all heard of it, yet trade continues," Lenoir said. "Are you not afraid of catching it?"

"It's gone now," Gerd said. "Been gone three years or more."

"The Inataari found a cure?"

Bevin shrugged. "Must've done. We stayed away for a year or so, but then we got word things were more or less back to normal, so we started up again. Been back there three times since, and she looked like the old Darry to me."

"Me too," said Stew, "only better, 'cause there weren't so many ships coming through as before. Makes it easier for a man to get what he needs." His leer threatened to steer them back to the subject of whores, but fortunately, Bevin had other things on his mind.

"Suppose this means they got it back again," he said.

"Captain won't go near any port that's got plague. Looks like we've seen the last of Darry for a while, lads. It'll be another year of timber and fur. Cheap Mirrhanese silk if we're lucky. Hope old man Tully's been saving, or we're out of work." He waved for the barmaid.

Lenoir eyed the approaching pitcher of ale irritably. Gerd's speech had already begun to slur, and Stew's grin had turned sloppy. Soon, they would be too drunk to be of any use. Lenoir could try to cut them off, but they would take it badly. Whatever else they knew, Lenoir would have to get it from them fast. "Is there anything you can tell me about the cure the Inataari found?"

"Not a thing," Bevin said. "We were on this side of the ocean when we heard the plague was done, and by the time we went back"—he shrugged and glanced at his mates—"I suppose we didn't care."

"What about your other shipmates?" Kody asked. "Any of them the curious sort?"

Gerd snorted into his flagon. "Doubt it."

"All the same," Lenoir said, "I want the names of every man who served on that ship four years ago."

The sailors laughed at that. "Couldn't do that sober, Inspector," Bevin said. "*Serendipity*'s a big girl. I'll give you those as I remember, but the rest . . ." He gestured at the small man. "What about you, then? Stewards keep track of who's who."

"The whole crew?" Stew shook his head. "No way. Ritter, maybe."

Bevin grunted. "Maybe, if you can find him."

"Ritter was purser back then," Marius explained. "I think he's with *Duchess of the Deep* these days."

"And the captain?" Lenoir asked. "Would he know?"

"*Serendipity*'s got a new master since then," Marius said. "As for Captain Hollingsworth, last I heard, he was dead."

"Reckon he still is," Bevin said, and his shipmates laughed.

Lenoir fought to keep his frustration from showing. He could not tell if he was on the verge of discovering something important, or merely chasing chickens round the yard. Moreover, he was out of questions; he had played every card in his hand, save one—the wild card. "Sergeant, you may let Harund out of the cuffs now. I am certain he will behave." The red-haired man said nothing, preferring to glare sullenly as Kody removed the iron cuffs. Lenoir met his eye just long enough to convey mild amusement at this childish display. Then he drew a roll of parchment out of his coat pocket and flattened it on the table. A charcoal sketch of the "reporter" calling himself Burell stared out at them. "Have any of you seen this man before?"

Lenoir watched closely as the sailors leaned over the sketch. Stew scrunched up his face, exposing his front teeth like a rodent sniffing at garbage. Harry gave a dismissive little snort and looked away in apparent boredom. Marius frowned, and Gerd's mouth drooped open a little. Bevin scratched his beard and shook his head. Even Zach came over to look, and as he drew near, he trod gently but unmistakably on Lenoir's foot. Lenoir turned to look at the boy, but Zach ignored him, his gaze riveted to the sketch.

"Don't know him," said Bevin. Gerd, Harry, and Marius grunted dismissals of their own. "I might've seen him," Stew said, "but I'll be buggered if I know where."

"Very well." Lenoir dragged a chair over from the adjacent table and plopped himself down. "In that case, we will drink a toast to your old shipmates on *Serendipity*—as many as you can remember. Zach, run to the dockmaster and fetch a ledger, quill, and some ink. It is time to practice your letters."

CHAPTER 16

"It's not going to be easy, Inspector," Kody said, scanning the page by the failing light of evening. He wiped a bead of sweat from his brow. It had been warm in the alehouse, though not unpleasantly so. Lenoir had not been sweating, but then, Kody was a bigger man, and his shirt looked to be thicker.

"We'll be able to find the ones who are still with *Serendipity*," the sergeant went on, "but the rest . . . Looks like sailors aren't much for keeping in touch. Fewer than half of these names have ships beside them."

"And lots of those ships aren't in port," Zach added. "Who knows when they'll be back?"

"Maybe if we had a dozen watchmen to help," Kody said, "but with the whole force tied up on quarantine duty . . ." He shook his head, looking uncharacteristically worried.

"If you are through enumerating the challenges," Lenoir said, "perhaps we could focus on what we have in hand." Turning to the boy, he cocked his head in the direction of the tavern from which they had just emerged. "Which one of them was lying about the sketch?"

Zach grinned, visibly pleased with himself. "Harry."

"Are you certain?"

"I'd bet a crown on it."

Kody gave the boy a skeptical look. "How can you tell?"

"He snorted when he looked at it. He does that whenever he's pretending he's got good cards. Like if you play a sword that knocks out his shields, he'll snort, as if he doesn't care, so everyone will think he has another good play to make. But it's a lie. If he really has good cards, he gets this nasty little smile on his face that he thinks no one can see."

"You got all that from one round of cards?" Kody asked, a hint of admiration creeping into his skepticism.

"He's really bad," Zach said solemnly.

"Nevertheless," said Lenoir, "you did well. Not everyone would have noticed."

"Bevin would have noticed," Zach said, "and the others too, unless they were too drunk."

Lenoir grunted. "True. They have been playing cards with Harry for years. If he was lying, they would most likely know it."

"If they knew, they didn't let on," Kody said.

"That is hardly surprising. Shipmates protect each other."

"Should we bring him in?"

"To what end? I doubt he would talk, not without resorting to some of the more persuasive interrogation methods, and we do not have enough evidence for that." Despite his earlier bluster, Lenoir was painfully aware of the limitations of Braelish law. "If this were Arrènes, perhaps, but I'm afraid your parliament is regrettably squeamish on such matters. I doubt the word of a ten-year-old cutpurse will suffice." Zach scowled, but did not otherwise defend his honor.

"We could follow him," Kody said. He sounded unhappy about the idea.

Lenoir considered. Even if Zach was right, and Harry was indeed lying about the sketch, there was no guarantee that following him would yield anything. Lenoir had already guessed that their killer might be a sailor. The fact that another sailor recognized his face proved nothing except that the two had crossed paths at some point. Harry's lie was similarly inconclusive. He struck Lenoir as the sort who would be uncooperative purely for the sake of it, taking petty delight in thwarting the hounds. He might not even know the killer's name. "We would do better to show the sketch around the docks," he said, thinking aloud, "starting with the names on our list. We will begin first thing in the morning."

"What about me?" Zach asked. "I could follow him."

The thought had already occurred to Lenoir, but there were risks. "Harry does not appear to be very fond of you, Zach. I'm not sure it is a good idea."

"I'll keep out of sight. It won't be hard—he's drunk half the time anyway. I'll watch the door from over there." He pointed to a rowboat bobbing noisily amidst the cluster of smaller vessels near the boardwalk. "I can hide in there, and when he comes out, I'll tail him. That way, if he meets up with the bloke in your drawing, I can follow *him* and find out where he stays. I come get you, you arrest him, and *wham!* Fort Hald!" Zach mimed the slamming of a prison door, then dusted his hands off for good measure.

"I doubt it will be quite that simple." Still, they could not afford to let Harry go completely, not if there was a chance he might lead them to the killer. Lenoir could try enlisting another hound, but the rank and file were not trained for undercover work; a watchman would blend in like a pigeon among ravens. Most of the sergeants were fools, and anyway, the chief would never agree to assign a second one, not with so many injured in the riot. As it was, the hounds could barely maintain the quarantine; any spare capacity would be devoted to maintaining law and order. Catching a killer came a distant second, for now at least. As for his fellow inspectors . . . Lenoir almost laughed out loud. *The Drunk, the Lout, and the Imbecile,* he called them. One day, he would write a play.

No, there were only two choices. Either Lenoir and Kody would have to split up, or they would have to take a chance on Zach. As for the boy, he would be taking chances of his own. Lenoir gazed down at him, irresolute. The eyes that met his were sharp, alert, almost disturbingly adult. But the rest of him—the flyaway hair, the scuffed knees, the restless, self-conscious way he kicked at the pitted planks of the pier . . . Clever he might be, but he was still, unmistakably, a child. "It could be dangerous, Zach. If he spots you . . ."

"He's just waiting for an excuse to wring my neck." Zach shrugged. "I know."

Lenoir sighed. It was unwise, unethical, and would almost certainly earn him a strong reprimand from the chief. It would also put the boy at considerable risk. Zach was the only person in Lenoir's life who might legitimately be considered a friend, for all that he was a child. Yet to assign him such a task would mean putting the case ahead of Zach's welfare. *Business as usual, then,* he thought with a twinge of bitterness. "Promise me you will be careful, Zach. I have enough on my conscience already."

The boy grinned. "Don't worry. I got you covered."

"That is not what I'm afraid of," Lenoir said, but Zach was already halfway down the pier, bounding away like the eager child he was. The setting sun traced a bloodred line around his silhouette as he stooped to grab the painter of the battered rowboat he had chosen as a hiding place.

"I hope you know what you're doing, Inspector," Kody said, swiping at his brow. He looked even more worried now.

Lenoir watched as the boy stepped into the shadowed belly of the boat and was gone.

*   *   *

"Kody." Crears held out his hand. Kody hesitated half a heartbeat, then shook it. He hoped Crears hadn't noticed the delay.

"Bit warm for gloves, isn't it?" the constable asked.

"They're to protect from plague." It was the truth, even if it deliberately gave the wrong impression. "You should be wearing some. The men too."

"I'll look into it," Crears said. "Where's the inspector?"

"Home, probably. He doesn't know I'm here." No point in lying about that, either.

Crears considered him in the wan glow of the lamplight. "What's up?"

"I'm here to see Merden. I thought of something later this afternoon, after we'd already left, and I wanted to run it by him. Might be nothing, but"—he shrugged—"worth checking out, anyway."

"It's pretty late."

"Yeah, well, the inspector didn't think there was much in it. You know how he is." Kody put on his best Arrènais accent. *"You may chase your tail if you wish, Sergeant, so long as you do it on your own time."* He shrugged again. "So here I am. On my own time."

He'd had the whole ride over to think about how he was going to explain his presence to Crears, and he figured his story was solid enough. It wouldn't be the first time Kody did some digging on his own after Lenoir had dismissed his ideas.

Crears had his back to the lanterns. A scarf shrouded half his face, and his eyes were lost in shadow. Kody couldn't tell if he was buying it. He glanced away, pretending to be interested in the nighttime arrangements at the barricade.

"Got you those guards you asked for," Crears said at length. "One out front, one out back. Merden should be safe enough."

"Thanks." The relief in his voice was unmistakable.

Hopefully Crears would put it down to the news about the guard. "See you on the way out," he said.

"Watch your step, Kody. Mood's mighty ugly around here."

Kody nodded. He paused a moment longer, so as not to seem like he was in too much of a hurry. He scanned the barricade one last time, threw a casual wave at the watchmen on duty, and struck off toward the main road.

A full moon glared down from above, bathing his path in cold silver. Kody glanced up at it, but had to look away. The glow was too much for him. It made his eyeballs ache, the way frigid water makes a tooth ache. Even so, he was grateful for its light. He'd forgotten to bring a lantern. Stupid of him, but he'd been . . . distracted.

It could be something else, he told himself for the hundredth time. People got headaches, didn't they? Got fever. Didn't mean they had the plague. It didn't mean *he* had the plague.

Three to four days before you started showing symptoms, Lideman had said. Five, if you were especially hale. Kody was especially hale. That meant it couldn't be the plague . . . didn't it? It had only been two days since they watched Oded treat the boy. Even if Kody had been infected then, he wouldn't be showing symptoms already.

Unless you caught it that first day. That very first day when he and Lenoir had met Lideman among the pestilence houses. Before they'd had scarves and gloves.

But that would be such bad luck. Such incredibly bad luck. That couldn't happen to him. It *couldn't* . . .

His heart thudded in his chest. In his throat. At his temples. He could feel it everywhere, as if it were searching for a means of escape. Kody jammed his hands in his pockets and quickened his step.

A low murmur guided him the final fifty paces or so to the tent that had once been Oded's. The crowd had only grown since the afternoon. They seemed more subdued than they had been earlier, though. News of Oded's death must have reached them by now, and it seemed to have inspired a somber mood. For the most part, people were seated, or lying down, and no one offered any resistance as Kody wove his way between them. They recognized him from before, most likely, knew he wasn't here to jump the queue.

Well, not exactly.

He nearly walked right into the hound guarding the door. Crears had told him to expect someone, but he'd been so lost in his head, he'd forgotten already.

The tent blocked out much of the moonlight, but even so, Kody recognized the man looming over him. There weren't many men who did that—*loomed*—and of those who did, only one had shoulders as broad as an oak tree.

"Hi Kody," said Innes. Thankfully, he made no move to shake.

Kody was glad they'd picked Innes. He was big enough to intimidate even the hardest criminal, and he wasn't easily spooked. That last bit was important, considering what he would be standing guard over, the kinds of things that would be going on in that tent. "I'm here to see Merden," Kody told him, hoping it was enough.

Innes just nodded. He wasn't the sort to question things too much, thankfully. He stood aside to let Kody enter.

A soft glow suffused the tent. Merden was bent over Oded's medicine table, studying it, making notes. A sliver of moonlight peeked through the slash at the back of the tent, where the killer had escaped. Merden must not have had time to repair it yet.

"Sergeant," the Adal said, straightening. He looked over Kody's shoulder, expecting to find Lenoir.

"I'm here on my own," Kody said. He swallowed, his mouth suddenly dry.

Merden waited.

"I . . ." Kody cleared his throat. His hands clenched

into fists at his sides. "I think maybe ..." He couldn't even say the words. His head felt as though it could float away at any moment, though whether that was fever or just plain panic, he wasn't sure.

"I see," Merden said, and Kody could tell from his tone that he did. "Sit down, please." He gestured at what Kody supposed was meant to be a chair, a tripod of sticks with a saddle of animal hide. It creaked when he lowered himself onto it, but it was surprisingly sturdy. Merden sat across from him. "Describe your symptoms."

"Headache. Light hurts my eyes. Fever, but not too bad. I'm feeling a little light-headed just at the moment. And before, I"—he hesitated—"I think maybe I sneezed up blood."

"Remove your scarf, please."

Kody complied. Merden held up a lantern and shone it right in Kody's face.

"*Hey!*" He threw his arm over his eyes. "Didn't you hear what I just said about light?"

"I heard. I needed to see if your eyes were bleeding, or your nose." Merden lowered the lantern. "You will be pleased to know they are not."

"Real pleased," Kody growled, wiping tears from his eyes.

"You say you think you may have sneezed blood. When?"

"This afternoon. Just as I was leaving here, in fact."

"And since then?"

He shook his head. "Nothing." That had to be a good sign, right?

Merden raised a hand to Kody's brow. His fingers felt cool. That wasn't such a good sign. "Definitely fever," Merden said, "though not, as you say, too serious. When did you first begin noticing symptoms?"

"Early afternoon, I guess. On the way to the docks." He shifted in his chair. The conversation felt oddly like a confession. "I guess if I think about it now, though, maybe it was this morning. That's when the headache started. I didn't think much of it at the time, because . . ." He shrugged. "I don't know. People get headaches."

Merden's amber eyes searched him. "You came alone. I assume that means you have not told the inspector of your condition."

"What condition? For all I know, it's just flu. No point in getting him all riled up for nothing."

"It is hardly nothing, Sergeant. Even if it were flu, that would greatly increase your chances of catching plague. You must realize that. And since it is summer, and there are no reports of flu circulating at the moment, I am not inclined to believe that is what we are dealing with."

Kody's stomach seized, as though he'd been punched. He swallowed again. "So, you think it's . . ."

Merden sighed. It was all the answer Kody needed.

His gaze dropped to the floor. The world seemed to tilt around him, as if he were a pocket of stillness in the midst of a storm. "Okay." He breathed in, out. Listened through the roaring in his ears until there was only silence. "Okay." He looked up. "So, I need the tonic, then, right?"

Merden rose and circled the table, chose a bottle from among many. "I have been preparing it all afternoon. It should work."

"Should?" The word had an ugly power to it. Kody felt light-headed again.

"It depends how far the disease has progressed, and on other things besides, things we cannot know. As Oded told us, not everyone can be cured this way. Some require stronger measures."

Kody shuddered. He'd seen what *stronger measures* looked like. If it was a cure at all, it was surely worse than the disease. That was his first thought, at any rate. Then he pictured the bodies they'd seen, black and blue and bloated, and thought, *Maybe not.*

"Three drops every hour until I say otherwise,"

Merden said, "starting right now. You will rest here. I will wake you in an hour for the next dose."

Kody glanced at the cot where the boy had undergone his treatment. Where he'd bucked and writhed and burst into shadow.

"Not there, Sergeant." Merden's deep voice carried a hint of amusement. "You would not find your dreams . . . restful. You will sleep on the ground, on a blanket. The night is warm. You should be fine."

Kody suddenly felt too tired to argue. He took the cup of water Merden offered him, downed it. It was so bitter that his throat closed up and his mouth started watering in protest, as if to banish the taste.

He curled up on the floor like a dog and closed his eyes.

He dreamed of his childhood, of summers by the lake and autumns picking fruit in his uncle's orchard.

When he woke, he was trembling. Or shivering. He couldn't tell. A hand was on his shoulder. Merden's.

"The fever grows worse," the Adal said. "That should not happen, not after three doses."

"Three?" Kody rolled over, squinting up at him. "I only remember two."

"Three," Merden repeated, "and you should be showing signs of improvement."

"In three hours?"

"Everyone is different, but Oded assured me that most patients show improvement within two hours." Merden shook his head. "I am sorry, Sergeant, but it appears you are not responding to the potion. You will need—"

Kody held up a hand. He didn't want to hear it.

A wave of panic crashed over him, frigid, airless, dragging the world out from under him. For a moment, he thought he might actually throw up. But he didn't. He just sat there, staring at nothing, his breath whispering darkly in his ears. Somehow—a hound's instinct, maybe—he'd known it wasn't going to be that simple. Not for him. He was special, apparently, and not in the way you wanted to be special. It would be so easy to hate the world for that, but what would be the point? It was what it was.

Kody made a decision. He pushed himself to his feet.

"What are you doing?" Merden asked warily.

"Going home. We've got a long day ahead of us tomorrow."

"You cannot seriously be thinking of leaving?"

Kody went over to the table, trying to identify the tonic amid the clutter. All the little brown bottles looked the same. His hand hovered over them, indecisive but steady. The sound of his breath in his ears was as thick as smoke. It was almost comforting.

"Sergeant, you are sick, and getting sicker all the time. You need treatment."

"I'm getting treatment." Kody chose a bottle at random. He figured Merden would stop him if it was a problem.

"It is not working."

"You don't know that," Kody snapped. "You just said it yourself—everyone's different. Maybe it just takes longer for the potion to work on me than it does on most people."

Merden sighed. "I doubt that, and even if it were true, it would still be unwise for you to exert yourself."

"I don't have a choice. We're canvassing the docks tomorrow. The inspector can't do it alone, and there's no one else to help him. Every hound in Kennian is busy enforcing the quarantine. You know that. I can't afford to take time off, no matter how sick I am."

Merden folded his arms. "And what about Inspector Lenoir? Or anyone else you come into contact with? Do you imagine I will let you go out there and infect others?"

"You think you can stop me?" He eyed the Adal's slender form meaningfully.

"I am quite certain of it, Sergeant." Merden's gaze was as level as his tone.

Kody looked away uneasily. "Look, I'm not even very contagious yet, if what Dr. Lideman told us is true."

"An *if* of some importance," Merden said dryly. "Besides, *not very contagious* is not good enough. We cannot take the risk of you breaching the quarantine your colleagues are working so hard to defend."

Clever, that—bringing his fellow hounds into it. Kody's mouth twisted bitterly.

"Your devotion to duty is commendable," Merden went on, "but there is too much at stake."

"But that's just my point! There's too much at stake, and I can't leave the inspector to go it alone." He had to make Merden see. *Had* to. His life, even Lenoir's, was a small price to pay if it helped them find out something useful about the plague. "You've got to help me, Merden. Help *us*. All I need is a few more hours. That's not too much to ask, is it? Give me something to manage the symptoms, and I promise I'll wear a scarf and gloves the entire time. I'll keep my distance as much as possible."

The soothsayer shook his head and opened his mouth, but Kody ploughed on.

"It's my job to risk my life. Lenoir's job too. This thing is bigger than us. You know he'd agree with me."

Merden looked away, still shaking his head.

"Just a few hours," Kody said again. "Just the morning. I'll come back tomorrow afternoon. I swear. I *swear*, Merden."

Amber eyes locked on to his. Merden's lips pressed into a thin line. "Very well," he said at length. "This is police business. The decision is not mine to take. But know this: if you are not back by afternoon, as you have sworn, I will no longer be able to suspend my conscience. I will alert your colleagues to the situation, and you can explain yourself to your chief."

Kody let out the breath he'd been holding. "Thank you."

Merden gave him an irritable look. "I would rather you did not." He headed over to the table. "I will give you something to manage the headache and fever. Dissolve a spoonful of the powder in liquid, at most every four hours. That means I am giving you three doses, since you will be back here by noon." He raised an eyebrow significantly.

"Got it."

Merden reached for a mortar and pestle. He paused. "Do not make me regret this, Sergeant," he said softly.

"I won't," Kody said. He prayed to God it was the truth.

CHAPTER 17

Lenoir took the long way in to the station. He had the streets largely to himself at this early hour; only the bakery on Little Oxway had its lanterns lit, washing the cobblestones in a weak glow. He closed his eyes as the scent of fresh bread filled his nose, warm and golden and comforting. He would have bottled that scent if he could, carried it with him through the day so that he could draw on it when he needed to. Instead, he turned a corner and it faded away, like a pleasant dream that he could not quite recall.

Chimes rang out from a nearby church, greeting the dawn. Their triumphant song frayed Lenoir's nerves. He had taken too much wine last night, and each strike of the mallet seemed to glance off the inside of his skull. More than that, the paean to God's glory seemed out of place on this gloomy morning, tasteless and unfeeling, like laughter at a funeral. Better for the priest to sound a toll for the hundreds who had perished last night, a single pang for each of God's children who had been carried off like notes on the wind.

On a whim, Lenoir turned left on Grantley. The avenue curved too far to the southeast, but it cut through the heart of the flower district, and the sight of summer roses would do him good. Even at this hour, preparations for the day's business were well under way. Clouds of color lined the street, tables and wagons loaded up with fresh blossoms of every size and shape. Young girls in dingy frocks stood by while their mothers filled baskets for them to carry, and little boys tied bundles with twine and cheap black ribbon. The black ribbon puzzled Lenoir until he noticed the signs: FUNERAL FLOWERS HERE. SYMPATHIES AND CONDOLENCES. CASKET FLOWERS AVAILABLE. Some tables even offered little pouches of lavender to be carried under the nose, to "ward off bad air."

You cannot escape it, he thought, *not even for a moment.* Each reminder of death was a reminder of failure. His failure.

Pride alone would make that a bitter draft to swallow. But something much more corrosive gnawed at Lenoir's nerves. He could not shake the thought that perhaps this case held the answer to a question that had hung over him for months:

Why did the Darkwalker spare you?

Lenoir had saved Zach's life and thwarted the necromancers, but surely that was not enough to atone for his sins? Surely his debt remained? Why, then, had he been given his life?

Perhaps it was not a gift at all, but a bond. An unspoken compact between Lenoir and whatever cosmic judge had decided to stay his execution. He had been set free on the condition that he repay his debt at the first opportunity. And now here it was, his chance to atone for his sins, and he was failing. The lives that were meant to pay for his own were slipping through his fingers. For them, there would be no second chance.

There is no redemption, the Darkwalker had said.

Lenoir was proving him right.

"Miracle tonic!"

Lenoir nearly jumped out of his skin.

A salesman darted out from behind his cart, waving a

brown glass bottle as though it were the Golden Sword itself. "Cure what ails you! Only half a crown!"

Lenoir glared at the swindler. "Have you no shame, sir? Profiteering on tragedy?" The furious tremble of his voice surprised even him.

The man blinked, taken aback. "Just trying to make a living."

"By peddling worthless concoctions to desperate people?"

The salesman just stared, as though Lenoir had lost his mind. *Perhaps I have,* he thought. A vulture this man might be, but there was nothing unusual in that. Was he really so different from the flower women with their lavender pouches and funeral arrangements? "What are you doing in the flower district?" he growled, irrelevantly. "You would have more luck plying your trade in the slums."

"Not worth the risk."

Lenoir frowned. "What do you mean?"

"Too much plague. Better to keep to neighborhoods like this, just on the edges of it."

A finger of ice slid down Lenoir's spine. "What do you mean, *on the edges of it*? We are well away from the Camp."

Once again, the man stared at him as though he were insane. "You been living in a cave, mate? It's not just the slums now. It's all over the poor district."

"But the quarantine . . ."

The salesman snorted. "Right. Might as well carry water with cheesecloth." Just then, he spotted another passerby, and he dove after her. "Miracle tonic! Only half a crown!"

Lenoir looked up, his gaze skimming over the windows of the flats above him. It did not take long to find what he dreaded: the black cloth dangling from closed shutters, just as he remembered it from his youth. *Plague here,* the cloth announced. *Stay away.*

"It's happening," he murmured.

He jogged the rest of the way to the station.

*   *   *

Lenoir found Chief Lendon Reck doing what he did best: stalking about the kennel barking orders.

"I don't give a damn *what* he told you, Stedman, *I* told you to bring them here—all of them! This isn't bloody optional, do you understand? We've lost a whole day! And you, scribe!" Reck jabbed a finger at a passing youth. "Send a messenger out to Barrier One right away! Tell Crears that the dozen men I promised him won't be coming, thanks to his cretin of a colleague in North Haven!"

The young man hovered uncertainly. "Er ... do you really want me to say that last part?"

"Of course not!"

The scribe scrambled away, Inspector Stedman following close behind. As he passed, Stedman gave Lenoir a look that said, *Watch out.* It was good advice; Lenoir had learned long ago that it was best to steer clear of Reck when he was in such a mood. Unfortunately, Lenoir did not have that luxury today. "Chief," he said, a little warily.

"Well, well. Look who's decided to pay a visit."

Lenoir winced. It *had* been a while since he had passed through the station. "Do you have a moment?" Reck gave him a scathing look, and Lenoir laughed humorlessly. "Very well, a foolish question. Nevertheless, I need to speak with you."

For a moment, it looked like the chief was going to tell him to take a long leap from a very high building. Instead, he motioned irritably toward the stairs. "Five minutes. Let's go."

When they reached the chief's office, Reck sank behind his desk with a windy sigh, as though he had not sat down in days. "Close the door."

Lenoir complied before taking a seat of his own. Reck had not offered, but he rarely did, and Lenoir rarely waited for an invitation. He settled against the creaking wood and watched as the chief rubbed his eyes, his temples, his jaw—the latter sporting at least three days' growth of beard. He looked as exhausted as Lenoir felt.

"You got something to say, Inspector, or did you just come to gaze at my pretty face?"

Lenoir had many things to say, but he hardly knew where to begin. "Has the quarantine been breached?"

"Breached? No, but it's leaking, and getting worse every day."

"Where is the plague turning up?"

"Where isn't it?" Reck gestured at a map of the city pinned to the wall behind him. "Fishering, Stonesgully, Houndsrow. That's as of yesterday morning. I'm sure we'll add more to the list today. Isolated cases for now, but that won't last."

"I saw a black flag on Grantley on the way in just now."

"Grantley? In the flower district?" Reck swore and shook his head. "First I've heard. If it's that far in . . ."

"General contamination cannot be far behind."

Reck rubbed his eyes again. "General contamination, is it? You've been spending too much time around physicians."

"It is a term I recall from my youth. Or at least, an approximate translation of it." He could still see the words on the front page of every newspaper in Serles, stamped in pitiless black ink. "We should shut down the port, Chief."

Reck looked up sharply. "What do you mean, *shut it down*?"

"If Kennian falls to the plague, the other port cities of Humenor will not be far behind." *Starting with Serles.*

"Hearstings would never agree. There's too much money involved, not to mention goods the city needs to survive. And even if he did agree, we could never make it happen. I don't have the manpower."

"Parliament could request the king to send the army."

Reck's eyebrows flew up. "Have you lost your mind? You want the army to take over Kennian?"

"If that is what it takes to preserve law and order, and to prevent the plague from spreading over the entire continent. You do not know what it will be like, Chief. You cannot imagine...." Lenoir closed his eyes and shook his head against the memories. Corpses stacked like firewood. Black smoke billowing over rooftops. Human ash drifting like snow over barren streets ... He had thought those images banished forever, but they returned to him now in a rush, every hellscape that had ever haunted his nightmares as a young man.

"It didn't happen that way before," Reck said. "The pox that hit Arrènes never came to Braeland. As far as I know, it never turned up anywhere else either, except a few cases here and there. Not even the neighbors got it."

"That was different. Serles was isolated because of the revolution. Shortly after the plague began, the navy blockaded the port to prevent rebels from entering. Very few ships got through. Even the main highways were blocked. Serles suffered alone. And besides, the pox was nowhere near as deadly as this ... *hatekh-sahr.*"

The chief frowned. "What did you call it?"

"*Hatekh-sahr.* It is the Adali name for the disease. It means *marks of the demon.*"

Reck grunted. "It's a demon, all right, and it's running rampant in my city. But I can't close the port, not with hounds. I'll speak to the lord mayor, but ..."

"But he is a fool."

Reck ignored that. "You getting anywhere?"

"Honestly, I do not know." This was why he had come—to update his superior, and to get a second opinion from a hound who had been on the job longer than any other man on the Metropolitan Police force. But now that the moment had come, Lenoir felt oddly detached. What did it matter anyway, with the plague slowly seeping out of the Camp and into the veins of Kennian proper? The worse the epidemic became, the more his task seemed petty and pointless. For the first time in a long time, he felt something like the old apathy creeping back in. How else to feel in the face of such futility? *So much for finding purpose in your work,* he thought bitterly.

Reck read it all in his eyes, and he did not bother with false comfort. Catching whoever was behind this was no longer his priority. "I hear you convinced Crears to turn Sergeant Innes into a bodyguard for some Adali witch-doctor."

"Innes and a pair of watchmen. It was generous of Crears to agree."

"That's one way of putting it. Did you pull rank, or just call in a personal favor?"

"It was necessary."

"And why is that? What are you up to, Lenoir?"

"Merden is a healer of some renown among his people. I believe he may be able to cure the disease using a remedy he learned from another Adali healer."

Reck's bushy gray eyebrows climbed his forehead. "That so? Cure it how?"

"It is"—Lenoir hesitated—"a traditional remedy. My hope was that once the cure had proven itself, the College of Physicians would be willing to reproduce it on a large scale."

"And?"

"I'm not sure. They remain . . . skeptical."

"I'll bet. But that doesn't explain the guard detail. You afraid this miracle cure is gonna start a riot?"

Lenoir blew out a breath. He had not even thought of that, but it was certainly a possibility. *Just one more thing to worry about.* "Innes and the others are there to protect Merden from a killer. You see, the other healer I mentioned—the one who taught Merden the treatment—was murdered yesterday morning."

"Murdered?" Reck frowned. "What's that about?"

"Four patients he had treated were also murdered. I believe the killer is the same person who started the plague. Or at least, he is part of the same conspiracy."

"Back up—did I hear you right?" The chief leaned forward in his chair. "There were five murders yesterday and I'm just hearing about it now? What in the below have you been doing out there, Inspector?"

Lenoir sighed. "I apologize, Chief. I should have updated you sooner."

"Damn right you should have. It's been three days, Lenoir. Three days of all-out chaos on my streets. I've had two murders—not counting the ones I didn't know about—and my best inspector nowhere to be found. I'd have had you hauled in by your bootheels if I wasn't up to my neck in shit." He shook his head, but Reck was too much of a hound to let his ego get in the way of good police work. He folded his arms and sank back into his chair. "All right, let's hear it. Everything you've got so far."

Lenoir began by explaining how he and Kody convinced Horst Lideman to let an Adali witchdoctor practice on his patients.

"I'll bet that was a tough sell," the chief said.

"Indeed, but I was convinced the Adali were onto something, and in the end, we were able to persuade Lideman to try. Oded performed his ritual on four patients, all of them terminal. But when Kody and I returned to the Camp the next morning, all four patients had died. At first, we thought the treatment had failed, but when we examined the bodies, we discovered signs of smothering."

Reck grunted thoughtfully. "Someone wanted it to *look* like the treatment failed. And when his ploy was discovered, he went for the witchdoctor instead." The chief studied him for a moment, and Lenoir could not help fidgeting a little under the scrutiny. *You should have seen that coming,* Reck's eyes seemed to say, but perhaps Lenoir was merely imagining it.

"We were able to get a description of the killer from one of Lideman's people," Lenoir continued. "I had a sketch done up, and Kody and I took it to the docks." He explained about Zach's information, and the story of *Serendipity* in Inataar.

"So you think the plague was brought in from Darangosai?"

"I don't know. There is so much that doesn't make sense. If what the sailors say is true, Darangosai has been plague-free for some time. Where did they obtain a sample of the infection, and how did they transport it without becoming infected themselves? Then there is the distance. Even if our guess is correct, and they used corpses to transport the disease, the crossing from Inataar takes at least three weeks, and often more. The corpses would have decomposed significantly on the voyage, yet the bodies Drem found in the Camp appear to have been fresh—a few days old at the most. I cannot account for it."

"Don't get bogged down in the details, Lenoir—that's not your style. We know it came in by ship. That gives you a place to start. The particulars don't really matter."

"I suppose not. What matters is *why* someone would do this, but I am no closer to understanding that."

"I'm not sure that's so important either," Reck said. "Whoever he is, the bastard is obviously insane. Who knows why madmen do anything? Just for the fun of it, sometimes."

Lenoir shook his head. "No, Chief, that does not fit. Aside from the fact that one man could not possibly transport this disease across the sea without help, the murders in the Camp were too calculated to be the work of someone purely bent on mayhem. There is an angle to this, I know it."

Reck considered him with an odd expression. "You're putting an awful lot of thought into this, considering how little is likely to come of it. That's not your style either."

Lenoir knew exactly what the chief was getting at, and it sat badly with him. It was not the first time Reck had taken a swipe at him for his erstwhile lack of enthusiasm for police work. True, Lenoir had changed, but he saw no purpose in dwelling on it, least of all now. "Once, perhaps," he said coolly. "But I trust you are not suggesting I should revert to old habits?"

Reck snorted. "Don't get your feathers in a fluff, Lenoir. I'm just saying you're overthinking it. It's like those jigsaw puzzles—you ever done one of those? My son used to be crazy about them. He liked to try to guess what the picture was after he'd only put a handful of the pieces together. He'd stare at them for hours, days even, just these little scraps of paint on wood, as though he could make sense of it. But he never did, not until he had enough of the pieces in place. You can stare all you like, Lenoir, but you don't have enough pieces."

"And how do you suggest I get them?" Lenoir asked irritably. He was not in the mood for folksy wisdom.

Reck, meanwhile, was not in the mood for impudence from his subordinates. "I suggest you do your job, Inspector. Take your sketch and head back to the docks. If you're lucky, you'll hook something. If you're very lucky, it will lead you to your killer. None of which will do a damn thing to keep the peace or stop the plague, so if you'll excuse me, your five minutes are up."

Lenoir sighed and got to his feet. "One more thing. If the Inataari did find a cure, perhaps we can learn what it was. Someone should dispatch a ship to Darangosai at once."

"I'll tell Hearstings, but I wouldn't pin much hope on it. Even the fastest ship in the navy couldn't get there and back in less than six weeks." He gestured at a ledger on his desk. "You got any idea how many people will be dead by then?"

Lenoir shuddered as the images accosted him again. Priests in waxed robes pushing handcarts. Packs of dogs roaming the streets, feasting . . . "Yes, Chief," he said softly, "I do."

CHAPTER 18

Zach woke with a snort. His cheek was pressed against something hard, and there was a faint rocking motion beneath him. He smelled fish. *Where in the below?* Then he remembered: *the rowboat.* He'd fallen asleep on the job.

Damn! He'd practically begged for this chance, and here he was, dozing off like a little kid up past his bedtime.

He sat up, rubbing an awful crick in his neck, and peered into the weak wash of dawn. To his surprise, the docks were already bustling. Fishermen, mostly, though it looked like the *Regent* was fixing to sail this morning, bound for shores unknown. Zach longed to go with her. It would be easy enough to sneak aboard. He could hide belowdecks and pilfer food and water, at least for a while. Then, when they were too far out to sea to turn back, he'd come out of hiding and offer to work in exchange for passage. They'd let him, probably. Or they'd toss him overboard. Zach reckoned it'd be worth the risk if it meant he got to see Inataar, or Mirrhan, or even Arrènes, where Lenoir was from.

Maybe next time, he told himself. Right now, he had a job to do—if he hadn't already stuffed it up.

He gazed groggily at the Port, rubbing one eye with

the backs of his knuckles to banish the sleep. The tavern looked deserted, but he knew better. The Port was the kind of place that never really closed. Men stayed up all night playing cards and whoring, and those who felt tired simply curled up on the floor, sawdust in their beards, for a bit of a kip. The question was, had Bevin and his crew left while Zach was having a kip of his own, or were they still in there?

As though in answer to his thoughts, the door opened, and a familiar figure appeared. The skinny bloke, Stew, emerged into the light, blinking and muttering to himself. He hovered in the doorway for a moment, as if to get his bearings, before tottering off into the morning. Feeling perfectly awake now, Zach crouched lower into the belly of the boat and waited.

A few minutes went by. Zach started to worry. Maybe Stew had been the last to leave? But no—here came Bevin and Gerd, arms draped over each other's shoulders, Bevin howling with laughter as usual. *Come on, Hairy,* Zach thought. *Come on out.* He refused to believe he'd missed his chance. If he had, he'd never be able to face Lenoir.

Gerd started off in the same direction as Stew, but Bevin paused just outside the door. He poked his head back inside and said something, and moments later, Hairy appeared.

Zach flicked his eyes skyward in silent thanks.

Hairy looked like he'd been run over by a stagecoach. His hair stood up at all angles, and his clothes were rumpled, as though he'd slept in them. Judging from the straw clinging to his shirt, he had.

The three sailors shambled off down the boardwalk. Zach started to climb out of the boat, but then Hairy stopped suddenly, as if he'd just remembered something. Zach dropped back down, wincing as the movement caused the boat to rock conspicuously. He waited until it leveled out a bit before peering over the gunwale. Hairy was saying something Zach couldn't hear, and he cocked his head in the direction of one of the piers. Bevin shrugged, and Gerd started off again, plodding along like a horse bound for the barn. Bevin said something and then turned away, leaving Hairy alone. The red-haired man changed direction and started up the pier.

Zach clambered out of the boat and followed, darting between the crates and stinking piles of netting that littered the wharf. He must have looked dodgy, scurrying along like a rat, but luckily, the fishermen and dockhands were too busy to notice. He kept far enough back that if Hairy chanced to look back over his shoulder, he probably wouldn't recognize Zach straightaway.

They were almost at the end of the pier when Hairy stopped, craning his neck to look up at a hulking ship with a trio of red masts poking up into the sky, the words *Duchess of the Deep* painted on the hull. He shouted something Zach couldn't make out, and a man appeared on the deck. While Hairy was absorbed in yelling up at the other man, Zach found a nice big coil of rope to crouch behind. One good thing about the docks—there was no shortage of places to hide.

"He's not here," the man on the deck called down. "Haven't you heard? He's with *Fly By Night* now. Has been for near half a year."

Hairy swore. He started to walk away, then paused and turned back. "What about Ritter?"

"What about him?"

"Durian's balls! Is he there or not?"

"All right, pipe down. I'll get him." The man on the deck moved out of sight. Hairy folded his arms and kicked at the crust of salt between the slats of the pier, waiting. Eventually, another man appeared up on deck.

"Harund?" He sounded surprised. "What are you doing here?"

Hairy scowled. "You want me to shout your business from down here, do you?"

"Wait. I'm coming." The sailor disappeared over the rail, only to reappear on the gangplank, making his way down. Zach tried to get a good look at him, but he didn't dare stick his head up too far, or he'd be spotted for sure. At least he could hear pretty well. "Haven't seen you in a while," the unfamiliar man said. He didn't sound too unhappy about it.

"Yeah, I missed you too," Hairy said sarcastically. "So Nash has gone over to another rig, then?"

"A while ago. So?"

"But the two of you are still tight?"

"Tight? I don't know. I see him now and then. Why?"

"Think you might see him today?"

There was a pause. "What's this about?"

"What's your problem? Simple question, isn't it?"

"Sure," said the other man. "Just curious, I guess."

"Well, you're not the only one. Hounds came around last night asking about him. Didn't know his name, but they had a real good sketch."

"Is that so?" The other man sounded worried.

"Didn't say what they wanted him for, but they were asking lots of questions about the plague, and *Serendipity* too."

The other man swore. "And they didn't say what they wanted?"

"Something to do with the plague. Seemed to think we could help 'em find a cure, or some such." He laughed contemptuously. "Talk about chasing the wrong rabbit."

"Yeah." The other man sounded distracted.

"Anyway, if you see Nash, better let him know the hounds are looking for him. I'd tell him myself, but I gotta get to bed. Head feels like a butcher's block." It sounded like Hairy was fixing to leave.

His companion, though, wasn't quite ready to let him go. "What did you all tell them, anyway?"

"The hounds? Not much. I'm the only one knows Nash, and I didn't say nothing."

"And the plague?"

Zach could easily picture the annoyed look on Hairy's face. "What about it?"

"Well, did you tell them about Darangosai?"

"Sure. So?"

"And did they think it was the same disease?"

"Not you too! What in the Dark Flame is everyone so interested in this bloody plague for?"

"I'm not," the other man said quickly—too quickly, it seemed to Zach. "Just wondering what the hounds are looking for, is all."

"Who gives a damn? To the below with 'em. I had half a mind to knock some teeth out, only I didn't want to spill my ale."

Zach snorted. *Was that before or after Sergeant Kody slammed your big ugly face into the table?*

"Anyways," Hairy continued, "I'm dead tired. Gotta get home. Just pass the message to Nash, all right? I owe him one."

"You owe everyone on the docks, I hear," the other man said dryly. "But yeah, I'll pass the message."

Zach heard footsteps, one set on the pier, the other on the gangplank, as the sailors parted ways. He shifted in his hiding place to make sure Hairy couldn't see him as he passed. Now Zach had a dilemma: keep following Hairy, because that's what Lenoir asked him to do, or stay with the other man, the one called Ritter? From the conversation, it sounded like Ritter would be seeing Nash before Hairy did, and wasn't the whole point of following Hairy to get to the man in the sketch?

Plus, this Ritter bloke sounded suspicious. Hairy might not have noticed, but Zach was pretty sure Ritter was sweating the fact that the hounds were snooping around, even though they'd been asking about Nash. Then there were his questions about the plague. Why should he care about that unless he was involved somehow?

Zach glanced back over his shoulder at Hairy's receding form. He bit his lip uncertainly. He looked back at the *Duchess*. Ritter had reappeared at the rail, and he was watching Hairy too. He looked anxious.

As soon as Hairy was out of sight, Ritter came back down the gangplank. That sealed it. The bloke was dodgy and no mistake. Zach could always find Hairy at the Port later on, if he needed to. For now, he would tail Ritter, and hopefully, that would lead him to Nash. Sure, it was a gamble, but if he got it right, Lenoir would be pleased, and that meant Zach would be one step closer.

To being a hound. To having a future. To having a *life*.

Most street kids didn't bother thinking about the future, not once they were old enough to understand they weren't entitled to one. But Zach was different. He was smarter. Better. He had *plans*.

You had to have plans if you wanted to be somebody someday. And Zach did want that, desperately. Provided he lived long enough. That wasn't a sure thing where he came from, but Zach didn't dwell on that.

One step at a time.

He peered around the crate. Ritter was nearly at the end of the pier.

"One step at a time," Zach whispered, and he crept out of his hiding place.

For the second time that day, Zach found himself crouched in the belly of a boat, fighting off sleep. He'd tailed Ritter to another ship, a trim, fast-looking vessel called *Fly By Night*. Ritter had disappeared inside about two hours ago, and Zach hadn't seen him since. He was so bored that he'd started counting seagulls. (It wasn't a very satisfying pastime; they all looked exactly the same, and they kept moving around.) He was getting thirsty too, and hot. He should have been hungry, but the smell of fish guts baking in the sun was too off-putting.

He was just about to give up when something finally started to happen. A bunch of dockhands showed up, milling around while one of their number boarded the ship. Zach could hear them talking among themselves while they waited.

"Better not be the same story as last time," one of them said.

"I'll tell you what," said another, "if one of those little buggers so much as sticks his head out of his cage, I'll twist it off for him."

"I'd like to see that," said a third. "Twisting the head off a monkey."

Monkey? Zach felt himself grinning. At last, something interesting!

"All right, lads," a familiar voice called. Ritter waved over the rail at the assembled dockhands, and they headed up the gangplank, each one trailing a dolly. They were gone for a while, and when they showed up again, they had crates loaded onto the dollies, and they started ferrying them off the ship. Zach couldn't help sticking his head up a little higher, hoping for a glimpse. He'd never seen a monkey before. Ritter, meanwhile, positioned himself at the bottom of the gangplank, making notes on a ledger as each crate went past.

It took forever. Somebody must have been starting a zoo or something, because even at one monkey per box, there were a whole lot of boxes. Zach had long since lost count by the time Ritter said, "That's enough—we don't want to overdo it."

The head dockhand gave him a mystified look. "There's gotta be at least two hundred more down there."

"I'm aware of that." Ritter's pencil continued to bob. "But we don't want to flood the market, not yet. The product has only just started selling. It's simple supply and demand, my good man. Too much, and the price drops. Too little, and we don't make enough profit. Find the right balance, and you're rich."

"*We*, is it? What's this got to do with you anyway, Ritter? This isn't your rig. How come Marsh's men aren't taking care of this themselves?"

"I'm doing Captain Elder a favor, that's all, while he and his crew take advantage of some well-deserved shore leave."

The dockhand shrugged. "Whatever you say. Where do you want 'em?"

"Warehouse 57, same as last time. My associates will pick them up from there."

The dockhand nodded and withdrew.

Once the crates had been taken away, Ritter went back up the gangplank. He stayed inside the ship for a while, and when he reappeared, he no longer had the ledger. He was whistling as he came back down, and he continued his happy little ditty all the way back to *Duchess of the Deep*.

"Huh," said Zach when Ritter had gone inside. So much for finding Nash. From the way Ritter had been acting earlier, Zach had been sure he was heading off to warn his friend about the hounds. Instead, he'd just been going about his business. *Well that's disappointing*. Maybe he should have followed Hairy after all.

Something puzzled him, though. If Ritter worked on *Duchess of the Deep*, how come he was unloading crates of monkeys from *Fly By Night*? Zach didn't know much about sailing, but he was pretty sure you could only work on one ship at a time.

He waited for Ritter to show up again, but he didn't. Meanwhile, Zach's curiosity started to tug at him. *Monkeys*. Whole crates of them, just sitting there in Warehouse 57.

What ten-year-old could resist?

It wasn't hard to break in. Warehouse 57 looked formidable, a grim brick structure with padlocked doors, but the small arched windows lining one side of the building provided Zach with the perfect entry point. The windows weren't big enough for a grown man to squeeze through, but Zach was a boy, and small for his age. He picked up a stone, glanced around to make sure no one was nearby, and threw it at the glass. He knocked out the jagged shards so he wouldn't cut himself. Then he grabbed an empty crate, clambered on top, and wriggled through the window.

It was hot in there, and dark, but there was enough light coming through the windows to see by. He spotted the cluster of crates near the doors and headed over, pulse skipping with nervous anticipation. The crates were about the size of a coffin. Zach couldn't see any air holes; he wondered how the monkeys breathed. He pressed his ear up against one of them, but he couldn't hear anything. Tentatively, he scratched the wood with his fingernails. "Hello?"

Nothing.

He groped around in the dark until he found a pry bar. It was heavy and rusted, but it would do. Zach wedged the thin end under the lid of one of the crates and cranked it. The nails popped free, and a two-inch slice of darkness appeared. Zach waved his fingers in front of the gap, but nothing happened. He sniffed at it, but the smell that greeted him wasn't fur or dung. It smelled more like grass.

Zach moved farther down the crate and leaned against the pry bar again. The lid creaked and rose higher, but there was still no sound.

Sod it.

Zach tore the lid free and looked inside. In the shadowed depths, he could just make out the shapes . . .

. . . of a bunch of dried plants.

"Aw, come on!" His voice echoed in the cavernous space, sharp and indignant. It was like finding spinach on your plate when you'd been promised sugar biscuits. He slammed the lid back down in disgust. He opened one more crate, just to be sure, but it was the same as before:

rows of dried plants tied in neat little bushels. *Spices and cotton, cotton and spices.* He could now add herbs to the list. Talk about boring.

Zach was still scowling as he squirmed his way back through the window. He was so annoyed that he didn't even notice the man lounging in the shade of the warehouse, and would have walked right by had a great paw not seized the back of his collar. "Hey!" He twisted to glare at his captor, half expecting to find Lenoir.

The face that loomed over him was not the inspector's. Bevin smiled, slow and nasty and full of teeth. "Hello there, little pup."

Zach's throat seemed to close up a little, but he swallowed through it and mustered every ounce of bravado he had. "You better leave me alone, Bevin. I got friends in the police."

"Oh, I know it." Bevin's grin widened, and he lifted Zach off the ground like a kitten by the scruff of its neck. "That's just what I'm counting on."

CHAPTER 19

"There's another one," Kody said, pointing. The scrap of black cloth dangled from a grimy window on the fourth floor. The window next to it also had a black flag, though whether it was the same residence, or a neighbor's, Lenoir could not tell. "That's eight now," Kody said.

Lenoir had no interest in listening to a running tally of death. "Perhaps you could turn your thoughts to more useful pursuits, Sergeant."

Kody scarcely seemed to hear him. "Panic's going to spread even faster now, with those flags popping up everywhere."

"And hounds wearing scarves and gloves wherever they go," Lenoir said, gesturing meaningfully at Kody. "Your attire is hardly going to inspire confidence in the public."

Kody gave him a dark look. "I shouldn't protect myself?"

"This is not the Camp. The risk here is minimal."

"Tell that to the people flying those flags."

Lenoir let the matter drop. If the sergeant chose to be overcautious, that was his business.

Kody brooded in silence for a time. After a few blocks,

he blurted, "Even if this Ritter fellow can help us find the rest of the old *Serendipity* crew, it's not going to be enough."

"We don't know that. At a minimum, it will give us a pool of potential witnesses who might be able to tell us more about the plague, where it came from, and perhaps even how the Inataari cured it. And, if we are very lucky, someone who can identify the man in the sketch."

"And if they can't?"

The sergeant was on thin ice now; Lenoir could feel his patience cracking. "You are unusually negative today," he said coolly. "I thought we had discussed this. There is no point in lamenting our situation. We can only hope for the best. If the sketch yields nothing, there is still Harund. Zach may yet find something useful by tailing him."

Kody said nothing. He had little faith in the boy, Lenoir knew. He believed Zach's age and delinquency made him unsuitable as an informant. That only proved how green the sergeant was. Zach's age and delinquency were precisely what made him so valuable. Necessity had taught the boy resourcefulness, and he knew how to play the child when it suited him. Zach had turned coal into diamonds more than once for Lenoir. He had also failed, sometimes spectacularly, but more often, he contributed some little tidbit, a piece of the puzzle that Lenoir would not otherwise have found. Lenoir would be more than grateful for a little tidbit now.

A shrill voice broke into his thoughts. "Protect yourself and your loved ones from the plague! Get the latest medical advice here!" A boy about Zach's age waved a newspaper over his head. About a dozen more of the papers rested by his feet, pinned under a rock. It looked like he had almost sold out, even though it was only midmorning.

"I'll take one of those." Lenoir flipped the newsboy a coin.

The boy caught it with a whoop, grinning from ear to ear. "Hot damn, I'm gonna sell out today! Plague's good for business!"

"Show some respect, boy," Kody snapped. "People are dying."

The newsboy gave him a sullen look and peeled another page off his pile. "Protect yourself and your loved ones! Latest medical advice here!"

Withdrawing a little for the sake of his ears, Lenoir unfolded the newspaper and scanned the page. "Let us see what the latest medical advice has to offer."

Remain indoors as much as possible, with all doors and windows firmly shut. Use a rag or similar means to block off any gaps or drafts. Ensure that a fire is burning at all times. Fire consumes the miasma and purifies the air. Take care, however, not to inhale too much smoke. If possible, add camphor or rosemary to the flames. This increases your protection.

"Miasma." Lenoir shook his head. "This country."

"They'd have a better explanation in Arrènes, I suppose?" Kody asked irritably. He had been reading over Lenoir's shoulder.

"A better explanation than mysteriously corrupted air? Is it even possible?" Lenoir snorted and kept reading.

Should you find it necessary to go out of doors, take precautions. Cover your nose and mouth at all times. Take a scarf—any fabric will do—and fold it to make a pouch, as shown in Diagram A. Fill the pouch with straw. This will act as a filter against the miasma. If possible, add rosemary or camphor to the straw, the latter in conservative quantities. Be aware that too much camphor can cause disorienta-

tion, shortness of breath, lethargy, reduced appetite, and rash.

Prevent bare skin from coming into contact with any foreign surface. Use a handkerchief or gloves to touch doorknobs and handrails. Close contact, including shaking hands, hugging, or kissing should be avoided at all costs. Should a member of the household become infected, that person should be isolated immediately . . .

Lenoir skipped to the end of the article. It was attributed to none other than Dr. Horst Lideman, Head of Medical Sciences, Royal Braelish College of Physicians. "Wonderful." He folded up the paper and jammed it in his pocket. "Now every household in Kennian will be burning a fire at all hours, many using a highly flammable substance." He drew a deep draft of gritty air. He would have sworn the soot was laced with camphor already, though that was probably his imagination.

They continued on their way, heading toward the poor district and the docks. They had passed through here only yesterday, but the plague had marched on overnight, annexing new territory and consolidating its hold over the old; the sunlight spilling over the rooftops revealed a rapidly decaying world. Anyone brave enough to be out on the street wore a scarf, many of them folded into the cunning little masks described in the *Herald*. No doubt the article had been carried in all the newspapers, and terrified Kennians were taking Lideman's word as scripture.

Shops in this part of town had been closed for days, but many were now boarded up. One shop, a cheap jewelry and watch repair, had a man seated out front with an old musket posed across his knees. Kody scowled when he saw it. "What's that about?"

Lenoir thought it rather obvious, but before he could say so, Kody was striding purposefully across the street, looking every inch the Stern Hound. He truly was in a mood today. Lenoir could only sigh and follow.

"Sir, would you mind telling me what you're doing with a firearm in public?" Kody jabbed an accusing finger at the musket.

The man in the chair tensed, peering up at Kody with suspicious eyes. "Protecting my shop. What business is it of yours?"

In answer, Kody flipped out his badge. The shopkeeper just laughed derisively and shook his head.

"Civilians aren't allowed to carry firearms within city limits," Kody said.

"Not bad enough you hounds abandon us, now you're hassling honest folk trying to protect what's theirs? Where were you last night, when Mrs. Peters's place got busted into?" The man gestured angrily at a shop down the street, where a stout woman hunched over a broomstick, sweeping up broken glass. Several panes were missing from her storefront window, dark squares gaping like missing teeth.

"Don't see you chasing down the thieves, either," the shopkeeper continued, "any more than you're chasing down the thugs who snatched Mrs. Feldman's handbag. I could give you a description, you know. Anyone on this street could. They set on her in broad daylight, bold as you please. And why not? Not as if there's any hounds nearby to stop 'em."

Kody pursed his lips and glanced down the street at the damaged shop. He had no answer for the shopkeeper, of course. The hounds *had* abandoned these people, albeit unwillingly.

"We understand your difficulties, sir," Lenoir said, "but we cannot have firearms in the street. Put your musket inside. Somewhere you can reach it quickly, if need be."

"What good is that? I don't plan on shooting it. I just want those crooks to see it, so they think twice about hitting my shop." The man hooked a thumb over his shoulder. "I got jewelry in there. Might not look like much to you, but it's worth a few crowns, and I'll be damned if I let some street thug make off with it just because you hounds can't be bothered to do your jobs."

"We're busy with the quarantine," Kody said. It sounded peevish and defensive, and it produced a predictable answer.

"Cracking good job you're doing too." The shopkeeper's voice dripped with contempt.

"We do not have time for this," Lenoir said. "Put the musket away, or it will be confiscated. Display a warning sign, or a length of pipe, or even a blade—I don't care. But no firearms. They are too unpredictable."

So saying, he turned and headed up the street to have words with the woman whose shop had been broken into. It would be a purely symbolic conversation, but now that he and Kody had identified themselves as hounds, they could not very well walk past a crime scene without saying anything.

The woman was stooped over a dustpan as Lenoir approached, chasing glittering fragments into its maw. Glass crunched under Lenoir's boots. "Mrs. Peters."

The woman straightened. "Yes?"

"Inspector Lenoir of the Metropolitan Police. I understand you have had a break-in." He glanced at what remained of the windows, but the name of the business must have been etched onto one of the broken panes, because he could not tell what kind of shop it was. "What was taken?"

Mrs. Peters leaned on her broomstick. She was about fifty, Lenoir judged, round and knobby, with a face like a root vegetable. "Laudanum, mostly. Some rubbing alcohol."

"You are an apothecary?"

"That's right. They took all my camphor too." She shook her head and emptied the dustpan into a waste bin. "People only started coming in asking for it yesterday, and already someone's taken to stealing it. Criminals aren't as dumb as you think." She resumed sweeping.

"Not all of them, anyway," Lenoir allowed.

"Anyone hurt?" Kody asked.

"No, thank God." Mrs. Peters glanced up from her sweeping. "Not everyone can say the same. I'm the third break-in on this street in as many days, Inspector. When are you hounds going to do something about it?"

"As soon as we can." A thin answer, but it was the only one he could give.

"I don't suppose you got a look at whoever did this?" Kody asked.

"Nope. Heard the glass breaking in the middle of the night, but by the time I came downstairs, they were half a block away. Just as well. All I had to defend myself with was an iron skillet. Not like Torben there. Least he's got a gun."

Not anymore. Lenoir did not have to look behind him to know that the other shopkeeper was still glaring after them. At least he had put his musket away.

"I am sorry for your troubles," Lenoir said. "We will do what we can."

Mrs. Peters gave him a wry look. She knew exactly what those words were worth.

Lenoir and Kody moved on. They made good progress, for there was little to impede them; the streets were largely deserted. With shutters closed, windows boarded up, and residents sheltering indoors, the city felt strangely anonymous. Ageless. Lenoir could not shake the feeling that he was walking back through time, each step bringing him closer to Serles—not the blooming beauty he had left behind, but the withered, diseased crone she had been during the revolution. Streets of brick and mortar devoid of life, a skeleton of a city with nothing flowing through her veins but a slow, invisible poison. The thought that someone had inflicted that poison deliberately was more than he could comprehend. *Perhaps the chief is right,* he thought. *Perhaps whoever did this is simply mad.* Lenoir was a practical man; he did not suffer from romantic ideas about tortured, twisted creatures hiding in laboratories and caves. Men, not monsters, committed crimes. Yet surely only an irredeemable psychopath could perpetrate an evil such as this.

They found *Duchess of the Deep* moored along the main wharf. She was an ungainly thing, a three-masted bark that sat high above the waterline. Her hold might be empty, but the thin line of barnacles on her hull told Lenoir that she never sat much lower. He did not know much about ships, but the *Duchess* did not look like one of the faster models. Most likely she kept close to home, bearing coal or timber or some other Humenori goods. All was quiet up on her decks, suggesting most of her crew was on shore leave. Lenoir pressed his lips together worriedly, a foreboding that proved justified when the sailor who answered Kody's shout said, "Ritter isn't here."

Lenoir cursed under his breath. "Where is he?"

"No idea." The man's irritable tone suggested he had better things to do than answer for the whereabouts of his shipmates. "And before you ask, I haven't seen Nash either."

Lenoir and Kody traded a blank look. "Who?"

"Never mind." He started to turn away.

"Why would we be looking for Nash?" Lenoir called.

"I don't know." The sailor made an impatient gesture. "It was just a guess, obviously a wrong one. Now are we done? I've got things to do."

"We're done when the inspector says we're done," Kody snapped.

Something nibbled at the edge of Lenoir's thoughts, but he could not quite make it out. "What made you think of Nash, when I was asking about Ritter?"

Kody threw him a puzzled frown, as if to say, *Where are you going with this?* Lenoir could not have answered him. Ritter was no one special, as far as they knew; just the former purser on *Serendipity*. They hoped to get a list of names out of him, nothing more.

"Look, forget I said it," the sailor said. "Just that someone came by looking for Nash this morning, and when he couldn't find him, he asked for Ritter instead. So when you come by looking for Ritter . . ." He shrugged.

Lenoir sighed. He had been grasping, and his fingers had closed on empty air. "Very well. Do you know when Ritter will be back?"

"Captain lets him sleep here, so probably by dark."

Lenoir nodded. He had only one question left. "The sketch, Sergeant."

"Right." Kody reached into his pocket. "One more thing. Do you recognize—"

A gunshot popped, and someone started screaming.

CHAPTER 20

Lenoir flinched and reached for his pistol. Kody swung the crossbow off his shoulder, his gaze raking the pier. The screaming seemed to be coming from somewhere behind them, at least one pier over, but the looming cliffs of timber and canvas blocked their view. Lenoir dropped to his haunches, trying to peer beneath the needle nose of a brig, but he saw nothing. The screaming went on, a sound more of fear than pain, reaching across the water with unsettling intimacy. A second gunshot rasped through the salt-crusted air, and then all was silent. The screaming had stopped.

"Shit," said Kody, and he bolted.

They raced up the pier toward the boardwalk, Kody cradling his crossbow, Lenoir cocking one hammer of his pistol, their boots pounding out an urgent rhythm beneath them. Shouts of alarm went up all over the docks. Lenoir spotted a sailor up in the rigging of a nearby clipper, shading his eyes as he surveyed the scene. "You there!" he called. "See anything?"

"Puff of smoke over there!" The sailor pointed.

"Anyone hurt?"

"Can't tell!"

They banked right at the boardwalk, heading for the

next pier. Just as they were about to reach it, the man in the rigging called out to them again. "Hey, someone's running down there!"

The sailor was too far away now for Lenoir to see where he pointed, but it hardly mattered—the pier ran only one way. That meant whoever was fleeing the scene had three options: board one of the ships, leap into the water, or make for the street, which would send him right past the hounds. Whatever he chose, he would be easy prey.

Lenoir and Kody turned right at the pier, heading back out into the bay. The scene that greeted them was one of confusion. Bodies cluttered the wharf, sailors and dockhands swarming out of the ships like ants rousted from their nests. Lenoir gritted his teeth in frustration. Not only did the crowd block his view, they were clogging the narrow pathway between the hounds and their quarry.

"Clear the way!" Kody cried. "Police coming through!"

Slowly, blinking like bewildered cattle, the sailors stood aside. For a moment, Lenoir feared the runner had escaped, boarding a ship unseen or simply melting into the crowd. But then someone cried, "There he goes!" A sailor perched in a crow's nest jabbed a finger excitedly. "Down there. Do you see him?"

A dark figure darted through the crowd, disappearing and reappearing between the bodies. Kody found a new burst of speed. "Somebody stop that man!"

The runner must have heard him, because he veered suddenly, heading up the gangplank of a four-masted bark. *Fool,* Lenoir thought in grim satisfaction. They had him now.

KaPOW.

Another gunshot sounded from behind. Lenoir whirled around. Over the heads of the crowd, he saw a puff of white smoke. *What in the below?*

Indecision cost him several seconds, but there was really only one choice. "Split up!" Lenoir pointed at the ship, then turned to pursue the shooter, giving Kody no time to argue.

Up ahead, the shooter tossed his spent musket aside, letting it skitter across the pier. He was faster without it, and he hit the boardwalk in a few short strides, disappearing moments later behind the hull of a ship. By the time Lenoir cleared the obstacle, his quarry had almost lost him, ducking through the double doors of one of the warehouses. *Has he trapped himself, or is there another way out?* Lenoir had no way of knowing. His quarry, meanwhile, had no way of knowing whether Lenoir had seen him go in. Lenoir could use that to his advantage— presuming the man was actually trying to hide, and not simply looking to break his pursuer's line of sight.

Lenoir paused outside the warehouse to catch his breath and let his swimming head settle. He was no longer in a hurry; either the shooter was hiding inside, or he had already fled out a back door somewhere, in which case Lenoir had already lost him. Better to let his breathing slow until it was not so labored that it would give away his position. Pinned down or not, his quarry was dangerous, for he might still be armed.

His breath recovered, Lenoir crouched and made his way to one of the windows. He dared not go inside, not yet; opening the door would leave him backlit, an easy target. Hopefully, he could catch a glimpse of the shooter through the window. Licking his lips, his fingers constricting unconsciously around the butt of his gun, he peered inside.

No such luck. The glass was encrusted with salt, leaving it virtually opaque. If the warehouse had been lit inside, he might at least have glimpsed a shadow, but as it was, the only thing casting a shadow was Lenoir. He ducked back down, cursing silently. *Now what?*

He leaned against the wall, the brick pressing against his shoulder blades, his heart thudding warningly in his chest. *You are being foolish,* he told himself. Armed or not, whoever was hiding in that warehouse was not gunning for Lenoir. Indeed, he was probably cowering in a corner somewhere, cursing his luck. The docks were thinly policed at the best of times, and these were hardly the best of times. The fact that Lenoir and Kody had been within earshot of the crime was pure coincidence, and only the most hardened criminals had the stomach to take on the hounds. *He is more afraid of you than you of him, Lenoir. Now get going.* Thus armored, he headed back to the doors.

He hesitated just long enough to regret sending Kody after the runner. With the sergeant to kick down the doors and cover his entrance, Lenoir would not have felt so vulnerable. But it was done now. He had no choice. Steeling himself, cocking the second hammer of his pistol, Lenoir shoved his way in.

Kody opened his mouth to say something, but Lenoir was already off, heading back up the pier after the shooter. Swearing, Kody turned and resumed the chase, thanking God with every step that he had Merden's headache powder to keep him on his feet. The runner had already disappeared, but there weren't many places he could go now that he'd cornered himself on that ship. Not that it made Kody's task easy. It was a huge vessel, and from the looks of it, there was no one else on deck. Kody could only hope that at least one sailor was still on board and could point him in the right direction, or he'd be searching cabins and cargo spaces all day.

He hesitated at the bottom of the gangplank, feeling exposed. But he hadn't seen a weapon on the runner, and anyway, he wasn't even sure he was chasing a criminal. The shooter had been on the opposite end of the pier; maybe this bloke was just running for his life.

Best not to assume, Kody thought. *Plan for the worst and hope for the best.* He paused a moment to catch his breath. Merden's medicine had brought the fever down, but he still felt a little light-headed, and a gentle throb still pulsed inside his skull. *Not exactly top shape for running a man down,* he thought bitterly. He started up the gangplank.

The deck was deserted except for a pair of seagulls complaining noisily on the opposite rail. Kody scanned his surroundings, his crossbow tracking left to right, but unless the man was pressed up against one of the masts, he wasn't here. Four sets of stairs led to raised platforms fore and aft, just high enough that Kody couldn't see more than a few feet over the top. Beneath each platform was a cabin, and another set of stairs led down below. The runner could be hiding anywhere.

Kody decided to start on high ground and work his way down. That way, the runner couldn't get off the ship without him seeing. Cautiously, he climbed the nearest set of stairs at the foredeck. A light breeze swept in from the bay, cooling his brow, but all else was still. He could see the raised deck at the stern of the ship from here, and it looked empty too. Time to search the cabins.

The doors of the forward cabin were locked. Kody was pretty sure he could bust through, but he decided to check the aft cabin first. He kept to the rails as he crossed the deck, and hunched low as he passed in front of the cabin windows to reach the door. His fingers slipped around cool iron, and he tugged ever so slightly. Open. Kody paused just long enough to check his crossbow and loosen his pistol in its holster before slipping inside.

He hurried away from the door, blinking furiously to help his eyes adjust to the gloom. Shadowy shapes crowded the interior: a table here, a writing desk there, a bookshelf with narrow slats to keep the books from tumbling out in a storm. Kody moved as silently as he could, but the boards creaked beneath his boots, conspicuous enough that he might as well have whistled a jaunty tune. He made a slow tour of the room, keeping to the walls to cover as much ground as possible with his crossbow, but it was too dark to see much of anything. He could scarcely identify the furniture, let alone a shape that didn't belong. *Back to the windows,* he thought. Putting the light behind him would help a little.

Just as he reached the windows, a cough seized him, so sudden that he actually staggered.

It was all the opportunity the other man needed.

Something blasted into him, knocking him backward into the windows. Glass shattered, wood splintered. Kody tumbled out onto the deck, his crossbow spinning out of his grasp. His head came down hard, and for a moment, the sky spun above him. The air was gone from his lungs, and he lay on his back like an upended turtle, blinking and gasping. He rolled onto his side in time to see the runner pick up a coil of rope and throw himself over the rail.

Kody clambered to his feet and reached for his crossbow, but the weapon had discharged when he hit the deck, and there was no time to reload. Growling, he slung it over his shoulder and staggered to the rail. The runner was climbing down the seaward side of the ship to a dinghy hanging ten feet below. Without thinking, Kody drew his sword and slashed the rope. The runner dropped, but he was already far enough down that the fall didn't matter; he landed messily, but safely, in the dinghy. He looked up at Kody, and the expression on his face was one of pure panic.

Kody reached for his pistol and pointed it. "Don't make me."

The man choked out a terrified sound and started to climb over the edge of the dinghy.

"Stop!" Kody cocked a hammer. The man continued to scramble, flinging wild glances back and forth between Kody's gun and the distant surface of the water. Jumping from this height might well break his legs, but allowing himself to be arrested didn't appear to be an option.

Kody's finger twitched on the trigger. But he couldn't

be sure of merely wounding, not with a weapon as inaccurate and devastating as a pistol, and he didn't really know who this man was. He wasn't the shooter; he might even be the intended victim. Swearing, Kody holstered his gun and climbed over the rail. *Nice move cutting the rope, genius.* There wasn't enough left for Kody to use. Gritting his teeth and bracing himself, he jumped.

His legs blasted into the dinghy, and he crumpled to the floor of the boat. An instant later, something connected with his head, sending a flash of agony through his brain, and for the second time in as many minutes, the world spun. He heard a frantic rasping sound, as of rope being cut. Kody started to his feet, but the dinghy bucked suddenly, dropping him to his knees. He had almost recovered when the rope snapped a second time. A pulley whirred, and the boat fell out beneath him. Kody seized the side of the dinghy as its nose dropped, and then he was dangling over the sea, his arms straining in their sockets. The boat plummeted, a counterweight for the fugitive as he rode the rope back up to the ship. A heartbeat later, the prow of the boat struck water, and Kody plunged into the cold and the dark, his mouth full of seawater and the taste of failure.

He found Lenoir on the boardwalk, alone.

"You lost yours too," Kody said. It was not a question.

Lenoir looked him over. "While you were swimming, it would seem."

Kody squinted against the pain in his skull. The gentle throb had reverted to hammer blows, courtesy of a boot to the head. He hoped Lenoir would assume it was seawater stinging his eyes. Part of Kody wanted to tell him right now. Just get it over with. But another part, the hound part, knew this wasn't the time. There was still too much to do, and the day was withering faster than the bloom on a morning glory.

It was past noon already. He'd broken his promise.

Merden would have told Crears by now. In which case, Kody reasoned, there was no point hurrying off to the Camp. He needed to stick with this. It was his only real hope. It wasn't like he expected a miracle—not really—but if there was even a hint of a chance they might learn something that could lead them to a cure . . . well, that was his best play, wasn't it? With all due respect to Merden's healing capabilities, if Kody didn't respond to the tonic, no amount of smoke and mirrors was going to save him.

A current of panic arced through him, bright and icy. He shuddered, then squared his shoulders.

Thinking like that doesn't get you anywhere, he told himself. *Focus on the task at hand.* "Did you get a look at him?"

"No. He escaped through the back door of a warehouse."

"Mine was a sailor, I think. He sure knew his way around a ship."

Lenoir nodded, as if he was not surprised. "The shooter as well. He knew which warehouse was open, and how to escape through the back loading doors. Obviously a local."

"What do you suppose was going on?"

Lenoir shrugged. "No way of knowing. Yet more evidence of the breakdown of law and order, perhaps."

"Probably just some stupid row." The thought of having been thrown through a window, kicked in the head, and dropped off the side of a ship because of some squabble between a couple of drunken sea dogs made his temples throb even worse. Surreptitiously, he reached inside the pocket of his trousers, and was relieved to find the powder still there, tucked into a small leather pouch. The seawater would have turned it into a paste by now, but hopefully it would still work.

Lenoir, meanwhile, looked pensive. "Possibly, though the choice of weapon would suggest not. An argument between sailors, no matter how heated, does not generally result in firing a musket. A knife to the belly would be much more likely. Same goes for a robbery."

Kody grunted. The inspector had a point. *What, then?*

"It doesn't matter," Lenoir said into his thoughts. "We did our duty—or attempted to, at any rate—but we are here for another purpose."

"Yeah, about that . . ." Kody withdrew a tattered sheet of paper from his other pocket—what was left of the sketch. The saltwater had not been kind. Torn, smeared, and creased, the drawing no longer resembled anything human. Unless their suspect had been run over by a wagon recently, no one was going to recognize him. "Sorry, Inspector."

Lenoir sighed. "There is nothing to be done about it now. We will have to get another one done as soon as we can. In the meantime, let us move on to the next name on our list. We might not have a likeness, but at least we can ask about the plague in Darangosai. First, however, we should pay a brief visit to your flat." The wry look returned, stopping just short of a smile. "You are somewhat less intimidating sopping wet."

Watching from a safe distance, Ritter blew out a long, relieved breath as the hounds withdrew. *That was too close.* He couldn't be sure how much the hounds had got out of his shipmate at the *Duchess,* but hopefully he'd managed to interrupt them before they'd shown off their sketch. The gunshot had worked its magic, and Marty had done his job, leading them on a merry chase. Ritter hadn't counted on having to fire a second time to cover Marty's escape, and that had very nearly landed him in irons. Luckily, though, a man in his position knew the docks like he knew his own cabin.

The hounds would be back, he supposed, but at least he'd managed to buy himself some time. As for what to do with that time . . . He'd have to get word to Nash. The hounds were becoming more than a nuisance now.

Ritter pulled the letter out of his pocket, the one he'd planned for Marty to give to Nash. Scanning it, he found the sentence he was looking for: *I might need you to deal with the hounds soon.* Ritter took out his pencil and crossed out the word "might." Then he scrawled out a similar note to Sukhan: *Time to deal with Marty.* This one Ritter would deliver himself, by way of a knot in the wall of Warehouse 57, but there was no hurry. Sukhan wouldn't come looking for it until nightfall anyway. And then the last loose end would be tied off, and it would be free sailing.

Ritter jammed the notes back into his pocket and headed off down the pier, whistling.

CHAPTER 21

"Aw, don't look at me like that, little pup." Cracked knuckles pushed a cracked flagon across the table. "It's nothing personal."

Zach scowled. "Is that supposed to make me feel better?"

"A man takes comfort where he can," Bevin said, and took a swig. "You should try the ale. It's the best on the docks."

"It's the only ale on the docks, and I still don't call it the best." Zach hadn't even tried it, but he was feeling contrary.

Bevin, though, was in his usual lighthearted mood, and he greeted the remark with a gusty laugh. "I'll have to remember that one! You're a clever little cuss, and no mistake." He saluted Zach with his flagon.

Zach grabbed his, saluted back—wryly—and took a long draft. It tasted like rotten nuts, and he felt his face scrunch up in disgust. *Thought so.* But what else could you expect in a place like this? His gaze took in the cramped space, with its stained rushes, sooty hearth, and cobwebbed rafters. He'd thought the common room of the Port was shabby, but it was practically a palace compared with this part of the inn. He hadn't even known this back room existed, and from the looks of it, no one else did either. Zach wasn't exactly finicky, but when you could make a game of counting the spiders living in the cracks of your table, it was time for a bit of a sweep. *What would Sister Nellis say if she saw this place?* The nun kept her orphanage spotless, and she was forever clucking over Zach's supposedly untidy bunk. *An offense to the Lord,* she called it. If a few creases and crumbs were an offense to the Lord, this place must have been enough to call down the wrath of the Holy Host itself. Zach pictured Durian astride his glowing steed, golden sword raised to the heavens, eyes blazing with righteousness. *Tremble, ye spiders! God's General is coming for you!* He snickered into his flagon.

"You don't seem that worried." Bevin sounded half puzzled, half admiring. "Either you're very brave, or you don't really understand your situation."

Zach shrugged. "What's to understand? You're holding me captive; I guess so Hairy can have a go at me."

"Captive? Now that's a bit dramatic. I'm just asking you to spend a few hours here with me."

"And if I refuse?"

"Wouldn't do you much good."

"Sure sounds like captivity to me."

"Similar, I'll grant you." Bevin cocked his head. "But it doesn't seem to bother you none."

Zach almost rolled his eyes. Bevin had a ripe dockside accent, just like Zach, which meant he should know better. "I'm an orphan from the poor district," Zach reminded him, since it seemed he needed reminding. "If I had a copper for every time someone's kept me someplace I didn't want to be, I'd have a mansion in Primrose Park, wouldn't I?"

Bevin smirked. "Just because it's not the first time doesn't mean it won't go badly. For all you know, this could be the worst fix you've ever been in."

"No," Zach said solemnly, "it couldn't." The scar on his wrist seemed to tingle when he said that.

The big man grunted, considering Zach with a newly appraising look. "Be that as it may, you're wrong—I'm not keeping you for Hairy. Not exactly, anyway."

"Then what am I doing here?"

"Like I said, it's nothing personal. Just business." Bevin shifted on the bench so that his back was propped up against the wall. He stretched, grabbed his flagon, and said, "You're a commodity, lad. Do you know what a commodity is?"

"Something valuable."

"That's right. Something *tradable*."

Zach took a noisy sip of his ale to cover his confusion. He was an orphan. A street rat with nothing to his name except what he managed to nick every now and then. How could he possibly be tradable? "You're gonna sell me to Hairy, then?" It was all he could think of.

"Not quite." Bevin smiled like a clever cat and took a pull of his ale. "You flatter yourself. Hairy might be chipped at you, but not enough to part with good coin. Besides, our Hairy is perpetually broke, isn't he? How's he gonna buy you? No, he's got to have a real incentive, enough to make him raise the coin he needs to pay."

Incentive. Zach didn't follow.

"Think about it." Bevin gave him an encouraging nod. "What happens when you've been sitting back here with me long enough?"

So, Bevin liked the same sort of guessing games as Lenoir. He wanted Zach to figure it out on his own. What was it with adults leaving little trails of grain for him to follow, as if he were a chicken being led to the coop? Why couldn't anyone just give a straight answer? "I don't know," Zach said sullenly.

Bevin clucked his tongue. "I'm disappointed in you, little pup. Here I thought you were *so clever*."

That stung. Zach knew he was being goaded, but he couldn't resist. "The hounds will come looking for me." He could hear the pride in his voice, and the threat.

Bevin heard it too, but it didn't have quite the effect Zach expected. The big man grinned, just as he had done back at the warehouse when Zach had mentioned the hounds. "Exactly."

"You *want* the hounds to come looking for me?" Zach was baffled. "But when they find you, you'll spend the rest of your life in jail. Have you ever been to Fort Hald?" Zach had, briefly, before Lenoir fetched him out. He still had nightmares about it. It was his visit to Fort Hald that had convinced Zach he needed to have *plans*. Street kids without plans ended up dead, or locked away in an iron dungeon full of crazies and hard-muscled men who looked at you like they thought you might make a decent meal.

"It'll take them a while to find you," Bevin said, waving vaguely at the filthy little den they were in. "Not too many people know about this place, and anyway, I doubt your inspector would bother to check the Port. It would be bloody stupid for Hairy to stash you in the one place they know he hangs around, now wouldn't it?"

"Hairy?" Zach was even more baffled now. "What's he got to do with it? You're the one stashed me here."

Bevin's smile widened. "Ah, but your inspector doesn't know that, does he? All he knows is that Hairy wanted to wring your neck. When he can't find you, who's the first person he's gonna suspect?"

At last, Zach understood—sort of. "You're trying to get Hairy in trouble."

Bevin's only response was a hitch of his flagon and a long, greedy pull.

"But why? I thought he was your friend."

Bevin belched. "Sure he is, but like I told you, this is business. Our Hairy owes me fifty crowns."

"Fifty crowns?" Zach wouldn't have guessed a bloke like Bevin came across fifty crowns in his whole life.

"Lot of money, isn't it? More fool me for letting him get in that far over his head. What can I say?" Bevin shrugged. "I like my cards, and so does Hairy. Only unlike our Hairy, I know how to play the game."

"But how is keeping me here gonna help? Nobody's gonna pay fifty crowns for me."

"Sadly, no." Bevin swiped the back of his hand across his mouth and swirled his flagon, gauging how much he had left. "But they might pay ten, and ten is better than none. I've been waiting years for Hairy to pay me back, but he just gets in deeper and deeper. Like I said, he needs an incentive. A little encouragement to take his responsibilities more seriously."

Zach reckoned he was the incentive, but he couldn't quite work out how. "So you figure if Inspector Lenoir comes after Hairy, looking for me, Hairy will . . . what?"

Bevin gestured at the walls. "Even Hairy doesn't know about this place. Old Molly keeps that information tight. I can keep you back here as long as I want and no one will know."

"I could scream."

"You could, but you'd regret it."

Zach scowled, but he knew Bevin was right. Screaming would be pointless—and painful.

"If Hairy knows you're missing, he'll know the hounds are coming for him. He'll panic. I *have* been to Fort Hald, you see, and so has Hairy. He won't want to go back. If he pays me, he won't have to."

Aha. Bevin was holding Zach ransom, only instead of collecting the ransom from Lenoir—which would never work—he was getting it from Hairy. The hounds would blame Hairy for Zach's disappearance. They'd come looking for him, and unless he paid Bevin off, he'd be in trouble. *There's a word for that,* Zach thought. Lenoir had used it more than once in his hearing. It was called . . .

"Extortion."

"A clever cuss," Bevin said, draining his flagon, "and no mistake."

"Won't that make things kind of awkward between you two?" Zach asked dryly.

"Things are already awkward. Cutting down his debt to me can only improve the situation." Zach couldn't tell if Bevin was being sarcastic, but it seemed pretty clear that he didn't care if Hairy was mad at him or not. Ten crowns were obviously worth more to him than a friend. "It's a tough world," Bevin said, almost apologetically. "Besides, Hairy doesn't need to know that I'm the one who took you. I'll just let on that I might, just might, know where you're to be found, and if he makes it worth my while . . ." Bevin shrugged. "He'll still be chipped, but it won't look as if I'm the one who set him up. He'll just think I'm taking advantage of the situation."

"Still seems like a lot of trouble to go to. I mean, why not just bust him up a bit?" It was common enough; Zach had seen it done a dozen times.

"Call me sentimental, but I just don't fancy getting rough with him. This way is easier on both of us."

"Unless he can't come up with the ten crowns. A broken arm is better than jail."

"That it is. But Hairy won't be going to jail—not on my account, at any rate."

"So you're bluffing."

Bevin grinned. "Hairy never could tell. Part of why he's so deep in debt."

"What if he can tell this time? What happens to me?"

"If Hairy won't pay, I got another buyer."

Zach's mouth dropped open. "*Another* buyer?" Durian's balls, how many enemies did he have?

"You remember our friend Augaud, don't you?"

Zach winced; he remembered the Lerian all too well.

Bevin smiled that clever cat smile again. "I might've let slip that I knew where to find you, if he fancied a little payback."

"Payback for what?" Zach folded his arms. "I didn't even take his stupid purse."

Bevin laughed. "Not for lack of trying."

"Still, what's he so sore about? Happens all the time, doesn't it? It's a tough world, like you said." Even Lenoir didn't hold Zach's stealing against him—most of the time, anyway. How else was a street orphan supposed to survive?

"Your mistake wasn't the stealing," Bevin said. "It's who you stole from. We sailors work hard for our coin. Life on the seas is bloody rough, and ship owners are stingy. We hoard every copper until we come back to port, when we spend it all in one glorious streak. Stealing from a sailor is foolish." Zach had just opened his mouth to point out that Augaud wasn't a sailor when Bevin added, "Stealing from a fur trader, though—that's *suicide*."

Zach clamped his mouth shut and squirmed in his seat. He remembered the look on the Lerian's face. And the knife at the Lerian's waist.

As though reading his thoughts, Bevin said, "A fur trader spends his life gutting creatures that can defend themselves a lot better than you, little pup." He mimed a jab and a twist, slashing his imaginary knife up the middle of whatever furry creature he was butchering in his head. "He slashes 'em open, spills out a steaming pile of guts, and then he takes their skin, and he saws it off, inch by inch. When he's done that, he scrapes off the little bits of meat—careful, meticulous, so he doesn't damage the fur. Then he stretches the pelt out like this, and he nails it up to let it dry." Bevin examined his fingernails. "Gets so much blood caked under there, he can't ever get it out. The smell of it never leaves his nose. But that doesn't bother him, not the fur trader. You ever seen a deer, lad?"

Swallowing, Zach shook his head.

Bevin closed his eyes wistfully. "Beautiful creature, that. Glossy coat. Big brown eyes. Dainty little hooves. Graceful as wind, they are." He opened his eyes, and they glinted with cruel amusement. "Fur trader will rip 'em open without a blink. Now you, little pup—I don't know when was the last time you saw yourself in a looking glass, but you got more of the rat than the deer. What do you think your life means to a fur trader?"

He's just trying to scare you, Zach told himself. Trouble was, it was working. "It was just a stupid money purse." The protest sounded meek and ridiculous, even to him.

"A man like Augaud spends four days out of five out in the woods, living rough, with not a soul to keep him company. He catches what he can, sells it for what he can get. He only makes it into town a few times a year, and when he does, he wants to spend his earnings on a bit of fun. Every coin in that purse represents a day of killing and a night spent shivering under the stars. And you want to steal from *him*?" Bevin shook his head. "Suicide."

Zach could picture it all so vividly: Augaud squatting over a campfire, meat roasting on a spit. A bunch of carcasses strung up in the trees, pelts nailed to tree trunks. Zach had always been a little afraid of the woods, even the ones in the park, but Augaud wouldn't be afraid. If anything so much as rustled a bush, the Lerian would whip around, knife glinting in the firelight, and slash its throat. Zach could almost feel the blood rushing hot over his hands. "You're gonna sell me to a man like that?"

"Not unless he outbids Hairy."

Zach took a long, slow drink of his ale so Bevin couldn't see his lip tremble.

Bevin must have seen it anyway, though, because he laughed. "Relax, little pup. I'm just winding you up."

Zach straightened a little. "So . . . you're not gonna sell me to Augaud?"

"Not unless he offered so much that I just couldn't refuse, but the odds are stacked in your favor. Hairy's got more incentive than the Lerian. Chances are he'll bid the highest. Fear is a much stronger motivator than anger."

Fury bloomed, warm and stinging, in Zach's cheeks. "Greed is a pretty strong motivator too."

"Like I said, lad." Bevin shrugged. "It's a tough world."

So much for *plans*.

"So that's it, then," Kody said, watching as the sun sank over the horizon, dissolving into a bloody haze of smog. "The day's gone." One would have thought he was scheduled to die at dusk, so despondent did he look.

"There is always tomorrow," Lenoir said, hoping he sounded more resolute than he felt. Ash pricked at his nose and stung his eyes, the fumes of a thousand fires as people all over Kennian tried to drive the plague out with smoke and superstition. A few miles away, in the heart of the Camp, Merden treated the sick—or at least attempted to—while Sergeant Innes and a pair of watchmen stood guard against a murderer. Constable Crears would be reinforcing the barrier for the night, with or without the extra watchmen Chief Reck had promised him. Meanwhile, in the poor district, shopkeepers and frightened residents huddled behind locked doors and boarded windows, waiting for packs of criminals to roam like wild dogs through the unprotected streets.

Death's banquet has three courses, the poet Irdois wrote. *First the flesh, then the marrow, and last of all the heart.* He had been writing about the revolution, how it sapped the courage and eventually the humanity of an entire nation. But he might just as easily have meant the plague. The occasion might be different, but the banquet was the same.

"I just wish I didn't feel so damned powerless," Kody said, massaging his temples with gloved fingers. They were dress gloves, Lenoir noticed, high-quality, made of soft kid leather. Expensive. He had never seen Kody wear them before. Most likely, the sergeant reserved them for special occasions. It surprised him that Kody would wear them for work like this, down at the docks. The pair he had been wearing earlier had got soaked when he tumbled into the bay, but why take the trouble to replace them, to find a handkerchief to replace the scarf? There was no plague at the docks, at least not so far as anyone knew.

Lenoir paused.

"Headache?" he asked, as neutrally as he was able.

"A bit, yeah." Kody had paused too, before he answered, a silence as swift and shattering as a lead ball.

Lenoir's breath quickened. "If you are feeling ill, Sergeant, you should report to Merden immediately. We cannot take any chances."

Kody met his gaze, and there was something in his hazel eyes that made Lenoir go cold. "Sergeant . . ."

Kody swallowed, looked away. "I was going to tell you," he said quietly. "As soon as we were through here. Now, I guess."

"Tell me what?"

Kody said nothing.

All the little pieces started to fall now, remembered images drifting through Lenoir's mind like the ragged bits of a torn painting. Kody sweating. Kody rubbing his temples. Kody in a foul mood, brooding and snapping . . .

"Are you . . . Sergeant, do you have . . . ?" Only a tremendous act of will prevented Lenoir from taking a step backward.

"Seems like." The reply was barely audible.

"Are you certain?"

Kody hitched a shoulder. He gazed out over the bay. "Merden thinks so."

"You've spoken to Merden about this?"

"Last night. I started feeling pretty bad about this time yesterday, so I thought I should check in . . ." Kody's voice had gone dull, as though he had spent every ounce of emotion he had.

Lenoir's blood roared in his ears. *He has it. Plague. Kody has plague.* It did not seem real, no matter how many times he repeated it in his head. "Why didn't you tell me?" He should be furious. He *was* furious. Kody had put him at risk. Had put the public at risk. But another concern took precedence, and before Kody could answer, Lenoir asked a different question. "Did he give you the tonic?"

Kody nodded. "I've been taking it, and some other stuff, every hour, or at least as often as I could without you seeing. Doesn't work, though. Merden says I need the other treatment. Today. Without it . . . Well, you know."

The words battered Lenoir like hailstones, swift and hard, leaving an icy feeling sliding down his spine. He could not believe it. That it should be *Kody*, of all people. He would have thought he was long past being disappointed by the injustice of the world. Not so, apparently. He could taste the outrage at the back of his throat, bitter as bile.

"I was supposed to go back this afternoon," Kody went on, "but then the shooting . . . I broke my promise. He'll have told Crears by now." He shrugged. "Doesn't matter, I guess."

Lenoir took a breath to compose himself. He could not afford to give in to fear or fury, not yet. The sergeant deserved better than that. "We must go," he said. "Immediately."

Kody held up a hand. "Thanks, Inspector, but you don't need to come along. You've got things to do. Besides, I don't think I even believe in . . ." Kody trailed off, his gaze going somewhere over Lenoir's shoulder. He frowned into the distance. "Look at that."

"Whatever it is, it can wait!" Lenoir snapped. "We need to get you to the Camp *now*."

"I know, it's just . . . Awful lot of smoke over there."

Lenoir glanced instinctively over his shoulder. "Never mind that, it is not our . . ." Now it was his turn to trail off, momentarily distracted by the magnitude of what he was looking at. In the midst of the general haze, a dark cloud swelled like an angry thunderhead. It was difficult to be sure, but he thought it was coming from near the market square. It was most certainly *not* coming from a chimney. "That one is out of control," he admitted.

"A whole building, by the looks of it."

Even as they watched, the cloud continued to grow, thick and malevolent. *A bad one,* Lenoir thought. A strange glow appeared over the rooftops, as if the buildings themselves were made of coal.

"It's really going," Kody said, his frown deepening. "I wonder if anyone— *Shit!*" A tongue of flame leapt into the sky, as brief and fierce as a flash of lightning. "I think we'd better check it out, Inspector."

Lenoir almost laughed out loud. "Have you lost your mind? You have other matters to attend to."

"Yeah, but look at that. It's bad. There are hardly any hounds in the city. They're gonna need our help."

"Then I'll go. You head to the Camp immediately."

"Just as soon as this is done. I'm not feeling too bad. You saw how I chased that bloke down on the pier. I can help."

"You *can*, but that does not mean you *should*."

"Why shouldn't I? It's my job. If I wasn't ready to die for it, I wouldn't be here."

Lenoir could not believe what he was hearing. Commitment to one's duty was well and good, but this . . . "This is not heroism, Kody. This is foolishness."

"I'm not trying to be a hero. I'm trying to be a hound."

"*Go.* That is an order, Sergeant."

Another flash of lightning, and this one came with thunder, of a sort—a distant *boom* sounded, as of something collapsing. The smoke rose higher, tumbling over itself. A glow like the inside of a forge soaked the sky.

Kody's eyes were pleading. "You know I'm right. You know it, Inspector."

Lenoir swore viciously. "Very well," he started to say, but Kody was already moving.

CHAPTER 22

They pounded up the boardwalk for the second time that day, but this time, there was no criminal to catch, no weapon to hand that would be any help. Technically, this was an affair for fire brigades and watchmen. But with most of the Metropolitan Police force manning the barricades, watchmen would be few and far between. Every pair of hands was needed. Even Kody's.

After a few blocks, they could hear the bells, shrill and urgent. Lenoir hoped he was right about it coming from the market district. At least then, some of the shops would be insured, and therefore protected by a fire brigade. Judging by what they had seen from the docks, however, the fire was already beyond the help of buckets and hoses. It must have started hours ago, while Lenoir and Kody were busy chasing the phantom shooter. *They will be at the fire hooks already,* he thought. He wondered how many buildings would have to be pulled down.

The closer they drew, the more difficult the going became. Streets that had been deserted a few hours before were now full to bursting. Fear of the plague could not possibly compete with something as titillating as the drama unfolding in the market district, and gawkers and gossips choked the narrow alleys. People stretched out of open windows like snails reaching from their shells, calling out to one another as they described the scene, real or imagined, in the distance. Lenoir and Kody jostled their way through the press, shoving and swearing and issuing the occasional threat. As if that were not bad enough, the way soon grew even more clogged as people fleeing the fire began to trickle out of the market district, only to become tangled up in the flotsam and jetsam of onlookers. Lenoir tried to imagine how a fire engine, even the hand-pulled kind, would negotiate its way through. *They will not,* he concluded. If they had not already arrived on the scene, they would never do so now.

"There." Kody pointed, and they banked west. Or at least they tried to; a small wagon stood in their way, the horse stamping and muttering agitatedly as its owner loaded up his belongings.

"Get this thing out of the road," Lenoir snapped. "The way must remain clear!"

The man barely glanced at him. "I'm almost finished. I'll not have everything I own burned to ash. I have six children to feed."

"The fire is blocks away," Lenoir said.

"You feel that wind? It'll be headed this way soon enough."

Kody grabbed the horse's bridle. "You heard the inspector. Move this cart now, or I'll move it myself." He gave no hint of illness now. His bearing was as straight and strong as always. It was as if the wind had filled his sails once again, however temporarily.

The man glared at Kody, but he did not dare to argue. Instead, he called up to an open window, and moments later, his family appeared. He loaded them into the wagon and trundled off down the alley.

"He's right, you know," Kody said. "The wind is going to blow the fire this way."

"All the more reason why the roads need to remain clear for the fire brigades."

A distant *roar* filled the air, as if a giant bellows had been stoked. Smoke rolled over the rooftops.

"Something just took light," Lenoir said. "Highly combustible, by the looks of it. A glazier, perhaps." There were several in the market district, including Willard's, a boutique famous throughout Humenor for its elegant glass chandeliers. Technically, glaziers were illegal within the city walls, along with foundries, smithies, and other businesses that stocked flammable materials. In practice, however, they were tolerated—an indulgence the city of Kennian might rue after today.

A few more twists and turns and they came upon it at last, a scene that would stay with Lenoir for the rest of his days. A towering inferno engulfed the entire row of buildings on one side of the street. The heat of it stung his cheeks, and an unpleasantly warm breeze ruffled his hair. For a moment, he could only stare, transfixed by the sheer enormity of it. It was as if he looked upon the below itself, at the flaming prisons every God-fearing man was taught to dread. Only instead of the souls of the damned, these flaming prisons trapped living souls. Lenoir could see at least three groups of them, perhaps eight people in all. They leaned out of windows, waved frantically from above parapets. *Where are the ladders?* It was a desperate, irrational thought. Lenoir could tell at a glance that most of the buildings were too far gone. Leaning a wooden ladder against them would simply be adding another log to the fire.

"Holy Durian's ghost," Kody breathed. "Where do we even start?"

The fire brigade seemed to be equally at a loss. A fire engine mounted on a skid pumped a feeble stream of water, but the tank was too small, the hose too short, to do much good. A pair of watchmen presided over a bucket line, but this too was an exercise in futility. The heat prevented them from getting too close; most of the time, the water did not even reach the flames. When it did, it hissed out of existence as though it had never been. Meanwhile, firemen scrambled around with ladders and blankets, trying to find a way to get to the people trapped inside. *They are already lost,* Lenoir thought grimly. Most likely the firemen knew it too, but they had no choice but to try. Lenoir squeezed his eyes shut in a vain attempt to banish the sting of smoke and despair.

Flames leapt into the sky, reaching precariously close to the jetties leaning out on the far side of the street. It was only a matter of time before the fire leapt the gap. Already, the lower floors of a building on the eastern side of the street had taken light, probably ignited by debris from the explosion that had blown out the windows on the ground floor of the building opposite. A great gaping maw fringed with broken glass was all that was left of the storefront, but Lenoir recognized it all the same. He had been right about the glazier: it was Willard's after all. *What a shame,* some distant, detached part of him thought. *It was the only true art in the city. . . .*

"Should we join the bucket line?" Kody's voice brought Lenoir back to the here and now.

"No point. It is a lost cause." In fact, it was worse than that; it was a waste of manpower. *As good a place to start as any.* Lenoir headed over. "You men—forget those buckets and concentrate on clearing the area!"

It took a moment for the watchmen commanding the line to realize who he was, but even when they did, they did not exactly rush to follow his orders. "The fire brigade told us to keep at it," one of them said.

"Are you blind, or merely a fool?" Lenoir pointed at the merciless wall of flames. "You have not made a dent in that fire, nor will you. It is too late for that."

"He's right," Kody said. "These buildings are lost. All we can do now is try to prevent it from spreading." As he spoke, a galaxy of glowing embers swirled above the burning buildings, threatening to blow onto the rooftops opposite.

"What do you want us to do?" the other watchman asked.

"Round up these men and start evacuating the adjacent blocks. Divide them into teams to cover as much ground as possible. Go, now!"

The bucket line began to break up—agonizingly slowly. Most of the men had been out of earshot of the exchange; they were confused about the sudden change of plans. Nor were they the only ones.

"Hey!" Lenoir turned and found himself nose to nose with a meaty fellow with close-cropped hair. "Just what in the below do you think you're doing!" He wore the livery of the fire brigade, and had some sort of badge pinned to his chest, proclaiming him chief of the Whitmarch Firefighters.

"Deploying your resources in a logical fashion," Lenoir said. "The buckets are a waste of effort."

"Who do you think you are?"

"I am Inspector Lenoir of the Metropolitan Police."

"I don't care if you're the sodding King of Braeland! I'm in charge here, and I say where and how my men are deployed!"

The watchmen were officers of the Metropolitan Police, and Lenoir had every right to give them orders—but it would do no good to say so. He needed this man's cooperation if he was going to achieve anything. "I apologize," he said. "But surely you must agree that it is too late for buckets. Our only course now is to begin making firebreaks."

The man scowled, and for a moment Lenoir feared he was one of those officials with more pride than sense. Then he said, "I've already sent my men for gunpowder. In the meantime, all we have is fire hooks."

"Then why are you not using them?"

"We are, on the other side of the block, where it meets Kingsway. But we don't dare start pulling things down here. The streets are too narrow—we'd just end up burying ourselves in rubble."

He is right. Lenoir swore under his breath and rubbed his jaw. "How long will it take for the gunpowder to get here?"

"Not too long. Our warehouse is down at the docks."

"The docks?" Kody echoed in dismay. "But aren't you from Whitmarch?"

"It's illegal to store gunpowder anywhere but the docks. Thought a police officer would know that. Anyway, it's not that far away."

"Farther than you think," Kody said. "The streets are jammed with people."

"And the more the fire spreads, the more wagons and handcarts there will be," Lenoir added.

The fireman shook his head in disgust. "Dammit, if people came to lend a hand instead of fleeing like a bunch of rats from a sinking ship . . ."

Lenoir was only half listening, distracted by a sudden scramble along the facade of one of the burning buildings. The firemen had finally found a place to lean their ladder, and were hustling a woman and her two children out of a window. *Thank God for that.* As for the other trapped souls, he could no longer see any sign. Either they had found a way out, or they had already perished.

Lenoir started to ask whether the rest of the block had been evacuated when he noticed a new tendril of smoke—on the wrong side of the street. "Look there."

Kody and the fireman followed his gaze, and they both swore. "There goes another block," the fireman said. "Damn this wind!"

"Can't you turn your hose on it?" Kody asked. "It would do more good up there than down here."

"Not enough water pressure. Can't get past the second floor."

"Buckets?"

"Not without more manpower. *Goddamn it!*" The fireman stormed off—to what purpose, Lenoir could not imagine.

"It's heading east," Kody said. "And we're not far from the poor district . . ."

At least in the market district, most of the buildings were made of stone and brick. Many had illegally built wooden jetties on top as a way of stealing an extra few feet of space, but at least the skeletons of the buildings could withstand the flames. The poor district, with its cramped jumble of wood and thatch, was little more than a pile of kindling. And beyond that lay the docks. Hemp and timber, tar and pitch, whale and linseed oil—a hundred substances just yearning to be set aflame, to burn hotter than the flaming pits of the below. *And then there is the gunpowder . . . enough for the entire royal navy.* "The fire must not reach the docks," Lenoir said. "If it does, this city will burn to the ground."

"All right, what do we do?" Kody asked. A sheen of sweat had broken out on his brow, soaking the hair at his temples into gentle curls. It was more than the heat of the fire.

He is getting worse, Lenoir thought grimly. The exertion was costing him. And if he was showing it, he was suffering it tenfold, for Lenoir had learned by now that Bran Kody was very good at concealing discomfort. He started to say something, then thought better of it. The decision had been made. There was no going back on it now.

"We need to clear the streets," he said, "and evacuate a wider perimeter."

"But how do we do both? If we evacuate, the streets will be even more clogged. The gunpowder will never get through, and then we won't be able to blast out firebreaks . . ."

Lenoir squeezed his eyes shut and tried to concentrate, to block out every thought that did not belong—of Kody, of plague, of regrets and rash decisions.

Think, Lenoir. Think!

He mapped out the area in his head, just as he had

done that day in Evenside, when he had been chasing down the art thief. The memory gave him an idea. "We will route them toward Kingsway," he said. "The avenue is wide enough to accommodate plenty of traffic. We will keep Aldwich and Baker's Lane free."

"What about the people who live on those streets? How are they supposed to get to Kingsway?"

"They go up."

For a moment, Kody looked blank. Then his eyebrows flew up. "On the rooftops? Is that safe?"

"The buildings along both of those streets are shoulder to shoulder and all of a level." That was why Lenoir had chosen them. "The evacuees need only to reach the adjacent building on the Kingsway side and climb down. Even a child can do it."

"They won't be able to bring their belongings."

"No, they will not, but it is better that than dying."

Kody was nodding now, his gaze abstracted. "And those who won't evacuate?"

"May God protect them, because we cannot. We don't have the manpower to force them."

"We don't have the manpower to do any of it, not yet. We'll need to get every man in that bucket line to recruit five more."

"Then we had better get started, Sergeant. Press-gang them if you have to. You have a badge and a pistol—do not hesitate to use them." He paused. "And Kody—"

But the sergeant was already gone, jogging over to the two watchmen organizing the former bucket line. "You two! New instructions . . ."

Lenoir found the chief of the Whitmarch brigade near his fire engine, waving his arms and shouting ineffectually about water pressure. *He has no idea what to do with himself,* Lenoir thought. He had seen it before. Fortunately, he could offer a solution. "You will never put it out," he said, "but we can use what manpower we have to clear Aldwich and Baker's Lane to make way for the gunpowder."

"Aldwich and Baker?" The man's brow stitched up in confusion. "Why them?"

Deep breaths, Lenoir. "It does not matter," he said through gritted teeth. "The point is, if we can block them off, the wagons will be able to get through. Post your men at the intersections. Have them tell anyone they see that the fire is only just behind them."

"But that isn't true."

Lenoir's hands balled into fists at his sides. It was all he could do not to grab the man and shake him until his teeth rattled. "No, it is not true. But if we simply ask nicely, the evacuees will go where they please, and one man at an intersection will not be able to stop them. If, on the other hand, a member of the fire brigade says that the street behind him leads into a blazing inferno, they will believe it."

"I suppose." The fireman grabbed a pack off the skid and produced a map of the old city. "So you want us here, and here . . ."

Looking at the map, Lenoir felt a stab of desperation. *So crowded. So narrow.* The flames would leap from rooftop to rooftop as easily as a sparrow flits between the branches of a tree. "We have no time to lose," he said. "Have you sent for the lord mayor?"

"Not yet."

"We must do so immediately. It will not be enough to bring down one or two buildings. We will have to demolish entire blocks of housing." For that, they would need the lord mayor's permission.

A great, tortured moan sounded from the western side of the street. "Look out!" someone cried. The horses harnessed to the fire engine whinnied and danced. Wood creaked, cracked, and finally collapsed in a roar as the innards of one of the buildings gave way. Windows blew out, and a hot wind rushed into the street. Lenoir threw an arm over his face.

"Time to move," the fireman said, grabbing Lenoir's arm.

He pulled away. "Give me a horse. I will ride ahead and find the gunpowder. Send the other horse with a message to the lord mayor."

The fireman did not look happy about leaving his fire engine behind, but it was useless anyway. Lenoir unharnessed one of the horses and slung himself gracelessly onto its back. "Remember, Aldwich and Baker's Lane must remain free."

"I'll take care of it. Just get us that gunpowder, Inspector, or nothing we do will be worth a good Goddamn."

Lenoir pointed his horse south and put his heels into it.

CHAPTER 23

Lenoir clattered down the cobbled street, moving at a canter until he reached the intersection, where he found his way blocked by a crowd of onlookers. He drew his mount up short. "Move aside! This area must be evacuated!" A few of the gawkers glanced at him, but most paid him no heed at all. Lenoir drew his pistol, tightened his hold on his horse, and fired into the air. *"Move now!"*

The startled crowd parted for him. As he rode through, Lenoir glanced over his shoulder and saw Kody and his press-gang making their way up the street. *Good.* The sergeant would have his work cut out for him, but Kody was a big man, and not shy about using that to his advantage. He would get the job done.

Lenoir steered his horse through the winding alleys until he found Kingsway. The largest thoroughfare south of the city walls, it cut a wide path through the heart of the old city, dividing Morningside from Evenside, from the Tower all the way to Kingsgate. Lenoir had thought to find the way relatively clear, but word of the fire's progress had obviously got out, for a steady stream of traffic flowed southeast, away from the market square. Horses and handcarts, wagons and sleds, Kennians had loaded up whatever they could find in their haste to flee. They would have to turn off Kingsway eventually, heading south to Tower Gate, or looping back around to Castlegate. For now, they formed a river of humanity, and Lenoir had to slow his horse to a trot to get through.

It was full dark by the time he reached the poor district, and still there was no sign of wagons bearing gunpowder. Lenoir veered east toward the docks. *I should have found them by now. Could I have missed them?* But no—he had taken the most direct route, and surely they would have done the same. Lenoir paused and looked over his shoulder. To the west, the horizon had an ugly red glow, though it was long past sunset. The wind blew into his face, carrying smoke and ash and giving wings to glowing flecks of debris. In the dark, it was easy to spot the places where new fires had sprung up. Lenoir counted three of them, one of which was not so very far from where he stood now. He closed his eyes, listening in vain for the sound of a demolition, as if he could will it into being.

Even this far away, the streets were filled with people. Lenoir moved upstream against the tide, guiding his horse at a walk. Most traffic was headed for the Tower Gate. They would take the Bay Bridge across the Sherrin, but then what? They would find themselves stranded in the marshlands, for the hounds would prevent them from heading farther west, toward the Camp. *Trapped between the hammer and the anvil,* Lenoir thought.

He passed the Firkin, Zach's favorite haunt. He hoped the boy was making his way to the Tower Gate along with everyone else. The last time Lenoir had seen him was at the docks, but that had become the most dangerous place in Kennian. *Zach is clever,* he told himself. *He won't allow himself to become trapped.* He needed to believe that, for there was nothing he could do to help the boy. He would never find Zach amid this river of humanity.

He had nearly reached the docks when he found what

he was looking for—after a fashion. A wagon emblazoned with the emblem of the Whitmarch Firefighters stood in the middle of the street, unmoving. And empty.

Lenoir rode up to it. "Who belongs to this wagon!"

"I do." A man in the livery of the fire brigade appeared beside Lenoir's horse. "Who wants to know?"

"Metropolitan Police. Where is the gunpowder?"

"Gone."

The air seemed to leave Lenoir's body. He stared, uncomprehending. "What do you mean, *gone*?"

"I mean gone. Bloody well *stolen*." The man gestured angrily at the street. "Gang of thugs was waiting for us, like they knew we was coming. I suppose they did, what with the fire setting half the market district aglow. Set upon us with swords and rifles. Took as much of it as they could carry in one wagon."

"One wagon." A timid little pang of hope lit up Lenoir's breast. "How many wagons were there?"

"Three."

"So one of them got away?"

"Yep. Took the long way, just in case there was more thieves waiting on Kingsway. He should be there soon, if he didn't have more trouble on the way. You never know, what with the streets being completely wild these days." The man glared up at Lenoir. "Not a hound in sight, least not when you need one. This city is paying something dear, and no mistake."

Lenoir could not deny it. "Which way did they go? The other wagon?"

The man pointed, and Lenoir took off at a trot.

It took him twice as long to retrace his steps, and by the time he had covered half the distance, he could tell something was wrong. Kingsway had become all but impassable. The smaller tributaries branching off were nearly as bad, with traffic at a virtual standstill. Refugees milled around in confusion, babies crying and goats bleating, trying in vain to find a way through. Overhead, a haze of smoke blotted out the stars. Lenoir abandoned Kingsway and continued to fight his way north.

He found the wagon at Orlister Plaza, adrift like a raft on a motionless sea. The driver was on his feet, his expression desperate as he sought a way through. It looked like he was trying to get to Smithrow.

"You there!" Lenoir fought his way close enough to shout. "This way! Baker's Lane is blocked off. You will be able to get through there!"

The driver shook his head; even at this distance, he could not hear above the babble of the crowd.

Lenoir tried again. "Baker's Lane! You will be able to get through!"

The man looked half hopeful, half suspicious. "Says who?"

Lenoir grabbed his badge and held it high. The man squinted, then sagged in relief. "Baker's?"

Lenoir pointed again, impatiently, and the driver nodded. He sat down and tugged at the reins. The draft horses shuffled about, but they had nowhere to go. Meanwhile, someone had climbed up onto the back of the wagon to get a better view. The driver tried to wave him off, but the man paid no heed, craning his neck as he peered above the rooftops. And now he was clambering up onto the barrels of gunpowder. . . .

Swearing, Lenoir grabbed his flintlock and fired into the air. "Metropolitan Police! You, get down from there! Clear a path for that wagon, *now*!"

With the right encouragement, the crowd managed to find enough space to let the wagon pass through. Lenoir rode in front, brandishing his pistol as though he might fire again, even though both barrels were now spent. So unencumbered, it took them less than five minutes to reach the roadblock at Baker's Lane. A pair of firemen barred the intersection. They were from a different brigade, Lenoir noted. That was well—the more manpower they could muster, the better. "We have gunpowder here," Lenoir said, "for the firebreaks. Let us through."

The firemen looked the wagon over. "You with the Whitmarch brigade, then?" one of them asked Lenoir.

"Metropolitan Police."

"Oh yeah?" The fireman looked relieved. "Listen, can you help us get some of these folk into a bucket line? We've been trying to round up volunteers, but nobody is willing. . . ."

Lenoir scowled. "Nor do I blame them. We have already determined that there is no further use in it. That is what the gunpowder is for."

The firemen exchanged a look. "That's not the orders we got."

"What orders? From whom?" A cold trickle of dread slithered down the back of Lenoir's neck.

"From our chief, but he had 'em from the lord mayor himself. All hands on deck, that's what we were told. That's why they closed the gates."

Lenoir jerked on his horse's reins so sharply that the animal backed up a little, nickering in protest. "What did you say?"

The fireman hooked his thumb over his shoulder in the vague direction of Kingsgate. "His Lordship ordered the city gates closed, so as to encourage people to help fight the fire."

Durian's ghost.

Lenoir felt sick. He had known Hearstings was a fool, but this . . . this was madness. He scanned the sea of people around him. *Trapped like rats inside twenty-foot stone walls.*

"Where is he?" *God as my witness, I will shoot him myself.*

His thoughts must have burned in his eyes, because the fireman actually shrank from him a little. "Not sure. Think he might have left already."

"Who is in command?"

"Chief of Police."

"Where?"

"Up there." The fireman pointed. "Addley, just outside the church."

Lenoir called over his shoulder to the wagon driver. "You will be fine from here. Hurry!" So saying, he blasted through the roadblock and headed for Addley.

He found Lendon Reck outside the church, poring over a map with a group of firemen. They wore at least four different liveries, representing brigades from all over the city. Reck barely glanced up when Lenoir approached, sparing only a fleeting look of surprise before continuing with his conference. Lenoir waited until they had finished, for he knew Reck would not tolerate any interruption.

"What are you doing here?" As usual, the chief did not trouble with niceties.

"Kody and I were in the area. Have you not seen him?"

"No."

"He cannot be far. I had him press-gang anyone he could find into helping with evacuations." Lenoir did not dare mention Kody's illness, not now. That would come later.

"Was that you who ordered Aldwich and Baker's Lane blocked off?" the chief asked.

"Yes."

"That was good thinking. It allowed us to get some gunpowder through, and I hear there's more on the way."

Lenoir nodded. "Only just down the road. The wagon should be here any minute."

"Good. Now if you'll excuse me, I've got a church to blow up."

"What, this church?"

"The very same. I'd be worried about my immortal soul, but I'm pretty sure I'll be fighting on the side of the Dark Flame anyway, when the time comes."

You and me both, Chief. "Has the fire spread so far already?"

"At this rate, everything inside the walls will be burnt to ashes by prayer day."

The walls. Lenoir felt the rage boil up inside him again. "Did you know Hearstings has ordered the gates closed?"

The chief had started to walk away, but Lenoir's words drew him up short. *"What?"*

"Some firemen just told me. It would appear His Lordship did not see fit to consult you." *Or even to inform you.*

Reck cursed expansively. "First the quarantine and now this! I ought to hang that piece of shit up by his—"

"Castlegate is closest, and the fields around Castle Warrick are a perfect place to shelter. I will try to get them to open it. Do I have your authority?"

"Much good may it do you. If the guards have got their orders from the lord mayor, there's nothing I can say will sway them."

"That is not what I meant, Chief." Lenoir rested his hand against the butt of his pistol. "Do I have your authority?"

Reck's eyes met Lenoir's. His mouth pressed into a hard line.

"If those gates do not open . . ." Lenoir did not need to finish. The riot in the Camp would still be fresh in the chief's mind, as it was in his own. *If the fire does not get them, the panic will. Scores will die at the gates.*

All around them, bells clamored and men shouted. Beneath that, the distant roar of flames, punctuated by the occasional crash of timber giving way. Yet in that moment, as Lenoir and the chief stared at each other, there was only silence.

He saw it the moment Reck decided. The chief's shoulders sagged, and he seemed to age before Lenoir's very eyes. "Would you really do it?"

"I don't know." He said it so softly, he doubted Reck even heard.

The chief looked away. "Blowing up churches and pulling guns on city guards. Aren't we a pair. Destined for the Dark Brigades and no mistake." He shook his head. "Go. Do whatever it takes to get those gates open. But remember, Lenoir, those men are just doing their jobs."

"I know. But, Chief . . . let me have your gun. Mine is spent, and there is no time. . . ."

Reck sighed and handed over his own flintlock. "God help us both." It sounded more like a verdict than a prayer.

Lenoir pointed his horse toward Castlegate.

If it had not been for the roadblocks, the journey would have taken hours. As it was, Lenoir had to argue his way through each checkpoint, glancing behind him every now and then at the angry glow staining the sky.

When he reached Castlegate, he saw that the guard had been doubled—to four. What had been a largely ceremonial position only hours before was suddenly all too real, and the four young men manning the gate looked equal parts determined and afraid. Lenoir could not blame them. Armed with muskets and swords, they were all that stood between thousands of terrified Kennians and the safety they sought. Worse, the gates had been designed to shut invaders out, not to keep city folk in, so the mechanism stood exposed, readily accessible to anyone brave or desperate enough to challenge the guards. *It's the Camp all over again,* Lenoir thought. It was only a matter of time until the blood flowed.

And you might be the one to start it.

Steeling himself, he edged his horse up to the gate and flashed his badge, letting the torchlight flame on its contours. "Inspector Lenoir of the Metropolitan Police."

The guards just stared at him, their muskets clutched

to their chests in white-knuckled grips. Behind them, the portcullis offered a tantalizing glimpse of freedom—or at least, of Meadowsmead.

"You must open these gates." Lenoir kept his tone as even as possible, wishing he did not have to shout. It would be better if the crowd could not hear him, but there was no avoiding it.

"Our orders are to keep them sealed," one of the guards replied. Raising his voice, he added, "For the good of the city!" Shouts and jeers answered from the crowd.

"The orders are a mistake," Lenoir said. "The bucket lines have been disbanded. It is too late to fight the fire."

"It's not too late," another guard said, scowling rebelliously through a patchy beard. *They are just boys,* Lenoir thought grimly. It did not make his task any easier.

"If people would just help, instead of running away, we could beat it," the first guard said.

"No, we could not." As if Providence itself had heard him, a distant *boom* sounded. "Do you hear that?" Lenoir gestured over his shoulder. "That is a controlled explosion. They are demolishing buildings in the market district. Our only hope now is to create firebreaks and let the fire burn itself out."

The guards only tightened up in front of the gate mechanism. "We have our orders from the lord mayor himself."

Lenoir sighed. *God and Durian forgive me.* He reached for Reck's gun.

"Ho there, guards!"

A trio of riders appeared on the far side of the portcullis, looking as though they wanted to get *in*. Distracted, Lenoir let his hand drop, leaning out from his horse to get a better view. Two of them seemed to be private guards of some sort, judging from their livery. As for the third, his face was instantly familiar, for it was forever engraved on Lenoir's memory.

The Duke of Warrick wore his customary scowl, the rugged angles of his features only sharpened by the torchlight. "Why is this gate closed?"

"Your Grace!" The guards bowed awkwardly, not daring to turn their backs on the crowd.

"Did you not hear my question?" Warrick did not raise his voice, but he did not need to; its flinty edge cut through the noise of the crowd well enough. The guards started to stammer out a reply, but at that moment, the duke noticed Lenoir. "You." His eyes narrowed sharply. "Lenoir, isn't it?"

"I am pleased you remember me, Your Grace." It was not false humility. Lenoir *was* pleased, for it meant he had succeeded in rattling the duke's cage. His Grace needed to know there was at least one man in the Five Villages who knew him for what he was.

"You are a difficult man to forget, Inspector," Warrick said with a wry twist of his mouth. "Still, I would not have expected to find you here."

"Nor I you, Your Grace."

Warrick waved a gloved hand in the direction of the market district. "I came to see the fire. From the castle, it looks as if half the city is aflame."

"And so it may be, if they do not make the firebreaks in time."

"They are demolishing already?"

"Already is half too late," Lenoir said.

"I see." Warrick squinted into the distance. "But that does not explain the gates."

"No sensible man can explain the gates," Lenoir said, making no effort to disguise his contempt.

Warrick arched an eyebrow. "You disapprove, I take it?"

On any other day, Lenoir would rather cut off his own arm than ask a favor of the Duke of Warrick. But with the city of Kennian burning behind him, and all these people trapped . . . "Your Grace, I beg you, order these gates opened."

Warrick regarded him detachedly. "By whose authority are they closed?"

"It was the lord mayor ordered it, Your Grace," one of the guards supplied, rather loudly.

"You would have me override his authority?" Warrick sounded faintly amused. "The Crown stepping on municipal territory . . . That is not lightly done, Inspector."

"I do not ask it lightly. Hearstings is a fool." At this point, Lenoir did not care who heard him. "He thinks closing the gates will earn him extra hands to fight the fire, but all it will do is condemn hundreds of people to death."

"Foolish indeed."

"A greater oaf has never held office."

His Grace let out a low, gravelly laugh. "Men of office are usually fools. You know it well, or I have mistaken you." He leaned in close to the portcullis. In the torchlight, his eyes seemed to take on a feverish gleam. "It is the fatal flaw of a system such as ours, Inspector. A man like Hearstings need not earn his position; he is born into it. Competence, when it arises, is merely a happy coincidence. But then, you are Arrènais. You hardly need me to tell you how backward this country is."

"Arrènes does not want for fools, Your Grace."

"Perhaps, but if Hearstings had to rely on the voices of these people"—he gestured at the crowd—"to keep his office, he might reflect on his decisions more carefully."

Lenoir snorted. How often had he heard such views expressed, and with what passion, before the revolution? The reality had proven infinitely less praiseworthy.

Warrick flashed a thin smile. "You think that such a flattering view of democracy cannot possibly come from a member of the aristocracy?"

"I think such a flattering view of democracy can only come from a man who has never lived in one. But that is a debate for another time, surely."

Warrick hardly seemed to hear him. He gazed over Lenoir's shoulder, into the red haze of the market district. "This city will learn its lesson," he murmured. "But not tonight. Not like this."

"Please, Your Grace," Lenoir said, "let these people out."

Warrick's gaze settled back on him. He considered Lenoir in silence, his thoughts carefully guarded behind those hard gray eyes. Then he swiveled his horse's head and withdrew beyond the reach of the torchlight. Lenoir slumped over his horse's neck, defeated.

The duke's voice reached back through the shadows. "Open the gates."

For a moment, Lenoir thought he had imagined it, for the guards just stood there, looking at one another. Then one of Warrick's retinue cried, "You heard His Grace! In the name of the king, open these gates!" The four young men scrambled to obey.

Lenoir permitted himself a moment just to *breathe*, inexpressible relief washing over him. Then he drew Reck's pistol, held it high, and addressed the crowd. "The gates are now being opened. They will remain open throughout the night, and everyone who wishes to pass may do so. You will move in an orderly fashion. Pushing and shoving will not be tolerated. Any person seen to be endangering those around him will be shot dead. Is that not so?" He glanced over his shoulder at the guards.

"It is!" one of them called back stoutly, and he even brandished his musket for effect. "Keep it civilized, or you'll wish you had! There's plenty of time for everyone to get through."

For once, Lenoir blessed the mindless obedience of young soldiers.

"Let's go!" another of the guards cried. "Move it nice and steady!"

And miraculously, the crowd did just that, shuffling soberly, quietly, through Castlegate, destined for the suburbs and the fields beyond. By the hundreds they came, then the thousands, as if every artery in the city had opened, lifeblood emptying to the low, erratic heartbeat of distant explosions. All through the night and into the dawn they flowed, then trickled, then seeped. The sun rose over a wounded horizon, gap-toothed against a bloodied sky. And when at last the terrible heartbeat ceased, and the flow stanched, a silence more terrible still settled like ash over the empty streets of Old Kennian Town.

CHAPTER 24

Lenoir slid off the back of his horse, his legs shaking beneath him. He had spent half the night astride that animal, and he would be hard-pressed to walk tomorrow. Still, looking at Chief Reck, Lenoir felt he had got the better end of it.

"Good work at the gates," the chief said, rubbing bloodshot eyes. His fingers scrubbed a white streak through the film of soot on his skin.

"I cannot take credit for it." Lenoir's gaze roamed over the smoldering rubble of Orlister Plaza. Only hours before, he had been obliged to fire his pistol to clear the crowds from this place. Now it stood an empty ruin, blasted apart to prevent the flames from continuing their voracious progress toward the poor district. "The Duke of Warrick ordered it open."

Reck's eyebrows rose. "Warrick, eh? Wouldn't have seen that coming." The chief smirked. "He must have loved overruling Hearsting's orders. No great affection between those two."

"In fact, I think he was loath to do it, though I'm not sure why." The duke's behavior was often enigmatic, but never more so than last night. There had been a moment when it seemed as though Warrick actually *wanted* those people to remain trapped, just to prove a point.

"Regardless," said Reck, "it's lucky he was there. He came to gawk, I suppose?"

"More or less."

"Hearstings came by too, though he had enough sense not to stay for long. I think he could tell I wasn't very happy." Reck gave a brittle smile.

"So," Lenoir said, "what now?"

"Nothing left to do but wait for it to burn itself out."

"How much did we lose?"

"Assuming it finishes off what's left inside the perimeter, practically everything from the market square to the poor district, from Kingsway east."

Lenoir swore.

"That's putting it mildly," said the chief. "Still, it could have been worse. We just barely had enough gunpowder to blast our way around it. If we hadn't managed, who knows where it would have ended. At the city walls, most likely."

Lenoir wondered how many had died. It would be a long time before they had even a vague idea, and they would probably never know exactly. Many of the dead would remain forever anonymous. But Lenoir had more pressing concerns now, like making sure Bran Kody did not join them.

"Where is Kody?" he asked. "I need to find him straightaway." He had already made up his mind to tell the chief *after* Kody had been treated. The last thing he needed right now was to waste precious time being reprimanded for his negligence.

"He's leading a search for survivors," Reck said. He shook his head. "That'll be an ugly job."

Lenoir cursed inwardly. Was the sergeant truly so cavalier with his life? Every hour counted. Every *minute*. They might already be too late, and Kody was leading a search for those who were already beyond help?

"An ugly job indeed," he growled, "and not one he needs to do personally. He has other tasks."

For some reason, the remark nettled the chief. "It's called compassion, Lenoir. Most people consider it a good quality. One of many good qualities he has. He's a damned fine hound."

"I know it," Lenoir said, taken aback.

"Do you? Have you considered telling him so once in a while?"

Lenoir felt himself flush, part anger, part embarrassment. "What is that supposed to mean?"

"It *means*, Inspector, that you've got a talented officer, and a good man, working under you, and if you're too damned busy penning your own personal tragedy to take notice, I'll assign him to someone else, someone who'll appreciate him a little more."

You had better do it quickly, because he's dying of plague.

The words were on Lenoir's lips, but he could not bring himself to say them. It did not matter anyway; the chief had already stalked off to speak with one of the firemen, leaving Lenoir alone with a thought too bitter to swallow.

He gave his head a sharp shake. He had to find Kody. It ought not be too difficult. If the sergeant was leading a search party, they would be moving slowly, systematically. So long as Lenoir followed a logical path, he would come across them soon enough.

He started off at the market district. What was left of it, at any rate. It was virtually unrecognizable now, a smoldering, gaping wound of ash and rubble. Lenoir moved along the edges, his mind struggling to process the destruction around him. *This city is paying something dear, and no mistake.* The words of the Whitmarch fireman, and no greater understatement had even been spoken. The plague did not march alone; it brought lieutenants, fire and fear and lawlessness, and together they had cut a wide swathe through the city. Kennian had suffered much, and there was no end in sight.

The despair that pooled at the bottom of Lenoir's belly was all too familiar. He had felt it as a youth in Serles, when his beloved city had been ravaged by war and pestilence. He would not have thought himself capable of feeling it again. Not for Kennian, a home he had adopted out of necessity more than choice. But he had lived here for over a decade, and in that time, she had found a home in him, as much as he in her.

The thought surprised him. Even the idea that he *had* a home came as something of a revelation. Perhaps he was not so rootless as he let himself believe; perhaps he had attachments, however subtle, that he did not pause to appreciate. *It is only in loss that we truly understand what matters to us,* he thought. No great epiphany, that, but Lenoir felt the truth of it now more than ever before.

Inevitably, that turned his thoughts back to Bran Kody.

He hardly needed the chief to tell him that Kody was a competent hound, a good man. Anyone could see that. Lenoir himself had said so many times—though he could not, admittedly, recall saying so to Kody. An oversight, perhaps, but surely the sergeant knew of his esteem? After all, had he not recommended Kody for promotion? Accepted him as his deputy? Surely that was evidence enough?

Not for the chief, apparently.

To be sure, the chief had witnessed more than a few barbed remarks directed Kody's way. Lenoir *was* hard on him sometimes, but how else was a young officer to learn? It was his supervisor's role to guide him, to correct him, and if occasionally Lenoir was less than delicate about it, well . . . no man was perfect.

He had made mistakes with Kody. More than a few, perhaps. He could admit it, at least to himself. Even so, the idea that the sergeant had a better alternative was laughable.

Whatever Lenoir's personal faults, his fellow inspectors could not possibly compete with him professionally, and that was what counted for Kody. The sergeant had specifically requested to serve under Lenoir, thinking that the best fit for his ambition. He would not thank Reck for assigning him to the Drunk, the Imbecile, or the Lout.

At least, Lenoir thought not. But how well did he really know Kody? How much had he *tried* to know him, in spite of spending nearly every waking hour beside him?

The answer to that, at least, was no revelation.

Too busy penning your own personal tragedy, Reck had said. There was something in that, perhaps. Lenoir had been so lost in his own head that he had failed to notice when his deputy contracted the plague.

And you consider yourself the finest inspector in Braeland.

That, perhaps, was the truly laughable part. Or at least it would have been, had it not very possibly cost Kody his life.

There is no redemption, the Darkwalker had said.

Perhaps you should have those words engraved on your tomb, Lenoir.

"Cure what ails you!"

The voice shattered Lenoir's musings as abruptly as a stone hurled into a mirror.

"Get your miracle tonic here!" The swindler he had seen that morning in the flower district was standing at the corner of Kingsway and Birch, waving his brown medicine bottles proudly. "Supplies limited!"

The despair in Lenoir's belly took light, flaming into rage. He stalked toward the man, his hands balling into fists. . . .

"Two crowns a bottle!"

Lenoir paused.

Two crowns?

In the flower district, the salesman had wanted only

half. *And did I not see him once before that, near the docks?* The salesman had offered it to Kody for a quarter.

Both times, the man had been shouting at random passersby, trying to drum up sales. Lenoir had not seen a single taker. This time, the salesman was addressing a veritable crowd of potential customers. The streets were near deserted, yet here were at least a dozen well-dressed people gathered around, waiting to shell out a small fortune for a single pint of liquid. Frowning, Lenoir made his way over.

"Pardon me," he said to one of the would-be buyers, a small woman with a mask over her face. She shrank from him, as if he were the plague incarnate. "Don't worry. I am not sick. I am curious, however, about this tonic. Is it not awfully expensive?"

"Worth every bit of it!" It was another customer who replied, a man hurrying away with his precious brown bottle tucked under his arm. "Cured my niece in three days. Got some for my sister now. If you can afford it, mate, you should get it while you can. I'd have bought some yesterday, but he was out. . . ." The man hurried away.

Out? Trade was obviously booming. *At two crowns a bottle, he will be rich in days.*

Lenoir's eyes narrowed.

Was it possible? He had more than one reason to hope.

"I will take a bottle," he called, and he fished in his pocket for his money purse. He had just enough, so long as the salesman was happy to take it in quarters and ten-ners.

The salesman did not recognize him, which was just as well. Lenoir was in no mood for smugness. He handed his money over and took his bottle.

A few blocks later, he came across Kody. He had been right about the sergeant being easy to find, but wrong about why. Kody was easy to find because he was not moving. He perched on the curb at the end of Barrow Street, head between his knees, ash dusting his shoulders like snow collecting on a forgotten gargoyle.

The sight of him, alone, forlorn, still as a tombstone, was a blow to Lenoir's stomach.

He started across the road.

Kody glanced up. The left side of his face was hideously bruised, presumably from where he had been kicked the day before. His eye had swollen shut, and one corner of his mouth had a grim downward turn. When he saw Lenoir, he raised a hand. "Stay back, Inspector." He had taken his handkerchief off. He held it in his left hand, balled up. Lenoir could see the blood, stark against the white cloth, from where he stood in the middle of the street.

"Nosebleed," Kody said. "I could almost tell myself the bruising was normal, but the nosebleed . . . Guess there's no doubt now." He brushed absently at his trousers, leaving streaks of ash the color of granite.

Icy fingers wrung out Lenoir's guts, but he shook the feeling off. He knew what had to be done. "Are you strong enough to walk?" he asked.

Kody tried for a smile. "It's only a couple of bruises. I've had worse."

"Then get up. I'm taking you to the Camp."

This time, the invading forces of God Himself would not be enough to get in his way.

Lenoir ducked through the tent flap and paused to let his vision adjust. In the gloom, he could almost feel the golden eyes upon him.

"You should be wearing a mask, Inspector," a deep voice chided.

"I was in a hurry."

"Do you bring news of the city?" Merden stepped into the glow of a candle. "We could see the flames from here."

Lenoir winced. He had been so preoccupied when the

chief described the extent of the damage that he had not even processed the full implications. "Your shop . . ."

Merden sighed. "I feared as much."

Though he had more pressing concerns, Lenoir could not help but ask, "Will you be all right?" The question seemed to take on a double meaning. Now that he could see Merden clearly, it was obvious that the soothsayer was not well. He had lost weight. In two short days (*Dear God, has it only been two days?*) Merden had gone from lean to thin, and it seemed to Lenoir that the light in his eyes had dulled somewhat.

"It is a loss, certainly, but I do not keep the truly rare items in the shop. I do not dare risk them falling into the wrong hands. The rest of my stock is of modest value, strictly speaking, and not so very difficult to replace. As for the shop itself"—he gave a weary shrug—"the insurance should almost cover it."

"You are insured? Your business must do very well indeed."

"My arts are rare," the soothsayer said, in the second tremendous understatement of the day.

"Indeed they are, and I would call upon them now." Lenoir gestured behind him. "Sergeant Kody is outside. I told him to wait while I checked your disposition."

While I checked whether you were busy practicing khekra, was what he meant.

Merden straightened, suddenly alert. "Bring him inside."

In the honeyed light of the candles, the sweat on Kody's brow stood out like a string of amber beads. His skin, pale where it was not bruised, swollen and streaked with ash, made him look half a corpse.

"You are late, Sergeant," Merden said.

Kody just nodded. He had spoken hardly a word since they quit Barrow Street.

"The bruising is from a blow to the head," Lenoir explained. "He was kicked yesterday afternoon."

Merden took Kody's face in his hands, tilted it to the light. He wrapped his fingers around the sergeant's wrist to take a pulse. Then he knelt and pushed up Kody's trouser leg. Lenoir sucked in his breath. Tiny blotches of red and purple smattered the sergeant's ankle, as if someone had dropped a jar of raspberry jam near his foot. Kody stared at it dully, as if he had known it was there, or at least expected it to be.

"The strain of running has caused his blood vessels to burst," Merden said, "and it is too thin to clot properly. Soon, it will take no impact at all for the lesions to form. We must begin immediately."

"Wait," said Lenoir.

Merden's eyebrows flew up. Kody just looked at him with that same dull expression.

"I have a theory," Lenoir said, "and if I'm right, the ritual may not be necessary." He produced the brown medicine bottle, handed it to Merden. "What do you make of this?"

Merden took it. "THIRMAN'S MIRACLE TONIC," he read with a frown. "What is it?"

"I bought it off a salesman on Kingsway. He had quite an enthusiastic clientele. He claims it can cure the plague."

"Does he?" Merden uncorked the bottle and took a sniff. "Interesting." He held the bottle to the candlelight, swirling it gently. "It smells similar to the remedy I am using, the one Oded taught me." Merden angled the bottle, his golden eyes narrowed. "It separates in a similar manner as well." He glanced up. "Does it work?"

"Something tells me it will."

"We must test it."

"Agreed." Lenoir's gaze slid to Kody.

The sergeant, for his part, eyed the bottle. "If it works, I wouldn't have to do the ritual?"

Merden shook his head. "Impossible to say until we try it. And consider—if it does not work, the delay may cost you your life."

"You do not have to be the test subject, Sergeant," Lenoir said, "but I wanted to give you the choice. I knew you would dread having to undergo the ritual. No offense," he added, glancing at Merden.

"None taken. It is quite unpleasant. I can readily understand why Sergeant Kody would wish to avoid it. But that does not mean it would be wise to do so."

"I'm doing all right," Kody said. "Those bruises on my leg can't be more than a couple of hours old. I still have time."

"You have done this well because you are a big man, Sergeant, and exceptionally fit. Your system held out longer than most. On top of that, my medicine helped to mask your symptoms. But you would be a fool to test the limits of your good fortune. The appearance of lesions means you have a day at the most."

"Two hours," Kody said. "That's how long the other tonic takes to show results, right? That's not so much time to wait. Besides, it has to be tested on someone. Might as well be me."

Lenoir could not help but admire Kody's courage. He knew what it was like to face certain death. He had not done so with half as much grit.

Merden sighed. He considered the bottle again. "It is certainly your decision, Sergeant. But it is a great risk."

Kody's mouth twitched uncertainly. "You say it smells like the other stuff?"

The soothsayer nodded. "On the face of it, I would say its basic ingredient is the same, or at least a cousin."

"What ingredient is that?" Lenoir asked.

"I do not know the name in Braelish. In Adali, it is known as *dwar*."

"*Dwar.*" Lenoir frowned. "Doesn't that mean *circle*?"

"I am impressed, Inspector. I did not realize you spoke Adali."

"I can count the number of words on my fingers."

"More than most Humenori." Merden swirled the

bottle, watched it separate and settle. "It does indeed mean *circle,* after the pattern it grows in. It looks a little like clover, in fact. We use it in many medicines, especially for traumatic injuries. It thickens the blood."

"What about Braelish medicine—would Lideman use it?"

Merden considered. "I cannot say for certain, but I would be surprised."

"But it's part of the recipe Oded gave you?"

"It is the main ingredient. We have been using it to treat uncomplicated cases. For most, it seems to be working." He sighed and glanced at Kody. "For most."

Kody looked stricken. "If it's practically the same stuff, does that mean this potion won't work on me either?"

"It is possible. For that reason, to be sure whether it works at all, we will need a second test subject."

We. The soothsayer had used the word several times. "Who is *we,* Merden?" Lenoir asked.

"I managed to find someone open-minded enough to assist me. I believe you both know Sister Rhea?"

"The nun from the clinic?" Kody asked.

"The same. She has taken over treatment of the uncomplicated cases, those who sought help straightaway. That gives me time to focus on the complicated ones."

Lenoir glanced around the tent uneasily. Now that he actually looked, he could make out the cot, the sickle of candles, the crystals . . . all of it. "So you have been spending the last two days . . ."

"Exorcising demons." He might have said "playing Crowns," so matter-of-fact was his tone.

Lenoir shuddered. "How many have you treated?"

Merden sighed and looked away, and Lenoir was reminded forcibly of Oded. "Perhaps fifty or so have received the tonic, not including Sergeant Kody. Of those, we have lost only one. As for the complicated cases, I have treated just under a dozen. It is"—he passed a hand over his eyes—"not sustainable. And yet, it is not enough. Not nearly."

"Sixty may not seem such a great number, but they are all of them someone's father, or sister, or grandmother."

"Or son," said Kody quietly.

Merden nodded, but he did not look comforted. "I am grateful for Sister Rhea. Without her help, we would not have been able to save even that modest number. If Oded had survived . . ." He did not finish the thought; there was no point.

"At least he was able to teach you what he knew," said Lenoir.

"Indeed, though I have adapted his technique somewhat." Some of the light came back into Merden's eyes as he explained. "Oded's treatment consumes too much time and energy. Isolating the soul is still necessary in the most severe cases, but if the patient is strong enough, and the treatment rapid enough, that step can be circumvented."

Lenoir had no idea what to say to that.

"Also, I have ceased the restorative spell entirely. It is too draining, and delays my recuperation for the next patient. Instead . . ." He trailed off, shaking his head. "Forgive me. I am wasting precious time." He handed the bottle back to Lenoir. "Take this to Sister Rhea. She will treat Sergeant Kody. As for the other test subject, tell Sister Rhea to administer it to the young woman I sent over a few minutes ago. She has not yet received treatment, so she will make a suitable test subject. If the bleeding does not slow within two hours, then the potion does not work." He turned to Kody. "In which case, Sergeant, I will hear no more protests." He pointed at the cot, in case there was any mistaking his meaning.

Kody nodded resignedly and ducked out of the tent.

"Good-bye, my friend," Lenoir said. "And thank you."

"You do not need to thank me. We all use our gifts as

we are able. My gift is for *khekra*. Yours is for thinking. Now go and think." Merden withdrew to the back of the tent, the shadows swallowing him whole. "And, Inspector — put on a mask."

CHAPTER 25

They found Sister Rhea stooped over a cot, helping an old man to drink. He made a face as he gulped it down, the nun cooing encouragingly with every swallow. "Inspector," she said when she noticed Lenoir. "This is a surprise." Then she saw Kody, and her eyes widened. "Sergeant, you look awful! Are you quite well?"

Kody smiled ruefully. "Not quite, no."

"The sergeant requires urgent treatment, Sister," Lenoir said. He held up the bottle. "Merden has asked us to test a new remedy."

"Oh?" She wiped her hands on her apron and came over. Taking the bottle, she eyed it warily. "Isn't that awfully risky, when we know we have something that works?"

Lenoir glanced over the cots, row upon row of them jammed into the space. Every bed was accounted for, and their occupants did not look much better than Kody. "Are you sure it works? It has only been two days. . . ."

"Yes, but the bleeding stops within hours, and their strength begins to return soon after that. It's a slow process, but the trend is unmistakable."

"That is good news. And the plant it uses—what is it called?"

"Hogsfoot." She smiled. "A modest name for a miracle, isn't it? Who would have thought that something so simple could be so important? We overlook God's gifts all too often. Or at least, we Braelish do. The Adali look more closely, it seems."

"Merden believes this new tonic is based on the same ingredient, or similar."

"Then why are we testing it? If it's the same, there is no need, and if it isn't . . ." She shook her head. "It really does seem risky. Are you sure this is what you want, Sergeant?"

Lenoir could tell from Kody's expression that he was not, in fact, sure. How could he be? He was gambling with his life. Such was his dread of *khekra*, however, that he did not hesitate. "Thanks for asking, but I just want to get it over with. If it doesn't work . . . we can always go back to Plan A, right?" He tried for a confident smile. He failed.

"Please, Sister," Lenoir added, "it's important. And there is more. Merden asked us to test a second patient as well, just to be sure." Rhea started to object, but Lenoir cut her off. "Just for two hours, Sister. He said that if the bleeding does not slow within that time, you are to put the patient on the old treatment."

"Did he say which patient?"

"Yes. The last one he sent here, a young woman."

Sister Rhea sighed. "Very well. I can't say I approve, but Merden is a miracle worker, and he's got us this far." She turned and waved at one of her volunteers, a figure at the far end of the tent.

The man came over, and when he stepped into the light, Lenoir recognized him as Drem, the man he and Kody had spoken with a week ago. The interview had been a brief one, owing in part to the fact that Drem had been so weak that he was scarcely able to carry on a conversation. And now . . . "You have recovered?" Lenoir asked, hoping he did not sound quite as surprised as he felt. Surprised, and relieved. Here was physical proof that survival was possible. Kody very much needed that proof right now. So did Lenoir.

"Not so strong as I was." Drem shrugged his thin shoulders. "But strong enough to help out."

"You are a brave man, to expose yourself again after what happened."

Sister Rhea smiled. "He is a brave man, though he's in no danger now, except perhaps from exhaustion. Once a patient has been exposed to the disease, he is immune."

"How can you be sure?" Kody asked. He was speaking to Rhea, but his eyes were on Drem, as if fixating on the hope he represented.

"That's usually the case with illnesses like these," said Rhea. "Either they kill you, or they cure you forever."

"No doubt, but even so . . ." If it were Lenoir, he would not be willing to bet his life on it.

As for Drem, he just shrugged again. "I choose to have faith. If it weren't for Sister Rhea, I would have died. It's my turn to give something back."

Lenoir could hardly believe he was talking to the same man. Drem still looked thin and washed out, but his posture was straight, his eyes bright and alert. He had obviously rounded the corner.

"So long as he doesn't push himself too hard, he'll make a full recovery," Rhea said. "And he gives the patients hope. In him, they see the possibility of a cure." She put a hand on Drem's shoulder and offered him the bottle. "Take this, please, and mix two doses." Drem nodded and headed off for the vestibule.

"Thank you, Sister," Lenoir said. He turned to Kody, put a hand on his shoulder. The sergeant blinked in surprise and looked down at it, as though some unidentifiable creature had just alighted there. Lenoir had never made such a gesture before, and it felt strange—false, somehow—to do it now. But it also felt necessary. "I will be back to check on you in a few hours," he said.

In the meantime, he had a physician to see.

"Hogsfoot?" Lideman sat back in his chair, his brow stitched up skeptically. "Is *that* what's in it?"

"Apparently so," said Lenoir.

"Remarkable." Lideman shook his head. "You have to give the Adali credit. They do find healing properties in the oddest of places."

"I take that to mean conventional medicine does not make use of this plant?"

"Hogsfoot? I should say not. If I've heard of the plant at all, it's only because my wife is constantly complaining about its presence in her garden. Did your witchdoctor say how it works?" He raised a hand in a staying gesture. "On second thought, never mind. I'm sure it's to do with some supernatural creature or another."

So much for giving the Adali credit. "It thickens the blood, apparently."

Lideman grunted. "That makes sense."

"Merden will be pleased you think so," Lenoir said dryly.

The physician at least had the grace to look embarrassed. "It's not that I doubt his talents, Inspector, or that of his predecessor. The tonic Oded gave me does appear to be working. But you must understand—"

"So you have been administering the tonic Oded gave you?"

"Yes, although we have only enough for two patients, according to the schedule Oded prescribed."

Lenoir frowned. "And you have not asked for more?"

"I wanted to make sure it was effective. . . ."

"That was two days ago. I'm told the effect is visible within two hours."

"Some improvement, yes, but hardly definitive—"

Lenoir shot to his feet. "I suggest you ask Sister Rhea

to provide you with more," he said coldly. "Her volunteers have been preparing it night and day since Merden gave them the recipe."

"But she couldn't have been sure it would work. . . ." He spread his hands feebly, as if to say, *You see my dilemma.*

"She took a leap of faith. Apparently, she considered it preferable to satisfying some sanctimonious code of ethics."

Lenoir left the physician sputtering behind him. He had not even told Lideman that Kody was infected. He did not want that pompous ass anywhere near the sergeant, he decided.

He returned to Merden's tent, but this time, he did not go inside. Instead, he approached the familiar figure standing watch a few feet away. "Sergeant Innes."

The big man turned, and Lenoir could not help taking a step back at the sight of him. Innes looked like an ogre at the best of times, but with his new miasma mask, he was the stuff of nightmares. The wooden face looked just human enough to be unnerving, with a grotesque knob at the nose and mouth where the straw filter was contained. The glass eyes were as dark and fathomless as those of a beast. Perhaps that was no bad thing; a frightening appearance could only help the sergeant do his job.

"Inspector." Innes's voice was oddly subdued through the filter. "How goes the hunt?"

"Better." At least, Lenoir hoped so. "And here?"

Innes shrugged. "All right. Had a tussle or two between folk anxious to see the witchdoctor, but nothing we couldn't handle."

"And you are checking everyone who goes in or out?"

"Even the patients. Good thing we got masks and gloves."

Lenoir nodded. As arrogant and narrow-minded as Lideman could be, there was no denying he cared about people's health. Lenoir was grateful he had provided the hounds with proper protection. "No sign of our man?"

"Nope. I reckon he figured out we were onto him and made tracks."

Lenoir could not decide whether that was a good thing or bad. It meant Merden was safer, but it also meant they had less chance of catching their quarry.

"Some pretty weird sounds coming out of that tent, Inspector."

Lenoir could well imagine it. "Adali medicine is . . . elaborate."

The glass eyes gazed down at him, dark and empty. "Reckon so," Innes said.

"We must take our salvation in whatever shape it comes, Sergeant." *Even if it is dark magic, or a miracle tonic sold on the street.*

"Reckon so." Innes paused. He shifted his bulk. "Kody looked pretty bad," he said. "He take a beating?"

"He was kicked in the head."

"Rough." Innes hesitated again. "I heard a rumor, Inspector."

Lenoir said nothing.

"Kody . . . Is he all right?"

Lenoir was not surprised that word of the sergeant's condition had already circulated among the hounds. *The only thing that spreads faster than plague is word of it.* "He is not all right, Sergeant," he said quietly, "but I very much hope he will be."

Innes nodded. "Me too."

A stretch of silence ensued. Lenoir and Innes gazed out over the somber movements of the Camp. "Do you mind if stand watch with you a while?" Lenoir asked at length. "I am waiting."

"Sure thing, Inspector. What're you waiting for?"

"A miracle."

*   *   *

"It's incredible," Sister Rhea said, taking Lenoir by the hand and leading him into the treatment area. She practically glowed with delight. "See for yourself."

For the second time in a year, Lenoir gazed down at the inert form of Bran Kody. This time, at least, the sergeant was not in a coma. He was asleep, his chest rising and falling peacefully, but his face was still half a horror, and the splotches peeking out from the cuffs of his trousers had darkened to purple. If there was a miracle here, Lenoir could not see it. "This is better?" he asked doubtfully.

"Oh, yes! The fever is gone, and the nosebleeds have stopped. And look at the hematoma on his ankle!"

Lenoir looked. "It is worse than ever."

Rhea smiled. "It looks worse, perhaps, but it's actually a good sign. When the bleeding is fresh, the bruise is red. This darker color means the blood has clotted."

Like a corpse, Lenoir thought before he could stop himself.

"And see here, the other patient . . ." Rhea led him over. Like Kody, the young woman was asleep. And like Kody, she did not look like a miracle. Alive, certainly, but her skin was ashen, and plum-colored arcs sagged beneath her eyes.

"The treatment works, then," Lenoir said, wishing he felt more confident about it.

Sister Rhea had enough confidence for both of them. "Better than the one we've been using," she beamed. "Much better! Where can we get more?"

"There is a man selling it on the streets."

The nun stared at him, astonished. "Just like that? Why, everyone must be buying it!"

"He has many customers, but the product is too expensive for most. He is charging two crowns a bottle."

"Two crowns!" A small, despondent sound escaped her throat. "Why, that's immoral!"

Lenoir could not disagree.

"The quantities we need . . . we'll never afford it!"

"You will not have to." Lenoir turned and headed for the tent flap.

"Where are you going?"

"To get you your medicine." Lenoir quit the tent in long, determined strides.

That tonic, and the man selling it, were about to become the property of the Kennian Metropolitan Police.

CHAPTER 26

Sergeant Ray Innes liked a good interrogation.

It was the part where all your hard work, all the scratching around in the shit with the chickens, started to pay off, and you got to see the pig you'd been chasing get a spit up the arse. He never got tired of watching them squirm. And by God, this one was gonna squirm and squeal like a hog at the slaughterhouse, at least if Innes had anything to say about it.

Kody was sick because of this bastard. Or at least, he was sicker because of him. Inspector Lenoir hadn't explained the whole thing (he never did) but from what he'd told Innes, this skinny bloke—the one Innes currently had by the scruff of his neck—had been hoarding a cure for the plague. A bloody *cure*. All those people dying, vomiting up blood and such, and this vermin was sitting on the one thing that could save them, just so he could make some coin.

It made Innes want to snap his skinny vermin neck.

The chief wouldn't like that, of course. Innes would get himself tossed on his ear, and maybe worse. It almost seemed worth it.

"Now this room," he growled, putting every lick of menace he felt into his voice, "is my favorite part of the station. We call it the Pit. Know why?" He steered the prisoner roughly over to the solitary chair in the center of the room and shoved him onto it. "'Cause it's where we roast the pigs." Bracing his hands on the arms of the chair, Innes leaned in close enough to smell the terrified man's breath. "That concludes our tour."

"Thank you, Sergeant." The voice came from over his shoulder, and there wasn't a hint of feeling in it. Innes couldn't tell if Inspector Lenoir was annoyed, amused, or something else. The inspector was wearing his interrogation face, smooth and unreadable. Trying to guess his thoughts was as good as trying to see through stone. The inspector was good at that—being intimidating without saying a word. Half the time, Innes figured, he didn't even realize he was doing it. You could look at him sometimes, and you knew he was thinking things about you. Those dark eyes, sharp and cunning, looking straight through you. You could practically see the wheels turning in his head. It was enough to make a man suck in his gut and stand up real straight.

Lenoir leaned against the wall near the doorframe, arms folded, looking at the prisoner with an unblinking gaze. As usual, he let the silence do his work for him, letting the tension coil around them like a snake slowly tightening its grip.

"I don't understand why I'm here!" The prisoner appealed to Lenoir with his gaze. "I haven't done anything wrong!"

The inspector said nothing.

"Seems to me you've done plenty wrong," Innes said. He knew his part in this. Enjoyed it. He was the heavy, a role he'd played from the day he joined the force, owing to his size. It came natural. That's why the inspector had chosen him, plucking him off guard duty and replacing him with a watchman. Because Innes was a first-rate heavy. He hadn't done many interrogations with Inspector Lenoir—Kody was a first-rate heavy himself, so the inspector didn't have much call to look elsewhere—but it wasn't like they needed a lot of practice together. The rhythm was always the same: the sergeant (or sometimes, the watchman) was the heavy, and the inspector was the cold, calculating one, a man who wouldn't be moved by tears or pleas or claims of innocence. Inspector Lenoir played that part better than any of them. It came natural.

"Leastways, you're a slimy bastard," Innes rumbled. "All those folks dying, hundreds every day, and all the while you've been sitting on the cure just so you could get rich."

"I haven't been withholding it!" The whites of the man's eyes showed, like a spooked horse, and his body tensed up around itself. "I've been offering it since the beginning! Selling it, sure, but that's not illegal, is it?"

Should be, Innes thought, but that didn't make it so. He wasn't sure what they could even charge the pig with. Course, that didn't mean much. Innes had never been much good at memorizing the rules. That was the inspector's job, and Innes reckoned he knew what he was doing.

He kept on. "Selling it, sure. For two crowns apiece. What kind of filth takes advantage of desperate folks like that?" He leaned in again. "You know how many hounds got plague on the barricades? The inspector here—his deputy got it. My friend. Got any idea how that feels?" He straightened, started massaging his hands, real slow and deliberate. "Makes you damned mad, I can tell you. Start looking for someone to blame. And now here you are . . ."

The man sucked in a few rapid lungsful of air, each one noisier than the last. He was on the verge of full-blown panic. *All right, Inspector, that's the meat, good and tenderized.* Innes stepped back. It was Lenoir's turn now.

"Are you Thirman?" Lenoir posed the question blandly, like he didn't much care about the answer.

"Me? No. Irving's my name, and I—"

"Quiet. Short answers, please. Nod if you understand."

Irving nodded.

"I wonder, Irving, why you did not see fit to inform anyone—the police, the College of Physicians, anyone—that you were in possession of a cure for the plague? Surely you can see why the sergeant here finds that upsetting."

"I . . ." Irving's glance cut between Innes and Inspector Lenoir, trying to decide which of them was scarier. He licked his lips. "The truth is . . . well, I didn't know. Not at first, anyway. I mean, you know, I *hoped . . .*" He trailed off with a weak little laugh.

"You mean you did not care," Lenoir said. "You informed no one of your miracle cure, but let the plague gather steam, until you had more customers than you could keep up with. By then, you were able to charge whatever you wished. No matter how exorbitant the price, there would always be someone willing to pay it."

"But I never lied about it." Irving looked pleadingly at Innes, as if he was going to find any help there. "I never lied. I said I had a cure. I shouted it from the streets!"

"At a minimum, as the sergeant has pointed out, you withheld your miracle cure, which should have been given to the authorities without delay. I have no doubt I can convince the magistrate that qualifies as criminal negligence."

The pig went white.

"However," the inspector continued, "I think it is a great deal worse than that."

Innes grunted. This sounded interesting.

"I have a theory. Would you like to hear it?" Without waiting for an answer, the inspector went on. "Having obtained the recipe for a tonic that cures a particularly horrendous strain of plague, one as yet unknown to Braelish shores, you saw a business opportunity. If such a plague were to break out in Kennian, you would have cornered the market on a product people would be desperate to buy at any price. You would become rich overnight. I don't know how you first came upon the cure, and it does not matter. I *do* know how you brought the plague over from Inataar."

Irving's eyes widened. "*What?* Are you crazy? You think I—"

"Four thousand people, at last count." Lenoir shoved himself away from the wall, and now he let the anger shine through, a sight all the more frightening for its abruptness. "That is how many you have murdered. Sadly, a man can only be hanged once."

"Wait a second, Inspector—are you saying this pig started the plague on purpose?" As a rule, Innes didn't lose his temper. If he wanted to knock someone's teeth out, he did it, and he didn't think much about it. Sometimes people needed to be taught a lesson. But he never lost his cool. He just did what needed to be done, because it needed doing.

This, though . . . He'd never heard of anything like *this*. It made his blood boil.

"All those people . . . Kody . . . so this piece of shit could get rich?" Innes took a step forward, and for a moment, even he wasn't sure what he meant to do. The prisoner cried out. Lenoir shot him a look.

With an effort, Innes straightened, his fingers twitching in and out of fists.

"That's what you think?" Irving's voice rose in pitch. "That *I* started the plague?"

The inspector tilted his head. All of a sudden, he didn't look angry anymore. He looked cool as mint, the wheels turning behind those dark eyes of his.

He doesn't, Innes realized. He'd been playing the prisoner all along. That was the thing about Inspector Lenoir. He knew how to play people.

"That's not even . . . I didn't . . ." The pig couldn't even finish a sentence. Talk about tenderizing the meat.

"You didn't?" The inspector's tone was guarded, like he could maybe, just maybe, be convinced. "Someone did. That much we are certain of. The plague *was* started deliberately, and at last I understand why. There was profit to be made, a great deal of it. From where I stand, it all points to you."

When a man sees his escape open up right in front of him, he takes it. "I'm not the only one making money!" Irving was quick to say. "Not at all! Truth is, I'm not even making that much!"

"Really." The inspector folded his arms.

"I'm just a salesman! There are a few of us who were given the product, and we've got a system between us. I work Morningside, south of Kingsgate. Farther north, that's a bloke called Freeman. And on Evenside, there's—"

"*Given* the product, you say. Who gave it to you? Thirman?"

"That's right! Thirman! It's his product. I just sell it. He's the one you want!"

In the end, if you did your job right, the pigs served one another up on a platter.

"Who is he?" Lenoir demanded.

"An apothecary up in Meadowsmead. Not far from here, actually. I can give you the address." Irving was really warming to his subject now. "He's the one making the real money, I'm telling you. Charges a nice shiny copper for that potion, and more every day. He's the real reason my prices have gone up so high . . ." He trailed off, seeing as how neither Lenoir nor Innes looked very sympathetic. He cleared his throat. "Anyway, like I said . . . he's the one you want."

"I will take that under advisement." Lenoir looked up at Innes. "Sergeant, I believe we are through here."

"Looks like there's more to our tour after all," Innes said, wrenching Irving up out of the chair. "Next stop, the Pen. Can you guess why we call it that?"

He processed Irving as quick as he could. It never

hurt to hang on to a prisoner for a while, even if he wasn't your man. You never knew what might come up down the road. Chances were he'd be out in a couple of days, though. It didn't look like he'd done anything illegal, and though there were ways of getting around details like that, Innes doubted the inspector could be bothered. He had bigger game to chase, like this Thirman bloke. "Should we bring him in, Inspector, or question him there?" Innes asked once he'd rejoined Lenoir.

"Let us start there, and see what develops. I have a hunch the chain is longer than a link or two. We know that the plague was brought in by sea, but we have not yet found anyone with an obvious connection to the docks. Until we link the tonic to the docks, we have not yet completed the chain."

"You don't think this apothecary bloke is your link?"

"It is possible, but how would a Braelish apothecary come across the secret to curing a plague from Inataar? We shall see what this Thirman has to say, but on the face of it, I am inclined to believe that he, too, is just an intermediary. In which case, we have a long afternoon ahead of us, Sergeant."

A cheerful little bell tinkled as they opened the door to the apothecary's shop. Innes gave the place a quick once-over, but he saw nothing to worry about. It was even sort of nice, with a flowering plant in the windowsill and a pair of plush chairs set in front of the counter. Meadowsmead was one of the posher suburbs of Kennian, sitting between the old city and the rolling green estate of Castle Warrick. Innes didn't expect any trouble here.

A thin man appeared from a back room, smiling warmly. He had a kindly old face creased with laugh lines, and his clothing was crisp and well tailored. He didn't look like a monster. "May I help you, gentlemen?"

Better hope so, Innes thought darkly. He was too experienced to be fooled by the apothecary's grandfatherly appearance. If Irving was telling the truth, this pig was responsible for thousands of deaths—or at least had stood by and gotten rich while it happened.

"Mr. Thirman, isn't it?" the inspector asked.

"That's right."

"Of Thirman's Miracle Tonic?"

"The same." The man's smile turned proud.

"I will have every drop of it in your possession, sir, and I will have the recipe too."

The apothecary blinked. "I beg your pardon?"

"You may beg it, but you are unlikely to receive it."

That was a good one, Innes thought. He'd have to remember it.

Thirman took a step back, wary now. "Who are you?"

"Perhaps you did not hear me. I want every bottle on the counter *now*, and if you are very lucky, you will not live out the end of your days in Fort Hald."

"I hope that's because you mean to see him hanged, Inspector." Innes leaned against the counter. It creaked under his weight.

Thirman paled. "You're police?"

Innes didn't answer.

"Please do not make me repeat my request a third time," said the inspector.

"You can't just confiscate my goods." The apothecary drew himself up, doing his best not to look scared. "I know the law."

"Do you? Excellent. Then you will understand when I tell you that those bottles are evidence in the investigation of a crime, one of the most heinous this city has ever seen. That entitles me to confiscate them. It also makes you an accessory to the crime."

"What crime? What are you talking about?"

"I am referring to the fact that this plague was manmade, for the purposes of making someone very rich."

"You getting rich by any chance, mate?" Innes asked.

Posh folk tended to be easier to rattle than the hard-bitten types hounds usually dealt with, but there were exceptions to every rule. Thirman raised his chin proudly. "I don't deny I'm making money, but since when is that a crime? My business is to sell remedies for illness, not to give them away for free. As for your allegations about the plague being man-made, I know nothing of that."

"I see," said the inspector. "And how did you come to be in possession of this wonder tonic?"

"Why, I made it, of course. It does say Thirman's Miracle Tonic on the bottle, after all."

The bloke wasn't exactly helping himself. Posh people were so proud.

"You discovered the recipe for yourself, did you?" Lenoir asked.

Thirman hesitated. Innes could tell he was thinking about lying. "No, I did not." He looked unhappy when he said that, so Innes reckoned it was probably the truth.

"Where did you get it?"

The apothecary looked away, embarrassed. He mumbled something Innes couldn't hear.

Neither could the inspector. "Pardon?"

"I bought it." Thirman scowled. "Satisfied?"

"Not remotely. When did you buy it, and from whom?"

"About a month ago, from a fellow calling himself Elder—though I don't think that was his real name."

"And why is that?"

"When I went looking for him the other day, nobody had seen him for a while, and when I started asking questions, it sounded like the Elder they knew didn't look a thing like the man I spoke with."

"Where did you go looking for him?"

"At the docks."

The inspector grunted, like he was feeling a bit smug.

"What made you think you would find him there?"

"He told me he was a sailor, although he didn't really look the part."

"How not?"

Innes didn't see why it mattered, but he reckoned Lenoir must have a reason.

"Well, I suppose he was a little . . . bookish."

"Not our man in the sketch, then," Lenoir muttered, as if to himself.

That meant there were others involved. Hounds called that a *conspiracy*.

"Could you describe him to a sketch artist?" the inspector asked.

Like Irving before him, Thirman was only too happy to turn the inspector's eye elsewhere. "I suppose so."

"What prompted you to go looking for this Elder in the first place?"

"To complain," the apothecary said. "He cheated me."

"Cheated you how?"

"He promised me I would be the only one with the recipe. I paid for that right. But now there are competitors poking up like weeds all over town."

The remark stuck in the inspector's craw. His eyes went cold. "I am very sorry to hear they are cutting into your profits."

"My profits are not as grand as you might think," the apothecary returned. You had to give it to the bloke—he had stones. "In fact, the margins are shrinking. Two weeks ago, I paid almost nothing for a pound of those herbs. Now I pay half a crown per bunch. *Per bunch!* It's obscene."

"This ingredient," Lenoir said, "it is Hogsfoot?"

"Hogsfoot?" The apothecary shrugged. "Possibly. That's not what Elder calls it."

"Show it to me."

Thirman ducked into the back room, and when he came back, he had a bundle of dried herbs. He didn't look very happy about handing it over. "Half a crown. Can you imagine? That makes it pound-for-pound the most expensive item on the market. Still, I suppose exotic herbs and spices are always worth a small fortune. Look what they're charging for cinnamon these days."

"What do you mean, *exotic*? This does not grow in Braeland?"

"Of course not!" Thirman laughed the way you do when something isn't the least bit funny. "Do you think I'd be paying half a crown per bundle if it did? It comes from Inataar. Brought in on the spice ships. That's where Elder got it. Angel wort, he calls it. Probably made the name up himself."

"Angel wort . . ." A glazed look came over the inspector, and he repeated the words in a near whisper. "Angel wort . . ." Abruptly, his gaze snapped back into focus.

Every hound knew that look. Innes could practically hear the *click* of something falling into place.

"Start with the cuffs, Sergeant, then round up the bottles. I will find us a cab."

"Haven't seen one of those in days, Inspector."

"There is a cab company just up the road. I will roust the owner. We must not dally at the station. In and out."

Innes glanced out the window. "Getting dark," he pointed out.

Lenoir turned and looked. He swore.

"First thing tomorrow?" Innes asked.

"Do you have any idea how many people will have died by then?" Lenoir snapped.

Innes didn't.

The inspector sighed and shook his head. "You're right, of course. Even if we skip the station, we will never reach the docks before nightfall." He rubbed the bridge of his nose, growling. "How in Durian's name did the day slip away so quickly?"

"They do that."

"We could fetch the dockmaster," Lenoir muttered. He was talking to himself again, trying to think his way around the sunset. "The ledgers will have what we need. . . ."

"When was the last time you slept, Inspector?" Probably wasn't any of his business, but if he had to guess, he would've said it had been a good long while.

The inspector gave him a sour look. Innes figured he was about to get an earful. But then Lenoir sighed and said, "Two nights ago."

"Thirty-six and counting," Innes said. "Tough to be sharp on those terms, Inspector." He shrugged. "'Course, it's up to you."

Lenoir's mouth pressed into a thin line. He was mad, but Innes didn't think it was directed at him. "First thing in the morning, then," Lenoir said. "As in, dawn."

Innes nodded. "Hope the sketch is done by then."

"There, at least, we need not worry. I know exactly where we are headed next."

"How?"

Lenoir flashed a rare smile. "Because of Zach."

"Who?"

"My informant."

"Oh yeah." Innes had met the boy once. Crafty kid. They all were, those street urchins. Leastways, those as managed to stay alive. "Where's he at these days?"

"I'm not sure, but if I know Zach, he is drinking ale and having a wonderful time."

CHAPTER 27

Zach drank his ale and thought dark thoughts.

The fire was his big chance, and he'd missed it. Bevin had been completely distracted, arguing with Old Molly and the others about whether they should make a run for it. Trouble was, Zach had been distracted too, mesmerized by the orange glow seeping through the warped windowpanes of Old Molly's room upstairs. He'd been a little bit afraid, but mostly, he'd been fascinated. And when he'd finally woken up to the opportunity that was in front of him, it was too late. Word came in that the fire had been contained, and that was it—the excitement was over, and Zach was herded back to the dark little room where he'd spent most of the past twenty-four hours.

His only consolation was that Bevin looked just as bored as he was. The big man flipped card after card, whizzing grumpily through a game of solitaire while Zach sipped awful beer.

"We could just forget about this, you know," Zach said, not for the first time. "If you let me go, I promise not to tell the hounds."

Bevin didn't even look up. "You keep trying, little pup." He flipped a card, scowled at it. "Bugger."

"What's taking so long, anyway?" It wasn't like Zach was in a hurry to be auctioned off, but he reckoned it would be better than watching Bevin get drunk. Again.

"Hounds must not have noticed you missing yet. Been a lot going on, in case you haven't noticed." He flipped another card. "Bugger."

"It could be a while, you know. Sometimes the inspector and I go weeks without talking." That was an exaggeration, but Bevin couldn't know that.

He didn't seem to care. "The patient cat gets the mouse." He scanned his cards for a move, but he didn't have one. Zach could see that from upside down.

"So we're just supposed to sit back here until then?"

"Pretty much."

Bugger.

Zach decided to try something new. "By keeping me here, you're killing people, you know."

At least Bevin looked up this time, if only briefly. "How do you figure that?"

"I got important information for the inspector about the plague. If he knew what I know, he could probably find a cure. You keeping me from him is costing people their lives."

Bevin snorted and flipped a card.

"It's true," Zach said. It was desperate, appealing to the humanity of a thug like this, but he'd already tried everything else he could think of.

"Yeah? And what information is that? What do you know that's so important?"

Zach hesitated. If he told Bevin what he'd learned, might it get back to Ritter and Nash?

"Well, now." Bevin put his cards down, eyes narrowing. "You really do know something, don't you?"

That was stupid. For all Zach knew, Bevin was in on it too. Ale and boredom had dulled his wits. *Not thinking like an inspector anymore, are you?* Aloud, he said, "Never mind."

"Oh, no—I'm not gonna let you off that easy. Most interesting thing I've heard all day. So tell me, little pup, what's your friend the inspector looking for, anyway? Why's he so interested in the plague? Last time I checked, hounds didn't go sniffing after diseases."

Zach had been thinking a lot about that, and he figured it couldn't hurt to tell Bevin what he'd concluded. "I reckon the hounds think somebody is behind it. Like when a building burns down, and somebody did it on purpose. That's called arse ... arse ..."

"Arson." Bevin laughed. "It's called arson."

"*Anyway,* I reckon this plague is the same thing. People are saying it was the Adali, but I bet it wasn't, and Inspector Lenoir is gonna prove it."

Bevin grunted. "So he figures it's one of us from *Serendipity,* 'cause we came across the plague in Darry? Thinks we brought it across the sea?"

"Well, did you?" Zach tried to ask the question the way Lenoir would have: cool, sharp-eyed.

Bevin smirked. "Not so as I've heard. That plague in Darry was years ago. Besides, why would we? Why would anyone?"

Zach couldn't answer that.

"So this important information you got, what is it?"

Zach studied Bevin. The big man was good at bluffing; one round of cards had been enough to convince Zach of that. But like Hairy, he had a tell: when he was lying, his right eye narrowed just a fraction, as if to say, *Are you buying this?* It was subtle, but Lenoir had taught Zach to observe everything, and that's what he did. Right now, he observed that Bevin's eyes were alert and round with interest. *Not bluffing,* Zach judged. He couldn't be absolutely sure, but he decided to risk it. Maybe he could learn something new. "You remember that sketch Inspector Lenoir showed you?"

"I guess."

"I found out who it is."

Bevin's eyes twinkled, and he sat forward a little in his chair. "Did you now?"

He's interested. There had to be a way Zach could use that to his advantage. "His name's Nash." Recognition flickered across Bevin's face. "You know him?" Zach asked, watching closely.

"Heard the name. Serves on one of the local rigs, I think."

"That's right. *Fly By Night*, at least these days. He used to serve on *Duchess of the Deep*, along with his mate, Ritter."

Zach felt pretty smug when Bevin's eyes widened. The big man gaped for a moment, then burst out laughing. "Well, well. You really *are* a little pup, aren't you? Gonna grow into a hound one day, is that it?"

"Maybe."

Bevin scratched his beard thoughtfully. "Nash, is it? And he's mates with Ritter, who was with us in Darry during the plague. I've gotta admit, that's quite a coincidence."

"Inspector Lenoir says *coincidence* is another word for an unsolved puzzle."

"Might be." Bevin sounded distracted. "Ritter always was a sneaky little cuss, but I never figured him for a killer."

Bevin had called Zach a *cuss* on more than one occasion, but there was something different in the way he said it now. "Sounds as if you don't like him much," Zach ventured.

"Nobody likes Ritter. He's no sailor, that one."

"He serves on the *Duchess*, doesn't he? And *Serendipity* before that?"

"As purser," Bevin said dismissively.

"What's that?"

"The money man. Just an accountant. You know what an accountant is?"

"Sure." He had no idea. "But he's an accountant on a ship. That makes him a sailor."

Bevin snorted. "You can throw a cat in water, that don't make him a fish. Hell, I reckon a cat takes to water better than Ritter. He was sick half the time, and had his nose in a ledger the other half. Counting his gold, that's what made him happy. Going over his numbers, whistling those stupid little tunes of his. If he could find a way to pinch your coin, he would. Dock you for any damned thing he could come up with, no matter how flimsy." Bevin's expression darkened, and he shook his head. "Landed more than one of our mates in debtor's jail. Lucky to still be around, you ask me. You'd think someone would've cut his throat by now." Judging from the look on Bevin's face, he wouldn't mind doing the job himself.

"Did he seem crazy?" Zach couldn't think of any other reason to start a plague on purpose.

"No more than a true sailor, and maybe less. The sea does strange things to a man's head. She sings to you, and sometimes it's all you can hear." His expression took on a faraway look.

Keep him talking, Zach thought. Some of this information might be useful to Lenoir, and besides, it might help him win Bevin over, get him to rethink his plans. "If Ritter and Nash really did start the plague, they must have a reason. Revenge, maybe?" Most of the violence Zach had witnessed could be put down to revenge. That, or money. Or revenge over money. *Which is how I ended up here.*

"Revenge on whom? The whole city?" Bevin shook his head and took a sip of ale. "Doesn't make sense."

"I guess not," Zach admitted. "But do you think he's capable of it? Starting the plague, I mean?"

Bevin shrugged. "Could be. Certainly never showed much empathy for his fellow man."

That's the fish calling the snake slimy. Zach thought about yesterday, tried to remember everything he'd seen and heard, right up to the moment Bevin nabbed him. One memory certainly stuck out. "Do you think it could have something to do with monkeys?"

"Eh?" Bevin looked at him as though he'd lost his coins.

Zach sighed. "Never mind."

"What's he up to?" Bevin scratched his beard some more, staring off into space.

The opening was too good to pass up. "If you let me go, maybe we can find out."

The look Bevin gave him was almost pitying. "Don't set yourself up for disappointment, little pup. Life's got heartache enough in store without you going looking for it."

No arguing with that, Zach thought bitterly. "Just sounded to me like maybe you wouldn't mind doing Ritter an ill turn."

"Wouldn't mind at all. I'd line up for it, tell the truth. But it's like I said, this is business. I'm a practical man, and there's no profit in revenge."

But what if there could be?

Zach drank his ale and thought.

CHAPTER 28

Lenoir stopped dead when he saw Kody.

The sergeant was perched on the edge of Innes's desk, sipping tea, the two of them gossiping like ladies at needlework. The left side of Kody's face looked every bit as ugly as it had the day before, and his normally square shoulders had a droop to them, like a beanstalk that wants water. Lenoir's already foul mood instantly became fouler.

"What in the name of Durian's Holy Host are you doing here?" he demanded from halfway across the kennel.

Kody actually looked surprised. "Where else would I be?"

"In bed, recuperating from plague!"

The whole kennel froze. At that moment, it would have been possible to hear a mouse washing its whiskers.

The station was virtually deserted, but every man and woman in the place, watchman or scribe or sweep, was now staring at Kody. And then at Lenoir. And back at Kody.

Kody flushed, the first hint of genuinely good color he had had in what seemed like forever. "Maybe we could talk in your office, Inspector."

"I would be delighted, Sergeant."

Together, they headed up the stairs, Lenoir venting his exasperation on the aging carpentry with every step. What in God's name was the matter with this man? Had he not learned his lesson yesterday? (No, Lenoir corrected himself, the day before. Where *had* these last couple of days gone?) The chief had not yet come in—or, more likely, had already gone out to the barricades—so Lenoir would not get any help there.

Kody did not even wait until the door was closed. "I'm fit for duty, Inspector."

Lenoir scowled. "According to whom?"

"According to me. And Merden." He drew a piece of paper from his pocket and offered it to Lenoir.

"You got a note from Merden?" Under other circumstances, it would have been amusing.

"I figured you wouldn't take my word for it." Kody took a sip of his tea, his features as calm and collected as half a gargoyle mask could be.

Lenoir looked over the beautifully flowing script. In writing, as in speech, Merden was brief and mysterious, leaving many questions unanswered. *Sergeant Kody is fit for duty. However, he should not run, lift anything heavy, or otherwise cause his heart rate to climb too much.*

"This is meant to convince me?" Lenoir growled, waving the paper. "What good are you to me if you cannot let your heart rate climb *too much*, whatever in the below that means?"

Kody sighed. "Listen, Inspector, I've spent the better part of the past twenty-four hours asleep, with a steady dose of tonic. The fever is gone, the bleeding has stopped, I've had plenty of time to rehydrate, and I couldn't sleep another minute unless you knocked me cold or drugged me, not with the bastard who did this still roaming loose."

"I am on the verge of a major break in this case," Lenoir said.

"You've already had a major break," Kody said, smiling. "You found a cure to the plague. If you hadn't, I'd probably be dead by now. Instead, I feel like I'm getting over the flu. That stuff is amazing." He held out his arm. "You see this cut? Merden made it this morning. Clotted up faster than anything I've ever seen."

"I am pleased to hear it, Sergeant, but I meant that I am close to finding out who is responsible for all of this."

Kody's smile vanished. "Why do you think I'm here?"

"Sergeant Innes is downstairs. Give me one good reason why I should not take him, a perfectly healthy specimen?"

"Because there's no one in all of Kennian who wants to find this bastard more than me. Or who deserves it more, if I may say so. Sir."

There, Lenoir could not argue.

"I appreciate your concern for my health," Kody went on, "but that's my business. As for whether I can hold up my end—you don't need to worry about that either."

Perhaps it was the look in the sergeant's eye, or the determination in his voice, or the thick thread of guilt that tugged like a taut fishing line at the bottom of Lenoir's belly. Whatever the reason, he found he could not deny Kody.

He sighed. "On your head be it, Sergeant," he said, and he gestured at the door.

"There." Lenoir dragged the ledger closer to the window and tapped it. "*Fly By Night*, provenance Inataar by way of Mirrhan, seven hundred crates angel wort." He read the date in the right-hand column. "Six weeks ago."

Kody forced himself not to squint in the cheerful morning sunlight. The headache was more or less gone, but for some reason, bright light still bothered his eyes. He couldn't let the inspector see that, though. He'd had a hard enough time convincing Lenoir as it was, and had endured nearly half an hour of barbed remarks on the way to the docks. If it hadn't been for Merden's note, he wouldn't be here, he knew.

Merden had taken some convincing of his own. The note Lenoir saw wasn't the first version he'd penned. The original started out, *Sergeant Kody continues to display remarkable bullheadedness and indifference to his health,* but Kody had managed to persuade him to stick to the facts. And the facts were that he could stand upright, could walk and talk without keeling over, and wasn't in any danger of relapse. There was nothing wrong with his mind, and he was no longer contagious. He wouldn't be joining the lads for a friendly game of dustball anytime soon, but even if he was at half strength, he'd still be stronger than Lenoir. As far as he was concerned, that meant he was fit for duty, and when he explained it that way to Merden, the Adal had reluctantly agreed.

"I owe you one, Merden," Kody had said.

The Adal had snorted and criticized Kody's maths.

Kody didn't much fancy the idea of being indebted to a witchdoctor, but there was nothing, *nothing*, he wouldn't do to get his hands on the sick bastard who had done this to his town. To him.

"Seven hundred crates," Lenoir repeated, "at a total estimated value of two hundred fifty crowns."

Kody frowned. "That's it?"

"My guess is it is worth even less than that. The value was probably exaggerated to avoid suspicion. If the herb is as commonplace in Inataar as its cousin in Braeland, it is probably worth next to nothing at its point of origin."

Meanwhile, it was apparently selling at half a crown a bushel in Braeland. Someone was getting very, very rich.

"Look here, Inspector," Kody said. "There are three different dates in the *unloaded* column. The last one was just yesterday."

"That's right." The dockmaster leaned in over Lenoir's shoulder. "Pain in the arse, that rig. Unloading in dribs and drabs, taking up space while I got others waiting out in the bay. She's paying the fees, but still . . . it's not right, treating her like a warehouse. She belongs out on the seas, not gathering barnacles at port."

Lenoir glanced back over his shoulder. "What do you make of that? Why wouldn't she unload all at once?"

"Most likely they don't want to pay too much for warehousing, and the crew said they didn't want to put all the product on the market at once. Building up demand, or some such." The dockmaster shrugged.

Fury flooded Kody's face. "Depraved sons of—"

Lenoir shot him a warning look. He didn't want Kody giving away too much. He was right, of course. They were finally homing in on a suspect, and the last thing they needed was to show their cards. Kody took a deep breath.

"When they unloaded yesterday, where did they take the goods?" Lenoir asked.

The dockmaster consulted the ledger. "Warehouse 57."

"Show me the ledger for that warehouse."

The dockmaster fetched it down and handed it over with a sullen expression. He still didn't fancy being ordered around. If Lenoir noticed, he didn't care; he scanned the columns again, looking back and forth between the two books. "It says here there are two hundred fifty crates remaining on board."

"So it does."

"And between these three columns, the number unloaded comes to four hundred fifty."

"That adds up," Kody said.

"Yes, but look here. According to the warehouse ledger, four hundred thirty-nine crates were checked in to Warehouse 57."

The dockmaster frowned. "Odd."

Eleven missing. Odd indeed.

"Could it simply be a clerical error?"

The dockmaster shook his head. "My people are careful about that sort of thing. That ledger tells the customs commissioner what he's collecting on. If he shows up at the warehouse and finds something else ... Best-case scenario, the difference comes out of our pockets. Worst case, my arse is in Fort Hald."

"And yet you failed to notice the discrepancy."

The dockmaster reddened. "Smuggling happens, Inspector. We do what we can, but I can't personally crack open every crate, or escort every load to the warehouse and guard it until the customs man arrives. All I'm saying is that it wouldn't be a problem of sums. If the figures don't add up, it means somebody's up to no good."

"So the question," Kody said, "is what was in those eleven crates?"

"Something they did not wish the customs collector to see."

But what?

Judging from Lenoir's expression, he had no idea either. "Who captains *Fly By Night*?"

"Captain Marshall Elder."

"Elder." Lenoir said the name like it meant something to him. "Where can I find him? On the ship?"

"You can try," the dockmaster said, "but I doubt it. I've been down there to look for him three or four times, and he's never there. Haven't seen Marsh since *Fly By Night* got back, to tell you the truth. No one has."

"Then who is dealing with the cargo?"

"His crew. What's left of 'em, anyway. When a ship comes into port, her crew scatter like dandelion fluff. Only a few stay behind to watch over the rig, and even those are ashore half the time. Most days, it's just the security guard they hired here in port."

"What about the first mate?" Kody asked.

"Haven't seen him in days."

Lenoir swore and rubbed his eyes. "What about the ship's owner? Where can we find him?"

"There I can help you. *Fly By Night* is a local girl, not

one of those foreign jobs. Like as not, her owner is a Kennian."

The dockmaster fetched another ledger. As he flipped through the pages, Lenoir asked, "You seem to know a lot about the comings and goings of the *Fly By Night* crew, considering how many ships you have to deal with every day."

"Marsh is a friend of mine, or at least I thought so. Damned rude, coming into port and not even saying hello." He shook his head and wet his thumb, flipping a page. "Then there's the business with his ship sitting idle. Not like him at all. I'll give him a piece of my mind, next I see him."

Something told Kody it was going to be a long time. "Here you go." The dockmaster pushed the ledger across his desk. "Third line down."

"Lord Kelvin Haughty," Kody read.

Lenoir frowned and looked for himself. "Hughley. Lord Kelvin *Hughley*."

"Oh," said Kody.

"We will pay him a visit presently," said Lenoir. "But first, I want to see that ship."

An empty ship is an eerie place. Like an abandoned house, or a temple long forsaken, its former inhabitants do not seem absent so much as invisible—watching, silent and unmarked, from a space the living cannot touch. Lenoir both loved and hated such places. Hated, because they oppressed his nerves, as if eyes followed him from every shadow. Loved, because they seemed to him almost alive, witnesses to the truths he sought. Capable, if he was clever enough, of telling him everything he needed to know. *Fly By Night* held the answer to the riddle—who had brought the plague, and how. She spoke to him, albeit in a language he did not understand. He could hear her whispering in the creak of timber and the soft sigh of the sea. Messages were hidden in the enigmatic geometry of her cargo hold, if only he could make them out.

Kody absorbed the scene differently. "This place stinks."

"Impressive analysis, Sergeant. Do be sure to mention it in your report." Lenoir held out the pry bar.

The sergeant snatched it up with a wry look and went over to the cluster of crates crammed in a corner of the hold. "I'm just saying, it doesn't smell like herbs to me. It smells like *piss*, and a whole lot worse." If he experienced anything more than olfactory distress at finding himself in the belly of the ship that had brought him plague, he gave no sign.

"Ship's holds aren't known for their pleasing perfumes," the dockmaster said. He adjusted the scarf on his face, perhaps hoping it might do a better job of blocking the smell.

Wood barked, and Kody pried the lid off the crate. "Herbs," he reported.

"Do one more, just to be sure," said Lenoir.

Kody pried open a second crate. "Same."

Lenoir nodded; he had expected as much. "At half a crown a bushel, these crates are worth at least a hundred crowns apiece."

The dockmaster whistled. "For a bunch of dried plants? Who knew?"

"Whoever shipped them across the Grey knew."

"Lord Hughley, I guess," Kody said.

"Perhaps." Lenoir was not so sure. To the dockmaster, he said, "You mentioned that you have found the ship deserted several times when you stopped by. Is that not unusual?"

"Yeah, it is. Most captains insist on at least one or two staying behind, plus a couple of guards. That's the way we prefer it on our end too, in case anything comes up. Like the hounds taking an interest, for example."

"How many men does it take to operate a vessel of this size?"

The dockmaster glanced around. "Rig like this? Crew of fifteen would be typical."

"Fifteen crew, and none of them aboard." Lenoir raised his lantern higher, chasing back the shadows. "You say you know Captain Elder well. What about his first mate?"

"Bird?" The dockmaster shrugged. "Enough to say hello."

If only we had the sketch. Something told Lenoir that the dockmaster would know their suspect too, whether it was Bird or someone else.

He turned full circle, letting the light spill over the timbers. Something against the near wall caught his eye: a thin white scar at about the level of his knee. He went to take a closer look. "There is a scratch in the wood here. Fresh, by the looks of it."

"Probably nicked it when we were unloading the crates," the dockmaster said.

"I don't think so." Lenoir moved the lantern a few inches to the right. "There are more over here." Transferring the lantern to his left hand, he held his right to the wall, pressing the tips of his gloved fingers against the wood. "Four parallel scratches, like claw marks. A cat, perhaps?"

"Could be, but I'll bet it was the monkeys. Filthy little buggers."

Lenoir whirled around, the light from his lantern slashing the darkness. "What did you say?"

"*This* was the ship with the monkeys in it?" In the glow of the lantern, Kody's scowl was truly frightening. "Why in the below didn't you say so?"

"How was I supposed to know you'd care?" the dockmaster said defensively.

Lenoir shook his head. The imbecility of the common man never ceased to amaze. "Why were they not listed on the manifest?"

"Because they weren't cargo. Not officially, anyway.

They were just pets. Belonged to Marsh, or so I was told."

"Told by whom?"

"Bird, the first mate."

"But you never confirmed this with the captain himself?"

"Like I said, I haven't seen Marsh since *Fly By Night* set sail a couple of months back."

"Where are the monkeys now?"

"No idea."

"That must be why it smells like piss in here," Kody said.

"Possibly." Lenoir had no idea what monkey urine smelled like, but to his nose, the stench in the hold was all too human. He made a slow tour of the area, scanning the floor, the walls, what remained of the cargo. In one corner of the hold, he found a series of barrels, most open and empty, a few still sealed. In another, the reek of urine was especially strong, as if it had been doused over and over. He found another series of scars in the wood, but these had not been made by claws. There were six of them, perfectly even cuts in two groups of three. Nearby, Lenoir found a dark stain on the floorboards. He drew his knife and scratched at it, producing a rust-colored sawdust. *Blood.*

Lenoir shone his light on the dockmaster. "Fifteen men to sail this craft, you say?"

"That's right."

"In that case," Lenoir said, "we are looking for four suspects, and one of them is named Bird."

"Only four?" Kody frowned. "What about the rest?"

"The rest," Lenoir said, "are dead."

CHAPTER 29

"Dead?" Kody blinked, surprised. "Not that I'm sorry to hear it, but . . . how do you know?"

"Because I read the signs," Lenoir said. He walked over to the cluster of barrels. "You see these? They are supply barrels. Food and water."

"So?"

"So, look how many are still sealed. The crew consumed only two-thirds of what they brought."

"Maybe they overestimated what they'd need."

"Not bloody likely," the dockmaster said. "Marsh is too experienced a captain to take up precious cargo space with supplies he didn't need."

So why all the uneaten food? Kody was beginning to see where Lenoir was headed.

"Then there is the urine smell, as you so cunningly observed. The stench is concentrated here, in this corner. Some animals instinctively urinate and defecate in a particular spot, but most are indiscriminate. That, and the smell itself, leads me to suspect it is actually human urine." He walked over to another part of the hold, shining his lantern against the wall. "As for these scratches, they are definitely human. Too even to have been made by anything but a knife, and clustered together in distinct groups of three. Someone was keeping count of something. The passage of time, for instance. One mark for each day, such as prisoners are wont to do."

"Someone was being held down here," Kody said.

"Exactly." Lenoir moved again, and this time he shone the light at the floor. "The blood soaked into the boards here may or may not be his."

Kody knelt beside the bloodstain. "If it is, this isn't where he died. Not enough blood."

"No. But my guess is whoever it was did not die violently, at least not in the conventional sense."

Kody looked up at Lenoir. "And you think that because . . ."

"Eleven crates, Sergeant."

"The missing cargo." Kody remembered, but he didn't quite follow.

"Eleven crates disappeared somewhere between this ship and Warehouse 57. And do you happen to recall how many infected corpses Sister Rhea's man collected?"

Kody swore softly. "Could it be a coincidence?"

"Possibly." Lenoir walked back over to the cargo, the two hundred–plus crates full of herbs. "It could also be a coincidence that these crates are approximately the size of a coffin. Or that the first load of cargo was taken off this ship six weeks ago—around the time bodies started turning up in the Camp."

"A lot of coincidences," Kody said, sighing.

"Too many to credit."

"But if it takes fifteen people to sail this ship, how did they manage?"

"Judging by the barrels, they were most of the way home before the crew started to perish." Lenoir turned to the dockmaster. "Is it possible that a skeleton crew could pilot the ship for a short distance?"

"Just barely, but yeah—it's possible, if they were close enough to home, and they didn't hit any weather. If they were gonna make it, this would be the season to do it."

"That is not a coincidence either. This was all meticulously planned."

The dockmaster looked grim. "So Marsh—he's dead, then?"

"I cannot be certain about anyone specific, but it does seem likely."

"Bird never said anything. Guess that means he's involved?" The dockmaster's hands were balling into fists at his sides. *There's a storm brewing there,* Kody thought. He understood it well enough. He was feeling pretty dark-minded himself.

"You think this Bird and his coconspirators infected the rest of the crew on purpose?" Kody could feel the anger boiling up again, like lava rising in a volcano. "Depraved doesn't even cover it," he growled.

"Depraved," Lenoir said, "and efficient. As I said, this was all planned very carefully."

"Where do the monkeys come into it?"

"Is it not obvious? The monkeys were the carriers. Bird and the others couldn't risk traveling for weeks on end with infected corpses, so instead they brought monkeys, something they could keep safely caged until the right moment. It explains everything—how they were able to find an infected host even though Inataar is plague-free, how the corpses came to be fresh in spite of a long sea voyage. Animals have been known to carry diseases to which they themselves are resistant or immune. Most likely, that is what happened here. They were kept segregated somewhere in the hold, separate from the crew, until Bird needed them. All he had to do was wait until the ship was most of the way home, stage a mutiny, lock the crew down in the hold, release the monkeys, and wait it out. In such close quarters with the animals, infection would have been inevitable. As long as Bird and his coconspirators handled the monkeys carefully, it would have been a simple matter to control who was exposed to the disease, and when."

A simple matter. Kody wasn't sure what infuriated him more: the ruthlessness of the crime, or the matter-of-fact way Lenoir explained it.

His thoughts must have shown on his face, because Lenoir sighed. "I do not mean to sound callous, Sergeant. But if we are to find these men, we must first understand them."

Kody knew he was right, but it still made him sick. "Are you sure about all this? What about the blood-stain?"

"We know at least one crew member had a knife on him when he was locked in the hold. Perhaps a fight broke out."

"Or maybe they managed to take out one of the monkeys." Somehow, the idea made Kody feel a little better.

"Perhaps," said Lenoir. To the dockmaster, he said, "This Bird, can you describe him?"

"Well, he takes after a bird, doesn't he? Or did you think that was his real name?"

Lenoir gave the man a sour look. "I did, actually. So, what—he has a long nose?"

"Long nose, beady eyes. Built like a beanpole. Has a weird, twitchy way about him."

Built like a beanpole. "Not the man Brice saw," Kody said.

"It would seem not. We must get the scribes to work on new sketches as soon as possible—of Bird, and of our original suspect."

"With the Inataari, that makes three out of four we should be able to spot easily enough."

"Perhaps if we had watchmen at our disposal." Lenoir sighed. "As things stand, nothing will be easy."

"And there's still the fourth man. We have no idea who he might be."

"We'll find out," Lenoir said. "And when we do, he will hang."

*   *   *

Durian's balls. Ritter lowered the spyglass. In the distance, the dockmaster and the hounds were reduced to specks as they climbed the gangplank up to *Fly By Night.* If they'd found the ship, they knew most of it already, and soon enough they'd know the rest. Out in the suburbs, Ritter could continue to pass himself off as Captain Elder, but down here at the docks, that wouldn't fly. He was known around here, and though there weren't many who could connect him to *Fly By Night,* it took only one. *I should have been more careful,* he thought. He could have hired someone else to oversee the cargo, someone expendable. That way, none of it could be traced back to him. But he'd been too excited, too tickled by his own cleverness, and now at least half a dozen dockhands could attest to his involvement. One of them might have mentioned him already, and even if they hadn't, the hounds would most likely interview the lot. They'd find out about Ritter sooner or later, and then it would be over. He'd already made enough money to walk away—more than enough—but there was a king's fortune still unsold. . . .

Damn! If only he'd given Nash the order days ago, the hounds would have been taken care of by now, the way Sukhan had taken care of the other loose ends. Nash would get to them eventually, but by then it might be too late. They'd already found the *Fly*, and thirty-six thousand crowns worth of goods were about to be seized. That thought alone was enough to make Ritter queasy. Worse, the hounds would certainly use the angel wort to make more tonic. They'd distribute it for *free*, dumping it on the market. They'd ruin everything.

Ritter figured he had about two, three days at most. After that, it would all be over. Most likely, he'd find himself in jail. Best-case scenario, the roaring market he'd carefully constructed for himself would collapse. Still, you could make a lot of money in forty-eight hours, if you knew what you were doing. *Volume is the answer,* he thought. Before, he'd been relying on fat margins. He didn't have time for that now. *Get it all out there, reduce the price, sell as much as you can, then disappear.* That was the only course left to him.

He had enough product, even without the remaining cargo on the *Fly*. He'd moved the last load out of Warehouse 57 as soon as he'd discovered the break-in, and that was as much as he could hope to sell in forty-eight hours anyway. With the supply side taken care of, he could concentrate on creating demand.

He had his monkeys, but letting them loose in an open space wouldn't do much good. It had taken days of being locked up in the hold with them for the crew to fall sick. The little bastards might bite one or two people if he got lucky, but that wouldn't be enough. Besides, it would take a few days for the victim to start showing symptoms, and Ritter didn't have that kind of time. He needed another plan.

Fortunately, Ritter was never short of plans.

All it would take was a handcart and a miasma mask. With so few corpse collectors making the rounds, he'd have no trouble finding households desperate to be rid of their dead. He'd have a barrowful in no time, and another after that. He could plant the corpses anywhere he liked. Out in the open, in untouched neighborhoods, where they'd create the most panic. A water well here and there, just to speed things along. It would take a couple of weeks for the plague to really get going, but that was all right. The deaths were just a side effect anyway. It was the *fear* he really needed.

Ritter glanced up at the sun. Early afternoon. If he could get a couple of loads of corpses by nightfall, he could distribute them under cover of darkness. *Perfect.* By this time tomorrow, if he planned his route well, every neighborhood in Kennian would be covered—starting with the richest. Then it would be too late to stop it. He'd have his demand, and every sprig of angel wort in Kennian wouldn't be enough to slake it.

You'll have to leave town, he thought. That was unfortunate. He loved Kennian; he hated to have to sacrifice her to the plague. There was no help for it, though. As much as Ritter loved Kennian, he loved gold even more.

One hundred seventy crates left, at a hundred and forty-four crowns apiece, minus Nash's ten and Sukhan's fifteen . . . Ritter did the maths, and decided it was more than enough to live on, even for him.

Whistling, he collapsed his spyglass and headed for Warehouse 49.

"I am very sorry, Officers, but His Lordship is unable to receive you today. Good morning." The chamberlain started to close the door.

Kody wedged his foot in the doorjamb. "I think maybe there's a misunderstanding here. This isn't a request."

The servant regarded him coldly. "There is indeed a misunderstanding, sir. I very much regret that His Lordship is *not able* to receive you."

"Not able." Lenoir narrowed his eyes. "Why is that, exactly?"

The chamberlain hesitated, and for a moment, Lenoir thought he was going to have to ask Kody to be even less polite. Then the servant lowered his voice and said, "His Lordship is not well, and we are under strict instructions to admit no visitors."

"Not well as in, has a bit of a sniffle? Or . . ." Kody shifted a little farther back from the door, as if he might catch plague a second time.

The servant made no reply, but he did not need to; Lenoir read the truth in the tense lines of the man's face. "I believe it is a little more serious than that, Sergeant."

Kody glanced up at the windows. "There's no flag. . . ."

"Of course not." An aristocratic household would

never advertise the presence of plague. Lenoir was surprised the chamberlain had admitted as much as he had. Perhaps he was hoping the hounds would insist the servants be sent away. If so, he would be disappointed; Lenoir had no legal basis for interfering. "How long?" he asked the man.

"Yesterday morning."

"And his condition?"

The chamberlain cleared his throat uncomfortably. "His Lordship's physician is . . . not optimistic."

"That is unfortunate." Lenoir paused, considering the man. "I have heard of a new medicine," he said, watching the chamberlain carefully. "A tonic sold on the street that is said to bring some relief to the afflicted. Have you not tried it?"

The chamberlain looked positively scandalized. "A miracle potion peddled by street hucksters? I think not. His Lordship is in the care of Dr. Ipsworth, the finest physician in Braeland."

"I see. And what treatment has Dr. Ipsworth prescribed?"

"I hardly think it appropriate for me to discuss such details."

"A harmless question, surely? The plague gains new ground every day. If I should fall ill, I would very much like to know what the finest physician in Braeland recommends."

The chamberlain glanced furtively behind him and narrowed the doorway to a crack, as if afraid the good doctor might overhear and charge him a fee. "His Lordship's chamber is purified continuously with camphor smoke, and the dark blood is drawn off every few hours."

Smoke and leeches. And they call the Adali superstitious.

Aloud, Lenoir said, "I will certainly remember it, and I wish His Lordship a speedy recovery. In the meantime, perhaps you can help me. I am trying to track down a

man called Bird, who is first mate aboard *Fly By Night*.
Do you know where I might find him?"

The chamberlain shook his head. "But perhaps Mr.
Garren can help you. He is Lord Hughley's personal secretary."

"Is he here?"

"Oh, yes. He is never far from His Lordship's side,
even now. I will fetch him from the study. Under the circumstances, I think it best if you remain outside the
manor."

Lenoir did not argue.

"So, that's odd," Kody said when the servant had
gone.

"What's odd, Sergeant?"

"Well, Lord Hughley has the plague."

"So it would appear."

"And the people treating him don't seem to know
much of anything about the miracle cure."

"No."

"The miracle cure that came in on Lord Hughley's
own ship. You don't think that's strange?"

Lenoir shrugged. "Not particularly. Most likely, His
Lordship is unaware that *Fly By Night* was in the business of importing angel wort."

"Unaware? How could he be *unaware* of the cargo of
his own vessel?"

"It happens all the time. Lord Hughley is a peer and
a parliamentarian. He has no need to involve himself in
the day-to-day of his business dealings. Why do you
think smuggling is so commonplace? It can almost never
be traced back to the ship owners. Men like Hughley
may or may not suspect what their employees are up to,
but so long as the money keeps coming in, many of them
prefer not to know. That way, if one of their captains is
caught smuggling, they can truthfully deny any knowledge of the cargo." Lenoir adopted a surprised expression. *"Opium? Why, they told me it was cinnamon!"*

Kody shook his head. "Just one more reason to love the high and mighty."

The door creaked, and a small, nervous-looking man appeared.

"Mr. Garren, I presume?"

"Clive Garren." The man stuck out his hand.

"Inspector Lenoir, and this is Sergeant Kody." Lenoir extricated himself from the man's sweaty grip. "I hope not to take too much of your time. We are trying to track down Captain Elder, or his first mate, Bird."

Garren's eyes flicked worriedly between them. "Are they in some kind of trouble?"

"Never mind that," Kody said. "Do you know where we can find them or not?"

"I have addresses for them, if that helps."

"Indeed it does," said Lenoir.

"Can't promise they're current. Sailors are creatures of habit, but if their favorite rooming house is full when they get back to shore . . . Anyway, let me just go fetch my files. . . ."

Garren disappeared back inside.

"You still think Captain Elder is dead?" Kody asked.

"I do, but I did not want to give too much away, in case Garren is involved."

Kody grunted skeptically. "Doesn't seem like the type."

"Perhaps not, but I am beginning to suspect our fourth man will not seem like the type. I have a hard time believing that this scheme was concocted by a bunch of sailors."

"Me too," Kody said. "Most sailors I've known have a hard time managing their money purse, let alone coming up with something as complex as this."

While they waited for Garren to return, Lenoir glanced up at the sky. Afternoon, and threatening rain. He sensed they had a long day, and possibly a long night, ahead of them. *You should not have left your coat be-*

hind, he thought. Reeking of smoke seemed the least of his worries now.

Garren reappeared with a ledger. As he was flipping through, Lenoir asked, "What can you tell me about *Fly By Night*'s cargo?"

"I'd have to look. Spices, usually, but every now and then they'd get their hands on some silk."

"And what about angel wort?"

Garren frowned and looked up. "Pardon?"

Lenoir scrutinized him carefully and decided the blank look was genuine. "Never mind."

"Here we are. Lionsvale Arms." Garren held out the ledger. "41 Court Street. Down in the poor district, I think."

"Provided it still exists." The fire had taken out half the area. "And what about the purser—do you have an address for him?"

"Marten? Yes, I've got it here somewhere...."

Two minutes later they were headed back down the drive, armed with nothing more than a couple of addresses that might or might not have survived the fire. Still, it was something.

"Why the purser?" Kody asked.

"A hunch."

"Based on what?"

"By definition, a hunch does not need to be based on anything."

Kody gave him a wry look. "Humor me? I did nearly die of plague."

"A scheme of this nature and complexity requires a calculating mind, one familiar with money and the basic principles of economics. It also requires someone in a position to convince captain and crew to take on an unfamiliar cargo, instead of what they were sent to purchase. Assuming Captain Elder was not a complete fool, he would not have taken the word of just any deckhand that there was profit to be made in a plant he had never heard of. Who could have convinced him to do it, at possible risk of his job? His first mate, perhaps. Anyone else?"

"His purser," Kody said.

"Satisfied?"

Kody rolled his eyes, apparently considering that his brush with death gave him license for minor insolence. Which, Lenoir supposed grudgingly, it did.

The sergeant led the way down the path, and when he reached the heavy wrought-iron gate, he swung it aside without visible effort, giving no sign of the weakness he must be feeling. That was good. They were getting close, and in Lenoir's experience, that usually meant one thing:

It was about to get ugly.

CHAPTER 30

Kody could tell from the stench that there was a corpse behind the door.

If the building hadn't been practically empty, somebody would certainly have reported it. As it was, Kody and Lenoir hadn't even been able to find the landlord. "I suppose I'll have to bust it in," he said with a sigh. He was pretty sure that would fall afoul of Merden's rules about exertion, but the Adal wasn't here to object.

"I doubt that, Sergeant, unless you imagine that Mr. Bird died of natural causes." Lenoir turned the handle, and the door creaked open just enough to reveal a slash of weak light. Kody started forward, but Lenoir raised a hand. "Get your crossbow ready."

"You think the killer is still in there? With a rotting corpse?"

"Most likely not, but we are closing in on some dangerous men, and I have a feeling we will be crossing paths very soon. It is better to be cautious."

Kody couldn't disagree with that. He swung his crossbow down from his back. "Ready?"

Lenoir cocked the hammer of his pistol and gave a short nod.

Kody burst into the room, crossbow leveled. He covered all the corners himself, not trusting Lenoir to do it properly. Only when he was satisfied that the tiny flat was empty did he allow himself to throw his sleeve over his face. "*Durian's grave.* I think I'm gonna throw up."

"That would hardly improve the smell," Lenoir said from behind his own arm.

It wasn't hard to find the body. The flat was barely big enough to accommodate a bed, a table, and a washbasin. Lenoir had scarcely crossed the threshold before he said, "Over here."

The corpse lay facedown near the table. From where Kody stood, he could just make out the awkward angles of the man's frame, as though he had tumbled out of a chair. Sunlight straining through a grimy window fell upon a stain on the floorboards. The dark spot was already moving with flies, and Kody said a silent prayer that he wouldn't have to deal with maggots on top of everything. He wasn't particularly squeamish, but there were limits, and little squirming sacs of goo were on the wrong side of them, especially when he already felt like something a cat retched up.

Lenoir wedged his boot under the corpse and rolled it over. Kody's stomach heaved at the smell, but he forced himself to get closer. "Throat cut," he said through his sleeve. "From behind, looks like."

Lenoir knelt. "A curved blade, I think."

Kody looked closer. There did seem to be a bit of a flourish at one end of the cut. "Could be."

"He knew his killer."

Lenoir's eyes were on the corpse, but there was no way he could draw that conclusion just from looking at the body, so Kody threw a glance around the room to find what Lenoir had already spotted.

Bed unmade. Pair of boots near the door. No sign of forced entry, but the door wasn't locked, either. How . . . ?

Then he noticed the jug on the table. "Two cups." He picked one up and sniffed it. "Mead."

"No signs of a struggle on the body. Our Mr. Bird was taken by surprise."

"Someone's cleaning house," Kody said. It was practically inevitable with conspiracies, especially when there was money involved.

"So it would seem," Lenoir said, standing. "Days ago, by the looks of it."

"And the smell of it." Kody considered the corpse. Tattoos covered his arms, and his head was close-shaven. "Tough-looking bloke. I'm guessing he wasn't much of an intellectual."

"Impossible to be sure, but I am inclined to agree. And our man in the sketch did not strike the witness as particularly educated either. Neither of them is likely to be the brains behind this operation."

"Maybe our man in the sketch is the one who took out Bird."

"Perhaps, but I doubt it."

"Why?"

The inspector's lips pursed in annoyance. On any other day, Kody knew, Lenoir would have ignored him, or ridiculed him for asking. But almost dying of plague had its advantages. Lenoir pointed at the body and said, "The curved blade. We have already determined that our man in the sketch is Kennian. It's possible that he has taken a liking to exotic swords, but it is much more likely that our murderer is the Inataari, since their kind are known to favor curved blades."

Kody did a quick tour of the flat, but found nothing of interest. A single canvas bag seemed to contain everything Bird owned in the world, which consisted of some well-used clothing, a well-used bones set, and a very well-used knife. "Guess Bird didn't earn that much," Kody said.

"Either that, or he did not manage his earnings well." Lenoir held up the money purse he'd found on the body and gave it a shake.

"Not much jingle there," Kody agreed.

"It would appear that Mr. Bird had not yet received his cut of the profits. My guess is that whoever did this was never planning to share."

"Might be more bodies in store for us today."

"Almost certainly. As for Mr. Bird here, he has told us all he can." Lenoir rose.

"So what next—the purser?"

"Indeed."

They made their way south, skirting the edges of the still-smoldering ruin that had once been the busier half of the poor district. The place was all but unrecognizable. Here and there, a familiar landmark—a church spire or a fountain—offered some sense of geography, but it was hard to believe this was the same neighborhood Kody and Lenoir had walked through so many times before. People had started to trickle back in, but most of them didn't seem to know what to do with themselves, wandering around with dazed looks, or picking aimlessly through the rubble in search of something left behind. *They started out with nothing,* Kody thought, *and now this.* Less than nothing. Was there even a word for that? *Destitute* seemed like an understatement. It was a potent reminder that whatever he had suffered, it couldn't compare to what many people in this city were going through.

According to Hughley's secretary, the purser of *Fly By Night* rented a flat in a three-story tenement on Hammond Street. The building was still standing, but Kody and Lenoir did not find a soul inside, and when they knocked on Marten's door, no one answered. Kody tried the knob, but it was locked. His shoulder seemed to give a subtle pang, like a plea for mercy, but there was no getting around it this time. Kody readied his crossbow, braced himself, and lunged.

The doorframe blasted into kindling on the second try, and Kody tumbled into a two-room flat with a generous window, curtains rolling in the ash-scented breeze. He paused to collect himself, just long enough to be annoyed that it was necessary, and gave the main room a quick once-over. Satisfied it was empty, he moved on to the bedroom. "Inspector," he called. "You'd better come here."

Kody kept his crossbow trained on the body just in case, but the man was lying facedown on the bed, and judging from the amount of blood on the bedclothes, he was almost certainly dead. Kody reached for his neck. "No pulse, but still warm. The blood too."

Lenoir cursed from the doorway. "We only just missed him."

"But how can that be? The door was locked. . . ."

Curtains rolling in the breeze.

Kody shoved past Lenoir and back into the main room. Sure enough, the window was open; he ran over and stuck his head out. A ladder leaned against the wall, reaching easily to the second-floor window from the lane below.

"Damn!"

If only they'd started with the purser, they might have caught the killer in the act. Still swearing, Kody went back to the bedroom. "He came in through the window."

"So I had surmised."

"A ladder." And why not? With no one around to report it, subtlety was superfluous.

"It would appear that Marten was expecting trouble," Lenoir said, gesturing at the clothes spread all over the bed. From the looks of things, the purser had been loading up a trunk when he'd been taken.

"Looking to skip town," Kody said. "Maybe he heard what happened to Bird."

"Or that the hounds were getting closer. Either way, he was aware of his situation."

He even had a knife strapped to his waist, for all the good it had done him. "Whoever got him must have been real quiet."

Lenoir rolled the body over. Kody looked first at the man's neck; sure enough, the throat was cut, that same little flourish on one side of the gash. Then he looked at the dead man's face. "Well I'll be buggered."

Lenoir looked over his shoulder, one eyebrow arched.

Kody pointed. "That's the bloke I was chasing on the pier yesterday."

He had the rare satisfaction of seeing Nicolas Lenoir look stunned. "Are you certain?"

"Well, he did kick me in the head, but yeah—I'm certain."

Lenoir looked back at the body. He was silent for a long moment. Then he swore softly in Arrènais. "Of course."

This time, Kody didn't bother to ask.

"A diversion," Lenoir said, and he actually sounded impressed. "That's all it was. There was no crime in progress, no sailor's squabble. That gunshot was designed to distract us from what we were doing."

Kody thought back to yesterday afternoon, though it seemed a lifetime ago. "We were going through the list of names from *Serendipity*."

Lenoir didn't answer. He sat on the bed, eyes closed, silent. Then he said, "*Duchess of the Deep.*"

Kody nodded. "I remember now. There must have been something on the *Duchess* they didn't want us to find."

"Something, or some*one*. We were just about to show them the sketch."

Kody lit up at the memory. "That's right! Whoever

we'd gone to see wasn't there, so I grabbed the sketch, and that's when the gun went off."

Lenoir swore again. "The list. I left it in my coat, back at the station. Do you remember which name went with which ship?"

"Sorry, Inspector. Too many names, and too much has happened since then."

"For me as well. But perhaps it doesn't matter. Something tells me our man in the sketch is connected to *Duchess of the Deep*. Since we have nothing else to go on, we might as well find out."

Kody trailed Lenoir out into the hallway. "Back to the docks, then?"

"So it would seem."

"What about the killer? Shouldn't we be focusing on him?"

"How do you propose we find him, Sergeant? Shall we walk around the poor district asking random passersby if they've seen an Inataari?"

"Why not? Someone must have seen him."

"And so?"

That caught Kody off guard. "Well, at least—"

"No, Sergeant, not *at least*. At most. *At most* someone might have seen him on the street. Where does that get you? Or do you imagine we can deduce his location simply because a witness placed him heading westbound on Hammond ten minutes ago? Unless you're feeling especially clairvoyant today, that is not a going to be a fruitful line of enquiry."

Kody scowled. "So I guess almost dying of plague doesn't buy much indulgence after all."

Lenoir's boots scraped to a halt. He turned. "Is that what you want, Sergeant? Indulgence?"

Just like that, Kody felt foolish and exposed, like a rebellious child facing a stern father.

"Perhaps you would prefer if I did not bother to point out when your impulses are illogical or counterproductive? That I did not expect you to think for yourself? Is that why you asked to serve under me? So you could carry on without learning a thing?"

Heat flashed over Kody's skin. He could almost have wished it were fever. "Of course not. I don't mind being told I'm wrong. I mind being talked to as if I'm thick as a stump."

Lenoir made a face, as if he'd swallowed something faintly sour. "I will admit that my tongue is occasionally more barbed than it needs to be. A bad habit acquired long ago, one I find difficult to break."

Kody stared. He could hardly believe what he was hearing. Nicolas Lenoir admitting fault? To *him*?

Maybe I'm in a coma again, he thought, *and this is all a dream.*

Lenoir sighed. "Let us make a pact, Sergeant. I will reflect a little more before I speak, if you promise to do the same. You have a perfectly serviceable mind, but you are lazy with it. You ask questions instead of seeking the answers for yourself. You follow your instincts blindly, without pausing to question them. You will never sharpen your critical faculties that way, and as for me, I will never have a moment's peace. For our mutual sanity, let us both agree to take an extra heartbeat to *think*."

Bran Kody had been called a lot of things in his life, but *lazy* wasn't one of them. Then again, nobody had ever critiqued his intellect before. The flush returned, whether with anger or embarrassment, he couldn't tell. Maybe a little of both. He opened his mouth to reply, but a shout from up the street cut him off.

"Let go!"

It was a woman's voice, shrill with fear.

"Leave me alone! *Help!*"

Kody spotted the woman just before she disappeared around a corner, dragged by an unseen assailant. "Hey!" He took three long strides, stopped. "You there!"

No answer.

Kody bolted, reaching for his crossbow as he ran. He could hear Lenoir shouting after him. Probably something about getting his heart rate up, but what was he supposed to do, just stand there and let a woman be attacked?

No, some things you didn't have to think about. Some things you just did. Kody wasn't going to apologize for following his instincts.

He was going to prove them right.

Lenoir watched Kody round the corner at the far end of the street, debating whether to follow. He could not keep up with the sergeant, not even now, and would not be much help in a physical altercation in any case. More to the point, he had a mass murderer to catch, and he was running out of time. In seizing the cargo of the *Fly By Night*, Lenoir had exposed his hand, giving the killer a chance to flee. He could not afford to be distracted by a purse snatching, or a lovers' quarrel, or whatever it was. The rational choice was clear: focus on the task at hand, and let the sergeant handle whatever little scuffle was occurring round the bend.

And yet.

Your job is to catch the killer. But is it not also to protect the weak? His hand drifted toward the butt of his gun, as if in answer. Cursing himself for a fool, he lurched forward.

The sudden movement saved his life.

Something brushed the back of his shoulder. Lenoir spun and found himself face-to-face with the man in the sketch. The sailor had been reaching for him with one hand, a knife clutched in the other, ready to ram the blade into Lenoir's back. *A straight blade,* some part of him registered. The man lunged.

Lenoir leapt back and drew his gun, but his attacker was ready, dropping the knife and pulling a pistol of his own in one fluid motion. Both hammers clicked back at the same moment. Lenoir and his attacker stood eye to eye, barrel to barrel.

The sun vanished behind the rooftops, plunging the street into shadow. *Another day dies,* Lenoir thought. *A bloody day.*

And it seemed the blood was not yet done.

CHAPTER 31

L enoir had heard of standoffs like this, but he had never experienced one for himself. There was no way he would get the drop on this man. The sailor outweighed him by at least twenty pounds, and there was a wild glint in his eye, like that of an animal cornered. It was impossible to know which of them had better aim, which of them had taken more lives, but the odds did not tilt in Lenoir's favor.

So what now?

Bereft of any better ideas, Lenoir started talking.

"You are a hard man to find."

"So are you. Lately, anyway." The hand holding the gun had a slight tremor. Fear or excitement? Lenoir could not tell.

"I did not realize you were looking for me. Worried I was getting too close?"

The man hitched a shoulder. The gesture was meant to look indifferent. It did not quite get there. "I wouldn't call it worried, but it's become inconvenient. *You've* become inconvenient."

"The woman at the end of the street," Lenoir said. "Your doing?"

"Your partner is a big bloke. Didn't fancy taking you both at a time." He flashed a thin smile. "Clever, right?"

"In a common sort of way, perhaps. But being clever is not really your role in all of this, is it? You are the muscle. The plague, the miracle tonic . . . those were not your ideas."

"What do you know about it? Think I'm not smart enough?" The man flicked the barrel of his gun irritably. "You know nothing about me, hound."

Are you trying to get yourself killed, Lenoir? There was little to be gained in antagonizing the man. Yet Lenoir could not resist the opportunity to get some answers at last. "I know you serve on *Fly By Night.* I know you murdered your captain and most of your crew."

"Not my fault Marsh was stupid. Didn't have to be that way. He could've come in on it. There's plenty to go around."

"Oh? From what I have seen, those who were promised a cut of the wealth were lied to." Lenoir held his breath, hoping. It was possible the man did not know his comrades had been murdered. If the sailor thought he was next, perhaps he might—

"They got a cut all right," the man said with a smirk, "just not the kind they was counting on."

Damn. So much for that idea. "What makes you think you have not been cheated like the rest?"

"Ritter and me go back. Way back. He owes me."

Ritter. The name flared in Lenoir's memory, but for a moment he could not place it. Then he remembered. *Duchess of the Deep.* The former purser of *Serendipity.* The last piece of the puzzle snapped into place. The picture was complete at last.

A pity about the gun in his face.

"So," he said, "what now?"

"Would've thought that was obvious, mate." The man's arm leveled out. The tremor was gone.

"If I die, you die."

"Maybe not. Maybe I'm the better shot."

"Possible, but irrelevant. Even a blind man could not miss at this range."

The sailor swallowed, but his arm did not waver. "And if I lower my gun, what then? You'll shoot me."

"I will not. You have my word."

He snorted. "So, what—you'll just let me go?"

Lenoir debated lying to him, but he sensed the sailor would not believe him anyway. "No, I will not just let you go. I will arrest you."

"No, thanks."

Lenoir took a long, steadying breath. If he let his frustration boil over, it would get him killed. "Listen . . . what is your name? Nash?"

The man blinked. "Who told you that?"

"I have an excellent memory when I need to. It comes with the job." *What made you think of Nash, when I was asking about Ritter?* Lenoir had asked the question at the *Duchess*, moments before the gun went off. He remembered the scene with perfect clarity now that he understood its significance. "It does not matter that I know your name. None of it matters, because it's over. Surely you can see that."

"It's not over." Nash's knuckles went white against the butt of his gun.

"Of course it is. Even if you manage to kill me, you gain nothing. We have seized the cargo of *Fly By Night*."

"Yeah, we know. Must've been real proud of yourselves, but it makes no difference to us. We got lots of product."

"Product that will be worth far less in a matter of hours. We are making our own tonic, you see. Gallons of it, to be distributed for free. Soon, there will be no one to sell to, and no money to be made. It is over."

"It's *not* over." There was a hint of desperation in Nash's voice. "There'll be plenty of buyers, more than anyone can satisfy. You think you've stopped us? All you've done is forced us to move faster."

"Nash—"

"Shut up, hound. I'm done talking." The tremor was

back in Nash's arm. It no longer mattered whether it was fear or excitement; they were equally dangerous now.

Lenoir's finger twitched on the trigger. If he pulled it, he was dead. If he did not, he was dead. There was no doubt in his mind that Nash was going to fire. Flintlocks were inaccurate and unreliable; there was a chance Lenoir might miss, or that his gun might misfire. Nash obviously preferred to take his chances with the flintlock than find himself in Fort Hald, and Lenoir could not blame him.

Something *clicked*.

For a split second, Lenoir thought it was the tumbler in Nash's gun releasing. Then a familiar shape strode into his peripheral vision, and he nearly swooned in relief.

"I usually prefer a crossbow, but it doesn't have that handy noise." Kody cocked the second barrel of his pistol, illustrating the point. "I wanted to make sure you understood your situation."

Nash opted for bluster. "Put it down, or he's dead."

"Let me help you out with the maths, mate. Between us, the inspector and I have four barrels on you. Unless you're real talented with that one barrel of yours, you've got a problem."

"It's over," Lenoir repeated.

"Put the gun on the ground, nice and gentle," Kody said. "Then back away."

Lenoir could see the whites of Nash's eyes. His lips pressed together. He twitched.

Lenoir fired.

The ball took Nash in the skull, shattering it into a red mist. The body went down like a sack of flour.

"Shit," said Lenoir.

Kody frowned down at his boots. "Well that's just great."

"We have bigger problems than your boots, Sergeant."

Kody ignored him; he was too busy wiping the toe of his boot on the underside of a windowsill.

Lenoir knelt beside the body, but he knew it was pointless. Nash was dead before he hit the ground. "We will not be getting anything more from him."

"You did the right thing, Inspector. He was going to shoot. If you hadn't pulled the trigger, I would have." Kody let down the hammers of his pistol and shoved it back in its holster.

Lenoir put his own gun away. "The woman you went after?"

"Took me a minute to figure it out, but every time I got close, they'd round another corner. Seemed a little too convenient, like I was being led on. Then I remembered the shooting at the docks, how it was all a diversion." Kody gave him a wry look. "It helped that I still had your voice ringing in my ear, telling me to question my instincts. Ironic, isn't it?"

"No. Coincidence is not irony, though it is commonly mistaken for such."

Kody rolled his eyes.

"Nash must have paid them." Lenoir nudged the dead man's knife with his boot. "He hoped to take me out quietly, then wait for you to come back."

"Then I'd get a knife in my belly."

"For you, Sergeant, I think he would have used the gun."

Kody gave a wan smile. "Wouldn't have needed to." He sagged against the wall. "One of the reasons I got suspicious was that I wasn't running nearly as fast as I wanted to. I couldn't."

Lenoir glanced at him. "Can you continue?"

"Are you kidding? When we're this close? With this one gone, that leaves the Inataari and the man in charge, assuming they're two different people."

"They are. The man in charge is Ritter."

Kody frowned. "Why does that name sound familiar?"

"The ex-purser of the *Serendipity*."

"That's it. So we've been on the right track for a while now."

"Perhaps, but that is not good enough. Even the name is not good enough, not anymore. We are running out of time."

"We can get a sketch of him done pretty quickly."

"It will be dark in an hour. A sketch will do us no good until morning, and besides—the odds of finding him that way are slim. He knows we are onto him."

"You sure?"

"When I told Nash we had seized the cargo on *Fly By Night*, he said, *We know.* Presumably, *we* includes Ritter."

Kody sighed. "He could be halfway to Berryvine by now."

"I don't think so. I think Ritter is making one last push before he goes into hiding."

"Oh yeah?" Kody inclined his head at the dead man. "Something he said, I take it?"

"He was convinced there were still more than enough buyers for his product. More than anyone could satisfy, he said." Lenoir closed his eyes, trying to dredge up every detail of the conversation. *"All you have done is forced us to move faster."*

"What do you suppose he meant by that?"

"There will be plenty of buyers, he said. There *will be*."

"Future tense." Kody sounded wary now. "That's odd."

"Indeed."

It did not take long for Kody to draw the inevitable conclusion. "Oh, God . . . you don't think . . ."

Lenoir opened his eyes. Something cold and heavy had settled at the bottom of his stomach. "Why not? He created a market for himself already. Why should he hesitate to expand it? It would be so easy."

Ritter had been careful the first time. He had chosen the Camp because it would be easier to contain the spread of the disease. After all, it would not do to kill off too many of his prospective customers. Now that he had been discovered, and there was no longer any question of holding on to his monopoly, Ritter had no incentive to show restraint. On the contrary, the more panic he could create, the easier it would be to move his product. And the best way to sow panic is to sow death.

"He is going to seed the city with corpses. Just like he did in the Camp, but with more bodies in more places." *So easy* . . . And once it was done, there would be no undoing it. It would take weeks, maybe months, for another shipment of angel wort to arrive. By then, it would be too late. Kennian would fall to the plague, and the rest of the Five Villages with it. *And after that, the neighbors. Sevarra and Kirion, and then Arrènes* . . .

Kody was upright now, eyes blazing. "We've got to find him. There's got to be a way."

Lenoir scanned the horizon, smudged with dusk and the lingering smoke of the great fire. Lights winked on in the distance, streetlamps and lanterns coming alive on hundreds of streets, in thousands of homes, as far as the eye could see, and beyond. Kennian had never seemed so vast. *We don't even know what he looks like.*

For a moment, Lenoir stood paralyzed, overwhelmed with despair. He had come so close to breaking this thing. So close to vindicating his life, to honoring the compact he had made, however unwittingly, with the Darkwalker on a cold autumn night. They had found a cure, had enough stock to keep the plague under control while another shipment made its way across the Grey. Cases outside the Camp were still relatively isolated, and Kennians were staying off the streets. The only people braving the outdoors were medicine salesmen and their desperate clients. That, and the corpse collectors . . .

Lenoir paused.

The corpse collectors.

Masked. Anonymous. And few.

"The station," Lenoir said, "quickly. Let us hope the chief is back."

"The chief? How's he going to help?"

"I'm not sure he can, Sergeant, but we have no choice but to try."

The fate of an entire city depended on it.

"I will take any spare capacity you have, Chief."

Reck scowled. "See any *spare capacity* on your way in, Lenoir? Because when I came in, all I saw was an empty kennel."

"I need men. Urgently."

"You and me both. In case you haven't noticed, we've been having a spot of trouble out there."

"I know who he is, Chief. The mastermind behind all of this. I can find him, if you just give me the manpower."

Reck sighed impatiently. "Look, I want to see this bastard hang as much as you do, but I've got bigger worries at the moment. I would've thought you of all people would understand that."

"No, *you* don't understand." Lenoir slammed his palms down on Reck's desk, upsetting an ink bottle. "This is not just about catching him. This is about stopping him. If we do not, thousands will die. Tens of thousands."

Reck stared at him as though he had lost his mind. "Kody, do you want to explain to me what in the flaming below has got into the inspector here?"

"He's going to do it again, sir," Kody said. He leaned over the desk too, shoulder to shoulder with Lenoir. "He's going to spread plague all over the city, unless we find him first."

"What do you mean, *going to*? Hasn't he already?"

"No, not at all!" Lenoir could hear how desperate he sounded, how frantic. It did not help his cause, but he could not stop himself. He could feel the seconds slipping through his fingers like fine grains of sand, each one as precious as a diamond. "What he did to the Camp was only the beginning. He wanted to keep the disease contained. It served his purpose to allow little pockets to spring up here and there, but that was all he needed to create demand. It's different now."

"Why? What's changed?"

"What's changed is that we know who he is," Kody said. "His time is almost up and he knows it, so he's doing everything he can to sell as much as possible before he makes a run for it."

"The best way to sell quickly is to create panic," Lenoir said, "and if you want to create panic—"

"You make it look like the whole city has come down with plague," the chief said. "I get it."

"He's going to do like he did in the Camp, with the corpses," Kody said. "Only more of them, in more places. And there won't be a river to separate them from the heart of the city."

"My guess is that he will pose as a corpse collector," Lenoir said. "That way, no one will take any notice of him."

Reck swore and got to his feet. "So how do we find him?"

"If it were me," Lenoir said, "I would start with the richer neighborhoods. Meadowsmead and Primrose Park."

"Makes sense. Folk there won't struggle to scrape together the coin. He'll sell quicker." Reck sighed again. "But even if we're right, that's still a lot of ground to cover."

Lenoir sagged against the desk, the enormity of it weighing him down. "Yes, Chief, it is. If we had the men, we could cover the local apothecaries he sells to. We could tear the docks apart until we found the warehouse with the rest of his stock. We could arrest every corpse collector in Kennian."

"But we don't have the men, so let's not waste time

with fantasies." Reck rubbed his jaw roughly. "I might be able to scrape together enough to do one of those things, and do it well. No point in spreading ourselves too thin to do any good."

"So which one?" Kody asked. "The docks are the surest bet."

"And the slowest," Lenoir said. "By the time he comes back for the angel wort, he will have done his work with the corpses, and we may never find out where he stashed them. If we truly want to stop him, we must go for the corpse collectors."

Kody's mouth pressed into a grim line, as though he had feared that answer. "It'll be like finding a mouse in a barn."

"That's one hell of a gamble, Lenoir," Reck said.

"Yes, it is, but I would rather take a chance on stopping him than be sure of catching him after it is too late."

Reck's gaze dropped to his desk, and for a moment he just stood there, head bowed in thought. Then he looked up and said, "Let's get on it, then."

They headed down the stairs to the kennel. "Where are we going to get the men?" Kody asked, glancing around at the empty desks of the sergeants and watchmen.

"I've got a few off shift, who should be getting a good night's rest." The chief made a sour face. "So much for that."

"That will not get us very far, Chief," Lenoir said.

"No, it won't. So we'll be using them as commanders, each one in charge of a unit."

"A unit of what, exactly?" Kody asked.

Reck spread his arms wide. "Behold your army."

Kody's eyebrows flew up. "Scribes? But, Chief—"

"They are just boys," Lenoir said.

"Don't be ridiculous. At least a third of them are women."

"Chief—"

"You got a better idea, Lenoir?" Reck asked impatiently. "You need eyes, and these fine people have 'em."

"We also need muscle," Kody said. "Ritter's not going to come quietly. Even the real corpse collectors might put up a struggle."

"That's where the off-shift officers come in. Each scribe gets a whistle. They see a miasma mask and a handcart, and they give that whistle a blast. Their sergeant or watchman comes running. That's it."

Lenoir grunted. "That is . . . ingenious, actually."

"So pleased you think so." Turning, Reck addressed the kennel at large. "Listen up, hounds! Drop whatever you're doing and gather round! You've all been temporarily promoted to watchmen!"

For a moment, no one moved; they just looked at one another, bewildered. A timid voice sounded from somewhere in the back. "What does that mean, Chief?"

"It means your night is about to get interesting."

CHAPTER 32

The shaft of light swung left to right, like the beam of a lighthouse, setting the cobbles aglow. The alley unfurled before them, a canyon of gloom flanked by rugged cliffs of stone. Above, dark windowpanes stared down, aloof and secretive. Lenoir paused, his lantern aloft, but nothing stirred. Apparently, the neighborhood was too rich even for rats.

"Shall I go take a look, Inspector?" The scribe hoisted his own lantern; its glare threw his angular face into sharp relief, giving him a ghoulish appearance.

"No. There is no one here. We move on."

The young man nodded. "You just say the word, though. I'm here to help."

"Yes, Riley, thank you." Lenoir tried to keep the impatience from his voice. The scribe was overeager, but that was to be expected. He had never been out on patrol before, and though he could not possibly understand what was at stake, he took his role seriously. Lenoir was grateful for that, even if he found the young man's presence more than a little irritating.

They moved back into the wan glow of the streetlamps. Still nothing stirred. It was barely past the supper hour, but it might as well have been thin of the clock, so quiet was the street. A growing sense of panic thrummed at Lenoir's nerves. He could not help imagining how many corpses Ritter might have collected by now, how many he might have distributed. Would he dump them into wells? God forbid, into the river? He shuddered, though the night was uncomfortably warm.

Something moved at the edge of Lenoir's vision. He whirled.

"Oh!" The figure threw her hands in the air, sending her lantern tumbling to the street with a mighty *clank*. "It's just me, Inspector!"

Lenoir was surprised to find his gun in his hand, trained on the startled scribe. He muttered out an apology and slipped the weapon back in its holster. Shaken, the young woman stooped to retrieve her lantern.

Get yourself together, Lenoir.

He continued up the street, Riley striding faithfully at his side, as though oblivious to the fact that Lenoir had nearly killed one of his colleagues a moment ago. "We'll get him, Inspector," the young man said stoutly. Lenoir's teeth ground together.

A shrill sound pierced the darkness. A whistle. In an instant, Lenoir was running. He dove through the shadows, pistol back in hand, blood roaring in his ears. The whistle blasted again. Shouts sounded from just ahead. *Please,* Lenoir prayed, *let it be him.*

No such luck. Lenoir knew it the moment he rounded the corner and saw them: the scribe, shining his lantern full upon his quarry; the corpse collector, arm thrown up to ward off the glare; the handcart, hearteningly, heartbreakingly empty.

"What's going on?" The corpse collector's voice was strangely muffled behind the mask. "Who are you?"

"Metropolitan Police," Lenoir said, without much conviction. "Remove your mask, please."

The man complied. He had silver hair and deep lines on his face, sixty if he was a day. As though Lenoir needed more proof that this was not the man he sought. "We need you to come with us. This young man will accompany you to the station."

"Why? What have I done?"

"Nothing, sir. It is a precaution."

"But I don't understand. What's this all about? Why, I'm a *priest*, you can't just—" The man protested all the way down the street, but he offered no resistance. Lenoir sent him off with only a single scribe. The priest was no threat, and Lenoir needed to keep as many of his team together as he could. He had already lost two scribes to escort duty; he could not afford to lose more.

"Just a few blocks left, Inspector," Riley said, "and then we've done Hollybrook."

"Yes, Riley, thank you."

"Where shall we go after that?"

Lenoir opened his mouth to respond, but found he had nothing to say.

"Well, if you do see anything, give a shout," Kody said.

The woman nodded and clipped the door shut, only too happy to get his swollen face out of her sight. He stood there on the stoop, momentarily lost in indecision, listening absently as the chain rattled and the bolt slid to.

What now?

His team had combed Primrose Park from end to end, and they hadn't found so much as a stray cat. *Maybe we should've started with the poor district.* Guaranteed, they'd find corpse collectors there, and plenty of them. *Too many,* the more sensible part of him put in. *You'd be hauling them in all night. Not nearly enough manpower for that.* No, Lenoir was right to start with the posh neighborhoods. Kody might have come up empty, but one of the others was bound to find something. "Bound to," he whispered, as if saying the words aloud could make it so.

"What's that, Sarge?"

"Nothing. Let's keep moving." He rejoined Patton at the bottom of the stoop. "We'll work our way back north, in case we missed something."

"Oh. Okay." The scribe shifted. "I just thought . . ."

"What?"

"Well, since we've already done our bit, maybe we should head over a few blocks, help out Sergeant Keane and the others?"

"We stick with the grid, Patton. That's how it works." Kody raised his lantern so the other scribes could see his face. "All right, hounds, that's enough loitering. We turn around and work our way back. Same pattern. Stay focused. I catch two of you on the same street, skulls are gonna crack. Got it?"

His team dispersed, melting into the side streets and alleyways. Kody started back up the avenue, and this time around, he was even more meticulous. The beam of his lantern scoured every stoop, every courtyard, every hollow. Not that he expected to find anything. If Ritter had spotted them, he would already have made tracks, and if he hadn't, he would be out in the open, not crouched in the lee of a town house stoop. After all, wasn't the whole point to dump the bodies where everyone could see them? *We should head back to the park,* Kody thought. *I'll bet that's where he'd do it. Or maybe Dressley Square. That would get plenty of attention come morning. Or . . . wait . . . the cathedral? Tomorrow's prayer day. For that matter, any church . . .*

He growled, grinding the heel of his palm into his eyes. There were just too many options. If they'd had every man on the force out there, maybe. But with a handful of watchmen and a few dozen scribes . . . It was worse than a mouse in a barn. It was a fly in a forest. *We'll never find him. We're sunk.* He couldn't even feel angry about it. Instead, he just felt sick.

Kody had just made up his mind to scrap the pattern and head straight for the park when he heard the whistle.

It was too distant to be one of his. Keane's, by the sounds of it.

"That came from Blackpoint," Patton said into his thoughts.

"Sounds like."

"Should we go?"

The whistle sounded again, shrill and insistent. Kody pursed his lips. *It's not ours. Keane will take care of it.* Then he heard something else.

KaPOW.

It lingered, drifting on the wind like a wisp of smoke. Patton froze. "Was that . . . ?"

"Yeah," Kody said, "it was." He started running.

The whistle had gone silent. For several agonizing seconds, the only sound was the pounding of footfalls as Kody headed toward the river. He didn't even glance behind to see if Patton was following.

It's got to be Ritter. By the sounds of things, he'd killed the scribe who found him. *If he gets away . . .* Kody pushed himself harder. The bridge was just ahead. The Minnow marked the boundary between Primrose Park and Blackpoint, between Kody's territory and Keane's. He couldn't be far now. Good thing too, because Kody wasn't going to be able to keep up this pace for long. As it was, Merden's injunction against running echoed in his ears.

Another whistle sounded. It came from the same spot, but had a slightly different pitch. A different scribe. Again and again it blasted, unmistakably urgent. The gun was silent, but that didn't mean the scribe was safe. Ritter might have spent his flintlock, but he was a sailor, and sailors always had knives. *Damn it, Keane, I hope you're on this.*

Kody could hear shouting now. It guided him around corners, through narrow alleys connecting wider streets. The voices were getting louder, but he could tell he was still at least a block away. He couldn't hear the whistle anymore. He tried not to think about what that meant. His blood roared in his ears, and his head felt like it could float away like a balloon at a fair, but he kept running.

He was nearly on top of the shouting now. He recognized Keane's voice, though he couldn't make out the words. There were at least two other voices, youthful and afraid. Scribes. If he kept on straight ahead, he would find them.

Kody veered left.

He couldn't have said why he did it. Maybe it was because the voices up ahead sounded so disorganized, so frantic. Maybe it was just instinct. Regardless, Kody found himself making a flanking maneuver, like a man trying to head someone off.

Which is exactly what he did.

The man almost barreled into him, all three hundred pounds of him. Kody spun his shoulders to avoid the tackle, and still had the presence of mind to stick his knee out. The impact sent a blaze of pain up his leg, but the fugitive caught the worse end of it, tumbling head-first to the pavement. Somehow, he managed to roll out of it, ending up in a wary crouch. Kody reached for his crossbow, some part of his brain registering surprise that a purser would be so agile. And meaty.

The figure snapped his arm out. Kody staggered. At first, it felt like he'd been stung by an insect, so small and burning was the pain. But when he reached up, he felt something buried in his neck, too cold to be anything but metal. He gripped it, ready to tear it out, but his attacker was back on his feet and there wasn't time. Kody leveled his crossbow. His attacker drew a knife, a big curved blade that gleamed wickedly in the glow of the streetlamp. *The Inataari.* He was at least six and a half feet tall, with long, narrow mustaches and the fiercest eyes Kody had ever seen. He took a step closer. Kody fired.

Somehow—Kody would never understand how—the

Inataari spun out of the quarrel's path. He whirled again, arms wide, and now the blade was coming at Kody in a flashing arc. He nearly fell on his arse trying to get out of the way. He grabbed for his gun, but the Inataari was on him again—how in the below did he move *that fast?*— and Kody had to throw himself against the wall just to keep his balance. He fumbled again for his gun. He'd just managed to pull back the hammer when his attacker blasted into him, grabbing his wrist and pinning him up against the wall. They struggled. It was like trying to wrestle a grizzly bear. Kody grunted and swore, but the Inataari was strong enough to best him on a good day, and this wasn't a good day. Kody felt himself being slowly overwhelmed. His vision swam with spots, and his knees weren't as sturdy as they should be. He was vaguely aware of a warm stickiness at his throat.

It is your blood, Sergeant.

For some reason, the voice in his head was Lenoir's.

There is a very small knife embedded in your neck.

Did the Inataari poison their knives? Or was that the Mirrhanese? Kody couldn't remember. His arm burned from trying to keep the blade away from his throat.

"Hey!"

The shout came from Kody's right. He knew the voice, but he couldn't place it.

Frantic footfalls against the pavement. An inarticulate cry, followed by a grunt as something crashed into the Inataari, hard enough to throw him off balance. Kody drove a knee into his attacker's groin, twisted out of his grasp, and fired. Something warm and wet spattered against his face.

The world swam. A gunshot sounded, as if from a distance.

Kody dropped into darkness.

CHAPTER 33

"Will he be all right?" Lenoir asked.

"Should be." Keane was making notes, but he glanced up long enough to give Lenoir a reassuring look. "He passed out, but he was awake by the time I found him. Didn't look too good if you ask me, but he got into the wagon on his own legs, so I guess that's a good sign."

"It's fortunate he did not bleed out." Lenoir had seen an Inataari throwing knife once, in a museum in Serles. They were a nasty bit of business, barbed in more places than was strictly necessary.

"Funny thing, that." Keane looked up again, his brow creased in puzzlement. "He didn't even lose that much blood. By the time I found him, you would've sworn that wound was hours old."

Lenoir blew out a breath, something between a gasp and a laugh.

Clotted up faster than anything I've ever seen. Kody's words as he praised the miracle potion, a medicine that thickened the blood. The sergeant's life may well have been saved by that tonic. Had he not contracted plague, Kody could easily have died from a knife wound in the street.

Now that, Sergeant, is irony.

Or was it justice after all, winking at them across the void of the universe? Lenoir shook his head in wonder.

He scanned the row of bodies before him. They lay side by side, ready to be loaded up into the wagon. Two of the dead were scribes. A third was missing most of his face—the Inataari, judging by the mustaches matted with gore. As for the fourth . . .

"We got him." Lenoir could scarcely believe it.

"Sure did." Keane put a boot to the corpse, as if for emphasis. The head rolled against the uneven cobbles, sightless eyes tracking across the sky.

Ritter. In the flesh at last. Dead flesh, thankfully. Lenoir had been right about all of it: the plan, the disguise, the neighborhood. The only thing he had not foreseen was the Inataari, though of course he should have. Ritter could have managed on his own for a while, but he would have needed help to drag a cartload of bodies all the way up to Blackpoint. "What exactly happened?"

"Scribe came across your man and his cart. Had a full crop of corpses with him. Reckon that's how the scribe knew."

"Where are the bodies now?"

Keane pointed. They had put the cart at the far end of the street, as far away as they could manage without losing sight of it. Even at this distance, Lenoir could see that it was full. Limbs dangled over the edges—an arm here, a leg there, bruised and swollen.

"Guess that means we managed to stop him in time," Keane said. "Unless he'd dumped a load already, that is."

"That would not have been possible. He would have had to wheel the corpses up from one of the infected neighborhoods. That would have been hard work, and taken hours, especially if he was trying not to attract too much attention."

Keane grunted, his pencil still bobbing. "Anyway, scribe sees them, blows his whistle, and takes one in the guts for his troubles." Keane indicated one of the bodies at his feet.

Lenoir knelt. If he had ever seen the young man before, he did not remember it. As for Ritter, he looked much as Lenoir had imagined him: small, pale, and rat-faced. He was perhaps a little more sinewy, a little more weathered, than Lenoir would have guessed, but the man was a sailor after all. He had been shot twice, once in the gut and once in the throat. Keane had unloaded both barrels on him. Lenoir would have done the same, and possibly run him through for good measure.

Still, gazing upon the corpse of his foe, a man responsible for so much death and destruction, Lenoir felt strangely hollow. There was no triumph, no sense of reckoning or redemption. He was relieved, certainly—but it was an exhausted sort of relief, as if a great wave had come and gone, leaving him scoured and empty.

Belatedly, he realized Keane was still talking. "We reckon the Inataari was keeping a lookout, ready to add some muscle if things went sour. Once he'd spent his barrel, they tried to make tracks, but Joyce here"—he indicated the body of the second scribe—"caught up with them around the corner. That's when he got it. Bastards nearly cut his head clean off."

Lenoir recognized the signature flourish of the Inataari's blade. He grimaced.

"They split up after that," Keane went on. "Kody caught up with this one first, and they tussled. Might've gone badly if Patton—that's him over there—hadn't showed up and given Kody a hand. Meanwhile, I got me this one." He shoved Ritter's corpse again. The head lolled to one side, leaving him face-to-face with his miasma mask. Vacant gaze met vacant gaze, each reflected in the glassy surface of the other. "You ask me," Keane said, "he got off light, considering what he did. If I had my way, we'd have fed him to the dogs in the Camp."

Lenoir could not disagree. *Sometimes, the best justice has to offer is vengeance.* In the end, justice had not even offered that. Nor was Ritter's bloody work complete. They had stopped him before he had managed to implement the last stage of his plan, but that would be no consolation to the sick and the dying, to those who would fall ill tomorrow, or the day after that. Hundreds of deaths had yet to be laid at Ritter's feet. Still, it might have been thousands had they not discovered the cure.

Speaking of which . . .

"Very well, Sergeant. Get these bodies loaded up and ready to go. As for Ritter's cart, leave a guard on it, and when you get back to the station, have the corpse collectors we rounded up tonight come up here and deal with them. Make sure everyone wears proper protection. Those corpses are highly contagious."

"Sure thing, Inspector. What about you? Where you headed?"

"To the docks," Lenoir said. "We have medicine to make."

The first rays of dawn filtered weakly through the salt-crusted window of Warehouse 49. Lenoir leaned against a wall, arms crossed, waiting. He had managed to roust the dockmaster hours ago, but it would be another hour or so before his crew started to arrive on the scene. Sailors were early risers, but the predawn hours belonged to the fishermen. *I like to keep the piers clear until the fleets put out in the morning,* the dockmaster had said. *Keeps the misunderstandings to a minimum.* Judging by the men Lenoir had passed on his way in—bleary-eyed, irritable, reeking of spirits—it was a wise precaution.

It had not taken the dockmaster long to locate the right warehouse, once he had Ritter's name to work with. Now it was simply a question of getting the angel wort out to the Camp, where it could be put to good use.

To do that, however, Lenoir needed hands, and plenty of them. That meant dallying about in this damp, stinking cave of a warehouse, idle and useless, while more pressing matters gnawed at his nerves.

Fortunately, he did not have to bear it for long. The warehouse doors creaked, and the first of the dockhands drifted in. He paused when he saw Lenoir, seemingly surprised to find him alone. "Good morning," the dockhand said, a little tentatively. Lenoir wondered what the man had been told about his first task of the day.

"You are earlier than I expected," Lenoir said. "That's good."

"Oh." The dockhand glanced around. "How many are we expecting?"

Lenoir shrugged. "You tell me. As many as it takes to load these crates up quickly."

"Where's the dockmaster?"

"I sent him off to round up some wagons."

"Oh." There was an awkward silence. The dockhand glanced behind him, at the door. "I suppose you're in a hurry."

"You might say that."

"Well, if you give me a hand, we could save time by getting 'em ready at the loading door. I mean, I know it's not your job and all, but if you're in a hurry . . ."

Lenoir considered. It was not the kind of task he would ordinarily consider, but he *was* in a hurry. Every minute they delayed was a chance for the plague to claim another victim. "I suppose they are not that heavy, considering the cargo."

"That's right. Most of the weight is in the crate itself." So he did know why he was here. That was good.

"Very well," Lenoir said, motioning for the dockhand to lead the way. They headed up the gangplank to the loading level. "Do you have a key for the loading door?"

He shook his head. "One of the other lads has got it.

He'll be along soon. But if we line the crates up nice, it'll make things go faster. Here, I'll take this end. That way, you don't have to walk backward."

Together, they hoisted a crate and started moving.

"You're a hound, then?"

Lenoir grunted, half in exertion, half in annoyance. He was not in the mood for idle chatter.

Taking the sound for assent, the dockhand went on. "Shouldn't you have a partner or something?"

"He is unwell." Following the dockhand's lead, Lenoir started to lower the crate, but it slipped from his grasp. He hissed in pain as a sliver the size of a toothpick sliced into his skin. "Stupid," he grumbled, picking at it. He should have asked to borrow a pair of the thick canvas gloves the dockhands wore.

"I got it," said the other man, bracing his hands against the crate to shove it into position. Lenoir noticed that this particular dockhand was not, in fact, wearing gloves. Perhaps his hands were so calloused that he did not need to. But no . . . looking closer, Lenoir saw that the man's hands were white and soft-looking. *Odd, considering his line of work.*

"Ready for the next one?"

Lenoir turned and started back.

A blow landed against the back of his skull, sending him staggering. He tried to regain his balance, but the floorboards swayed beneath him. He fell to one knee. Then came another blow, harder than the first. Lenoir's face hit the floor. He tried to move, but his head was full of cotton, and the cotton was soaked in blood. He could not see properly. He was so tired. . . .

"Now what?" a voice above him muttered. Something *clicked.*

I know that sound, thought Lenoir, but he could not place it through the fog in his brain.

"Well, shit," said the voice. "I suppose if I shoot you, every rat on the docks will come running." The click sounded again, followed by a long stretch of silence. Then a pair of hands grabbed Lenoir under the armpits and started pulling.

Soft hands, Lenoir thought. *Too soft to be a dock-hand...*

His attacker dragged him, puffing and cursing, across the floor, until he found a dark corner behind some crates. There he deposited Lenoir, positioning one of the crates to hide him from view. At first, Lenoir thought his attacker meant to flee, but instead he heard footfalls tracking back and forth across the space, as though searching for something.

"Aha!" the voice said. "That'll do." A bright, cheerful whistle went up from the lower level, accompanying the footfalls back up the gangplank.

On your feet, Inspector. Lenoir struggled to a sitting position, but his skull was throbbing, and the floor still seemed unsteady. He reached up and touched the back of his head; his fingers came away smeared with blood. The wound was in nearly the same spot as he had taken the rock a few days before. *You must get up. If you don't get up, you will die.* His thoughts were still foggy, but he knew that much.

He tried to brace himself between the crates and the wall, but his boots slid weakly out from under him. And then his attacker was back, standing over him with a pry bar. He looked mildly put out to find his victim conscious, as if he did not fancy the idea of caving a man's skull in while he was looking on. Lenoir did not think for a moment that would stop him, however.

"You don't have to do this." The words came out slightly slurred.

"I'm afraid I do. I've got a nice big wagon out there, and a couple of pairs of hands to help me load it. Can't have you getting in the way. I'm sure you understand."

"It's over. Ritter is dead."

The counterfeit dockhand blinked. Then he burst out

laughing. "Poor fellow. You really don't have a clue, do you? I'd love to explain it to you, but I'm afraid I haven't got that kind of time." He raised the pry bar.

An arm snaked suddenly round the man's neck from behind. He gasped. The pry bar clanged to the ground.

"Hello, Ritter," said a voice. "Got something for you, from me and the lads."

The man's eyes went wide. He started to speak, but it turned into a grunt as something drove into his back. Another impact, and another, the man's body shuddering with each blow. His mouth hung open, his gaze fixed on the ceiling. Then the arm drew away, and Lenoir's attacker slumped to the ground. Behind him stood a large, bearded man holding a knife wet with blood.

"You're one lucky hound. I reckon you had about half a second left to live."

Lenoir recognized the man, but for a moment he could not place him. Then a familiar voice called, "Bevin?"

The man looked over his shoulder. "Best you stay down there, little pup. No need for you to see this."

"Is Inspector Lenoir up there with you?"

Bevin grinned. "That he is."

A pause. "Is he all right?"

Bevin extended a hand. Tentatively, Lenoir took it. "He's fine, lad," said Bevin. "Leastways, he will be."

"Thank you," Lenoir said once he had regained his feet. He leaned heavily on one of the crates. It was all he could do not to vomit.

"Believe me, hound, it was my pleasure." Bevin wiped the blade of his knife against the edge of one of the crates. "Ritter had that coming, and then some."

"Ritter . . ." Lenoir gazed down at the dead man. "Are you certain?"

"I'd know him in my sleep. In my nightmares, more like. Coin-snatching little weasel was the bane of my existence for nigh on three years. Mine and every other honest sailor on *Serendipity*."

Lenoir shook his head. "Then whom did we take down in Blackpoint?"

The question was directed at the air, but it was Bevin who answered. "Don't know about all that, but one thing I can say about Ritter: he never did for himself what he could con another man into doing for him."

That fits, Lenoir thought. The crew of *Fly By Night.* The apothecaries and the tonic salesmen. Even Nash and the Inataari. All of them had been foot soldiers in Ritter's army, manipulated in one way or another to serve his ends. He had used direction and misdirection at every turn, herding all those around him. *Herding even you, Lenoir.* It was impressive, in its way.

"Inspector?"

Lenoir shuffled over to the edge of the loading platform. Zach stood below, gazing up with a worried expression. "You don't look so good. Is that blood?"

"Don't worry, Zach. I will be fine. I just took a blow to the head."

"Again?"

"So it would seem."

"Better watch you don't get punch drunk," the boy advised.

"I shall certainly try," Lenoir said wryly. "And where have you been?"

Zach opened his mouth, then paused. He shifted a little. "Hanging around with Bevin. You know." He scrutinized his boot.

There is more to that story, Lenoir thought. But it would have to wait. "How did you find me?"

"We didn't," Zach said. "Not exactly."

"We were following Ritter," Bevin said. "Your little pup here figured he was into some nasty business, so I offered to help."

Zach snorted.

"That is, I agreed to help, for a small fee."

"A fee?" Lenoir arched an eyebrow.

"The lad's idea."

Lenoir looked down at Zach. The boy took a renewed interest in his boots.

"A commission, like," Bevin went on.

"A commission from the Metropolitan Police. For killing a man. What an interesting idea."

Bevin shrugged. "Had no choice, did I? He was about to bash your head in. But anyway, that's not what the payment is for. It's a finder's fee, if you will. You obviously didn't have a clue where Ritter was, seeing as you thought he was dead. I found him for you."

"So you deserve a commission."

"Plus future considerations."

Lenoir's other eyebrow flew up. "Such as?"

Bevin grinned like a cat washing cream from its whiskers. "Seems to me the little pup here is onto a good thing. Wouldn't mind a little work like that thrown my way now and then. I'd be a real . . . what's the word I'm looking for . . ."

"Ass," Zach said. "Ass something."

"Asset," said Bevin.

"Yeah, that's it." Zach looked up at Lenoir and smirked.

Lenoir wrestled down a smile of his own. "I will consider it."

The big man jammed his knife back in its scabbard. "You do that, hound. You owe me, remember."

"I have a feeling you will help me to remember."

"Count on it. Now . . ." He clapped his hands together. "What do you say we have ourselves a little celebration? The Port is always open."

"Tempting," Lenoir said dryly, "but I will have to pass."

"Need to see a physician?" Zach asked.

"I do, but first, these crates need to be loaded into wagons and sent to the Camp."

"Oh yeah?" Zach glanced up at the cluster of coffin-sized crates. "Sure are a lot of 'em. What's in 'em, anyway?"

Lenoir ran his hand over the rough wooden surface. "Life, Zach. What's in them is life."

EPILOGUE

L enoir stared out over the faces of the crowd, trying his best to keep his expression neutral as the lord mayor droned on and on about courage, sacrifice, and a host of other qualities but thinly represented on the stage—least of all by His Honor. The speech had gone on for more than ten minutes, and Hearstings gave no sign of winding up. At first Lenoir had been merely bored, but the more the lord mayor talked, the angrier Lenoir became, until it was all he could do to keep still.

How dare you speak to these people about courage, when you fled the city during the fire? How dare you speak to them of sacrifice, when they have lost so much? You, who abandoned the Camp to plague, and the rest of the city to mayhem? You, who did not liberate a single resource to find a cure?

He glanced away, half afraid the crowd would read his thoughts in his eyes, and found himself meeting the gaze of another official on the stage. The Duke of Warrick wore a look of elegant contempt. He shook his head almost imperceptibly, as if to say, *Can you believe this drivel?* That only stoked Lenoir's rage; he felt his jaw go taut, and his hands balled into fists at his sides. The duke's lip curled smugly. He looked away.

This city will learn its lesson, Warrick had said on the night of the fire, as he watched the city burn. His Grace was not a man given to idle words. The exchange still nibbled at the edge of Lenoir's consciousness, but he was not ready to deal with it just yet.

The sound of his own name cut through his thoughts.

"Inspector Lenoir, please step to the dais."

Under cover of applause, Lenoir took a deep breath. *On your best behavior, Inspector.* He glanced at the chief for added inspiration. Reck wore a perfect mask, utterly impassive. Lenoir did his best to imitate it. He approached the podium.

Hearstings was draped in the trappings of his office, looking even more pompous than usual. His mustaches had been waxed to points, and the shine off his forehead was enough to blind a man at close range. Lenoir took petty satisfaction in seeing the tiny beads of sweat gathering at the lord mayor's temples as he suffered under the afternoon sun.

His Honor assumed an air of profound gravitas. "Inspector Lenoir, your tireless efforts to bring the monster responsible for these crimes to justice, and your pivotal role in identifying the cure for the terrible disease that has ravaged our city, are quite simply an inspiration. You have done tremendous credit not only to yourself, but to the entire Metropolitan Police force, and on behalf of the City of Kennian and all those assembled here, I offer our heartfelt and eternal thanks."

More applause. Lenoir fixed his gaze somewhere over the lord mayor's shoulder. He thought about strawberry tarts.

"In recognition of your tremendous contribution, I hereby present to you this key to the city. With it, you have the right to enter any public building, and open any of the city's gates."

Lenoir could not help it; his gaze strayed to Warrick. The duke did not look over, but his lip curled again, this time in a smirk.

Belatedly, Lenoir realized that His Honor was holding out a ridiculously large key. He took it, gazing helplessly at the polished brass whorls and wondering what he was meant to do next. The idea that he might be expected to speak struck him with sudden and sickening force. Clutching the key to his chest, Lenoir did the only thing he could think of: he bowed.

There was an awkward pause. Chief Reck began to clap, loudly. The lord mayor joined in, if a little bemusedly, and the audience soon after. The Duke of Warrick contented himself with a nod. To the crowd, it would seem a dignified gesture of acknowledgment. Lenoir knew the duke too well for that, however. Warrick was mocking him, if subtly. He was mocking the entire assembly. Lenoir might have joined in, were he not too uncomfortable with the idea that he was in sympathy with the Duke of Warrick, however briefly.

"You survived," Reck said when the handshakes were done and the crowd had begun to disperse.

Lenoir glanced over at Hearstings. His Honor was prattling away at a visibly disinterested Warrick. So much the better. Lenoir might have a chance of slinking away quickly. "It was a near thing, Chief," he said. He sounded as bitter as he felt.

"Be that as it may, I'm grateful. I don't need any more drama."

"I cannot disagree with that."

He started to say more, but Hearstings wedged himself between them and grabbed Lenoir's hand yet again. Apparently, he had been abandoned by Warrick, and could again bestow some of his time on the little people. "Really, Inspector, jolly well done! You single-handedly saved the day!"

His palms were even sweatier than his forehead. Lenoir squirmed free as quickly as decorum would allow. "Hardly single-handed, Your Honor. Aside from the many hounds who played a role, there are those in the Camp whose efforts to heal the sick have saved many lives. In particular, a pair of Adali healers—"

"Yes, I heard about that." Hearstings thumped his shoulder. "Just goes to prove that there are always a few good ones, eh?"

"I'm afraid I do not follow," Lenoir said coolly.

"Not that I blame the Adali, mind you. Not their fault their traditions are unsanitary. I mean, one could hardly expect those backward tribes to understand that burning bodies causes plague."

Lenoir stiffened. "You cannot possibly be suggesting—"

"Sergeant Kody!" the chief bellowed, loud enough for Lenoir to start.

Kody bounded over dutifully, looking remarkably hale for a man who had recovered from plague and taken a knife to the throat only two weeks before. A small bandage and a jaundiced hue around his eye were the only remaining signs of his ordeal.

"Your Honor," Reck said, "this is Sergeant Bran Kody. He was at Lenoir's side for the entire investigation. In fact, he actually caught the disease himself, but soldiered on anyway. . . ."

By the time Reck had finished singing Kody's praises, Lenoir's temper had cooled enough that he was able to bid the lord mayor a polite, if starchy, farewell. "Thank you, Chief," he said as he watched Hearstings's receding back. "You narrowly averted a diplomatic incident." Reck just rolled his eyes.

Lenoir turned the brass key over in his hands, feeling foolish. Sunlight brushed the metal in liquid gold, polishing the rounded edges of the lion motif.

"What're you going to do with it?" Kody asked.

Lenoir shook his head.

"You'll display it, at least," Kody said.

"Oh?" Lenoir looked up. "Why would I do that?"

"Well, it's an honor, isn't it?" Kody said.

"Is it?"

"Yes, Inspector, it is," Reck said. "It's a symbol. Symbols are important."

Lenoir looked back down at the key. "You're right," he murmured, more to himself than the chief. "They are." And suddenly, he knew just what he wanted to do with it.

"I wonder, Inspector, how many times I need to remind you to wear a mask."

Lenoir hovered under the tent flap, scanning the shadows. Seeing the cot empty, he stepped all the way inside. "The danger is not what it was," he said.

Merden *tsked*. "We are running low on tonic already, and it will be several weeks yet before we receive another shipment of angel wort. We cannot afford to be cavalier." He stepped into the candlelight, and Lenoir winced inwardly. Though he knew it was impossible, he would have sworn the soothsayer had lost weight overnight. "Besides," Merden said, "I doubt you would find the illness a pleasant experience, curable or not."

"I daresay Kody would agree with you." Lenoir glanced around the empty tent. "Taking a break?"

"Believe it or not, my services are not required just now."

Lenoir's eyebrows flew up. "Not at all? That is certainly good news."

"A temporary lull, no doubt, but yes—welcome news indeed."

At last, we are bringing it under control. The number of new infections dropped every day, and with the College of Physicians finally on board, they had been able to get tonic to nearly everyone who needed it. The number of cases requiring Merden's . . . *special talents* . . . had been greatly reduced. "You can rest," Lenoir said. "At last."

Merden slumped into a chair, gesturing for Lenoir to do the same. "I have been trying, but believe it or not, I cannot sleep."

"Nor I," said Lenoir, though he doubted they suffered from the same ailment. Night after night, Lenoir found himself staring at the ceiling, his mind raking through the details of the case, dwelling on every clue missed, every opportunity squandered, every bad decision that had cost time and lives. Of all the mistakes he had made, his failure to stop Oded's murder weighed heaviest on his mind. And it could have been still worse. If Kody had not recovered . . .

It did not bear thinking of.

"It has been a long time since I have been so thoroughly outwitted, Merden," he sighed.

The soothsayer cocked his head. "Outwitted? How so?"

"Ritter planned everything so carefully. Not only did he create demand for an otherwise worthless product, he founds ways of making money off the indirect effects as well. Did you know that when we raided his cabin, we found documents tying him to florists, funeral parlors, tombstone makers . . . He had even lined up buyers for his infected monkeys."

Merden grunted. "An astute businessman. But I still do not see how he outwitted you."

"He predicted every move we would make, and he was ready for it. He had me chasing shadows and decoys. Every time I got close, he would throw someone else in my way, someone he had paid or conned or otherwise manipulated into acting for him."

"A shepherd as well as a businessman."

"A shepherd?" Lenoir grunted, dropping his head onto the back of the chair. "An odd analogy."

"I do not see why. A shepherd leads his flock. He directs their movements, for good or for ill. He can lead them to green pastures, or he can lead them to slaughter. This Ritter was a shepherd of men."

"A shepherd of shadows," Lenoir said bitterly. "I should have seen the pattern."

Merden laughed. "Such hubris, Inspector."

Lenoir sat up, scowling. "What is that supposed to mean?"

Merden's golden eyes held him, unfazed. "You must think awfully highly of yourself, to imagine that you could discern a pattern from what you had before you. Frankly, I am amazed you caught him. Though not quite as amazed as I am that you found a cure."

"You already had a cure."

"A much less potent one, and less sure, as your sergeant unfortunately discovered. I would not have been able to do much good on my own."

Lenoir snorted. "And you accuse me of hubris. You saved over a hundred lives, Merden. Is that not good enough for you?"

Merden closed his eyes and knit his long fingers over his chest. "Perhaps there is no such thing as *good enough* in our lines of work."

In all the speeches he had listened to that afternoon, Lenoir had not heard words so wise as those.

"Still," Merden went on, "the value of what you have done cannot be denied. I believe it solves a mystery that has troubled my mind for days."

"Oh? What mystery is that?"

"Why you are still alive."

Lenoir blinked. "I beg your pardon?"

"You were marked by the Darkwalker. A sentence of death. No one ever escapes his vengeance, yet here you are. In nearly a thousand years of oral history, there is no precedent for it. You promised to tell me the tale, but you did not."

A shiver of dread rattled Lenoir's shoulders. "I was spared," he said quietly.

"Plainly. The question I have been asking myself is, *why*?"

"And you think you have an answer?"

"I do. I believe you were spared so that you could stop the plague. Settle your account, as it were."

"I had a similar notion," Lenoir admitted. "But perhaps that was merely wishful thinking. Vincent is the champion of the dead. Why should he care if thousands die of plague?"

"You forget, Inspector, it is not the Darkwalker who decides. He is merely an instrument, one without will of his own. Someone, some*thing* else, decided you should live."

"It." Lenoir's voice was barely above a whisper now. "He referred to his master as *it*."

The golden eyes opened. Merden sat up. "You *spoke* to him?"

"I did." Lenoir had done more than speak to Vincent. He had helped him. Fought alongside him. They had been, however briefly and improbably, partners. But Lenoir did not have the energy for that tale now. "He said *it* no longer sought my death."

"It," Merden said pensively. "Your god, perhaps. That would explain the desire to save lives."

There was a thought. Lenoir had long since given up hope of being right with God. The idea that he could be called upon to do His work . . . "Does God require a mortal instrument?" *And if He did, would it be me? Or was it some kind of test?*

Merden waved an indifferent hand. "Your guess is as good as mine, Inspector. The southern god has never made much sense to me."

Nor to me, Lenoir thought. *Not for a long time.*

"Regardless, whatever *it* may be, you have obviously served it well."

"You sound so certain."

"I am." Merden gave him a long, level look. His mouth quirked just short of a smile. "Perhaps you will sleep better tonight."

"Perhaps." Lenoir did not hold out much hope. No matter—he was used to it. "In the meantime," he said, leaning forward, "I have something for you."

Merden took the proffered gift with a bemused expression. "What is it?"

"The key to the city."

"What is it for?"

"It is a token of gratitude, in recognition of great deeds on behalf of the city. It was given to me by the lord mayor. But it should have been given to you."

Merden arched a coal black eyebrow. "Indeed? According to whom?"

"According to me."

"I see." Merden examined it, looking every bit as nonplussed as Lenoir must have looked that afternoon. "What shall I do with it?"

"You can enter any public building, or order any gate opened."

"Do your public buildings truly have such enormous locks?"

Lenoir smiled. "It is not really meant to be functional. It is a symbol."

Merden's expression cleared. The Adali put great store in symbols, their spiritual leaders most of all. "A mark of respect, then."

"Indeed. Now you are twice *mekhleth*. To your people, and to mine."

"In your eyes, maybe."

Lenoir slumped low again, resting his head against the backrest of his chair. "Is that not enough?"

The soothsayer's smile came through in his voice. "Perhaps it is."

ABOUT THE AUTHOR

E. L. Tettensor likes her stories the way she likes her chocolate: dark, exotic, and with a hint of bitterness. She has visited fifty countries on five continents, and brought a little something back from each of them to press inside the pages of her books. She lives with her husband in Bujumbura, Burundi.

ALSO AVAILABLE FROM

E. L. TETTENSOR

DARKWALKER
A NICOLAS LENOIR NOVEL

Once a legendary police inspector, Nicolas Lenoir is now a disillusioned and broken man. Ten years ago, Lenoir barely escaped the grasp of the Darkwalker, a vengeful spirit who demands a terrible toll on those who have offended the dead. But the Darkwalker does not give up on his prey so easily...

When Lenoir is assigned to a disturbing new case, he treats the job with his usual apathy—until his best informant, a street savvy orphan, is kidnapped. Desperate to find his young friend, Lenoir will do anything catch the monster responsible for the crimes, even if it means walking willingly into the arms of his own doom.

"Wonderfully weird...a riveting read."
—Kings River Life Magazine

Available wherever books are sold or at
penguin.com

R0193